The Last Hostage

Also by John J. Nance

Pandora's Clock
Medusa's Child

The Last Hostage

John J. Nance

DOUBLEDAY
New York London Toronto Sydney Auckland

PUBLISHED BY DOUBLEDAY
a division of Bantam Doubleday Dell Publishing Group, Inc.
1540 Broadway, New York, New York 10036

Library of Congress Cataloging-in-Publication Data

Nance, John J.
The last hostage / John J. Nance.
p. cm.
I. Title.
PS3564.A546L37 1998 97-44861
813′.54—dc21 CIP

ISBN 0-385-49055-0

Printed in the United States
February 1998

10 9 8 7 6 5 4 3 2 1

To George Wieser and Olga Wieser
of the Wieser and Wieser Agency in New York

The catalysts

ACKNOWLEDGMENTS

Being a professional author is seldom a solitary pursuit. An impressive retinue of marvelous people are required to support the work of the author from conception to publication, and many kindnesses are needed along the road of research and review.

It all begins with family, and the love and support of my wife, Bunny, who shoulders the thankless task of working on the ideas and the raw copy as it comes out of the computer.

But my works would not be possible without my agents, Olga and George Wieser, to whom this book is dedicated.

My thanks as well to my editor at Doubleday, Shawn Coyne, whose strategic suggestions and outstanding ideas added immeasurably to the force and excitement of this work. My thanks also to my publisher, Arlene Friedman, Chief Editor Pat Mulcahy, and Matthew Shear, my paperback publisher at St. Martin's. My appreciation also to Helen Verno and Winifred White-Neisser of Columbia TriStar Television, and to producer Bernie Sofronski—my partners in bringing this work to the screen.

Before anyone in New York or Hollywood sees a page, my business partner and primary editor, Patricia Davenport, has spent untold hours working on the manuscript, and the end result would be impossible without her.

Thanks as well to retired FBI veteran Larry Montague, who helped make sure the Bureau is presented correctly in these pages, and to my friend and neighbor, Federal District Judge Frank Burgess, who helped this lawyer vet the legal side of the equation.

University Place, Washington
October, 1997

The Last Hostage

PROLOGUE

Near Ft. Collins, Colorado. 11:43 P.M.

The unkempt head of Bradley Lumin swam into perfect view in the high-powered rifle scope, the crosshairs holding steady just behind his left eye.

With great care, the shadowy figure holding the Winchester 30.06 chambered a round and clicked off the safety. He took a deep breath and moved his index finger next to the trigger. For hours he had remained hidden in a row of low, scraggly trees some thirty yards away, patiently waiting for the occupant of the ramshackle trailer to plop himself in front of his aging computer. Every night Lumin's pattern was the same, though this time later than usual.

The image in the scope wavered momentarily as the heavyset man adjusted the yellowed undershirt he was wearing and scratched himself, then leaned forward again into the crosshairs.

Bradley Lumin, I sentence you to death.

A sudden shiver ran the length of the sniper's body, and he relaxed his finger and pulled his eye away from the scope for a second to regain his composure, the weak light of a quarter moon revealing a pair of angry eyes within the cloak of a black ski mask, dark coat, and pants.

In the far distance he could hear the never-ending stream of traffic between Cheyenne and Denver whining up and down the Interstate, five miles removed from the scruffy farm that Lumin had rented for his sudden exile from Connecticut. And from the nearby town of Ft. Collins, the gunman heard the wail and warble of an electronic siren as authorities responded to another emergency.

He took a deep breath and raised the 30.06 again to eye level, steadying his aim in the crook of a branch, bringing the crosshairs to rest once again on the left side of Lumin's head. His index finger caressed the trigger lightly, looking for the right position, then touched it in earnest, the ball of his finger against the cold steel of the trigger, feeling the resistance from the springs within as he checked the target once more and began to squeeze.

ONE

Aboard AirBridge Flight 90, Colorado Springs International Airport, Gate 8. 9:26 A.M.

The captain was late.

Annette Baxter, the lead flight attendant on AirBridge Flight 90 to Phoenix, tossed back her shoulder-length red hair and studied her watch as she turned toward the cockpit. She could see the copilot's left hand adjusting things on the overhead panel as he ran through his preflight procedures, but she could see that the left seat—the captain's seat—was still empty.

As small as AirBridge was, there always seemed to be a new pair of pilots up front on every other leg. Annette paused and closed her eyes briefly, trying to recall the copilot's name. He was barely in his mid-twenties and already a two-year veteran of AirBridge, sandy-haired and almost too cute to be acting like such a gentleman. Yet he had shaken her hand on boarding and greeted her with perfect formality. She'd had to suppress a giggle.

David! David Gates, like the musician. She smiled to herself. The real David Gates was closer to her generation. Probably even a grandfather by now. This right-seater was just a kid. She leaned into the tiny cockpit and gestured to the empty captain's seat.

"David, who's our captain today, and is he planning on joining us sometime before takeoff, or is he going to meet us in Phoenix?"

The young copilot looked around with a startled, defensive expression, and she held out her hand in a stop gesture.

"I'm *kidding*! I've got a weird sense of humor. You'll get used to it."

"I'm sure he's on his way," Gates said with obvious caution. "I saw him in operations."

"Oh, good. I was worried he might be stuck in traffic, or something worse." She patted his shoulder, cautioning herself not to act too motherly. She refused to think of herself as motherly. "I'm not panicked. I'm well aware we've still got twenty or thirty seconds before we're late and our airline goes bankrupt as a direct result."

There was a tentative smile from the right-seater.

She tossed her hair again and leaned in farther. "So, who *is* the supreme commander today?"

"Captain Wolfe."

She paused involuntarily. "Ken Wolfe?"

"Yes . . . you know Ken?" he asked.

She nodded, her eyes focused outside the copilot's window. "We've flown together many times. How about you?"

Gates nodded. "Several times." He watched her carefully, but added no more.

Annette looked at him and straightened up with a thin smile. "Well, if Ken slips in without my seeing him, tell him I'll be up shortly, and tell him we've got a legal celebrity aboard today in first class. In the back, however, we have a well-dressed 'Mikey.' He hates everything. I expect him to be trouble."

"You need me to come back and talk to him?"

She shook her head, trying not to smile at the image of the baby-faced five-foot-nine first officer reading the riot act to the very senior, very demanding, very self-important stuffed shirt in 6C.

"No, it's not that bad, yet. I can handle him with whips and chairs. I just need to brief the captain."

"Who's the celebrity?" the copilot asked.

"It's a surprise. I'll brief both of you later."

"What's a surprise?" A deep male voice filled her left ear as Annette turned to find Ken Wolfe standing in the cockpit door.

"Ken! Good to see you. I was just . . ." she gestured toward the copilot as she realized she was blocking his way. "Here . . . let me move into the galley."

"You were talking about a surprise?"

She nodded. "I'll let you get settled, *then* I'll tell you."

He smiled and nodded as he moved into the cockpit. He placed his flight bag to the left of the captain's chair and turned to greet the copilot with a handshake before sitting down.

Ken Wolfe let his eyes move with practiced familiarity around the cockpit as he completed the mental transition to airline captain, his mind focused exclusively on the task of orchestrating an airline flight. It was a comforting ritual, the copilot briefing, the flight attendant briefing, the cockpit setups, and the paperwork duties. Even the presence of a malcontent businessman in coach as reported by Annette had an element of comfort about it—a business-as-usual veneer.

"You need me to come back and talk to the man?" Ken asked.

"David, here, made the same offer," she replied, arching her thumb at the copilot. "No, but something tells me our long-suffering passenger will feel even more deprived if he doesn't succeed in having a really bad day. He wants a meal, not peanuts, he hates our coffee, he doesn't like the 'feel' of the seats, he's angry I told him to turn off his cellular phone, and he's upset I won't let him keep his briefcase at his feet during takeoff."

"Oh, is that all?" Ken replied, forcing a smile. "Any idea who the S.O.B. is?"

She smiled and nodded. "His name is Blenheim. The jerk runs a Canadian Rockies bus tour outfit in Seattle. He's sort of a travel agent, and he's livid because we didn't give him first class for free. But, to balance the equation, we've got a celebrity legal eagle in first class who's a real gentleman. That's the surprise."

The captain looked puzzled. "I'm sorry . . . who're you talking about?"

"Well-l-l," Annette stretched the word and handed the man's business card to the captain as if it were a trophy.

Ken smiled at her before looking down at the gold seal that adorned the upper left-hand corner. It was the logo of the United States Department of Justice. His eyes moved to the clear, black type in the middle of the card. He blinked and looked again.

"Rudolph Bostich."

"I read earlier this week," Annette was saying, "that he's the front-runner for Attorney General of the United States. The President is supposed to be submitting his name to Congress this week."

She watched the captain for a few seconds, puzzled at his silence. "You okay?"

All the blood had drained from Wolfe's face, and the hand holding the card was shaking slightly. Annette heard him take a ragged breath and swallow hard.

"I'm okay, Annette. Just a scratch in the throat," he said in a strained monotone before looking back at her suddenly, modulating his words. "Where is . . . Mr. Bostich?" He smiled a partial smile that wasn't real, his eyes vacant and distracted.

"He's in seat One-A, Ken. Should I relay a message or something?"

"No!" Wolfe handed back the business card as if it were a spider and shook his head vigorously, his response sharp. "No, please don't."

She started to say something else, then backed through the cockpit door in alarm as Ken suddenly threw off his seatbelt and lunged toward her, questioning through tight lips, "Anyone in there?" with a quick gesture toward the forward lavatory located just behind the cockpit.

Annette glanced at the lavatory door in confusion. "It's empty," she managed, but he was already brushing past her to slip inside. His face was pasty.

She heard the lock slide into place, followed immediately by the sound of vomiting.

TWO

Aboard AirBridge Flight 90. 9:44 A.M.

With a late departure behind them, first officer David Gates made the 'flaps up' call as the powerful 737 climbed southbound a thousand feet above the suburbs of Colorado Springs, soaring into the clear blue sky with an amazing view of Pike's Peak on his right.

This was David's leg, and he relished the chance to fly the Boeing and revel in the feel of her—yet a corner of his consciousness was working on the problem of what in the world had been going on with the captain back at the gate.

"Roger, flaps up," Ken Wolfe repeated. "I'm setting speed two-ten knots, and level change."

Even his voice sounded different now. Not exactly carefree, but calm and collected, where he'd sounded haunted and distracted just minutes before.

Why? Just because a national figure had come on board?

But Gates just couldn't get the captain's sudden trip to the lav out of his mind. Departure time had come and gone, but the captain had remained inside. David had left his seat then and tapped on the lavatory door to ask if everything was all right. The captain's pained voice from within had been really unsettling—more of an agonized whine than a voice. David was prepared to alert crew scheduling that they might have a sick pilot to replace when the lav door opened suddenly and Ken Wolfe emerged, looking strangely fit and serene. He'd smiled at his copilot and slipped back into the left seat as if nothing had happened.

"Are you okay, Captain?" David had asked.

Wolfe had looked at him, his eyes staring right through the copilot for several uncomfortable seconds before he smiled a sort of determined, jaw-setting smile, and motioned toward the back with his thumb. "I feel better now, David. Better than I've felt in years."

"Good. I was getting worried."

"Sometimes," Ken began, "God gives us strange and wonderful opportunities, don't you think?"

The voice of the Denver Center controller cut into David's thoughts.

"AirBridge Ninety, Denver Center, good morning. Turn right now to a heading of two-six-zero, climb to and maintain flight level three-three-zero."

Instinctively, David's finger caressed the transmit button in case the captain failed to reply. Most AirBridge copilots were used to Wolfe not responding to radio calls, even though the captain was supposed to be talking to the controllers whenever it was the copilot's turn to fly. Throughout his yearlong tenure at AirBridge, Ken was often moody, often distracted, some days saying almost nothing, other days talking nonstop. He was courteous enough, but the unpredictability of his moods had become an uncomfortable legend, and flying with him meant extra stress.

But today, Ken's voice replied instantly. "Okay, Denver, a heading of two-six-zero and up to three-three-zero for AirBridge Ninety."

David engaged the autopilot and checked the settings on the autoflight panel. They were moving at two hundred fifty knots now, almost five miles per minute, beginning the familiar trek over Durango, Colorado, and Four Corners to Phoenix.

David glanced over at the captain, wondering again about Ken's state of mind. He knew the captain had been hired as the new airline expanded, and he knew Ken came from Connecticut. Other than that, Captain Wolfe's background was a blank.

David realized the captain was looking back at him with what appeared to be a relaxed smile.

"You wondering why we're carrying a full load of fuel this morning?" he asked.

"We're tankering because it costs more in Phoenix than in Colorado Springs?"

Ken nodded as he returned his gaze to the instruments. "Yeah. But this is nuts to have more than four hours fuel aboard out of the Springs."

He looked back at the copilot. "David, have you flown this particular aircraft recently?"

The copilot shook his head, as much to clear away the disturbing thoughts as to reply. "No, I don't think so."

"So, you're not aware of the oil leak problem we've been having on number two engine?"

David Gates looked cornered. There had been nothing in the log book about number two engine, but it wasn't unusual for AirBridge pilots to verbally pass on maintenance concerns that probably should have been entered in the maintenance log. Not a legal procedure, but all too common in smaller airlines, or so he'd heard. AirBridge was his first airline.

"I . . . hadn't heard about any oil leak, and the maintenance log showed nothing. I'm sorry if I missed something."

Ken looked up at the overhead panel and reached for the FASTEN SEATBELT switch. He cycled it twice, sending a two-chime signal to the cabin crew indicating their passage through ten thousand feet, then glanced back at the right-seater.

"You didn't miss anything. No one has written it up yet, including me, but we're all suspicious. Either a main oil seal is going, or something else is happening out there. Last week it started making strange noises in flight and I seriously considered shutting it down."

David was silent for a few seconds, the image of the powerful CFM-56 jet engine hanging in his mind. "The engine instruments didn't give you any indication of what's wrong?"

Ken shook his head and shrugged his shoulders, "Not a clue. We'll just have to watch it closely."

On the flight attendant jumpseat by the forward entry door, Annette glanced at a small panel of colored lights on the ceiling and shook her head in disgust. Just after the ten thousand foot chimes, someone had already punched a passenger call button.

She leaned over to see around the forward cabin divider—just as the man in 6C reached for the call button again.

Annette took her time unbuckling her seatbelt and folding the aft-facing seat before moving quietly through the first class cabin into coach and kneeling beside the man's seat.

"You called, sir?" she asked in quiet, discreet tones.

The man's voice boomed back at her, loud enough to be heard in the forward section of the coach cabin.

"Does it meet with your *royal* approval now, madam, that I get up and get my computer out of the overhead so I can get some work done?" he asked in a demeaning tone. "I could also use a vodka tonic, if it wouldn't be too much trouble to ask you to do your job."

Annette looked at the carpet for a few seconds and cleared her throat, before looking back up at him.

"You'll have a chance to order a drink in a few minutes when the other flight attendants begin their service, sir. Right now, the seatbelt sign is still on and I must ask you to stay seated. *I'll* get your briefcase down for you, though, if you'll answer a question for *me*."

"What?" There was sudden suspicion in his eyes.

"Have you ever flown commercially before?"

Several passengers in nearby seats suppressed smiles, one actually chuckling out loud at her question.

He leaned back and snorted to emphasize a practiced look of disgust as he checked a large, gold wristwatch. A Rolex, she noted.

"That's an inane question, woman! I own a tour company. I fly commercially all the time."

Annette nodded. "Well, anyone who's in the travel business and who uses this airline system on a regular basis should be aware of a few basic procedures, such as all the rules you seem to be angry with me for enforcing."

The man came forward in his seat, his eyebrows raised, his squarish face turning slightly purple. "How dare you lecture me?" he said in a loud, outraged tone.

Annette smiled at him. "And how dare you fly on a discounted ticket and beat up on *me* for not giving you first class?"

"That does it. When I get to a phone in Phoenix, sweetheart, you're toast!"

"Why wait?" Annette said as sweetly as she could manage. "There's a phone in your armrest. In the meantime, if you undo that seatbelt before the light's out, the first officer will come back with a set of plastic handcuffs and we'll have the FBI meet you in Phoenix. Understand?"

Annette ignored the man's obscene retort and walked back to the first class galley, pulling the curtain behind her before turning off the smile and clenching her fists in the privacy of the small cubicle. There was no point in bothering Ken Wolfe with the latest installment of the man's temper tantrums. In little more than an hour the boor would be off the airplane anyway, and then she could spend her ground time writing a report to cover herself when the inevitable "fire-the-bitch-or-else" letter arrived in AirBridge headquarters.

"Did you feel that?"

Ken Wolfe's face was a mask of concern as he looked at his copilot.

"What?"

"That vibration? It's faint, but repetitious."

David cocked his head and closed his eyes for a few seconds, trying to discern what the captain was sensing amid all the normal vibrations of a jetliner in flight. His eyes came open just as quickly.

"I . . . don't feel anything unusual, but . . ."

"You may not be attuned to that particular range of vibration," Ken offered.

"Maybe not. Was it a ratcheting?"

Ken nodded. "Yes, but very faint. It happens every few seconds. *There!* Feel that?"

David looked even more concerned than before. "I don't . . . well, maybe."

"In the background," Ken prompted, "a kind of distant grinding or growling, coming and going."

"Yes! I *do* feel it," David replied.

Wolfe nodded as he leaned over the center console to study the engine instruments, then looked up.

"Okay, I need you to go back quietly and take a look at the engines through the cabin windows. Look at the front and the tailpipe area, and see if you see anything unusual."

David nodded and left quickly, closing the cockpit door behind him, as Ken studied the instruments, paying particular attention to the oil pressure, then suddenly pulled out the emergency checklist. He opened it to the tab marked "Precautionary Engine Shutdown" and scanned the items, then reached up and pulled back the throttle for number two engine.

Thrust lever, close, he intoned to himself.

He reached down behind the center console and wrapped his index finger around the start lever for the same engine.

Start lever cutoff.

With a singular motion, he pulled the lever out of the detent and lowered it to the cutoff position, stopping the engine.

Within thirty seconds the copilot was back. "What happened?"

Ken looked up at him with a worried expression. "Almost the second you left, the temperature started climbing out of limits. No excess vibration, but the oil pressure was dropping as well. I had to shut it down."

David slid back into the right seat and put on his headset as fast as possible. He had never shut down an engine before in any airborne aircraft. Despite all the training efforts to make a shutdown routine, he realized adrenaline was pouring into his bloodstream.

"So, you want me to declare an emergency?"

Ken Wolfe smiled slightly. "First, I want you to fly. It's your leg. I'll keep working the radios and declare the emergency in a minute."

"We're going back to the Springs, right?"

Ken was shaking his head. "We're already closer to Durango, Colorado, so that's our nearest suitable airport."

David looked over at Ken in mild disbelief, trying to interpret the look of grim determination and the slight smile on the captain's face.

"Ah, Captain, do we have maintenance at Durango?"

"Nope. There's a maintenance shop there, but it's not ours." Ken looked over at David, catching his eyes. "You're not suggesting we pass up the nearest suitable airport and go back to base just to save money, are you?"

David shook his head instantly. "No, no. I . . . I didn't mean that."

"The FAA says with an engine gone, you head for the 'nearest suitable.' "

"I know. I know."

"The *company*, on the other hand . . ."

David had his hand out in a stop gesture. "I really wasn't suggesting that. I was just thinking out loud. Durango's fine. Would you program the computer for me, direct Durango, please, and get us a clearance there?"

"And declare an emergency?"

"Yes, sir. Declare the emergency, let the passengers know, then alert the company."

Ken nodded as he punched the transmit button.

In the rear galley, flight attendant Kevin Larimer had been tracking the copilot's movements in the cabin. He'd seen him lean over several passengers to look at the right wing, and he'd felt the momentary fish-tailing just before the copilot turned and reentered the cockpit.

He glanced at his fellow flight attendant, Bev Wishart, and raised his eyebrows as the 737 yawed again, dislodging the heavy beverage cart they'd been loading. It began rolling slowly across the galley floor toward the right rear service door, where Bev caught it with a muttered curse. She set the foot brake before looking up at Kevin and frowning.

"Turbulence or technique?" she asked.

Kevin smiled at her and arched a thumb toward the front end of the plane. "They're probably up there rocking it back and forth on purpose, just like that Gary Larson cartoon."

Bev tossed her hair back and laughed as Kevin watched her, happy for the momentary license to do so. A smart, buxom blonde, she was married to a lucky American Airlines pilot and therefore untouchable, though Kevin had quietly longed for her during their multiyear friend-ship. Bev's huge eyes, which permanently radiated a look of surprise, were her best feature. He realized with a small start that they were now focused on him.

"Do we have a problem, Kev? You're looking concerned."

"Ah, I'll check."

He turned to reach for the interphone.

The P.A. system came alive at the same moment with Ken Wolfe's voice.

"Folks, this is the flight deck. You may have noticed a small sideways motion in the aircraft a minute ago."

The voice was deep and steady and reassuring.

"We decided to temporarily shut down our right engine because of some indications in the cockpit that may or may not be accurate. Whenever we're unsure, we err on the side of caution, and that's what I'm doing. Now, there's nothing to be alarmed about, but we're going to have to make what we call a precautionary landing at Durango, Colorado, and have the problem looked at. We'll keep you informed, but in the meantime, I'd like everyone to stay on the aircraft and in your seats while we're on the ground. Also please understand that this aircraft can safely fly and land, and even take off, on one engine, but you wouldn't want us to fly with this problem without checking it out."

The end of the P.A. announcement was punctuated by the sound of a half dozen flight attendant call chimes reverberating through the cabin.

AirBridge Airlines Dispatch Center, Colorado Springs International Airport. 9:57 A.M.

The dispatcher for AirBridge Flight 90 ended his call to the airport manager in Durango and sat back trying to define exactly what was bothering him. In an emergency, captains could decide to divert anywhere they thought appropriate. But Durango was an odd call.

Flight 90 couldn't have passed the halfway point between the Springs and Durango at the moment the engine was shut down, so why not return the passengers to Colorado Springs where they could be rebooked quickly? Durango was going to be a costly decision.

Verne Garcia stood up and unplugged his headset, his eyes on Judy Smith, the current director of flight control, who was apparently deep in thought at her desk a few feet away across the crowded dispatch control room. He moved quietly to her side, wondering if she'd had time to read the requisite e-mail message on her computer in the midst of watching over sixty other flights.

"Judy, you saw my note on Ninety?"

She shook her head and immediately looked down at her computer screen.

"Durango?" She looked up at him. "Why the hell Durango? You suggested they come back here, I hope?"

Verne nodded. "Yup. And he said Durango was the nearest suitable field."

"BS!"

"I know, I know, but I'm only the dispatcher, and Captain Wolfe has already started his descent."

The DFC had been reaching for her headset to call the crew, but Verne Garcia's words stopped her.

"Ken Wolfe?"

"Yeah. Why?"

She sat back with a puzzled expression on her face. "That's not like Ken. I know him. His decisions are usually very conservative, he's very . . . careful to find out what the company wants." She gestured to the computer screen. "This says it's a precautionary engine shutdown. What happened?"

"Oil pressure dropping, temperature rising. Bad engine getting worse."

"Has maintenance been watching that engine lately?"

"Not as far as I know, but you're asking the wrong guy."

Judy grimaced as she checked the time. "And, of course, we don't have maintenance at Durango, so no one can sign it off even if it's okay. In a word, we're screwed."

"That's a phrase."

She smiled. "No, it's a reality."

"I've already talked to maintenance. They're getting a couple of mechanics ready to fly to Durango."

"Damn!" Judy Smith launched her pencil at the far corner of her desk before looking back at Garcia. "You alerted passenger services?"

"Of course, Judy. I'm not new to this."

She held out the palm of her hand. "I'm sorry. This just has me boggled. I was in such a good mood, and now we've got to send someone over to rescue a hundred or so furious passengers at outrageous cost, and none of them will love us for it. It would have been so easy if he'd just come home, but I know Ken must have had his reasons."

"Probably, " Verne replied absently, startled at the odd look which suddenly clouded Judy's face.

THREE

Aboard AirBridge Flight 90, Durango–La Plata County Airport, Durango, Colorado. 10:14 A.M.

David Gates finished the last item of the shutdown check and looked at the captain, who was studying the maintenance log.

"You going inside to call dispatch?" David offered.

Ken's eyes remained on the log. "Not yet. But I do have a quick mission for you."

"Okay."

Ken raised his head and looked the copilot in the eye. "There's a small maintenance shop at the south end of the field run by a jet mechanic I know and trust. Gus Wilson is his name. Get someone to run you down there, find Gus, and tell him I need him to look at our engine before we declare this flight a lost cause."

"Ah, you mean he could legally sign it off, even though he's not one of our mechanics?"

The captain was nodding. "He could. *If* our gauges are lying."

"But, you said the gauges were showing—"

"David, just go get him, okay? We can discuss the finer points when we get him here."

The copilot hesitated, then began unstrapping the seatbelt. "The south end, you said?"

"Yeah. Gus Wilson. Big guy. Tell him to hurry. I'm probably wrong, but before the company flies another aircraft in here to pick these folks up, I want to try."

David got to his feet carefully as he gestured toward the captain's side window. "We're lucky we've got the only jet in our fleet with built-in stairs. You don't normally find portable stairs big enough for a Boeing on a private ramp."

"You're right. We're lucky, " Ken replied without enthusiasm.

David opened the cockpit door and slipped past Annette Baxter, who was on her way in. She turned and watched the copilot momentarily as he paused in the front entryway to put on his hat, then disappeared down the stairs, a pained expression covering his face.

Strange, she thought. He was probably just reacting to the tension of the moment. After all, having a planeload of passengers angry and ready to strangle you could be a pretty good tension builder.

She turned and entered the cockpit.

"So, exalted leader of the pack, what's the plan?" she asked. "I can report that the natives are staying in their seats just as you commanded."

"Feed and water them, Annette." His voice was firm and steady, devoid of emotion. "Keep them as happy as possible while our copilot scares up maintenance. There's a good chance this is all a false alarm and we can continue on."

Annette cocked her head. "Really? After an engine shutdown?"

"Only if it was a false indication."

She smiled at him. "If you do decide to go on, I assume you'll explain it to our nervous passengers."

Ken Wolfe turned slightly in his seat to look at her. "How nervous are they?"

"Sounds like an Ed McMahon line."

He looked lost. Annette began gesturing in the general direction of Hollywood. "You know, the Carson show? A few years back? Johnny would say, like, 'It's cold,' and Ed would say: 'How cold *is* it?' "

For a few seconds, Ken regarded her in stony silence, then shook his head. "Of course. I'm sorry, Annette, I'm a little distracted."

"Understood," she replied.

He turned to look out the side window, his voice bouncing off the glass as he reached around the center pedestal for the P.A. handset. "I think I'll talk to them now."

Annette nodded and backed out as Ken slowly raised the microphone to his mouth and closed his eyes, carefully considering his words before punching the button.

"Folks, this is your captain again. While we're waiting for maintenance to evaluate our problem, I wonder whether we've got any other pilots

aboard who might want to take a quick glance at the cockpit. Even if you're not interested in visiting, please indulge your captain's curiosity. I'm told that no flight ever departs these days without at least one pilot in the back. If that's you, please ring your call button, and one of our flight attendants will escort you up front."

In the forward galley, Annette looked up at the P.A. speaker in surprise, aware that a single call chime had rung in the cabin.

That's not like Ken not to warn me, she thought.

She looked down the aisle, feeling a little irritated and off balance. Kevin was already approaching a passenger who was rising from seat 18D to take advantage of the invitation to the cockpit. Kevin reset the overhead call button and motioned the young man toward the cockpit as Rudy Bostich caught Annette's eye.

"Yes?"

"I hate to bother you, but is there anything I can do to help? You know, file charges against the malfunctioning engine, get a court order to clear the runway?"

Annette laughed and shook her head. "Not yet."

"I'll admit the question springs from self-interest," Bostich continued. "I have a speech to deliver in Phoenix in two hours, and I'm getting a bit nervous about getting there."

"An official function, Mr. Attorney General?"

"Thanks, but the title's very premature. No, just a legal seminar. The world won't end if I don't make it."

"Well, we're waiting for a maintenance man, and we can't legally leave until he gets here. I just don't know how long it'll take."

Rudy Bostich smiled. "Okay. Sorry to bother you."

"No bother at all."

·

AirBridge Airlines Dispatch Center, Colorado Springs International Airport. 10:25 A.M.

Judy Smith, the director of flight control, slipped in behind Verne Garcia's chair and put her hand on his shoulder, feeling him jump slightly at her touch.

"Verne, we're going to launch the replacement flight in about ten minutes. Are you talking with Wolfe yet?"

Garcia looked around and shook his head. "He was supposed to call me on a land line as soon as he got on the ramp in Durango. I just spoke with the manager of the facilities there, and he says the copilot left the airplane about ten minutes ago, but I haven't heard from him either."

Judy straightened up and pursed her lips in thought. "Okay. Well, when he does decide to talk to us, tell him the cavalry is coming, and we're sending two maintenance guys with the flight."

She began to turn away, but Garcia caught her arm.

"Ah, Judy?"

"Yeah?"

He glanced around in search of overt eavesdroppers, but all the other dispatchers were engaged in their own telephonic battles. His eyes shifted back to her.

"I noticed a few minutes ago you kinda reacted a little when I told you Ken Wolfe was the captain. Is there a history here I don't know about?"

She regarded him in silence for a few long seconds. "Why do you ask?"

He shrugged again. "Well, when I gave him his paperwork earlier, at the counter, Wolfe looked a bit strange to me. I mean, I'm sure it's nothing, but it was like he was somewhere else, you know? He had a kind of distant, disengaged look. But, I've only been around here since last August, and I don't know everyone's story."

Judy unconsciously drummed her fingers on the side of the cubicle as she probed the dispatcher's eyes.

"He seemed distant, huh?"

"Very. Is that significant?"

She shook her head with unconvincing slowness as her eyes wandered to the far wall of the room. "Ken Wolfe is a bit of a mystery around here, Verne. He's a nice guy and a competent captain, but he has a strange capacity to worry copilots. It's like he's three or four different personalities, one light and friendly, another moody and unresponsive, yet another scared and suspicious. I'm . . . not sure what to make of him, but regardless of the turbulence, he's always been a team player as far as dispatch is concerned."

"I see."

"I'm sure what you observed was more of the same."

"Okay. I just thought I'd mention it, you know?"

Judy smiled absently and turned away, then turned back suddenly.

"Verne . . ."

"Yeah?"

"Tell you what. Call that manager again. Tell him to please go out to our aircraft *right now*, and tell Captain Wolfe personally to leave the cockpit and come call me."

Aboard AirBridge Flight 90, Durango–La Plata County Airport, Durango, Colorado. 10:28 A.M.

With a cart in the aisle in the middle of a drink service, Annette had not been expecting to hear the sound of the cockpit door being slammed hard enough to echo back through coach. She turned and looked toward the front of the cabin, startled to hear the public address system click on, and listened as Wolfe's voice filled the cabin.

"Folks, this is your captain. I've got good news. Maintenance rushed out here and found the problem to be a simple electronic circuit board that was giving us bad indications in the cockpit. With that, we're cleared to go. Your first officer is already getting the clearance from air traffic control, and as soon as our flight attendants can get the cabin buttoned up, we'll be on our way to Phoenix, with great apologies for the unscheduled stop. Flight attendants, please prepare the rear doors for departure and crosscheck. Forward stairs and door are already secured."

Annette glanced back at her compatriots, satisfied to see that Bev and Kevin were already pulling the serving cart to the rear galley. She walked to the front of the coach cabin and turned around, smiling at the sea of puzzled faces, pushing the volume of her voice to the limit.

"SORRY ABOUT THE DRINK SERVICE, FOLKS." Her voice wouldn't carry the entire length of the cabin, but the majority would hear her, she figured. "WE'LL GET TO YOU RIGHT AFTER TAKEOFF."

The sound of the left engine winding up began to reverberate through the fuselage as she moved forward to double-check the left front door. Sure enough, Ken had closed it and armed the emergency slide just as the procedure required.

Annette moved into the first class galley and stood for a second in thought, her mind uncomfortable over something she couldn't define. Maybe it was the truncated drink service. She hated to leave half the passengers wanting. Or maybe it was just being in Durango that was surreal. She had bad memories of Durango and a weekend gone bad there a few years before, an embarrassing experience with a new boyfriend who was supposed to be single.

She could understand the captain being anxious to go, but the speed with which everything had come together surprised her. When had the mechanics come aboard to sign the log book, for instance?

I must have had my back turned longer than I thought!

She'd gotten lost in the monotony of a drink or meal service many times before, the almost comforting chants reduced to second nature: *What would you like to drink, sir? Will that be with cream and sugar, or just cream? Would you like pretzels or peanuts? We have three kinds of beer, sir. They cost three dollars per can.*

The second engine was starting now, the whine of the turbine blades accelerating up the audible scales.

She heard the engines stabilize as she locked the compartments in her galley, then realized she had never offered coffee or soft drinks to the pilots. She felt the jet begin to taxi as she reached around and tried to open the cockpit door.

It was locked.

The 737 was turning to the right aggressively as it moved out of the ramp area. Annette braced herself against the motion.

The sound of the interphone call chime broke her thoughts, and she glanced toward the ceiling. The red light indicated the rear galley was calling. She moved to the forward entry door and lifted the handset. "You buzzed?"

"Annette, this is Kevin. Where is the guy in Eighteen-D?"

"What do you mean?"

"Well, he isn't in his seat, and his wife is worried."

"Eighteen-D?"

"The captain asked about other pilots aboard, and that guy came forward. Remember?"

"Yeah. I do now. Could he be in the restroom?"

"Not back here. We checked."

"Hang on a second." Annette leaned toward the forward restroom door as the 737 lurched slightly to the left, almost throwing her off balance. The unoccupied sign was showing. She raised the handset.

"He's not up here, either. Stand by and I'll call the cockpit."

It took several pushes of the call button before Wolfe's voice filled her ear.

"Cockpit."

"Ken? This is Annette at the door. Can I come in?"

There was a small hesitation before he spoke, and then the voice was strange and stressed.

"Ah, I'd . . . rather not right now, Annette. We're . . . a bit crowded in here. I decided to give our guest pilot a shot at the jumpseat."

She smiled, feeling relieved. "Good! That's what I was calling about. His wife feels abandoned."

"He says to tell her he'll be back a little later. He's having fun."

"Okay. When you're ready, what do you want to drink?"

More silence.

"Ken?"

"Ah, Annette, let's clear this line for now. I'm pretty busy."

"Sure. Sorry about that." Annette replaced the handset with the distinct feeling that somehow she'd accidentally crossed a line and asked too much. It made no sense, but somehow she felt guilty.

Two chimes sounded from the cockpit, the signal that they were ready for takeoff. Annette sat in the folding jumpseat behind the cockpit and fastened her seat belt almost as a reflex.

Why would he take a passenger in the cockpit jumpseat without telling me? And in the aftermath of an emergency landing.

Maybe that was the cause of the nagging discomfort.

No, she had already felt that way before the call about 18D.

A half mile distant a panicked man was spilling out the front door of the Durango Flying Service and racing up to the passenger side of an arriving pickup truck, his eyes flaring wide.

"Are you with AirBridge?" he asked the uniformed pilot who was climbing out of the truck.

"Yes, sir. What . . ."

"You've got to help me! My wife is on that airplane, and it's taking off without me!"

"What are you talking about?"

"Your . . . your flight, that diverted in here? He's leaving. The captain asked me to run an errand, and while I was off, he started up and taxied out."

"Wait a minute, you mean Flight Ninety?"

"Yes!"

"He's not going anywhere, sir."

"Yes he is! He's already on the runway!"

Suddenly the wave of noise from two turbojet engines at full power washed over them, the aircraft itself invisible behind the building.

The man from the truck suddenly broke away from the distraught passenger's grip and raced around the side of the building to the ramp, looking for the familiar shape of the 737.

The ramp was empty, and that made no sense. The aircraft had diverted in with a shutdown engine. No way would it be taxiing anywhere, unless to some maintenance facility on the field.

Maybe that was it! He looked to the north, his mind struggling with the fact that no maintenance shops stood on the north end. There was, however, a jetliner out there, and it was beginning to move. The tail was clearly visible now in the distance, gaining speed in what had to be a takeoff roll.

And that tail was attached to AirBridge 90.

First Officer David Gates stood in complete shock as his aircraft lifted off without him, the gear retracting on schedule, the 737 gently banking toward the west as it gained altitude.

And for a moment—for just a moment—he seriously entertained the ludicrous thought that perhaps the captain had simply forgotten that his first officer wasn't aboard.

FOUR

Aboard AirBridge Flight 90. 10:44 A.M.

The call from the rear galley was a welcome interruption, and Annette pressed the intercom handset to her ear just as two chimes sounded, indicating they were climbing through ten thousand feet.

"Annette? You there?" Kevin was asking.

"I'm here. What's up?"

"Bev and I are worried about one of our groups. The one in the front part of coach."

Annette rubbed her eyes as she tried to remember the people.

"Which group, Kevin? I recall we have a high school band aboard."

"Yeah. The band is sitting in rows thirteen through twenty, but there's another group from row eight on back, about twenty-two people. We need to pay special attention to them. I got a chance to talk to them briefly after we landed, but with this sudden departure they're probably freaking out by now."

"Why? Why would they be freaking out?"

There was a low laugh on the other end. "Because it's a graduation flight, Annette."

"Another high school group?"

"Nope. A fear-of-flying clinic."

She closed her eyes and shook her head. "Wonderful."

Annette replaced the handset and got to her feet, surveying the first class cabin. A striking young woman in the seats across the aisle from Rudy Bostich looked up at the same moment and smiled as Annette moved toward her, kneeling alongside her seat, calculating the considerable expense of the woman's elegant red suit and dangerously short miniskirt.

"Can I get anything for you before I start the service?" Annette asked.

The woman smiled again. "No, I'm fine. Just some coffee when it's convenient." She inclined her head slightly toward the coach cabin. "I, ah, heard the boor back there bitching about everything. I'm aware you're under more than a little inordinate stress."

Annette rolled her eyes and smiled. "Comes with the job."

"I was just wondering if this happens very often?"

"You mean . . ." Annette indicated the coach section with a flick of her eyes.

"No, I meant the, what did the captain call it, precautionary landing? Engine shutdown?"

"Oh." Annette shook her head vigorously. "First time for me, and I've been with this airline for three years, since the day it started flying, and with TWA for twenty years before that."

The woman nodded, her eyes drifting away toward the forward entry door.

Annette stood, but felt an immediate tug on her right sleeve.

"Ah, excuse me," the woman began again. "May I ask you another dumb question?"

"Actually, there are no dumb questions," Annette responded. "Ask away."

"Are there other entrances to the cockpit?" She inclined her head toward the cockpit door a few feet away.

"Other entrances?"

"Yes. Hollywood always shows pilots climbing up through hatches in the floor, and I was just wondering."

"Nope. Only that door."

"Okay. Thanks."

Annette took a step toward the galley, then turned back and knelt beside the woman again.

"Why do you ask?"

The woman tossed her head as if dismissing her own curiosity, and motioned toward the cockpit door with a chuckle. "I guess I wasn't paying attention. When we were on the ground, I saw one of the pilots leave, but I missed it when he came back. I just wondered if he came in another door."

Annette smiled at her, covering a feeling of sudden confusion. Seat

1C had a perfect view of the entry door, but if she'd been looking out the window, she could have missed him.

"Well," Annette said at last, "all it takes is a momentary distraction." She smiled and added, "Besides, pilots are inherently sneaky. We have to watch them every second." Annette stood up and straightened her skirt. "You can be sure of one thing, though. It takes two pilots to fly this aircraft, so if we're airborne, he's up there."

"Oh, I'm not worried. I was just curious."

Annette moved quickly into the galley and pulled the curtain behind her. She leaned against the slightly curved surface of the right galley door and tried to focus on the fact that several unusual things had happened, and were pushing her off balance. The rhythms were wrong and it was rattling her, getting in the way of her normal sequencing. Should she be starting the drink service now, or what? It was ridiculous to have to think about it. Her service sequence was second nature.

Annette turned her head and glanced at the cockpit door, which was visible around the corner of the galley curtain. The pilots should be almost at level-off and ready for something to drink, she decided.

She moved across to the interphone panel and pressed the captain call button, relieved that Ken Wolfe answered almost immediately.

"Ready for drinks, gentlemen?"

"Hold on," Ken said. The line went silent for a few seconds. "No, Annette. Thanks, but we're just fine."

"Okay. Would you open the door for a second, Ken? I'd like to come up."

More silence, and her stomach tightened with each passing second. Something was definitely not right. This wasn't like Wolfe. Why would he hesitate before opening the door?

Finally Ken's voice returned.

"Annette, ah, I'm expecting some turbulence up ahead. Why don't you take your seat, and make sure the folks in the back sit down as well."

"Okay, Captain, but please unlock the door for a second."

"Not now, Annette."

"But—"

"Later, okay?" There was an edge to his voice she hadn't heard before. She tried to reply, but for some reason her voice wouldn't come, and she replaced the handset with rising apprehension.

AirBridge Airlines Dispatch Center, Colorado Springs International Airport. 10:45 A.M.

Judy Smith heard something ceramic breaking and looked up to see Verne Garcia leap to his feet and gesture to her frantically, his eyes wide. She moved quickly to his side as he covered the mouthpiece and turned to her, barely glancing at the broken cup on the floor, the blood draining from his face.

"Judy, we've got a big, big problem. Flight Ninety's gone airborne and left the first officer behind!"

Judy stood in confusion for a few seconds, wondering how Garcia could have garbled his words badly enough to convey such a bizarre meaning.

"Ninety's airborne and the first officer left something behind?" she asked.

"No, no, no! The captain and the flight are airborne. What they left behind was the copilot. There was no maintenance signoff as far as we know, either. I have him on the phone here. He's on the ground in Durango and panicked."

"Which copilot? A deadheading copilot?"

"The copilot assigned to that flight. He's on the ground in Durango and on line eight. The plane is in the air without him."

"How in hell could that happen? The *copilot?* No way!"

"I'm not kidding, Judy. Please pick up an extension."

She lunged for the telephone on the next desk and punched the appropriate line.

"This is the director of flight control. Who's this?"

"First Officer David Gates, ma'am."

"Where are you?"

"Durango. On the ground. The flight's left without me. As far as I know, the only pilot on that plane is the captain, and I don't have any idea why he'd leave unless he was forced to."

"Forced? You mean, hijacked?"

"I . . . I can't figure out any other explanation." The voice on the other end was anguished and tinged with panic, the young pilot's breath coming in short bursts as he ran through an explanation of his fruitless trip to the south end of the field and the utter shock of finding the airplane poised for takeoff when he'd returned.

"Wait a minute. There was no mechanic?"

"There was a mechanic; I mean, there is a maintenance facility there, but this Gus I was supposed to find died several years ago, so I wasn't able to get anyone to come look at the engine, and when I got back, Ken had left me and a passenger and was at the end of the runway."

"You said a passenger was left behind, too?"

"Yes, ma'am. I'll put him on in a minute. His wife's still on the aircraft and he's very upset."

"How long ago did the airplane leave?"

"Five minutes max."

"Hold on!" Judy turned to Verne Garcia. "Get Albuquerque Center on the horn. Find out if they're working Ninety, and where he's going. Get me the controller."

"Got it." Verne Garcia turned away and began punching numbers into his phone as Judy turned back to the conversation with a shaken David Gates.

"David, is it?"

"Yes. David Gates."

"Okay, David. Did you see any indication that someone might have slipped on board?"

"No. The plane was beginning its takeoff roll when I spotted it. But there was no security on the ramp. Anyone could have boarded. There were line boys around, but I haven't asked them."

"David, this is very important. What, exactly, makes you think he was hijacked?"

"There's no other logical explanation. No one in his right mind would fly a two person airliner without a copilot unless he was forced to do so, or it was a war and someone was shooting at him."

Judy felt her mind race through a variety of possibilities. The copilot was right. No other rational explanation existed. If the flight was airborne without a copilot, then it had to have been hijacked, and they had a major problem.

"What do you want me to do?" Gates was asking.

"Give me the number where you are, stay right there by that phone, and . . . ah . . . don't talk to anyone about this yet."

"Don't worry, I won't! You want me to put on the passenger who was left?"

"Tell him I'll call back. Not now."

"Okay, but he's really, really worried. His wife's on that aircraft."

Judy replaced the phone and glanced over at Verne Garcia, who was talking urgently into his handset. Several off-duty dispatchers had begun to congregate in the area, each of them straining to hear what was happening. She turned and surveyed who was available, and pointed to the nearest one.

"Jim, get the FBI on the phone and stand by for me to come on the line. Jerry, will you go to my desk and get the emergency procedures manual and start going through the hijacking procedures? Rashid, are you working any flights?"

"No. What do you need?"

"Call the chief pilot, the VP of operations, and corporate communications. Fill them in."

"On what, Judy? I don't know what's happening."

"Oh, sorry. Okay, everyone, gather around. Here's what we've got so far."

Albuquerque Air Route Traffic Control Center. 10:50 A.M.

Air traffic controller Avis Bair took another sip of coffee and double-checked the altitude block on AirBridge 90. As cleared, the pilot had leveled at flight level two-one-zero, twenty-one thousand feet above the four corners area of northwestern New Mexico and northeastern Arizona and checked in with the usual expressionless, deep male voice. It was curious, she thought, that his emergency diversion to Durango had ended so quickly. At least 90 was taken care of now and on his way, leaving her free to deal with a developing conflict between an American jet and a United jet, with one overtaking the other at the same altitude, both bound for Los Angeles. The guy in the lead was being a genuine slug and flying much too slowly.

Avis had poised her finger over the transmit button when an alarm suddenly sounded in her ear. A small phosphorescent information block next to AirBridge 90's target began flashing simultaneously, displaying a transponder code she had never seen in actual practice.

7500!

Obviously a mistake, she thought, but just in case, there were specific procedures to follow. She felt a sudden rush of adrenaline as she glanced to her left, curious as to whether the beeping alarm had attracted anyone else's attention.

It hadn't. No one else was looking her way.

Avis leaned forward and studied the data block on the screen again, double-checking that it said what she thought it said.

Seven-five-zero-zero.

She pushed the transmit button. "AirBridge Ninety, Albuquerque Center. I show you squawking seventy-five hundred on your transponder, sir. Is that correct?"

She felt her heart beating loudly as she waited for the answer.

"Affirmative, Center. I am purposefully squawking seventy-five hundred. I have an uninvited guest in the cockpit."

Avis sat back, suddenly filled with adrenaline. The real thing! This was the real thing! Seventy-five hundred meant a hijacking, and this was a commercial airliner.

She swiveled around and shouted at her supervisor, then turned back to her scope.

"Roger, AirBridge Ninety, I do copy that the seventy-five hundred squawk is valid. Please maintain flight level two-one-zero and stand by."

Aboard AirBridge Flight 90. 10:55 A.M.

Her hands were shaking slightly, but Annette struggled to hide her apprehension as she did a quick drink service for her first class passengers. She had returned to the galley to think when she heard the engines throttle back and Ken Wolfe's strained voice on the P.A.

"Folks, this is the captain. We have a small treat for you today. I know we're running late getting you to Phoenix, but since air traffic control is slowing us down for traffic flow into the Phoenix airport, and since they're taking us right over Monument Valley, Utah, we've gotten ap-

proval to go down for a closer look. We'll get you into Phoenix just as soon as they let us, but in the meantime, enjoy the view which will be coming up in about five minutes."

Annette pulled the interphone handset from its cradle and punched the cockpit call button. Ken answered rapidly.

"Ken, I need to talk to you."

"So talk, Annette."

"In person."

"Why?"

"As your lead flight attendant, I want to come into the cockpit and talk with you right now. Ken, what's going on?"

"Annette, coming up right now could prove a bit difficult. What, exactly, are you concerned about?"

She leaned against the forward door with the phone pressed to her ear, wondering if she was having some sort of paranoid delusion. Maybe it was ridiculous to be worried, but the fact remained that refusing her entrance to the cockpit meant that he had something to hide, and she could feel herself panicking. She knew Ken Wolfe to be changeable and distant, but he wasn't the type to shut out his flight attendants. There could be several reasons for the refusal, none of them good.

What if he's got that other pilot flying in the right seat illegally, and he doesn't want me to know? We'd be at risk. I'd have to do something.

"Captain, please let me speak to David."

There was a chilling pause. If David was on the jumpseat instead of his copilot's seat, he might lie about it to protect the captain and himself. It was illegal for any pilot from another company to occupy the captain's or copilot's seat in a commercial jet.

"He's busy, Annette. He'll talk to you later."

"*Now*, please. I want to talk to him now. Or isn't he in the right seat? Ken, dammit, level with me!"

Another long pause, then the click of the push-to-talk button. Ken Wolfe's voice was suddenly different, carrying a more authoritative tone.

"Okay, Annette. You're right. Listen carefully, because I'm under some tight constraints here. David isn't here."

"Wh . . . *what*?"

"Someone else is up here, and he's insisting on telling us where to go."

Annette closed her eyes, trying to find a better explanation than the one now looming in her mind.

But nothing else fit. She had to ask, though the words threatened to choke her. "Ken?"

"Yes."

"Are we . . . are we hijacked?"

Another chilling pause that seemed to last forever.

"That's affirmative, Annette. Back there in Durango. He suddenly barged in and slammed the door and put a gun to my head. Well you did, damn you!" Annette heard the volume of his voice diminish as he addressed the occupant of the right seat.

"Oh God, Ken. One person?"

"Yep, and he's waving a gun at me right now to end this conversation. He says that you must not tell the passengers. He says he's not going to hurt anyone, but he demands to go where he demands to go."

"Where? Cuba?"

"I don't know, Annette, other than Monument Valley. First he wants to see Monument Valley up close. Then he'll let me know, and I'll let you know. In the meantime, keep quiet about this."

"How about Bev and Kevin? They need to know what's happening."

"No. I'll be listening to this channel, and so will he. You can't tell them. He says you can't tell them anything."

"Is it the guy in Eighteen-D, Ken? The guy you asked to come up? His name is Beck."

There was no response.

"Ken? Are you still there?"

There was a click, indicating the interphone had been disconnected. She looked at the handset like it was a ticking bomb, then replaced it slowly in its cradle, trying to imagine the man in 18D as the hijacker.

The image didn't fit. Not with such a young face and a pretty young wife back there in 18E.

Annette entered the galley feeling dizzy. She pulled the curtain behind her, vaguely aware that the 737 was decending, her mind whirling.

She could see the desert floor getting closer outside the small window in the galley door as a feeling of helpless confusion paralyzed her, the same question running over and over in her mind:

What on earth do I do now?

FIVE

Albuquerque Air Route Traffic Control Center. 10:58 A.M.

"AirBridge Ninety, please state your intentions."

Avis Bair released the transmit button and glanced up at her shift supervisor, who was staring intently at the large, circular computer display screen. The portly senior controller pointed a pudgy finger at the target marked AB90 and shook his head.

"Eight thousand and still descending." He turned to Avis. "And you didn't clear him down?"

"He never asked. He just started down on his own. I've got him on a discrete frequency, and shipped three other flights to the next sector."

"This is really weird. What the hell is he up to?"

"I haven't a clue. He's not talking."

"What's ahead of him out there, Avis?"

"Wide open terrain for the most part. Base altitude of the surrounding desert is about five thousand feet, but some of those buttes—the Mittens, for instance, in Monument Valley—stand over a thousand feet high."

"Weather's still clear?"

"Severe clear. Visibility unlimited. He should be able to see the obstacles ahead, and it looks like a controlled descent."

"Try him again, Avis."

"AirBridge Ninety, Albuquerque Center, radio check."

There was silence for several seconds before the sound of a radio transmitter being keyed filled their headsets and an overhead speaker, the sound of occasional static interlacing the words.

"Okay, Albuquerque, AirBridge Ninety here. You're probably wondering what we're doing?"

Avis glanced up at the supervisor with raised eyebrows as she keyed the transmitter.

"That's affirmative, Ninety. We see your descent. Could you state your intentions?"

"My guest up here wants to do some sightseeing, then go to Salt Lake City. He'll let me know what else he wants on the way. Then I'll let you know."

"Is your . . . *guest* . . . on the frequency?"

There was a long pause before the speaker crackled to life again.

"Affirmative, Albuquerque. He's armed, and he's listening to every word and telling me what to say."

"And there's nothing we can do for you at the moment?"

"Ah . . . since you asked . . . he's telling me that he wants you to have the Attorney General of the United States standing by ready to talk to him, and he wants—demands, that is—the Stamford, Connecticut, D.A. and the head of the Colorado State Patrol to be standing by, along with both a Colorado state judge and a federal district judge."

Three other controllers had gathered behind Avis and her supervisor. All of them exchanged long, incredulous glances as Avis scribbled down the demands.

"Understood, Ninety. We'll do our best. You're cleared now to any safe altitude above seven thousand feet. Maneuver at your discretion. Please advise when you're ready to head for Salt Lake."

"Roger, Albuquerque. I'll do what I can."

Avis looked up at the supervisor. "Is the FBI on line yet?"

He nodded. "They're setting up communications now through Washington."

AirBridge Airlines Dispatch Center, Colorado Springs International Airport. 10:58 A.M.

The Spartan office that housed the dispatch and control functions for AirBridge Airlines was becoming more crowded by the minute. The chief pilot and the vice president of operations were huddled in a corner urgently briefing the airline's president while a dozen other employees ranged back and forth grabbing every phone not already in use. In the background, four dispatchers were trying to keep the airline running while keeping an ear cocked for the latest word on Flight 90. None of the other flights had been told anything.

"Judy, David Gates wants to talk to you again from Durango."

Judy turned away from the cadre of business suits and glanced at Verne Garcia, who was gesturing to one of the blinking lines. She hesitated, then moved to her small desk and grabbed the receiver.

"DFC here."

"Ms. Smith?"

"It's pretty busy here, David. I need you to stand by. I expect the FBI will be calling you in a few minutes."

"I know, but there's something else I think you need to know."

"What?"

"The passenger whose wife is still on the plane? I didn't know this, but Ken asked him to get off. He was looking for pilots."

Judy rubbed her eyes and tried to make sense of the copilot's statement.

"What do you mean, David? Who was looking for pilots?"

"Let . . . let me put him on. You really need to hear this."

She heard the phone being handed over, and a new voice filled the line.

"This is Johnny Beck."

Judy introduced herself. "Mr. Beck, I'm very sorry we left you behind. Can you tell me how it happened?"

As he talked, Judy began making her trademark doodles on a legal pad, a steady flow of circles and triangles.

Just as suddenly, she stopped.

"Wait a minute. The captain asked you to do what?"

"I was talking to him in the cockpit, and he told me he'd forgotten to pick up his new flight plan, and would I run in and get it for him."

"And that's when you left the plane?"

"Yes, ma'am. But no one in this office knew what he was talking about, and when I headed back outside, the door was closed and the engines were starting."

"Was there someone else in the cockpit, or standing in the doorway, when you were there, Mr. Beck?"

"No. No one was around but the captain and me."

"You're sure?"

"Yes."

"How about on the ramp, say, at the bottom of the stairs?"

"No, ma'am. I was the only one near the aircraft when I got off."

Judy closed her eyes and tried to envision the scene. He had gone inside, made some inquiries, then returned. He had gone inside looking for a flight plan that Ken Wolfe should have known wouldn't be there. Dispatch wouldn't be sending a new flight plan to an aircraft that maintenance had yet to examine.

"How long were you inside, Mr. Beck?"

"Not more than three minutes, four tops. Ma'am, Nancy . . . my wife . . . is on the airplane. She's pregnant and probably worried silly about me, since I didn't come back aboard." His voice broke slightly, the stress and worry clearly audible. "Where are they now? Are you sure they're okay?"

Judy calculated the time it would take for the ground crew to move the stairs and the flight attendant to close the door, let alone the time it would take to start the engines. Three minutes would barely be enough.

"Mr. Beck, are you sure he had an engine running when you returned?"

"Yes. Yes, absolutely. But where are they now?"

Judy realized she had been only half-listening to his question.

"I'm sorry, Mr. Beck. The aircraft's headed for Phoenix right now, and we'll get this figured out and get you two back together as soon as we can." The lie rolled too easily out of her mouth, she thought, but what *should* she say? Your lovely wife is a hostage of some unknown maniac who's commandeered one of our jets?

No, a lie would do for now.

Judy thanked him and replaced the receiver with her eyes riveted on the group of senior executives in the corner.

Judy felt a cold buzz erupt somewhere in her body. It spread rapidly outward, making her legs feel weak, and she held the corner of her desk as she sat down. Verne Garcia's words were all too fresh suddenly in her memory: *Wolfe looked a bit strange to me*, Verne had said. *It was like he was somewhere else, you know? He had a kind of distant, disengaged look.*

There were two pilots aboard, and the captain had managed to get both of them off the airplane.

Why?

She rubbed her eyes and shook her head slightly to expunge the small wave of apprehension.

FBI Headquarters, Washington, D.C. 11:00 A.M. MDT, 1:00 P.M. EDT.

Agent Clark Roberts took the hijacking alert from the FAA Command Center in Virginia and began carefully following the established procedures, notifying the appropriate superiors and the field office in Denver and the resident agency office in Colorado Springs. He'd already started the search for the FBI's nearest hostage negotiator when another agent leaned in the door.

"We've got a demand from the subject. You on a first name basis with the Attorney General of the United States?"

Roberts frowned and narrowed his eyes.

"*What?*"

"He's demanding a line to the Attorney General, the Stamford D.A., and the head of the Colorado State Patrol, along with a state judge and federal judge."

"*Who* is?"

"The hijacker."

"You kidding?" Clark Roberts watched the other agent shake his head. "You're *not* kidding! Lord. A demand like that means it's political."

"Also, he's headed to Salt Lake City. I checked a second ago. We've got an agent there who's trained."

"Good!"

"But . . . it's a she."

Roberts looked at the other man carefully. "A woman?"

He nodded. "You want to call?"

"When did we train a female negotiator?" Roberts asked.

"We've got several of them, but that's not her primary job, Clark.

However, she has a degree in psychology and she worked as a psychologist for three years before she became an agent at the Bureau. Our esteemed deputy director said to tell you we go with her."

"This lady have a name?"

"Here's her number in Salt Lake. Agent Katherine Bronsky. I already dialed her beeper and gave your number. We're setting up a command post of sorts at the airport, with the help of the airport police, and she needs to be out there yesterday."

"How much experience does Agent Bronsky have?"

The other agent looked at Roberts with a guarded smile and waited a few seconds before answering. "Seems she's in her second year as a basic agent, but they let her take the hostage negotiator school at Quantico earlier than normal about a month ago because of her previous experience."

"Oh, Lord."

"Hey, maybe she'll bring a fresh perspective. And after all, we don't even know if the hijacker is male or female."

"It would be politically incorrect of me to object on the basis that a marginally qualified female has no business dealing with a hijacker of any gender, so I won't."

"Good. I didn't hear you not say that."

Clark Roberts shook his head. "How long before the aircraft can get to Salt Lake?"

"At least a half hour."

"And how long before we're set up there?" Roberts added.

"At least a half hour."

"Did I ever tell you you're a joy to work with?"

"No."

"Good. Don't hold your damn breath."

Aboard AirBridge Flight 90. 11:05 A.M.

"Folks, this is your captain again. Put down whatever you're reading and look out of either side of the aircraft. You're about to get a spectacular view of the historic buttes which make up Monument Valley. You've seen them in a thousand Western movies, now we're going to see them up close."

Annette looked once more into the frightened eyes of her two coworkers as they stood in the rear galley where she'd briefed them on the hijacking. "I've got to get back up there before he looks through the peephole."

Bev nodded as Kevin pointed to the side of the aircraft. "I don't know what the hell this excursion has to do with anything, but I want to see it."

Annette hurried back up the aisle, almost missing the voice of the young woman in seat 18E.

"Miss, please! Could I talk to you?"

Annette turned, startled to find herself facing the wife of the young pilot who had entered the cockpit back in Durango. She felt her stomach tightening as she wondered again whether he could be the hijacker, and whether she, too, might be involved.

"Yes?"

"I'm Nancy Beck. My husband went up front when the captain asked if anyone wanted to see the cockpit back in Durango. I haven't seen him since then, and I just . . . you know, want to make sure he's riding on the jumpseat up there."

Annette forced herself to smile. "That's exactly where he is, Mrs. Beck."

She smiled and sat back, looking relieved. "Thanks a lot."

Annette nodded, hesitated, and shifted her weight as she tried to decide how to phrase the question she'd been turning over in her mind.

"Mrs. Beck, your husband, is he, ah . . ."

"I'm sorry?" she said, leaning toward Annette, looking puzzled.

"I'm sorry. I forgot what I was going to ask."

Nancy Beck nodded as Annette turned and moved back to first class and into an empty row of seats to peer out the window. The 737 had been rocking and bucking gently in the turbulence from thermals, rising columns of hot air from the rapidly heating desert below, but she was unprepared to see the landscape shooting by in such a crazy blur.

She moved closer and slid into a window seat, astounded to see how low they were, a cold knot of fear compressing her stomach.

There was a blur to the left, to the front of the aircraft. Annette looked forward, instantly overwhelmed by the great looming presence of the West Mitten as the huge butte rushed past the window less than a thousand feet to the side, its summit towering considerably higher than Flight 90 was flying.

Her hand fluttered involuntarily to her mouth as the aircraft flew by in a partial left bank, bouncing in the pronounced rough air.

Annette jerked her head to the right in time to see the other great butte filling the windows, seemingly close enough to touch, the texture of the rocks on the near vertical walls visible in great detail and relief, the speed and proximity leaving her little doubt they were about to crash.

She snapped her head back to the left again, spotting the visitor center on the ridge line, mentally bracing for an impact she knew instinctively they couldn't survive. It wasn't an internal scream of fright, merely a split-second acknowledgment that they were about to smash into the terrain at several hundred miles per hour.

Instead, there was a sudden acceleration of the engines and a sharp pull up, and in a split second the rim of the valley flashed beneath them at tree top level.

No impact.

The 737 whistled over a dirt road, then a highway, finally beginning a sharp right climbing turn as the desert floor dropped away.

Suddenly there was intense commotion throughout the cabin, as if everyone had exhaled at the same moment. Annette could see members of the high school band gripping their armrests in confusion, unsure whether to be scared or exhilarated. But the fear-of-flying group was faring poorly, and watching her with wide-eyed intensity—a dozen sets of eyes flaring like a squadron of startled owls, each trying to decide whether the chief flight attendant was amused or terrified, so they could follow suit.

The verbal reactions registered in her mind, but it was the unruly Blenheim in 6C leaning inside the first class curtain whose voice assaulted her the moment she stood up and moved back to the aisle.

"Stewardess, what in the hell is that idiot up there doing?"

She shook her head, her voice still a hostage to shock, the same question echoing in her own mind.

Annette moved toward him, her face ashen, her voice barely a squeak.

"Sir, I'll try to find out what happened. I warned you to stay seated."

The man's eyebrows were fluttering angrily, hiding his obvious fright, but he nodded and sank back in his seat as his hands fumbled with the seatbelt.

Annette could hear a low rumble of conversation from the coach cabin as she turned away and moved quickly forward into the entry way to pick up the interphone handset, her finger jabbing repeatedly at the captain call button, not caring whether she irritated Wolfe or the hijacker.

"Yes?" Ken's voice sounded testy.

"What in heaven's name was that all about? You've scared the hell out of everyone, Ken."

"No choice, Annette. At least I kept us flying. It's too complicated to explain."

"Ken, you've got an airplane full of traumatized people. We couldn't have been five hundred feet off the ground."

"Two hundred, actually."

"Good Lord!" She rubbed her temple, her eyes fixated on nothing.

"Annette, he's telling me to go to Salt Lake City now, so it'll calm down."

"I hope so. Do we know what he wants?"

"World peace, a chicken in every pot, and death to criminals. I don't really know yet."

"You're going to need to talk to the passengers, Ken. You need to level with them."

"Why?"

"Because they're scared to death. *I'm* scared to death. Not knowing what's going on is worse that hearing that we're hijacked."

"You sure about that? *You* know the truth, Annette, but did it keep you calm?"

"I . . ."

"I'd wager it didn't."

"You've got to tell them something! Make up a story that it's okay to buzz a national monument and play chicken with mountains. Something. We're getting unanswerable questions back here."

"Deal with it, Annette. I can only do what this man wants."

"He's got a gun?"

"Worse than that. He's got a load of plastic explosives in his checked baggage. He's also got an electronic trigger in his hand called a dead man's switch."

For what seemed like an eternity, she couldn't make her voice work. A gun was bad enough with a single pilot aboard. Explosives too?

"What . . ." she swallowed, trying to clear her throat of the boulder-size lump. "What should I do back here, Ken?" Annette forced herself to breathe. She could feel the muscles in her diaphragm shaking uncontrollably.

"Stay off the interphone for one thing, Annette. No distractions, no trying to open the door. You might startle him, and if he lets go of that switch for any reason, we're dead."

SIX

Salt Lake City. 11:10 A.M.

Kat Bronsky pulled the damp towel from her head and dabbed at the few remaining drops of water on her body as she examined herself in the full-length mirror. Twenty-five minutes in a hot shower had probably been too much of an indulgence, but it felt wonderful, especially after being jolted awake by a grating alarm clock she hadn't meant to set before 10:30 A.M.

"Not bad, young lady. Not bad," she said at last as she tried to flatten her slightly overfed belly with her right hand. She arched her back and squared her shoulders. "This is how I'm going to look in two more months, fellows. At thirty-two, a sex goddess at last," Kat chuckled to herself. "Yeah, right!"

She was pleased the diet was working, but she wasn't exercising enough, and she resolved to work out sometime during the next week.

Maybe.

She turned sideways, carefully examining her profile, satisfied with the unruly cascade of chestnut-brown hair brushing her shoulders and the outline of her breasts.

The previous night's research marathon at the FBI's Salt Lake City field office had given her a morning off, and she wasn't due in before noon, but there was plenty of paperwork waiting for the office's newest agent and she was still enthused enough to look forward to it.

Kat began opening a new package of bikini panties as she glanced at the clock.

Jeez, it's after eleven!

She pulled on the panties more hurriedly than she'd planned and adjusted the elastic, then examined her reflection again, determined to ignore the fact that she still wasn't quite ready to wear something so skimpy.

Her new nationwide beeper sat on the counter, paid for by the FBI. Its presence thrilled her—an affirmation of her position as an FBI agent. She grinned as she picked it up and clipped it to the waistband of the bikini bottoms, then turned to the mirror with her arms over her head.

The perfect undercover ensemble! About as subtle as a SWAT team.

A loud alarm pulsed from the beeper at the same moment and Kat jumped slightly in reaction, feeling vaguely embarrassed, as if whoever had sent the message had also been watching her seminude self-appraisal.

The screen showed an urgent message from FBI headquarters in Washington and a number to call, and she moved quickly to the bedside telephone to make the connection, scribbling down the initial details about the hijacking of an AirBridge flight and the plan to set up a command post at Salt Lake City International Airport.

"I'll be in my car in ten minutes," she told her counterpart in Washington. "I'll call you on the way."

She hung up the phone feeling exhilarated.

Wow! The real thing.

She was now officially on a case as an FBI hostage negotiator. The thought made her smile as she replaced the receiver and began a tug-of-war with the nearest pair of pantyhose while plotting what clothes to grab.

Something businesslike, she concluded. *Okay, a pantsuit.*

Kat reached in the closet for the chosen ensemble with her mind racing over the seriousness of the situation, the thought sobering her instantly and draining her excitement away. This was dead serious. An airline hijacking could easily demand every bit of skill and training she had as a psychologist, and anything she did would be subjected to the intense scrutiny of both her bosses and the media. The FBI had very few female hostage negotiators in the first place. Worse, just one mistake in dealing with the hijacker and she could lose everyone on board.

Kat took a look at herself in the mirror as she put on her blouse and began fastening the back, her fingers uncharacteristically fumbling with the buttons. She felt a bit shaky, and that fact sent a cold chill up her spine. The only thing that might be standing between disaster and a peaceful surrender would be her voice. Her voice, her steadiness under pressure, and her intellect. She had to be cool.

Okay, I'm scared. I'd better admit it right now. She forced herself to take a deep breath and focus.

I'm scared, but I know what I'm doing.

Kat let several seconds tick by before glancing at her watch. Twelve minutes had already elapsed. A quick dab of lipstick, eyeliner, and blush, and she grabbed her keys and purse and headed for the door, quietly pleased by the dead weight of her Glock 40mm handgun as it bulged against the leather.

Aboard AirBridge Flight 90. 11:14 A.M.

"Sir! Sir, please sit down!" Annette jumped to her feet as a coach passenger came through the dividing curtains into first class at a brisk walk, his face contorted in a frown. She raised her hand as he came to a halt just short of the galley and pulled something from his shirt pocket, holding it up for her to see.

"I'm with the FAA, miss. Dudley Harris. I need to talk to your captain, right now."

She read the name on the identification card as he continued.

"I'm a maintenance inspector, but I can still file violations, and you're required to admit me to the cockpit on request."

Annette studied the man for a second, then gestured toward the forward entry alcove. Harris followed.

Annette molded her back against the forward entry door next to the interphone panel and motioned Harris to within inches of her face as she held her finger to her lips.

"What is it?" he asked in a suspicious tone.

"Mr. Harris, there's something I have to tell you," she said very softly.

He pulled back slightly. "I'm sorry, what? I'm having trouble hearing you." His voice was softer, too, but still loud enough to startle her, and she motioned for quiet again as she leaned forward to speak directly in his ear.

"Mr. Harris, the passengers have not been told, but we've been hijacked. There's a hijacker in the right seat in the cockpit with a gun, claiming he has a bomb in the baggage compartment."

The FAA inspector jumped back, his eyes wide, mouthing the word, "Hijacker?"

Annette nodded solemnly, and leaned toward him again.

"The captain told me the hijacker is listening on the interphone."

Harris took a deep breath and looked around toward the closed cockpit door before replying. He turned back to Annette, alarm showing clearly on his face.

"I—I had no idea."

She shrugged. "He said not to tell anyone."

The sound of a call chime reverberated through the airplane and Annette checked the ceiling call lights, startled to see it was the cockpit call button that had been pushed. She swallowed hard and motioned to Harris to wait as she picked up the handset.

"Hello."

"Annette?"

"Yes, Ken."

"I heard voices outside the door. What's going on? Is that sorry son of a bitch Rudy Bostich acting up?"

"Bostich? Ah, no, captain. You mean the guy in coach?" She looked at Harris in confusion, her mind whirling around his reference to Bostich as she raised the receiver to her lips again. "There's an FAA inspector here who didn't appreciate your tour. He wants to talk to you, but—"

"But you told him we've been hijacked, didn't you?"

"I had to, Ken."

There was silence for a few heartbeats as Annette held her breath.

"Is he still there?" Ken asked.

She nodded silently, before remembering to speak the words. "Yes. Yes, he is. He's right here with me."

"Well, I'm instructed to tell the FAA to go back to his seat. I've . . . I've got to hang up now."

Annette replaced the receiver and relayed the message to Harris, who raised the palms of both hands.

"I'm gone, but I'm in Twenty-two-C if you need me."

"Thanks, Mr. Harris."

The inspector moved through the first class cabin and headed back to his seat, leaving Annette with a desperate, hollow feeling that only increased when the sound of the P.A. filled the aircraft once more.

"Okay, folks, this is captain. Here's the deal. What I couldn't tell you a while ago was that we've had a forced change of plans. I'm not going to sugarcoat this for you. We've been hijacked, and the hijacker is sitting right next to me holding a gun."

There was a low, collective gasp throughout the cabin.

"What's worse, he claims he has a bag full of explosives in the baggage compartment, and he's holding an electronic trigger. If he lets go of that trigger, we've had it. Therefore, I caution everybody to remain seated, remain calm, and under no circumstances whatsoever should anyone try to intervene. Even if you could successfully overpower him, if his fingers leave that electronic trigger, it's all over."

Annette stood in shock watching the equally horrified expressions on the faces of her passengers. There had been a few short cries in the coach cabin, but now there was stunned silence as the captain continued.

" 'Scuse me just a second folks. What?"

The captain's question seemed to be partially off microphone, as if listening to the hijacker's response. There were the sounds of a voice murmuring in the background as the hijacker spoke, then Ken's voice returned to the P.A.

"Folks, the man tells me to assure you that he has no intention of hurting anyone on board, but that he's had to use real explosives just to make sure no one fails to believe him. He says—What? I can't hear you."

There was silence as the captain kept the P.A. button depressed, but every few seconds Ken would interject an "okay" or "all right" as the hijacker told him what to say. Annette turned and looked at the cockpit door, which was fairly easy to hear through. Countless times on the forward jumpseat she'd been scared to death by various warning horns going off in the cockpit during landing and wafting clearly through the door. If she could hear warnings, maybe she could hear the hijacker's voice, too.

She remembered clearly the voice of the young man from seat 18D, the other pilot. If he was the hijacker, she had to know.

Annette moved quietly to the cockpit door and put her ear against the surface as Ken began speaking once more.

"Sorry for the delay. I'm trying to relay exactly what I've been requested to relay. He says that he'll tell us what he's demanding a little later, but in the meantime, he's ordering me to fly us to Salt Lake City, and that's where we're headed right now. He also says—hold . . . hold on."

Annette listened for the hijacker's voice as Ken began listening again to instructions. She could hear him saying "right" and "okay" every few seconds, but even with her eyes closed to help sort out the sounds, she couldn't make out the second voice.

"Okay, I got it. All right, folks, the word is that he's demanding certain actions by various governments, including the U.S. government, in trying to right a terrible wrong. He says he knows what he's doing is a capital crime, but the crime he's trying to address is far worse. I'll tell you more when I'm permitted to. In the meantime, stay very calm, and again, do NOT try to be a hero. It could get us all killed."

The P.A. clicked off, but no additional sounds came from within the cockpit. Annette pulled back from the door and slid over to her jumpseat as a flight attendant call chime rang from the passenger cabin. She wondered why the hijacker was speaking so quietly. Obviously, whoever he was, his vocal range was being masked by the sound of the engines and the slipstream in flight. Listening through the door was going to shed no light on who—or what—they were facing.

· · ·

The call chime had been ringing repeatedly for the last thirty seconds. A distinguished-looking silver-haired woman in row nine was jabbing the overhead call button as if she were trying to kill it, and as Bev approached, she could see the alarmed passenger was none other than the leader of the fear-of-flying group.

Bev knelt beside her in the aisle, trying to keep her voice down.

"Mrs. Gates, are you okay?"

The woman turned to the right, startled to see Bev. Her eyebrows were flaring, and with a flick of her right hand, she pulled her reading glasses free, allowing them to drop on the cord around her neck as she took a quick breath, her voice coming in cultured intensity.

"Certainly not! Good heavens! I told these people this would be a calm flight, and then I led them into the middle of a nighmare."

"I'm awfully sorry—"

"I'm sure you are, but the fact remains, I've spent the past three months calming down twenty-two people who have just been returned to the status of emotional basket cases."

As Bev tried to respond, an older gentleman in the seat behind leaned forward and grabbed Mrs. Gates's elbow, his voice calm and gravelly.

"Elvira, my wife and I may be having a small coronary episode back here, but I take exception to being referred to as a basket case."

Elvira Gates turned and flashed the man a wide-eyed look, before a small smile spread across her face.

"Very well, then *I'm* the basket case!"

"We're all doing quite well back here, Elvira," he added.

"How could you be?"

"You told us even hijackings almost always end peacefully. Don't they?"

"I said that?"

"You did."

Mrs. Gates suddenly nodded. "Of course they do, Jack. I'm sure we'll be fine."

The man patted her elbow and sat back as Elvira Gates leaned toward Bev, her voice a whisper.

"When we get out of this, I may have to take my own course."

Salt Lake City. 11:27 A.M.

Trapped by the third interminable stoplight in a row, Kat Bronsky pounded the dashboard of her aging Volvo in disgust, and remembered she'd promised to call headquarters on the way. The traffic light turned green just as she pulled out her flip-phone, and she punched in the Beltway phone number with one finger of her right hand as she let out the clutch, steered with her knee, and shifted to second with her left hand.

A horn blared on her left as she drifted into the adjacent lane.

"Okay, your horn works. Now try the lights!" she yelled the words to the windshield, being careful not to actually look at the alarmed driver as she grabbed the wheel and swung back in her lane, holding the phone against her chin and shoulder.

"Not enough hands, that's the problem," she muttered.

"Hello? I didn't understand that," a voice on the other end replied in a puzzled tone.

She hadn't expected Washington to answer so fast.

"Ah, sorry. Kat Bronsky here. I'm en route to the airport."

"Okay, Kat. How long?"

"Ten, eleven minutes. You say we're set up in the airport cop shop?"

"That's right. You have the location?"

"Yes. Been there, done that."

"What?"

"I said I've *been* there."

"A lot of static on this line, Kat. I heard you then."

"What's the latest? Do we have anything yet on the subject?"

The agent filled her in on the demands relayed by Albuquerque Center, as well as the strange buzzing of Monument Valley and the copilot's abandonment in Durango.

Kat glanced at the receiver with raised eyebrows. "He *left* the copilot?"

"That's our information. And the hijacker apparently kicked a private pilot off, too."

"That's worrisome. Maybe the hijacker is also a pilot and didn't want company."

"We don't know, Kat. We're trying to talk to the copilot right now. Everything's secondhand."

"Can you have the copilot and the passenger standing by to talk to me the second I get to the command post?"

"Should be able to do that."

"And, of course, it's critical that I get an ID and a profile on this suspect the instant you get one."

"You understand, Kat, that right now we don't have a clue. The hijacker hasn't even been described by the captain, except that he's apparently a male."

"No threats yet?"

"A gun in the cockpit. That's all we have from the FAA."

A huge semi was slowing in front of her on a four-lane road with too much traffic on the left to go around. Kat hit her brake hard and balanced the phone on her shoulder again as she downshifted and tried to scan the side mirror to clear the left lane.

"Dammit. Hold on."

A final car shot past on the left and she accelerated into the clear lane and regained speed before grabbing the phone again.

"Okay. What I was saying . . . see if you can find what military air assets I have to work with. Are there any fighters in the area that could shadow him if we need them? I assume you're letting me call the shots on this?"

Another driver decided to slow in front of her and Kat shot to the right lane and swerved back to the left, deftly passing the slug.

"I'm the agent in charge, Kat," the voice in Washington said. "You know the negotiator's role. We'll do this in complete accordance with standard procedures, and you'll have me and the rest of the bureau standing by to help."

And standing by to take over in a heartbeat if they think the broad is going to screw it up, she thought.

"Okay. Have someone hold a receiver out to me as I come in the door at the command post. I'll talk to you then. In the meantime, it's the night of the driving dead out here."

"I didn't catch that. What about tonight?"

"No, I said it's—there's heavy traffic out here."

"Okay. Talk to you in a few minutes."

Aboard AirBridge Flight 90. 11:29 A.M.

The sight of the lead flight attendant shooting down the aisle headed to the rear of the cabin alarmed every passenger who glanced up. Her eyes were wide with obvious fear, her eyebrows betraying shock and urgency, her demeanor leaving no doubt she wasn't going to stop to answer questions.

Annette reached Kevin and Bev and fairly yanked them into the aft galley for a quick conference.

"Ken is all we've got, and I can't make out the hijacker's voice, so I have no idea who we're dealing with, but I suspect it's the young man who responded in Durango when Ken asked for pilots to come forward. His name is Johnny Beck. His wife's name is Nancy Beck. She's in Eighteen-E."

Bev's eyes widened. "You're kidding, right?"

Annette shook her head.

Bev glanced up the aisle. "I helped get their bags in the overhead, Annette. He couldn't have been sweeter, to his wife or to me."

"Could have been an act. Besides, where is he?"

"Could we have left him behind in Durango?" Kevin asked.

"How?" Annette countered. "He never got off as far as I know."

Bev raised an index finger. "But his wife was frantic, remember? She thought he had. That's when I called you. She freaked a minute ago at the hijacking announcement, and I don't know what to tell her. She's scared to death her husband's up there and in danger."

All three of them looked forward toward the seat that held Nancy Beck. Bev was shaking her head. "Either he's still up there and being held at gunpoint too—"

"I asked, Bev," Annette said, "and Ken told me he was up front. Then when I asked if he was the hijacker, he disconnected. It has to be him."

Kevin's teeth were grinding. "If so, I can take the bastard if we can get the door open fast enough."

"That's not our job!" Annette snapped, regretting her tone instantly. "I'm sorry, Kev. It's just . . . you know, we're not supposed to play Rambo up here."

"Annette, did you see how close we came to the Mittens?" Kevin asked.

Annette nodded as Bev chimed in. "It was far too close, Annette. If he's forcing Ken to fly crazy, he'll kill us if we don't overpower him."

The three of them stood in silence for nearly a minute before Annette took a deep breath and spoke. "Okay. If Beck—that pilot—is on this aircraft, then he's the hijacker. If he was left behind, the company should know it by now, and someone else slipped aboard."

"Had to," Kevin added. "I did a seat count. No one else is missing. It was either him, or someone from the ground in Durango."

"What do we do, Annette?" Bev asked.

"We go to the ET maneuver and phone home. You two please hold the fort back here. I'll get on one of the seat phones and call the company."

Kevin was nodding. "Ken Wolfe's experienced. He'll keep us safe."

Annette hesitated and Kevin noticed.

"What, Annette?"

She shook her head as if clearing cobwebs. "Oh, nothing."

"Come on, what? Something crossed your mind then that really had an impact."

She looked up at Kevin and studied his eyes for a moment, then glanced at Bev. "Just . . . just something that happened back in the Springs I don't understand." She told them about the captain's reaction to Rudy Bostich, and his apparent recovery before departure.

"That's why we were late?" Bev asked.

Annette nodded. "Whatever his upset with Bostich, I'm sure it has no connection to being hijacked, but it was really, really strange. A few minutes ago when Ken asked about the misbehaving S.O.B. in Six-C, he slipped and used Bostich's name."

Annette hurried back up the aisle, feeling her heart pounding every step of the way as her peripheral vision took in her traumatized passengers, some glancing over their shoulders at her, some sitting with their eyes straight ahead, and several using the seat phones.

She turned to a well-dressed young man in a window seat with one of the phones to his ear. He looked startled, and she heard him say "Just a minute" to someone on the other end.

"The phones are still working, right?"

Chris Billings nodded cautiously, holding the receiver as if he expected her to yank it away.

"My, ah, family," he said, gesturing with his eyes to the phone.

"Tell them you'll be fine," Annette replied as she turned and resumed the trek to the first class cabin.

The rows of first class seats on the right side just forward of the bulkhead were unoccupied and she eyed them carefully as she returned to the forward galley looking for her purse. Her American Express card was hard to find as usual, but she fished it from the depths of the purse finally and dropped it in the pocket of her uniform skirt, then moved back down the aisle to slip into one of the unoccupied seats.

A large man in a pullover shirt and jeans had been watching her from the left side of the same row, and she smiled thinly at him now as she held a finger to her lips and pointed to the phone.

He nodded. He understood.

The process seemed to take forever. She swiped the card and waited for the direct number to crew scheduling to ring as she glanced anxiously toward the cockpit, trying not to think about the implications.

"Crew Scheduling."

Annette changed ears and glanced around, keeping her voice as low as possible.

"Can you hear me?"

"Hello. Crew Scheduling." She could hear the usual beeps warning that the call was being recorded.

"Can you *hear* me? This is Annette Baxter aboard Flight Ninety—"

"Last chance. This is Crew Scheduling. Anyone there?"

"Damn!" Annette punched off the call and went through the process again. Once more the number rang and a voice answered.

"Crew Scheduling."

"Can you hear me now?"

"Sure can. Who's this?"

She rattled off the basics.

"You're calling from Flight Ninety? Jeez, Annette, hold on. I'll get the DFC. Don't go away."

There was nothing but line noise for what seemed like minutes as she pressed the receiver to her ear, trying to keep her voice low as she muttered into the unresponsive handset.

"Come on, dammit! Hurry!"

The sound of the P.A. system clicking on reached her ears, and she glanced up instinctively at the ceiling speakers as Ken Wolfe's voice filled the cabin.

"Folks, this is the captain, again. Our hijacker has issued an order I'm required to communicate to you."

There was a voice on the line again.

"Hello? Is this Flight Ninety?"

Annette took a quick breath. "Yes. This is Annette, the lead flight attendant."

"This is the DFC, Annette. Judy Smith. What's going on up there?"

"So, folks, it's unfortunate if this causes you any grief or inconvenience . . ."

"Judy, please listen! We've been hijacked out of Durango. Someone forced the captain to take off without the copilot, and—"

"We know, Annette. Tell me what's going on up there at the moment."

". . . but now I'm going to have to reach over and pull a specific circuit breaker that will . . ."

"I will in a second, but I need to find out something. Did we leave a passenger behind in Durango? If we didn't, then I know who the hijacker is. Otherwise it was someone on the ground. Do you know?"

". . . cut off the telephones for now."

Annette pressed the handset tightly to her ear, listening for an answer.

"Hello? Judy, did you get that?"

The captain's words had been slow to penetrate, but suddenly the fact that he'd cut off her call in midsentence penetrated her consciousness and she felt her heart sink as she slowly dropped the handset to her lap.

A cockpit call chime echoed through the cabin, and Annette

jumped from the seat and moved to the forward entry door to lift the intercom handset.

"Yes, Ken?"

"Where were you, Annette? I've been ringing for you."

She could imagine the hijacker listening to every word. Her phrasing would have to be very nonthreatening. "I've still got passengers to take care of, Ken, and they're scared to death."

"Collect all the portable cellular phones on board, Annette. Now."

"What?"

"Portable cellular phones. All of them. That's what he's ordering."

"It'll take a while, Ken."

"Just do it. He's irritated enough as it is. When you have them, call me. And Annette. He's got a little pen-like thing up here that vibrates if anyone is using a cellular, so caution everyone not to try holding back. If anyone keeps a cell phone and tries to use it, he'll know it immediately."

SEVEN

CNN Headquarters, Atlanta. 11:30 A.M. MDT, 1:30 P.M. EDT.

The secretary to the vice president of news programming left her desk and opened the door to her boss's office.

"Julie? I apologize for breaking in, but could I talk to you for just a second? It's urgent."

Julie McNair nodded and excused herself from an immaculately groomed young man sitting in front of her desk, then followed her secretary to the outer office, pulling the door closed behind her.

"This better be good."

"It is," the secretary began, "and I hate to interrupt a job interview, but you remember the applicant from Phoenix two days ago?"

Julie thought for a second. "Chris someone, right?"

"Chris Billings. He's on line three insisting that I get you on the phone instantly because—"

"*That* won't make him any points."

The secretary raised her hand. "Wait. He says he's in the middle of a major breaking story. He's on an airplane."

Julie pointed to the phone. "I'll take it."

The secretary punched up the line and handed it over her desk.

"Okay, Mr. Billings, what's up?"

"I'm hijacked."

"Say again?"

"I'm in a commercial aircraft, and we've been hijacked. The flight is AirBridge Ninety." He filled her in on the basics and Julie McNair's eyes widened as she leaned over the desk, grabbed a pen, and scribbled a note on the back of an envelope: *Get the control booth—tell them stand by to go live this line.*

The secretary read the note and nodded as she dashed from the office.

"Okay, Chris. You say you're calling on a seat phone?"

"Yeah, and it'll cost a fortune, but—"

"Don't worry, we'll pay the bill. I'm going to put you on live."

Billing's voice interrupted her.

"Forgive me, Ms. McNair, but we have to reach an agreement on something first."

His words stopped her for a second as she wondered why a job applicant who wanted to be a CNN correspondent would demand money up front for a story. He should know they didn't pay money for stories. Besides, this was a perfect opportunity for a live audition.

"Ah, what agreement would that be, Chris?"

"Have you hired anyone yet for that news position?"

"No."

"Good. I want that job. I'm good, I'm the best applicant you have, I'm sick of Phoenix and local news, and, well, I want the job. Hire me right here, right now on the terms we discussed for the money you advertised, and the story is yours."

"That's a form of blackmail, Mr. Billings. I don't appreciate—"

"*Please*, Ms. McNair! It's not blackmail, it's called bargaining power. I didn't have it the other day. I do now. I could call the other nets and make the same offer, but I dearly want to work for CNN."

"The other nets would tell you to go to hell."

"I don't think you really believe that, and neither do I. I'm not selling a story, I'm selling me. Look, I'm a damn good reporter, but I haven't had the chance to prove it at network level. Have you looked at my tapes?"

She sighed. "No, frankly, I've been too busy with interviews."

"Okay. Hire me right now for a six-month trial. Your word will be good enough. If you really like what I do for you on this story, waive the trial period and bring me on in full. But please give me a shot."

"Or you walk with this story, right?"

"Ms. McNair, you're a professional broadcast journalist, too. What would you do?"

Julie McNair ran it over in her mind. She'd always loved making decisions under pressure. Network broadcasting was a highwire act without a net, so what the hell. Even if she screwed up she could bury him for six months and hire someone else.

"Okay, Mr. Billings, you got a deal."

"Chris."

"Chris. You're hired, Chris. Now can we get this story on the air before it gets stale?"

"I'm your man, Ms. McNair. I'm standing by."

AirBridge Airlines Dispatch Center, Colorado Springs International Airport. 11:30 A.M.

Within twenty minutes, the senior executives of AirBridge Airlines had come together to form a crisis management team, taken over a glassed-in conference room adjacent to the dispatch center, and summoned the chief pilot and his boss, the vice president of operations. With several of the executives milling around in animated conversations on desk phones, two others using cellular phones, and the company president huddled with the corporation's general counsel in the far corner, only the chief pilot was looking up when the director of flight control entered the room wearing an ashen expression.

Judy Smith caught the eye of the tall, distinguished-looking senior pilot and moved quickly to his side.

"Steve? Got a moment?"

The captain looked haunted. He had been chief pilot during a hellish year of constant financial pressure and management demands to keep the airline running with a minimum number of pilots. Even if his pilots worked for free, they'd be costing too much money in the eyes of the company, or so he'd complained at every opportunity. The job was wearing him down, and cumulative fatigue was underscored by the dark bags under his eyes.

"Something new, Judy?" he asked.

She inclined her head toward the hallway. "Could we . . . talk out there?"

Captain Steve Coberg satisfied himself that the others in the room were all occupied before following Judy into the hallway and around the corner out of view.

"What's up?" he asked.

She looked him squarely in the eye and said nothing for a few seconds.

"Steve, how well do you know Ken Wolfe?"

Coberg cocked his head suspiciously. "Well, he's one of my pilots, of course. What are you getting at?"

"I think you already know, Steve. I think we both know there are some real concerns here. I know Ken fairly well in an over-the-counter way. I respect him, but there's no avoiding the reality that Ken Wolfe is a very stressed man, and I do not understand why."

He spread both his hands in the air in a constrained gesture.

"Judy, Wolfe went through hell before he hired on here. Let's just leave it at that, okay? There are things that aren't really material to this discussion that make him the way he is."

"What things, Steve?"

He rolled his eyes toward the ceiling and snorted as he raised his hands in a gesture of frustration, then looked back at her. "Things the man asked me not to go blabbing around this airline. Things that caused him great pain. Things that are none of your damn business in dispatch, okay?"

Judy studied her shoes for a second in thought. She snapped her eyes back to Coberg's suddenly. "I wonder if these things he doesn't want us to know about might explain his strange behavior around here."

Coberg sighed and gestured again.

"Look, I know he's a moody bastard, but what can that possibly have to do with a . . . a hijacking?"

"Ken's had a lot of complaints from fellow pilots, hasn't he?"

There was another long hesitation as he studied her eyes. "You know I can't discuss that sort of information." Coberg watched her eyebrows flare slightly as she moved imperceptibly closer.

"Steve, I've talked to a bunch of the copilots who've been flying with Ken this year. They all say he's a good stick-and-rudder guy in the cockpit, a by-the-book captain, but he's driving them crazy out there. Are you going to tell me you haven't noticed?"

"We get crybaby copilots whining about captains all the time, Judy. You probably don't understand that."

"You ever hear of People's Express, Steve?"

He snorted again. "People's *Distress,* we used to call them. Of course."

"Well, I was a Boeing 727 captain for what you call People's Distress before we collapsed in the eighties. I do understand, thank you very much."

"Sorry, Judy. I didn't know. I was with Eastern. We didn't like you folks very much."

"I understand that. I also understand that there's been a steady stream of worried copilots coming upstairs to tell you the same things they tell me." She began counting off points on her fingers. "They describe Ken as distant, distracted, distraught, and inconsistent, they say he misses radio calls, that he's moody, which you already pointed out, and I know for a fact that in crew scheduling's point of view, he's undependable because of all his sudden sick calls. That's hardly a normal profile. If I'm hearing these things, Steve, you're hearing them."

Coberg sighed and looked pained. "God sake's, Judy, of course the man's moody." Coberg turned and shoved his hands deep in his pockets as his eyes studied the far end of the hallway. He looked at the floor then, then back up at Judy, speaking at low volume. "Judy, four years ago, he lost his wife to a car crash. Two years ago, his only child, his little eleven-year-old daughter, was kidnapped, raped, tortured, and murdered back in Connecticut. He's in agony every day about that. The man's lost everyone close to him in this world. He has a right to be moody."

Judy knew her mouth was hanging open, her eyes huge, but she couldn't help it.

"My God, Steve!"

"See, that's the type of reaction I think he wanted to avoid around here. That's why he asked me not to tell anyone."

"Did you know about this when you hired him?"

Coberg hesitated, then nodded. "Most of it, yes. He'd been flying for a regional airline back east. Part of the Davidson empire of small airlines. I assume you know about Tom Davidson?"

Judy nodded. Davidson was a familiar name in the Wild West post-deregulation airline world. He was also one of AirBridge's biggest stockholders.

"Well, Mr. Davidson called me personally and told me the story.

He explained that the murderer had gone free on a technicality and said he was worried about Wolfe living there in Connecticut." He stopped for a moment and then continued. "Mr. Davidson asked me to make a place for Ken Wolfe at AirBridge and sent me his file. I couldn't see any reason to refuse."

Judy studied the chief pilot for several seconds before replying.

"Has Ken Wolfe been in counseling, Steve? Did Davidson tell you whether he had?"

Once again, Coberg sighed heavily and glanced around in frustration before locking his eyes on hers again. "Judy, the man's an excellent pilot, and we're desperate for excellent pilots. The suits in this airline are on me every time we cancel a flight because I can't get enough pilots hired who'll stay here for the peanuts we pay. I can't be concerned whether a good pilot's seeing a shrink or not, as long as he does his job. That's a personal question."

"*Counseling*? Whether an upset captain needs counseling is a *personal* question?"

"Yes, dammit!"

"But Steve, if you haven't noticed, he's flying our airplanes. He's flying our passengers. Should he be? Regardless of what Mr. Davidson wanted, did anyone check to make sure Wolfe was getting psychological help?"

Coberg snorted. "Is this going somewhere?"

"Yes."

"Well, *where*, then? Tell me!"

"How'd the hijacker get on board, Steve?"

Coberg stared at her in silence for a few moments before shrugging his shoulders. "*What*?"

"Exactly what I asked. How did the hijacker get aboard that aircraft?"

"Hell, Judy, why ask me? *You* told *us* what happened."

She shook her head. "No, I briefed you only on what I had so far, that the aircraft landed unexpectedly in Durango and apparently was commandeered by someone while the copilot was off running a very strange errand, and a passenger who happens to be the only other pilot on board was also sent off the airplane."

"And?"

"And the captain just happens to be our ranking problem child, with a file of worrisome feedback on inconsistent behavior that's probably several inches thick."

Judy saw his eyes narrow as he squared his shoulders and stepped back slightly.

"Judy, I don't like the implications here."

"Steve, if a hijacker was lying in wait, how'd he know our flight was going to make an emergency landing in Durango? Who would plan a hijacking in Durango, for God's sake? There's not enough commercial traffic through there. Have you asked yourself that question?"

"Well, he couldn't know, of course. Even the captain didn't know, which means the hijacker must have made a spur-of-the-moment decision. I mean, who knew Wolfe was going to lose an engine?"

"Wolfe didn't lose an engine. He shut it down. Wolfe shuts it down and then decides to go to Durango. You get it? *He* decided. He was the only one who could have known."

Steve Coberg's eyes narrowed under a furrowed brow as he thought about the contradiction.

"Well, I suppose the hijacker could have already been on board."

"Maybe he was. But the only other individual we've talked to who went to the cockpit was the pilot left behind, and he told me he saw nothing suspicious before the captain tricked him into leaving."

"Tricked?" Coberg's face betrayed total shock. "Jesus, Judy! What are you suggesting? You telling me you suspect the hijacker is Ken Wolfe's *accomplice*? Hell, the man's depressed. He's not a criminal."

"I don't know, Steve. I don't know the answer. But I do know something's very wrong here, and my guy Verne Garcia even commented on how distracted Wolfe was this morning at the desk."

Suddenly, Coberg was glancing in both directions down the hallway before looking at her, his voice kept very low.

"Judy, you can't repeat unfounded suspicions like this to anyone!"

She bristled. "Well, if *you* can't explain it, and *I* can't explain it, someone's got to be told."

"But you've got nothing!"

"I've got loose ends that don't fit and a captain who probably shouldn't have been flying, and we need to know—*they* need to know in that room there—what we might be dealing with. And hey, Steve. You think *that* will get you in trouble? Just try taking the blame for letting the suits in there get blindsided."

Coberg was breathing hard. He paused to wet his lips, his voice coming low and urgently to her ears.

"Judy, look. He was all right to fly, okay? I had no reason to ground Wolfe. We did everything right with him, but you're gonna screw around and second guess me and get me in real trouble here. Don't forget, Tom Davidson *personally* asked me to hire Wolfe."

"And that means what?"

"Well," Coberg gestured wildly to the ceiling, "if AirBridge is made to look stupid for hiring Wolfe, it reflects on Mr. Davidson."

"Can you prove Davidson made that call to you?"

Coberg looked shocked. "Well, no . . ."

"Steve, men like Tom Davidson are too smart and powerful to leave themselves open for blame. If the decision to hire Wolfe blows up in our faces, you can bet Davidson will have no memory of that call."

Coberg began to protest, but Judy raised her hand to silence him.

"Look, I'm not trying to get you in trouble, Steve, but either I'm going to tell them about Ken, you're going to tell them, or we'll do it together. Forget Davidson. This one's at your doorstep."

Again he regarded her over an endless bridge of awkward silence.

"You're serious, aren't you?" he said at last.

"Dead serious. We're going to do it right now."

Steve Coberg swallowed loudly and took a deep breath as he rubbed his chin and glanced in the direction of the conference room.

"Okay. Okay, we do it together."

"Good."

"Ah, I'll tell them his background problems, you tell them what Verne saw today."

"Okay."

"But please don't say he shouldn't have been flying."

She nodded slowly. "Steve, I think they're going to figure that one out all by themselves."

Aboard AirBridge Flight 90. 11:40 A.M.

Annette paused halfway up through the coach cabin to look back at Bev and Kevin, who were watching her from the rear galley area. There was a thin, supportive smile from Bev, but Kevin seemed angry.

Annette looked inside the plastic trash bag she was carrying. There were perhaps ten cell phones already, and more to come, since she had obeyed the hijacker's relayed orders and used the P.A. to ask everyone to surrender all their phones. Any cellular signal from the cabin, she had told them, could be detected by their captor.

She had seen ads for the type of cellular signal detector Ken had mentioned. They did exist.

"Ma'am?" She turned toward the familiar face of the young man she'd seen using the seat phone earlier, and realized with a start that he was reaching into her bag to get one of the cell phones.

Annette yanked the bag away.

"Hey! What do you think you're doing?"

"I've got to borrow one of those! I'm a CNN reporter. I was on the air when they pulled the plug."

"No! Jeez, didn't you hear what I said? The hijacker can detect if a cell phone's in use, even back here. We can't afford to upset him."

The thought of angering some psychopath in the cockpit with a bomb trigger in his hand was a terrifying presence in her mind, and she wondered if the passengers could sense her massive upset.

Chris Billings motioned her closer, his voice a whisper.

"You don't understand. I'm trying to tell the world exactly what's happening."

Annette leaned close to keep her voice low. "Why, sir? Why is that important enough to risk a bomb?"

"For rescue purposes in Salt Lake. It's vital the FBI know details, or they could make a fatal mistake."

She pulled back, shaking her head. "We can't take the chance. The safest way to deal with a hijacker is play it the way he wants it."

She resumed the trek forward toward first class, collecting several more phones before stopping in front of Rudy Bostich's seat.

Bostich was smiling up at her and holding out one of the smallest phones she'd ever seen.

"They'll be making these as surgical implants in the next few years, I guess," he said with a worried chuckle as he placed it in the bag. Annette smiled back as best she could, her eyes memorizing his familiar face, her mind trying to imagine what he could have done to so profoundly upset Ken Wolfe.

Rudy Bostich had noticed the frightened, faraway look on her face as he read her nametag.

"Are you okay . . . Annette, is it?" he asked.

She drew a sharp breath, nodded her head and tried to smile. It was an unconvincing performance, and they both knew it.

"I'm . . . just worried, like all of us," she said.

"Do you have any idea what the hijacker wants?" he added.

She shook her head and tried to force a smile.

"Not yet."

Bostich shifted in his seat and raised a finger. "Ah, you know, it would probably be better if you didn't tell the captain or the hijacker that I'm aboard, since we don't know what's going on. Just a precaution. The idea that there's a federal prosecutor on board, you know, could be a target."

"I understand," Annette replied, trying to keep her expression neutral while the memory of handing his business card to Ken Wolfe in Colorado Springs, and Ken's strange reaction to it, flashed across her mind.

"I'll make sure no one tells the hijacker," she said.

Annette turned in confusion and retreated into the forward galley, pulling the curtains behind her, and drew a ragged breath. The plastic bag of cellular phones was still dangling from her right hand and she hadn't even noticed. She placed it in the corner of the galley, against the right front door, and at the same moment remembered her incomplete phone call to operations. She'd tried to find out whether a passenger had been left in Durango, but had they heard her?

Probably not, she decided, but even if they had the answer ready, how could she get it?

The kid from CNN is right, she thought. *The FBI needs to know what's happening.*

Annette looked at the cockpit door and tried to imagine the cellular signal detector going off. What would the hijacker do if he thought someone was communicating with the ground without his permission? Was there somewhere around the airplane she could use the phone without the vibrator activating?

He'd have Ken call me on the interphone, she decided. *He'd yell at me not to try again. That's all.*

Annette made sure the curtains to the galley were pulled before leaning down and digging out the smallest phone she could find. It was the one Bostich had handed her, and she slipped it in her apron pocket before picking up the bag and moving to the interphone panel.

Ken answered immediately.

"I've got the phones in a bag here by the door. You want them up front?"

"I'm going to unlock the door, Annette. Open it just far enough to toss the bag inside, then shut it immediately. Look only at the floor. He says if he sees the whites of your eyes, he'll shoot. He doesn't want you identifying him. Understand?"

"Yes, but Ken, can I come in and talk to you?"

"No! Do you understand the procedure?"

She looked back toward the cabin, wondering if anyone was listening to her side of the conversation. The woman in 1C was watching the cockpit door, but Rudy Bostich was out of sight behind the partition dividing first class from the forward entryway. Annette kept her voice as low as she could.

"I understand the procedure, Ken."

Annette picked up the bag of cell phones as the click of the electronic door lock release reached her ears. She moved to the door and put her hand on the handle, which was on the right side, the hinge on the left. She pulled it open less than twelve inches. In her peripheral vision, she was aware of the back of Ken's head in the captain's chair as she reached in and quickly dropped the bag on the floor just inside the door, but from her position at the right edge of the doorframe, the copilot's seat was invisible.

There was another familiar object visible in the few seconds the door was ajar, and her mind raced to consider the possibilities: The crash axe sat in its storage harness on the left sidewall just inside the door.

Could I grab the axe before he could stop me? she wondered. *But what then?*

Annette closed the door as fast as she could, then moved back to the interphone panel, her knees shaking at the mere thought of attacking someone with an axe.

She picked up the interphone handset and pressed the button.

"Okay, Ken. They're all there."

"Thanks, Annette."

"Ken?"

There was no answer.

"Ken, please answer me."

The interphone transmit button finally clicked on.

"What?"

"Ken, is he listening?"

"Yes, but we're getting close to Salt Lake City. We don't have much time left. There's much to prepare for, and even I don't . . ." His voice trailed off.

"Don't what, Ken? Don't what?"

"Never mind. I'm being told to shut up. Go sit down and strap in. It'll be easier that way."

A cold chill began creeping up her back.

"What will be easier, Ken? What is he planning?"

There was no response, except for the sound of the interphone button being released in the cockpit.

Annette sank into the forward jumpseat, a hand over her eyes, the phone clutched tightly to her ear. *It'll be easier that way*, he had said.

The sound of the P.A. clicking on stunned her.

> *"This is the captain again. Everyone in this aircraft, flight attendants included, must be seated and belted in immediately. Do not get out of your seats for any reason!"*

Annette jumped to her feet and moved into the forward portion of the first class cabin as she felt the aircraft enter a sudden bank to the right. The eyes of a dozen frightened passengers were on her as she realized they were still banking, still rolling to the right. She caught a glimpse of tree-covered mountainsides thousands of feet below, filling the right-hand side windows of the 737.

The roll was continuing!

Annette braced herself with a firm hand on the edge of the overhead compartments. She had planned on walking through the cabin, checking on seatbelts, then briefing Kevin.

They were still rolling, almost through ninety degrees. She was looking straight down on the trees below.

Straight down!

Trees continued to move vertically in the windows on the 737's right side, from the bottom to the top, as the roll continued. A squadron of sunbeams shot through the left side windows at a wild angle, raking the cabin with as many shafts of moving light as the jet had windows.

What on earth is he doing?

She realized they were rolling upside down. Trees and rocks and meadows were moving at a crazy angle out of the top of each window frame, giving way to an upside down view of the horizon as she felt herself getting light on her feet and . . . *floating!*

We're completely inverted!

There were brief screams and gasps throughout the cabin as the 737 continued to roll through the inverted position.

Annette realized she was completely weightless. Blue sky and upside down clouds were visible through the right side windows, and the trees and mountainsides were appearing from the top down through the windows on the left side, all of them still moving as the roll continued.

She heard the engine power being throttled back, and the sound of an increasing slipstream as the aircraft sped up, its nose pointed slightly down as it continued to roll past 270 degrees, three quarters of the way around.

And within a few seconds, normal gravity returned and the sky repositioned itself correctly in both sets of windows as the 737 returned to level flight.

Once again the P.A. clicked on, barely overpowering the deafening sound of cries from the passengers and her own pounding heartbeat. The voice was strained and curt.

> *"People, I'm told to tell you that was just a sample of what will happen if anyone disobeys this guy's orders. Don't even think of trying to interfere. Stay seated. Stay calm. Stay out of it, or he'll put us through far worse than what you just experienced."*

AirBridge Airlines Dispatch Center, Colorado Springs International Airport. 11:40 A.M.

With the connection to AirBridge 90 broken, Judy Smith replaced the handset and looked around at the faces of the chief pilot, the VP of operations, and the company's president. The three men had followed her from the conference room when the excited crew scheduler had burst in and summoned her.

"What, Judy? *What*?" Steve Coberg asked.

She shook her head. "I lost the connection. We can replay the tape, but she asked the question 'Did we leave a passenger behind . . .' and then I lost her. I never heard what she was referring to."

Judy followed them back into the conference room, aware that a stern-looking man from corporate headquarters she recognized as one of the company's attorneys pointedly closed the door behind her. She heard the distinct sound of the door lock clicking into place, and she noticed that the curtains between the conference room and the dispatch center had already been drawn. When they were completely isolated, the man moved to the head of the table and introduced himself as the airline's vice president-law as he looked squarely at the chief pilot.

"Captain Coberg, is it?"

"Yes, sir."

His gaze shifted to Judy, and he spoke her name with a question mark.

"Yes," she replied.

"Okay. What you two were just telling us—these *concerns* you had about the captain's reaction to a terrible personal loss—can never leave this room. Any unfounded speculation or observations about the emotional stability of one of our pilots is proprietary information, and in fact, it's not even information. It's just dangerous gossip."

Judy started to speak, but Steve Coberg cut her off.

"We have no intention of letting that out of here, Mr. Wallace. But we felt these were observational details that the senior leadership needed to know."

The lawyer straightened and snorted, a stormy look on his face.

"Yeah, we really need to know after the fact that this captain may be a loose cannon in a financially marginal commercial airline operation with a gazillion dollars of liability exposure in a volatile stock market."

Coberg glared at Judy, then raised both hands in a gesture of puzzlement. "Well, are you suggesting I shouldn't have said anything to this group? I mean, these are just background worries, but I don't want the senior leadership to be, well, blindsided if anything ever came of it."

"Did you think he should have been grounded, Captain?" Wallace snapped.

"Well, no, of course not. If I thought Captain Wolfe wasn't fit to fly, he would have been grounded."

Wallace scowled. "That's exactly the point, Captain. Officially, this man had no problems whatsoever that would have left you or any other employee of this airline with any doubt about his capabilities, *because*"—he emphasized the word and drew it out—"*because* . . . if you officially *had* held such doubts, you would have officially removed him from flying."

"Sir," Coberg began, but the lawyer's hand shot up to stop him.

"To do any less than ground a legitimately questionable captain would be considered gross negligence, even if his problems ultimately have nothing to do with the way this man handles this hijacking. You operations people need to remember that there's a country full of rabid plaintiff's attorneys out there who'll sue us in a heartbeat on the mere suggestion that a captain wasn't absolutely perfect. An ink smudge in his log book from thirty years ago may be thrown back in our faces in court. Even God might not know about it, but we're supposed to, and we can't go around talking about unfounded concerns because some damn four-striper didn't smile enough at the cute dispatcher when he picked up his papers this morning."

"*Mr.* Wallace, I take offense at that!" Judy snapped, trying to control the anger that had already been coursing through her mind.

"What, dear? At being cute? Fact of life. You are."

James Ryder, the president of the airline, sat forward slightly and tugged at Jack Wallace's coat sleeve. "Enough, Jack. This is the damn nineties, and girls are sensitive."

"So are women, sir!" Judy replied. "I didn't think our company endorsed sexual harassment, even by officers."

Ryder sighed and raised his hand in apology. "I'm sorry, Ms. Smith. Women, of course. I meant to say women." He sat back and sighed. "Of *course* we don't tolerate sexual harassment here."

Jack Wallace shrugged as Judy drummed her fingers on the desk and spoke up.

"So, Mr. Wallace, you're saying that whatever information we actually had from observing our crews, we're not supposed to report it, and therefore—"

He slammed his fist on the table to cut her off.

"Dammit, Ms. Smith, there *is* no information unless you acted on it. You understand? If you knew, any of you," he pointed his index finger at Judy, moved it to the chief pilot, then back. "If you knew that this captain had real, genuine, nonspeculative, emotional problems that, without question, were materially affecting his ability to fly safely—not just his ability to baby-sit copilot egos—you should have canned him or grounded him instantly. That's what a court would say. That's what a jury would say. And that's what the damned press will go clucking about later on, even if every last person gets off that airplane unscathed. So if you didn't determine whatever you saw in this captain sufficiently worrisome to cause you to act, you saw nothing, and there was nothing to report. Understand? There are no shades of gray here."

"But what if someone asks us officially how he seemed this morning?" Judy asked, fixing the lawyer with a hostile gaze.

"Such as?"

"Such as the FAA. Such as the FBI. Such as a court, asking us under oath."

Wallace stared back at Judy with equal hostility and disdain before answering. His words were assembled with obvious care.

"I would never instruct you to lie, Ms. Smith. Remember I said that. But I will always tell you to be absolutely, positively sure that what you say under oath comes from hard facts that you absolutely knew at the time, and not from opinion or casual observations of an AirBridge pilot, or anyone else."

Steve Coberg shifted uncomfortably in his chair and spoke up. "But what about written reports from other pilots?"

Wallace shifted his gaze to Coberg and studied him for a few seconds, then smiled and looked down at the table briefly before snapping his gaze back with enough force to cause the chief pilot to flinch.

"What reports would those be, Captain?"

"Well—" Coberg began, but Wallace quickly cut him off.

"I would be very surprised and distressed if you, or your boss,"—Wallace flicked his eyes momentarily at the vice president of operations, who was cringing—"would permit anything resembling such reports to be in the official files of this airline. I'm sure if I came upstairs this afternoon to look through your file cabinets, I would find no such files in existence. Isn't that right?"

Wallace kept his eyes locked on Steve Coberg for several awkward seconds until the pilot swallowed loudly and nodded.

"Good." Wallace looked at James Ryder, who nodded his assent. "That closes the subject," Wallace continued. "We have an aircraft in the control of an unknown hijacker who has obviously overcome by force any reasonable resistance of one of our finest captains. We should be focusing on that reality, and that reality alone."

EIGHT

CNN Headquarters, Atlanta. 11:40 A.M. MDT, 1:40 P.M. EDT.

The director leaned toward the interphone to speak into the anchor's ear.

"We lost Billings. The line just went dead. All we can do is wait for a callback."

On the monitors, the director could see the anchor nod as he waited for a commercial break to end.

"We've got a freeze-frame of Chris Billings from the demo tape he left," the director continued, "and we'll rerun the audio."

A voice from the director's left caught his attention.

"That shot's up on five, Bob. That one okay?"

The director turned to look at the wall of monitors, studied the face of the young newsman, and flashed a thumbs up.

"Okay, here we go."

In the studio, the anchor looked up and resumed his steady gaze at the live camera.

> "We have an extraordinary breaking news story we began reporting to you less than fifteen minutes ago, involving a hijacked commercial airliner—AirBridge Airlines Flight Ninety—bound from Colorado Springs to Phoenix with a hundred and thirty passengers and crew aboard. Also on board that aircraft is CNN correspondent Chris Billings, who, up until a few minutes ago when the connection was lost, had been able to maintain telephone contact from his seat."

The screen dissolved to the still picture of Chris Billings as his voice filled the control room explaining the unplanned stop in Durango, the strange and frightening low pass through Monument Valley, and the sudden announcement that the aircraft had been hijacked.

> "At this moment, Reid, none of us on board this flight really knows what the hijacker wants, or who he might be. None of us in the coach cabin saw anything unusual before that startling announcement. The captain has told us that the hijacker is holding a gun on him in the cockpit and has placed explosives in the cargo hold. Here's part of the captain's announcement a few minutes ago."

There was a short pause and the scratching of the telephone handset against the speaker on the portable tape recorder as Billings held them together.

"*. . . He says that he'll tell us what he's demanding a little later, but in the meantime he's ordering me to fly us to Salt Lake City . . .*"

Billings's voice came on the line again.

> "Every few sentences the captain would pause, apparently listening to orders from the hijacker. The most fascinating aspect was when the captain mentioned what he knew so far about the hijacker's demands."

"*. . . certain actions by various governments, including the U.S. government, in trying to right a terrible wrong. He says he knows what he's doing is a capital crime, but the crime he's trying to address is far worse. I'll tell you more when I'm permitted to. In the meantime, stay very calm, and again, do NOT try to be a hero. It could get us all killed.*"

> "So, all we really know is that we're being diverted to Salt Lake City by a hijacker who says he's trying to right a wrong involving . . ."

Billings's voice ended abruptly as the screen dissolved back to the anchor.

> "And as we said before, we lost contact with correspondent Chris Billings at that point. CNN has also learned that the hijacker is

demanding that the Attorney General of the United States and a federal judge be placed on standby to talk to him, apparently when the aircraft reaches Salt Lake City. Additionally, we are told by sources close to the White House that the man most likely to be nominated this week to replace the retiring U.S. Attorney General is on that aircraft. Rudolph Bostich, the U.S. Attorney for Connecticut, was en route to Phoenix, Arizona, for an American Bar Association convention."

Salt Lake City International Airport. 11:45 A.M.

A small conference room adjacent to the offices of the airport police department had been pressed into service as a command post by the time Kat Bronsky arrived. Frank Bothell, a thirty-year FBI veteran, looked up from a commandeered desk as she walked in. He motioned her over as he finished a phone call.

"Yeah . . . yeah, that's what I need." He held his hand over the mouthpiece and looked up at Kat. "It's Washington. I've already got things in motion. I'll brief you in a minute."

She smiled and patted his shoulder, suppressing the overwhelming feeling of relief that he was already there. The worry over how to diplomatically take over and organize an airport full of male officers in ten minutes or less had dominated her thoughts during the drive over. Now she'd have solid help. Tough and kind at the same time, Frank Bothell was a man who genuinely liked working with women, though he cut them no slack as professionals.

Suddenly he was off the phone, leaving FBI headquarters on hold.

"Okay, Kat. Give me your laundry list."

"First thing I need, Frank, is the chain of command. Who's in charge?"

He nodded. "Overall local tactical command? I am. Negotiating and strategic planning based on your assessment of the hijacker? You are. Two of our other agents are inbound to help. I'll get everything ready to receive the airplane and coordinate with these folks," he turned to a startled looking airport police sergeant standing beside him. "Bill, was it?"

"Yeah. Bill Lipsky."

"Okay. Kat, Bill. Bill, Kat."

They shook hands quickly as Frank Bothell continued. "When it comes to dealing with whoever is in that cockpit, that's your baby, Kat. You tell me what you need, when you need it, and give me directions on what to do or not to do. I'll try my best to make things happen the way you want."

She bit her lower lip and nodded. "Okay."

"If you tell me to storm the airplane, though, we'll need approval from Washington. I've got the Bureau's SWAT team coming and they'll be backed up by the Salt Lake City Police. Washington has alerted the Bureau Hostage Rescue Team as well, and will launch them if necessary. Other things I can do locally."

"I need to talk to someone in the airplane as soon as possible. How do we do it?"

Bill Lipsky sighed. "I've got an FAA man coming down right now to help with that. When they get within, say, ninety miles, we can hook you up directly over the aircraft's radio. On the ground, we can run a special hard-wire phone out to the aircraft if the hijacker will let us, or we can plug into the plane's interphone system by the nose gear and talk to them over that."

Kat nodded. "Or you could hand them a cell phone through the window or use a radio walkie-talkie. A digital cell phone would be better for privacy, though, if we can't do a hard-wire. I don't want the media broadcasting what we say."

"Okay," Bill Lipsky looked over his shoulder and motioned another airport officer over. "I'll get someone searching for one."

"Okay," Kat unfolded her arms and stood away from the desk she'd been leaning on. "Frank, before I talk to Washington, what do we know about the hijacker?"

"Nothing yet. We've got an urgent request to the airline for the names of all aboard, including crew, and we've got a team standing by in D.C. to run the backgrounds as soon as we get them. Did you hear about CNN having a reporter aboard, and the wild fly-by through Monument Valley?"

Kat shook her head no, and Frank filled her in. "The reporter was cut off in midsentence. They could have run past the max range of the radio phones," Frank added. "Or—"

"Or the hijacker ordered them turned off, which would be significant," Kat finished.

"Did you know that the hijacker's demanding the Attorney General and a federal judge and several others be kept on standby?"

She nodded. "I heard." She fixed the senior agent with a steady gaze, eye to eye. "Any gut feeling whether this could be a Waco or Ruby Ridge thing?"

"No. It's all guesswork at this stage."

"I mean, asking for federal and state involvement sounds purely political. This isn't the anniversary of one of those disasters, is it?"

"Not that any one of us can recall, Kat. Nothing that's dear to those maniacs. Headquarters is doing a full check, and Clark Roberts is waiting for you on one of the lines there." He gestured to a telephone. "But I agree, it sounds damned political to me."

Kat kept her expression neutral. If this was political and the hijacker suicidal . . .

A cold apprehension gripped her. Dealing with unbalanced humans was one thing. Bargaining with rabid political zealots was entirely another. She mumbled a small prayer that it wasn't the latter.

Kat looked quickly at the faces around her. Frank Bothell was calm and collected. Bill Lipsky, the tall, tanned young police sergeant, had a wide-eyed expression of serious alarm; but several other police officers in the room were obviously pumped.

And they're all looking at you, girl! she thought.

Kat turned toward Bill Lipsky, the police sergeant. "Okay," she said with as much authority as she could muster, "someone please try to get me a briefing on the amount of fuel aboard that aircraft and its range. I need aviation maps and a list of airports they can use in the surrounding multistate area. And, if you can manage it, get me an aircraft flight manual for that precise model."

"You got it," Lipsky said.

"Frank, could you push them to get me a radio hookup to the aircraft as soon as possible? We need to know what we're dealing with." She started to turn toward the phone, then looked back at him. "And as soon as you know where you're going to park them on the airport, let me know."

"Why, Kat?" Frank asked with one eyebrow raised.

She looked him squarely in the eye and smiled. "Because I can't build the trust of a hijacker by hiding in a windowless office. I'll need to be out there at some point where the man can see me."

"You're assuming the S.O.B. is male."

She chuckled. "Most S.O.B.'s are."

Frank rolled his eyes. "You worry me, Bronsky."

Aboard AirBridge Flight 90. 11:45 A.M.

Annette had made her way back to the interphone panel as soon as the 737 righted itself, and Ken had answered rapidly.

"You've got to understand, Annette. I've got to do what he tells me as safely as I can. Go sit down now and pray."

"Is he listening, Ken?"

"Yes."

"Okay. Mister hijacker, will you please tell us what you want?"

"ANNETTE! Jeez, what are you trying to do? Thank God he found that amusing."

The cockpit interphone clicked off for a second, then back on.

"Annette, look. Go back and sit down and keep an eye on Bostich."

Annette took a deep breath and pressed the interphone button harder.

"What about Bostich, Ken?"

"Say again?"

"You said to watch Mr. Bostich. I'm asking you why. What does he have to do with anything? Is this something personal?"

There was a lengthy pause. "Hold . . . hold on." His voice diminished as he talked to one side of the interphone handset, apparently to the hijacker.

"Can I tell her? I mean, what the hell's the point of keeping my crew in the dark?"

More silence, then Ken's voice on the line.

"All he'll let me tell you is this. This whole thing is about Rudy Bostich. Bostich isn't the noble individual he appears to be. That's not my deal, that's his."

"I . . . I don't understand, Ken. If it's about Bostich, why is he hijacking all of us?"

"Enough, Annette! I've got a guy with a gun and a bomb up here, and we're not going to antagonize him, okay? Enough. Go sit down."

"Ken,"

"Now, Annette. NOW!"

"Okay. Okay, I will."

She replaced the handset and moved into the front of the first class cabin in total confusion as the P.A. clicked on.

"Ah, folks, all flight attendants are to be seated immediately in the nearest seat. I'm ordered to tell you that, crew. Do it now!"

A large, masculine hand reached out from nowhere and gently guided Annette into one of the plush first class aisle seats. She let herself settle back and closed her eyes for a second before looking over at her rescuer, who was trying to help her with her seatbelt.

"Thank you, Mr. Bostich," she managed.

He smiled thinly. "Don't mention it. The hijacker is probably watching through the peephole."

She drew a long, uneven breath.

"Anything I can do for you, Annette? By the way, I wish you'd call me Rudy."

Annette turned and looked him in the eye, her resolve hovering on a knife edge of momentary indecision. She was supposed to "watch" Bostich. Did that include talking to him? Why shouldn't she warn a future U.S. Attorney General that he was the apparent target of a hijacker? Prosecutors always had criminals in their past crying foul play. Maybe he would know what this was really all about.

After all, it isn't Rudy Bostich who's hijacking this aircraft, is it?

"Mr. Bostich . . . Rudy . . . I'm not sure how to say this, but the hijacker is saying this whole thing is about you."

"*What?*"

"That's all I know."

Rudy Bostich swallowed hard and looked at the cockpit door, then shook his head.

"That makes no sense. I have no idea what he means."

Annette's eyes remained fixed on the back of the cockpit door as she sighed and nodded her head. "In any event, we've got to get word to the FBI and my company."

Rudy Bostich looked puzzled. "How?"

She fished his tiny cellular phone from the pocket of her flight apron and slipped it in his hand, feeling, more than seeing, the confused look on his face.

"I . . . thought you said . . ."

Annette nodded again. "I did. And I think he probably does have a cellular signal detector up there. But I'm guessing he wouldn't blow us up over the first unauthorized use."

Rudy Bostich looked at the phone in his hand as if he'd been handed a live grenade. "Don't you think the FBI already knows, with the unplanned flight to Salt Lake, that there's a hijacker up here?"

"I'm sure they do know," Annette said. "But they need to know exactly what's happening up here, and I need some information from them."

"What do you mean?" he asked.

She explained her worries over the young pilot from seat 18D.

"I saw him go forward to the cockpit back there in Durango," Bostich said. "I think I heard him go down the stairs, too, but I'm not certain."

"If he didn't leave the airplane, Rudy, then he's the hijacker."

Rudy Bostich was shaking his head. "No. No, I got a good look at him. He's very young, probably late twenties, and I know I've never seen him before. I can't imagine why he'd have a problem with me. It's got to be someone else."

"You have other enemies?"

He snorted and laughed, then raised his hand in apology. "I'm sorry. That sounded derisive. It's just that my job is putting people on trial and helping to ruin their lives for what we believe they've done. There are probably a hundred or so hardened felons out there who would consider it an honor to kill me slowly."

"Does the name Ken Wolfe ring a bell, Rudy?" Annette had to know if Rudy and Ken had a history.

He shook his head at first. "Ken Wolfe? No, I can't say it does. Who is he?"

"Ah, he's our captain, and I just . . . wondered if you might know him. That's all."

Rudy Bostich shook his head in the negative. "Not that I can recall. Where's he from?"

"Colorado, I think."

"Name's not familiar, Annette."

She pointed to the cell phone in his hand, as much to change the subject as to make contact. "Could you give it a try, Rudy?"

He looked at the phone again, as if surprised it was still in his hand. "Yeah, ah, how do I get in touch with the FBI, though?"

She looked over at him, surprised at the question. This was a federal prosecutor.

"You dial nine-one-one, I suppose, and ask to be transferred."

He swallowed and nodded slowly, his eyes still on the tiny cellular phone. "Okay. Okay, I'll give it a try."

Annette shifted forward on the seat.

"Where're you going?" he asked.

"To check on the people."

"But Annette, he said—"

She cut him off. "Rudy, this is still my cabin, and I'm still responsible for all of you. It's a balance of risks, okay?"

"But what if he detects the phone and comes charging out of the cockpit?"

"You hear the cockpit door open, hide the phone. There's no way to know where a signal came from."

Rudy Bostich nodded and slowly opened the phone's keypad as Annette moved into the aisle, trying to suppress a sudden flash of disappointment at his timidity.

NINE

FBI "Command Post," Salt Lake City International Airport.
11:50 A.M.

"Agent Bronsky? If you'll pick up the phone and punch line twenty-five, Approach Control says they'll have the aircraft patched in momentarily."

Kat flashed a thumbs up to the airport police officer and turned to a technician who had been working to specially equip one of the desk telephones.

"Ready?"

He nodded, pulling off a headset. "We're wired. I'll be running a tape as well as piping the line back to Washington as you requested."

She sat down and adjusted herself in the chair, taking time to breathe deeply before lifting the receiver and punching the appropriate button.

"Agent Bronsky here."

"This is Salt Lake Approach. Stand by. We're going to patch you through."

"Approach, who's doing the talking aboard that aircraft?"

"Far as we know, one of the pilots. We gave him a heading direct Provo a few minutes ago and the response was completely professional. I'm sure we're talking to a pilot. In fact, we're ready for you to give him a call."

Kat adjusted the handset against her ear. "AirBridge Ninety, how do you read me?"

There was silence on the line for a few seconds, then the sound of a transmitter being keyed.

"This is AirBridge Ninety. Who's calling?" The voice was deep and steady.

"Is this the captain?"

Another pause.

"Who's calling? Who are you?"

"This is Kat Bronsky. I'm an FBI agent, and I'm talking to you through Salt Lake City Approach Control's radios. I'm at Salt Lake International. Now, can I please ask to whom *I'm* speaking?"

"This is the captain of Flight Ninety. You understand our situation?"

"Not well enough, sir. I take it you have an uninvited guest in the cockpit with you who's on channel?"

"That's correct. We've been squawking seventy-five hundred, and he's fully aware of what that means."

"And this is Captain Wolfe?"

Several seconds ticked by as Kat waited for the calculated effect of letting both hijacker and captain know that the FBI had already done their homework on the crew.

"Yes. Ken Wolfe."

"And, Captain Wolfe, does the person in the cockpit with you want to tell me his name?"

"Hold on." Twenty seconds went by before the transmitter was keyed on again. "He says no, he doesn't want to give his name."

"Okay, Captain. We can work with that. Will he talk to me directly?"

Another pause, equally as long.

"He says no. I'm supposed to relay."

"Understood. Well, the first thing I need in order to help is to have some clear idea of precisely what he wants. We understood your earlier relayed transmission regarding the various officials he might want to talk to, and we're working on that, but I need to know precisely what else he wants so that we can try to meet those requests."

There was no response for more than thirty seconds.

"I asked him. He says to tell you he wants love and charity and peace in our time, Agent Bronsky. He wants . . . murderers executed for their crimes, pedophiles permanently locked away where they can't hurt little girls and boys, lying prosecutors exposed for what they are, and—what was the last one?"

The transmitter keyed off, then on again. "Oh yeah. He wants stupid, criminal-loving judges thrown off the bench. All of his demands, he's telling me, are achievable, and I tell you, the safety of every person on this airplane depends on his instructions being followed to the letter. I—what?"

Kat could hear some mumbling in the background while the captain held down the transmit button.

Good thinking, captain! she mused. *Now maybe I can hear what the hijacker's saying, too.*

The voice was too far in the background to understand, but it was there.

"Okay, Agent Brasky, was it?"

"No. Bronsky."

"Right. Bronsky. He says to tell you he has nothing left to lose, and you can consider him completely desperate. He's armed, and he's got us wired to blow up if he lets go of an electronic trigger he's holding. There are explosives in the forward baggage bin. He says to tell you that he'll issue more instructions one by one, and if any one of them is not agreed to immediately, we're . . . we're dead."

Kat nodded. Standard ploy. Hijacker loads on the initial threats of violence to establish his dominance over the situation.

"Okay, Captain. You can tell him, if he's not listening to my voice, that we will follow each and every instruction to the best of our abilities, and we'll keep you informed on exactly what we're doing. We do not want him to be surprised or concerned. Our policy is to give a hijacker what he wants as long as he shows his good faith by progressive release of the passengers and crew, and as long as no one is harmed. Tell him that whatever he wants, what *we* want is a quick and safe ending to this with no one, including him, getting hurt. Do you think he understands that?"

In a moment, Ken answered. "He says yes, but any tricks or attempted tricks will be fatal. If he asks for the Attorney General and you put someone else on the phone pretending to be the Attorney General, he'll trip the switch and we're—I hate this reference but I'm supposed to use it—we're toast."

"Understood. Reassure him that we will not betray our word, nor any agreements we make. If we say it's a deal, it's a deal, and the full faith and credit of the U.S. government will back it. He's got to agree, however, to wait and talk if he's got any concerns. No one will be sneaking up on you, but something unforeseen could happen that might frighten him, and we've got to be able to have the chance to explain it rapidly. Will he agree to ask first about anything he doesn't fully understand?"

"He says yes."

"Okay," Kat said. "I know you're on your way here. We'll talk more on the ground, but I would like to understand, as clearly as I can, what, precisely, he wants us to do first?"

"Give me a phone number. A land line. He wants me to call you from a cell phone."

Kat looked up at the technician, who scribbled an area code and number on the pad in front of her. Kat read it into the phone.

"Stand by. I'll call you."

A long minute and a half crawled by before the appropriate line lit up, and Kat grabbed it.

"Agent Bronsky here."

"Okay, Agent Bronsky. Here's the deal. The first instruction is this. The FBI must proceed to a trailer park south of Denver and arrest the occupant of a particular trailer."

Kat scribbled the address as it was read.

"Okay. But what if we find more than one person there?"

"Wait a second."

Kat put her hand over the mouthpiece and turned to the technician. "You getting all this?"

He nodded vigorously as the captain's voice returned.

"Okay, he says pray you only find one person there. You're looking for a heavyset male. Any other person would probably be a kidnap victim."

"Okay."

"And, the suspect must be formally booked into a federal holding facility on federal charges of kidnapping and murder. A federal grand jury will have to be brought together in a matter of an hour or so, and they must hand down a formal indictment. And a full trial must be guaranteed. For anyone aboard this airplane to live through this, each and every step must be accomplished."

"Does he want to give me the name of the person he wants arrested, Captain?"

There was another pause of several seconds duration.

"He says to tell you again that there's only one humanoid organism in that trailer. When you've arrested it, he'll have further explanations and instructions."

"Can he tell us who this individual kidnapped and murdered?"

"Negative. Not until the man's arrested."

Kat looked over at Frank Bothell, who had already picked up the open line to FBI headquarters. He raised and lowered his eyebrows and shrugged his shoulders, a signal Kat understood well. Maybe it could be done, maybe it couldn't. Stall in the meantime.

"Captain, tell him we're starting the process immediately. As soon as you're safely parked down here, we'll talk further. Would you see whether he will permit us to run a private telephone line straight out to your aircraft?"

"I'll ask him. I'll let you know when we're parked. And Agent Bronsky?"

"I'm here."

"Do not, I repeat, do not even think about shooting tires or blocking the airplane or any other direct physical interdiction. He's serious. He'll detonate his bomb if you try."

"I understand. I'll be right here standing by on your air traffic control frequency if you need me. Just let the controller know, or call the same number on your cell phone."

"Roger," was the only response.

"Kat?" Frank Bothell's voice reached her from across the small room.

Kat stood and handed the phone to an airport police officer who had been standing nearby. "Re-establish the line with Salt Lake Approach and stay glued to this, please. Tell the controller to let you know the instant the captain wants to talk to me. Also, keep this other line open in case he calls by cell phone."

The officer nodded and slid into the same chair Kat had occupied as she moved to Frank's side. "What's up?"

"I've got the two men in Durango you wanted to talk to on line twenty-three, and Salt Lake Air Route Traffic Control Center just called to let us know that another airliner saw Flight Ninety doing aerobatics on the airway a few minutes before you started talking to him."

"Aerobatics?"

"Aerobatics are extreme flight maneuvers likes rolls and loops and—"

"I know the term, Frank. What *kind* of aerobatics?"

"Apparently they're flying slow, and they rolled the aircraft," he replied, indicating the maneuver with his hand.

"So we've got a wild, illegal buzzing of Monument Valley . . ." Kat began.

"I'd call it more of a surface level fly-through. He was down between those giant buttes."

"Okay, and now he's rolling the aircraft. Does that suggest to you what it suggests to me?"

Frank nodded tentatively. "You're the psychologist, Kat. I'm just a federal cop. The roll sounds like a fight in the cockpit. I don't know what to make of the Monument Valley thing." Frank studied her eyes. "But . . . you're discerning something else."

She nodded. "It's not a fight. It may be something far more dangerous. He could be demonstrating a feeling of liberation which would be inconsistent with his demands so far, or he could be trying to scare everyone aboard. I'm only sure of one thing, Frank. We've got to get that airplane on the ground and keep it nailed there. Whatever's going on, the flying is dangerously unpredictable. They get in the air again, we could lose them."

"Meaning?"

"The hijacker says he's a desperate man and he's demonstrated a type of physical control over the plane that tells me he isn't afraid of the technology. It also tells me he isn't necessarily afraid of dying, and if he's suicidal, he could take them all down in the blink of an eye."

"A purposeful crash, you mean?"

"Frank, from ten thousand feet above the ground, a seven-thirty-seven pushed over to the near-vertical can impact the ground in less than fifteen seconds, and the captain might not be able to prevent it."

"Wonderful. What do you suggest?"

"A heartfelt prayer that he's really going to land."

Kat picked up the telephone handset and punched the button for Durango.

Aboard AirBridge Flight 90. 11:50 A.M.

As Annette sat down again, a heavily perspiring Rudy Bostich slammed the tiny flip-phone back together with obvious irritation and sat looking stunned.

"Can't get through?" Annette asked him from the adjacent seat.

Bostich slowly shook his head no.

"It'll probably improve in a few minutes," Annette added. "We're coming up to the Wasatch Mountains right now. As soon as we get to the other side, you should be able to reach a cellular antenna."

Rudy Bostich was staring at the cockpit door, his eyes wide.

"Rudy?"

There was no response.

"Rudy, is . . . is there anything you're not telling me here?"

He turned toward her suddenly, his face frozen in a panicked expression.

"Annette, you said the captain's name is Ken Wolfe, right?"

She nodded cautiously. "Yes."

"And you said he was from Colorado?"

Annette studied his eyes. There was panic there, and another cold chill began to make its way down her spine. "I think he *lives* in Colorado, Rudy. I don't know anything about his background."

"Could he . . . could he be from Connecticut?"

"Rudy, why are you asking?"

"Does he . . . *did* he . . . have a daughter? Has he ever talked about losing a daughter?"

"Losing? You mean to illness?"

"Whatever."

"Mr. Bostich, you're obviously really worried about something here. What is it? Please tell me."

Bostich was gripping the arms of the first class seat hard enough to whiten his knuckles, his gaze forward.

"Look," Annette began, "I don't know him well enough to know whether he's ever been married. I've heard rumors that he had a terrible family tragedy somewhere, and I recall his saying something once about hating to miss autumn on the East Coast, but I don't know for sure."

"I remember that voice," Rudy said. "It *is* him."

"Ken Wolfe?"

Bostich nodded.

"What about him, though? Are you enemies or something?"

"In a way, yes."

Annette sat in shocked silence, her mind racing through the possibilities. What were the odds of a hijacker who hated Rudy Bostich jumping on perhaps the only aircraft in commercial aviation flown by a captain who was also angry with the same man?

"Annette?"

Bostich's voice didn't penetrate the kaleidoscope of thoughts going through her mind. Annette got to her feet and moved quickly to the galley in search of her purse. She fumbled for several seconds in the bottom of the bag, her fingers closing finally around a single key that had escaped its side compartment.

She moved out from behind the galley privacy curtains. She could feel Rudy Bostich's eyes on her from his window seat, but she didn't look at him. She knew he'd be frozen to his seat, too afraid to interfere.

For several minutes there had been no P.A. announcements and no particular sounds from the cockpit. They could be in flight anywhere, from all appearances, and the apparent normality of the scene made her apprehension seem even more ridiculous.

Annette moved to the cockpit door and put her hand on the doorknob without making a sound.

She rotated the doorknob very slowly, very gently, until it stopped.

With surgical care she lowered the nose of the key into position and gently rested it in the mouth of the keyhole. Slowly, very slowly, she pressed the key forward, letting the internal probes of the tumblers click along the teeth of the key one at a time, none of them producing enough sound to be heard against the slipstream of the jet.

Finally, it would go no farther.

If I'm wrong, I could get a bullet in the face.

The thought stopped her momentarily as she raced over the logic again.

No, I know I'm right. But I have to see for myself.

Annette looked down. The key was firmly in place.

Oh God, how do I do this? Do I yank all at once, or pull slowly?

It would take several seconds of clicking and turning sounds if she turned it slowly, she realized. The only way to maintain surprise was with a quick pull.

The 737 hit a short stretch of turbulence and Annette braced herself against the restroom door with her shoulder.

Now!

She twisted the key hard in her hand and felt the latch give as she pulled the door open.

Ken Wolfe's head whipped around toward the entryway at the noise with a look of horrified surprise as he recognized Annette and what she had done.

She stood in shock, her mouth open, groping for words. Ken was sitting in the left seat as she had expected.

The right seat was empty.

"What the hell are you doing, Annette?" Ken asked, his face turning red.

She swallowed hard. "The question is, what the hell are *you* doing, Captain?"

A thin smile played across Ken's face, then disappeared as he looked forward at the instruments, then back at her.

"Hand me that cockpit key, Annette. Then back out, close the door, and call me on the interphone."

She was breathing rapidly, her head swimming. Her own voice sounded distant.

"Ken, whatever you think you're doing, you're scaring the hell out of—"

His booming voice cut her off. "DO EXACTLY AS I TELL YOU! I'm not kidding about the explosives."

Annette saw his left hand leave the control yoke and come around to show her he was holding a small black object which looked like the remote arming device for a car alarm system.

"This is a trigger, Annette. There's a real package of plastic explosives in my bag in the belly bin. If I'm incapacitated and let go of this for a second, it's all over. We explode. Besides, there are no other pilots aboard. So try to overpower me and everyone dies. Now GET OUT!"

"Ken, WHY? Why are you doing this?"

"Go, dammit. GO! Call me on the interphone."

Annette handed him the key and backed out in confusion, fairly slamming the cockpit door.

She felt her hand at her mouth, her entire body shaking.

She paused, then moved to the interphone.

"Okay, Annette, now calm down."

"I don't understand this," she began, her voice shaking. "You're

. . . hijacking your own aircraft? *Why*, Ken? *Why*? What about your career?"

"Annette, you want answers, and I'm not ready to give you answers. But I do have a question. Do you really know who that scumbag is in first class?"

The words rolled off her ears at first. Her mind was dominated by the question *Why?*, her mind racing to find some rationale.

"What?"

"Do you know who Bostich is?"

"Yes. He's probably going to be the next U.S. Attorney General."

"Not if I can help it."

His words sent a jolt down her spine.

"What are you talking about, Ken?"

"Bostich is the cause of this, Annette. Whatever happens, don't you ever forget that."

She felt completely overwhelmed. The captain's words were making no sense.

"What do you have against Mr. Bostich?"

"Don't call that animal 'mister' in my presence, understand? Bostich is the cause of all this. I'll explain later—to everyone. Meantime, you keep that bastard under tight control. He's involved in this. He's a damn criminal! Serve him nothing. Give him nothing. Tell him nothing. Tell that pile of walking shit to stay in his seat or the captain will arrest him on the spot and the hijacker may shoot him."

"Hijacker? But *you're* the hijacker, Ken."

"That's the point, isn't it?"

"What's the point? Dammit, what *is* the point? I don't understand the point! I don't understand what you want." She felt tears on her cheeks.

Pilots could be trusted. Pilots didn't turn on their crews. She couldn't have spent a quarter of a century trusting her life to pilots and accept this.

This just can't be happening!

TEN

FBI "Command Post," Salt Lake City International Airport.
12:10 P.M.

Agent Kat Bronsky replaced the telephone handset and sat back in stunned silence, the voice of the abandoned copilot in Durango still playing in her mind. His description of the captain's strange behavior in Colorado Springs had created a small knot of fear in her stomach, and it was growing.

She glanced around the twenty-five-by-thirty-foot room at the various desks. Agents were hunched over telephones and computers in all directions and several airport police officers were moving in and out on various errands, all in feverish preparation for the arrival of the hijacked airliner.

The adjective seemed too precise. Kat drummed her fingers unconsciously on the rim of the desk, rolling the concept over in her mind, trying to decide why it felt so wrong. She'd learned to trust her gut reactions, and her instincts and intuition seldom failed her. But now, real lives were in the balance. She hoped she had the courage to keep listening to herself.

Kat sat forward suddenly, grabbed the telephone handset, punched up the line to Salt Lake Approach, and asked the controller for reconnection to AirBridge 90, as she turned toward Frank Bothell.

"Frank, you want to put on a headset? I'm going to talk to him again."

He turned and nodded cautiously.

Ken Wolfe's voice replied within thirty seconds.

"Captain, this is Agent Bronsky. I've been ordered by my superiors to speak directly to your hijacker. Put him on, please."

Kat could see Frank's eyebrows rising in her peripheral vision.

The reply from the cockpit of AirBridge 90 came almost instantly.

"No."

Kat drummed her fingers on the back of the receiver for a few seconds in thought. In the distance, Frank Bothell huddled over a desk, his hands pressing both sides of a headset to his ears. He caught her eye and arched both eyebrows, but she looked away, not wanting to be dissuaded.

"Captain, you know from your training that in a situation involving the hijacking of a civil aircraft in the United States, we are required to validate the presence of the hijacker, as well as validate the presence of any weaponry as best we can. So far, I've heard only your voice, and while I know the hijacker is sitting next to you, we absolutely must talk directly to him and hear his voice before we can begin to comply with his demands. This is not optional, do you understand that?"

Nearly thirty seconds ticked by before the frequency came alive with the captain's voice once again.

"Are you nuts down there, Bronsky? Don't you understand the basic situation here?" Ken Wolfe asked. "This fellow isn't in any mood to be dictated to, and he doesn't give a damn about your requirements."

"Captain, ask him if he really wants us to meet his demands."

More silence.

"He says that's a dumb question. Of course he does, but he doesn't want to talk to you. He wants me to do the talking."

"Captain, I know he's listening, so I'm going to say this right to his ear. Sir, if you refuse to talk to me, no one in Colorado is going to be arrested, and no one in the United States government is going to lift a finger to even consider your demands, regardless of your threats, because we don't officially believe you exist. To change that, all you have to do is talk to me. Just a few words. I need you to help me so I can help you. Okay?"

No response. Kat felt her heart pounding. She was all too aware of the chance she was taking, but she had to know.

A full minute ticked by, then two. Kat found herself longing to hear just the captain's voice again, anything to confirm they were still okay.

My God, what if I just pushed a madman over the edge?

The sound of a transmitter clicking on filled her ear, and for a moment she was too lost in relief to realize she was hearing a new voice. Gruff, deep, and masculine, it growled at her.

"Listen you stupid broad. I don't wanna talk to you or anyone! The captain will relay for me. You put this kind of pressure on me again, I'll detonate this seven-three and you hotshot feds can spend the rest of your lives wishing you'd listened to me."

Silence again.

Kat snapped her head around toward the technician. "You get that?"

He nodded, "Loud and clear."

"Agent Bronsky?" The captain's voice had returned, and Kat pressed the phone hard to her right ear.

"Go ahead, Captain."

"I hope you're satisfied with that answer, because you really made him mad. I'd recommend you not try that again if your purpose is helping us survive this."

"We've filled the square, sir. We'll talk with just you from here on."

Kat replaced the receiver and glanced at Frank Bothell, who looked deeply worried as he pulled off his headset. He stood up and moved to her side, speaking quietly.

"What in hell was all that about, Kat?"

She looked him in the eye. "I was following a hunch, Frank."

"You needed the bastard's voice on tape that bad?"

She nodded. "I'll fill you in shortly."

Frank nodded and began to turn away, then looked back at her, speaking softly out of the corner of his mouth as he leaned near her shoulder. "Don't freelance too much, Kat. The world, and more important, the Bureau, is watching, and you're the new kid on the block. Okay?"

"Okay."

As Frank moved away, Kat caught the technician's eye and walked quickly to the desk holding his recording equipment.

"Larry, can you run an analysis on both those voices?" she asked.

"What, you mean a stress analysis?"

"That, and more. Can you digitalize the voices and run a comparison of the voice prints?"

The technician studied her face, trying to discern her meaning.

"I'd have to feed this through the phone to the lab in D.C. I don't have the equipment here."

"Okay. As soon as you can."

"But, Kat, you've got to tell me what you're looking for."

"Just tell them to compare the voice prints, analyze the stress in each, and make certain we're . . . dealing with two different larynxes."

The technician drew back slightly and searched her eyes. "You want to make certain the voices come from different people?"

She looked down at the table and nodded. "Don't make a big deal of this, okay? Just get it to the lab guys with that request. This is just a precaution, not a theory," she fibbed.

The technician took a deep breath and nodded. "Okay. You've got it. It's a simple procedure."

"How long?"

"Ten minutes. Fifteen on the outside."

"Let me know."

Kat walked quickly across the room to where Frank was huddling with several newly arrived members of the Bureau's Regional SWAT team.

"Frank? Can I borrow you for a minute?"

He turned and gestured to the three men. "These fellows are providing the SWAT team from Salt Lake Police, Kat."

She smiled at them and raised an index finger. "Forgive my manners, gentlemen. We'll meet formally later." She grabbed Frank's arm and steered him a few feet away.

"I need some quick research done without raising questions. Do we have agents at AirBridge headquarters in Colorado Springs, yet?"

Frank nodded. "Two agents. They arrived maybe five minutes ago and checked in with me. Why?"

"How can I reach them?"

Frank sighed and looked down for a moment before finding her eyes again. "Kat, tell me what you want them to do and I'll make it happen, but don't be coy with me. I need to know exactly what you're thinking."

"I'm not being coy, Frank. I'm being cautious. Something's very wrong here."

"What?"

"About the captain. About this whole scenario. Something doesn't ring true and I need as much information about this captain as I can get."

Frank massaged his chin for a few seconds as he studied her face. "Okay, Kat, spit it out. What do you suspect?"

She looked around, then sighed deeply. "I'm sorry, Frank. I don't want to jump to conclusions, but I just talked to the copilot who was left behind in Durango, and I talked to the passenger they left. Frank, this captain was acting very odd this morning in Colorado Springs on the aircraft and in Durango. There's reason to believe that he may have been trying to get rid of any other pilots, including passengers who were pilots."

"Why?"

"I wish I knew. There's apparently a big-shot politician on board, but I don't know for certain that he's got anything to do with this."

Frank was nodding. "Yeah. Rudy Bostich, U.S. Attorney from Connecticut. He's up for Attorney General."

She nodded. "Frank, the copilot said that the captain came unglued this morning when he discovered Bostich was aboard. He witnessed some very weird reactions at the gate in Colorado Springs, and then there's this sudden engine shutdown out of the blue, and a convenient hijacker, and he gets all the pilots off the plane who might be able to land it."

"What's the bottom line here, Kat?"

Kat studied his face for a few seconds before answering. "I think the captain may be alone in that cockpit."

"I'm not following you."

"It's possible the captain is the hijacker."

"Jesus Christ!"

"Larry's feeding the voice tape to the lab right now to find out. I need background on this guy, any evidence of instability, or myopic allegiance to some weird cause."

"Kat, are you saying that second voice sounded phony to you?"

"Not really, but everything else points to the possibility, and whoever owns the hijacker's voice knows about airplanes. Did you catch his reference to the Boeing?"

Frank looked puzzled. "What reference?"

"The average person would call it a jet, or a jetliner, or a Boeing, or if they were really specific, a seven-thirty-seven. He called it a 'seven-three.' That's pilot talk, Frank. If there's a second person on that flight deck, he's either a pilot or he's very knowledgeable about the aviation community."

"That's hardly conclusive," Frank replied.

"But it's consistent with the impression we already had that the hijacker is not afraid of aviation."

An airport police officer appeared at Kat's side. "Excuse me, Agent Bronsky?"

Kat kept her eyes on Frank Bothell as she waved the officer away. "Not now, please."

Frank exhaled sharply. "Kat, if that's true—"

The officer raised the palm of his hand to get her attention. "Agent Bronsky, I'm sorry, but you've got a call, and it's really urgent."

She glanced over at him with obvious impatience. "*Who*, for God's sake?"

"The aircraft. The captain wants to talk to you. He's on a cell phone and he's yelling."

Kat stared at him in silence for a heartbeat before lunging at the nearest telephone.

"Agent Bronsky here."

The sound of Ken Wolfe's voice blew back through the receiver instantly.

"Get these damn F-sixteens the hell out of here! Do you hear me, Bronsky?"

Frank picked up an extension to listen in as Kat looked at him in confusion, her right hand in a questioning gesture. He gave her a wide-eyed shrug in return.

"Captain, what are you talking about?" Kat asked.

"I told you no tricks, no fighters, no nothing! You make these guys go away. You're gonna get us killed."

"Captain, what's going on up there?"

"What do you think, Bronsky? You sent fighters, the hijacker is upset about the fighters. I want you to stop endangering us. Understood?"

"Captain Wolfe, tell me precisely what's happening."

"Dammit, he's threatening to kill us because of these F-sixteens!"

"We did not order fighters, Captain. *Tell* the man that."

"Cute, Bronsky. You arrange for the Air Force to launch two fighters to shadow me and then pretend you don't know? That's a real trust buster. He's real impressed. He's waving the trigger around. With him in the right seat and you down there playing games, we're probably doomed."

Kat cupped her hand over the receiver. "Frank!"

He was already nodding as he punched up a clear line on the telephone desk set and began punching in numbers. "I know, I know. I'm checking."

Kat closed her eyes and tried to focus on the scene in the cockpit, and the mind behind the hijacking.

"Okay, Captain, look. We all know that sometimes the right hand and the left hand do not communicate. I honestly do not know where those fighters have come from or what they're doing there. Are you saying they're in formation with you?"

"That's right, Bronsky. As if you didn't know. Off to my left. He wants—hold on—he says he wants them to land at Salt Lake City International Airport, and before we even think about landing, he wants to see those two fighter pilots on the ground standing outside their planes."

"Affirmative, Captain. We're working on it."

She whirled around toward the adjacent desk again. "*Frank?*"

Frank Bothell pulled the receiver from his ear and rolled his eyes.

"Goddammit! Headquarters called the Air Force without telling us. The fighters are from Hill Air Force Base in Ogden. I'm calling them off."

Kat shook her head and repeated Wolfe's orders. "Frank, he's demanding the F-sixteens land here at Salt Lake International."

Frank nodded and pressed the phone to his ear again to issue the urgent instructions as Kat hunched over the receiver again, her eyes closed.

"Okay, Captain, tell him we're relaying the message right now. It will take a couple of minutes to reach them."

"They'd better hurry—he's waving the damn trigger around again."

There were some banging noises, then Captain Wolfe's voice in the background. "I told you . . . stop doing that. Please. They're complying. There's no sense in this."

There was silence on the other end for several long moments.

"One more slip, Bronsky, and he says he'll activate the trigger. *Please*, don't give him any more reasons!"

AirBridge Headquarters, Colorado Springs, Colorado. 12:10 P.M.

The Director of Flight Control, Judy Smith, spotted the two dark-suited men the moment they entered the building. When they were scooped up by the company's general counsel and escorted toward the second floor, she knew they were FBI agents. And they were about to be presented with a whitewashed version of Captain Ken Wolfe from a chief pilot who had undoubtedly been manicuring his personnel files. There would be no reference to instability, mood swings, copilot complaints, or the overall feeling that was eating her alive that the hijacking was somehow a product of the hell Ken Wolfe had been living. There would be only the feigned wide-eyed innocence of a chief pilot who was very worried about one of his best and most senior employees. The dog and pony show would take, what, five minutes? She wondered if veteran agents would be able to see through it, and the answer was obvious: Not in time.

Soon, the two men were back, shaking hands with the chief pilot in the hallway outside dispatch and heading for the parking lot, a folder in the hands of one of them.

Judy watched them get in a black sedan.

There was a long drive leading past the rectangular operations building to the opposite end, where the drive rejoined the road and passed a rear entrance. The rear entrance was the only way out of the building on that side, and the only one without surveillance cameras—a door smokers used to catch a quick cigarette without invoking the wrath of their nonsmoking coworkers.

She quickly pushed back her chair and got to her feet, smiling at one of the dispatchers who happened to look up. The hallway was empty, and she moved as fast as she could toward the far end.

She pushed open the door, relieved that no one was lounging outside. Above her, the back side of the building contained no windows, and no way for the senior executives to see what she was doing.

Judy positioned herself in the middle of the drive just as the black sedan turned the corner. The two men braked to a halt, one of them rolling down the passenger side window as she moved to his side.

"Are you gentlemen with the FBI?"

The passenger nodded, his eyes on her identification badge. "Yes, ma'am. And you are . . . ?"

She introduced herself and pointed to the car's rear door.

"Get me out of here quickly. I need to talk to you in private."

Aboard AirBridge Flight 90. 12:12 P.M.

For almost five minutes after closing the cockpit door, Annette had sat on the jumpseat in shock. When she felt the 737's engines throttle back for descent, she grabbed the P.A. microphone.

"Ladies and gentlemen, this is your lead flight attendant. We're going to be landing soon at Salt Lake City International, but due to the uncertainty of our situation, I want you all in a brace position. Take off your shoes now, take all sharp objects out of your pockets, and listen closely as I give you the basics of what to do."

The call chime from the cockpit rang. Annette ignored it and read through the list of procedures for passengers to follow.

"This is also known as the 'grab your ankles' position, but that's only to get your head down and secure so if we come to a rapid halt, your head won't be propelled into the seatback in front of you."

The cockpit call chime began ringing almost continuously.

"I'll give you the brace command just before landing, but if anything odd happens in the meantime, get into the position on your own, and wait for—"

The P.A. system was suddenly snatched from her control as Ken pushed his microphone button on the flight deck, overriding hers.

She replaced the P.A. microphone and reached for the handset.

"*What*, Ken?"

"What the hell are you doing?"

"Taking care of my passengers!" she said as calmly as she could.

"I told you to stay down."

"I guess you'll have to shoot me, then, because I'm going to do my best to keep these people safe."

"Annette, I'm warning you—"

"Let me take care of my job, dammit! You don't want to talk to me, you don't want to explain, you just want to terrify our passengers, and I'm not going to sit on my butt and let them be unprepared."

"Unprepared for *what*, Annette?"

"I wish I knew, Ken."

"All I'm going to do is land. Then we sit while I negotiate and make threats. Is that so difficult to understand?" Ken's voice had lost some of its bite.

"Threats, Ken? Is that all they are?" Annette pressed.

"Well . . . not really. I've got the bomb trigger. I *could* set it off. I will if I don't get what I want."

"So what do you want, Ken? What on earth do you want?"

"Justice, Annette. There are little girls out there who're going to be murdered if I don't succeed."

"What . . . what are you talking about, Ken? You're trying to prevent a murder by threatening to kill all of us?"

"*ENOUGH*, Annette! Sit down."

She felt her heart pounding, her hands shaking. Her voice had been too loud, and she could see the alarm in the eyes of the female passenger in 1C who had overheard much of the exchange.

"Annette, you push me too far, you'll be responsible for killing everyone on board. Now cool it! Get them prepared if you're determined to play stewardess games, but don't push me any more. Is that clear?"

"Very clear," she said quietly.

Annette replaced the handset and forced herself to jump to her feet and move into the first class cabin.

Rudy Bostich motioned her over urgently. The cell phone, she noticed, lay unopened in his lap. As she leaned toward him he caught her left arm in a vice grip and guided her down to the adjacent seat.

"That hurts, Rudy."

"I'm sorry. But you were talking to the cockpit. Wolfe doesn't know I'm aboard, does he? You didn't tell him, did you?"

She hesitated, studying his eyes, aware that his face was contorting in pure fear.

"Back in Colorado Springs, Rudy, I showed him your card."

"Jesus! I asked you not to let him know."

"I showed him before we took off. I said nothing more, but he already knew, and the hijacker knows."

"Oh, God!" he said, his right hand shooting to his mouth. "Oh, my God."

"Look, Rudy, we've got a big problem."

Bostich was nodding, his eyes on the forward bulkhead. "I know. I know. He's up there alone, isn't he?"

She nodded slowly, wondering if he'd overheard her conversation on the interphone, or somehow figured it out by himself. "He says you're responsible for all this, Rudy. I have no idea what he means."

He was staring out the window and chewing on the knuckles of his right hand as she stood up. "Rudy?"

He didn't respond, and she hesitated only a few seconds before turning toward the right side of the aisle and meeting the gaze of the frightened passenger in 1C, who was trying to ask several questions at once.

Annette put a reassuring hand on her shoulder. "I'll be back in a minute and we'll talk."

The woman nodded.

There were three other first class passengers besides Bostich. They were all apprehensive, all trying to catch her eye. She raised her hand in another wait gesture and shot through the coach cabin, purposely catching the eye of Nancy Beck, whose imagination was obviously running wild.

"He's okay. I can't tell you more," Annette said, her eyes recording the look of terror on an older woman several rows back in an aisle seat who had a fist stuffed in her mouth, her body visibly shaking.

Annette gathered Bev and Kevin into the rear galley and filled them in on what lay beyond the cockpit door, watching the blood drain from both their faces.

"My God, he's gone mad!" Kevin gasped.

Annette shook her head. "It involves Bostich, but neither of them will tell me anything, though Bostich asked if Ken had lost a child, and was he from Connecticut."

"He is," Bev said. "He's talked about that. I don't know about losing a child, though."

"Okay, look," Annette said. "We've got a bunch of terrified passengers all hunched over in a brace position and expecting the worst. We've got to handle that."

"Let's go," Kevin replied, gesturing to the cabin.

Annette led the way back up the aisle with Kevin and Bev on her heels. She found the frightened woman she had seen earlier in row 12 and sank to a knee beside her.

"Are you okay?"

She looked up and shook her head no.

A distinguished man in his seventies sitting next to her raised up slightly and leaned toward Annette.

"Miss, she's terrified, and I can't talk her out of it. Neither can Mrs. Gates."

"Is she your wife, sir?"

"No, we're just sweethearts. Look, when we signed on for this graduation flight with our fear-of-flying group, we thought it would be kind of a gentle exposure to your world, but I think all this is a really bad idea."

Annette stared at him uncomprehending for a second.

"A bad idea?"

"I'll agree it's a very clever training course you've devised, and you've all been staying in character really well, but I'd appreciate your ending this now. Jenny, here, thinks it's real, and I can't convince her otherwise."

"Ah—"

"Truth is, scaring us all to death is not the best way to make us like flying on your airline."

"Sir—"

"I want you to ask the captain to please stop the show. He's got some of us really deeply alarmed."

"Sir, I hate to tell you, but this isn't an act. We really have been hijacked."

The man sat back as if she'd punched him in the nose.

"This is *real*?"

Annette nodded.

"There really *is* a hijacker in the cockpit?"

Annette nodded again.

"Well!" The man stroked his chin for a few seconds and looked out the window before turning back to his seatmate, whose fist was still pressed against her mouth, her eyes scrunched tightly shut.

"Jenny, are you still terrified?"

She nodded.

"Good," he said. "I'm going to join you."

ELEVEN

Aboard AirBridge Flight 90. 12:20 P.M.

Ken Wolfe felt his left hand shaking slightly on the control yoke as he waited for the two Air Force F-16s to leave the perfect formation they'd been maintaining to the left side of his 737. There was a dull ache in his head, but he ignored it. No use asking Annette for aspirin. All sympathetic connection with her was gone. He was the enemy now.

There!

The lead F-16 suddenly bobbled, then stabilized. He could see the pilot looking down, one hand against his helmet in an involuntary response to a radio call.

Just as quickly, the two F-16s banked left, away from the 737, and plugged in their afterburners to streak off to the northwest toward Salt Lake City, some thirty miles distant.

What now, Ken? he thought.

He could imagine the frightened people behind him in the cabin, and the traumatized, angry flight attendants. He could imagine the kicked-over anthill AirBridge headquarters must have become. The word had probably been relayed as well to Tom Davidson back in Connecticut, and that triggered a significant pang of guilt. Davidson had found him the AirBridge job, helped him relocate, cared about his welfare—and this was his repayment?

Ken shook his head and refocused on the frenzy of activity ahead as the FBI tried to figure out how to foil the hijacker. He had to foresee their every move and block them, like a high-stakes chess game with a sudden death ending. He had to make this work for Melinda.

She would have been in junior high this year. She would have been blossoming into a young woman, with her whole life ahead! The same internal voice that never left him alone taunted him again, as it had every day since her murder.

Concentrate, dammit! Stay ahead of it, or they'll find a way around you.

Ken pulled the throttles back and continued the descent, calculating the altitude loss necessary to bring the jet down to a thousand feet above the ground just before the Salt Lake International runways. He'd kept the speed less than three hundred knots since Monument Valley, but now he slowed even more, noting that the fighters had already disappeared in the distance. They would be touching down within a few minutes, the pilots undoubtedly told to scramble out of their cockpits in accordance with the hijacker's instructions.

He thought about the preparations the FBI was rushing to make, and the nets they were preparing to ensnare him, from psychological games to wearying delays. So far, he'd been far too predictable, too busy issuing threats and flying to think ahead, think it through, figure out how to finish what he'd started.

The thought scared him suddenly, as if he'd already failed to anticipate some critical move against him. All the FBI had to do was get ready to hold the airplane on the ground and talk him into surrender. They would have no incentive to expose Bostich nor to bring in the human garbage that had murdered Melinda. They'd be too busy plotting to storm the aircraft with guns.

Ken Wolfe looked ahead to the northeast at the line of mountains bordering Salt Lake's east flank, the Wasatch Range. The ridgeline north of Ogden was sharp and high, rising from the plains to snow-covered peaks. He calculated the altitude of the highest ridge and filed it away. It would do fine.

FBI "Command Post," Salt Lake City International Airport.
12:32 P.M.

Frank Bothell lowered the telephone handset and looked across the desk at Kat.

"The two F-sixteens are on the ground, Kat. The pilots are getting out."

She nodded. "Good. Where's Flight Ninety?"

"On final approach. All other air traffic is halted."

"We have media helicopters around?"

Frank spoke a few words into the phone, paused, then turned back to her with a nod.

"Two of them, both cooperating with Approach Control, and both hovering at a distance."

"But they're broadcasting TV pictures live to the world, right?"

"Like I warned you."

Kat turned to one of the airport officers. "I need to look out a window."

The officer inclined his head toward a distant office. "We've got CNN on in the other room, Agent Bronsky. They've got the picture live from one of the choppers. It's also on the local channels. That's your best bet, because you can't see that runway from this side of the airport."

Kat followed him down a hallway and into a well-furnished office.

"Our chief's," the officer explained. In the corner, a console television was showing the live shot of the AirBridge 737 as it approached the airport, less than a mile out, descending steadily toward the runway. At the same moment, the jetliner appeared to level off.

"What's he doing?" one of the airport officers asked.

"He's going to fly over the airport and check that the fighter pilots are out of their planes," Kat replied, her eyes glued to the screen.

From the helicopter's vantage point at least a thousand feet in the air, the 737 could be seen clearly crossing the threshold of the runway roughly five hundred feet above the surface, its landing gear still retracted. The camera followed it steadily and began pulling back, showing the runway beneath as the jetliner flew above the three-mile ribbon of concrete. When the Boeing was past the halfway point, Kat could see the shape of the two grounded F-16s slide from right to left along the bottom of the picture.

The voice of the CNN anchor accompanied the fly-by with continuous narration.

> "There are one hundred and thirty people aboard this jet, we are told, and as the FBI and other authorities wait for the captain to

land, there is still no word on what individual or individuals may be responsible for what is, in legal terms, an act of air piracy."

Suddenly, the 737's nose pitched up as it crossed the departure end of the runway and began to gain altitude, still flying north.

"Is he going to turn back, or what?" Frank's voice rumbled gently in Kat's left ear. She jumped slightly. She hadn't seen him come in.

Kat looked back at the screen. "I'm sure the tower's cleared him to circle to land. He should turn in either direction pretty soon."

Still the 737 bored north, climbing steadily, as Kat straightened and watched with growing apprehension.

"He only needs to be fifteen hundred feet above the airport," she said, "and he should be there by now. Why isn't he turning?"

A phone rang in on the desk of the police chief as they watched the 737 climbing sharply now. Someone answered the phone and turned immediately toward the two FBI agents.

"Agent Bronsky? The captain's on the cell phone again and wants to talk to you."

Kat took the receiver as Frank moved to a second phone by the couch. She could hear the captain's voice even before she pressed it to her ear.

"You there, Bronsky?"

"Yes, Captain. Where are you going? The two F-sixteens are on the ground, just like you asked. The pilots are outside. Didn't you see them?"

"We saw them, Bronsky. We also saw the other vehicles lying in wait."

"What are you talking about? There are no vehicles lying in wait! We've kept our word."

"Has the vermin near Denver been arrested?"

Kat looked at Frank and cupped her hand over the receiver as she repeated the question. He shook his head no.

She turned back to the phone. "Captain, they're working on it. We only agreed to do that some twenty minutes ago. We've got to have some time."

Aboard AirBridge Flight 90. 12:36 P.M.

As the 737 climbed away from Salt Lake City International Airport, the terror gripping the heart of Rudolph Bostich blocked out all memory of the cell phone in his lap—until Annette sat down heavily beside him.

"Have you gotten through on the phone yet?" Her tone was tense and urgent, and he raised himself up from his semibrace position to look at her closely.

"No, I . . . frankly, forgot. Where are we?"

"Getting too close to the mountains and flying north. Why, I don't know. Try the phone now, please. Ken's not talking to me."

"Who should we call now?"

"The FBI, same as before. Wouldn't they be handling things down there?"

Rudy Bostich nodded and fumbled with the phone as he pushed the operator button. He asked for emergency connection with the nearest FBI office as soon as a voice came on the line.

FBI "Command Post," Salt Lake City International Airport.
12:36 P.M.

The news that the FBI was working on making the demanded arrest in Colorado had not been received well in the cockpit of Flight 90, and Kat braced for what she assumed would be a renewed round of threats.

Kat had asked for more time, and the captain's voice had come back on frequency anguished and demanding.

"I know this routine, Agent. Stall, stall, and stall again. I expected that, but this time it won't work. The penalty for not doing precisely as he dictates will be the loss of everyone on board. Do you understand that, Bronsky? Every man, woman, and child on this aircraft—including me—is going to die in just a few minutes unless he has the assurance of the Attorney General of the United States that the murderer he told you to capture will be arrested, indicted, and tried. DO YOU UNDERSTAND, DAMMIT? HELP ME UP HERE!"

"Yes, Captain, we understand. Stand by."

Kat could hear Frank punching in a number as she held the receiver in silence, trying to imagine the scene in the cockpit of Flight 90, thinking about every word he'd said. Her suspicions had to be right. They were shadow boxing, talking around the real issues, getting nowhere, and Wolfe was getting dangerously frantic. If she had any hope of getting to the heart and soul of what was behind it all, the pretense had to be dropped.

Kat glanced at Frank and grimaced.

"What, Kat?" he asked softly.

She covered the mouthpiece. "I have no choice, Frank. While you're trying to get the A.G., I've got to challenge him."

He moved closer to her with a receiver in his hand and a worried expression on his face. "What do you mean? What are you considering?"

"I've got to call his hand. I've got to stop the playacting."

"You mean, who the hijacker is?"

She nodded, and saw Frank swallow hard.

"Your show, Kat," he said at last. "We teach you the procedures, but we hired you for your intellect and instincts."

She smiled at him. "Please remember that at my disciplinary hearing."

Kat adjusted the phone in her hand and pressed it against her mouth, letting her eyes focus on the desktop. "Okay, Captain, let's drop the facade. You're holding all the cards and I know it. I need to know what you really want and why."

Wolfe's voice shot back immediately. "Why are you aiming that at me, Bronsky? It's not what *I* want, it's what *he* wants. You heard him."

"No, Captain Wolfe, I heard *you*. Only you."

There was a long pause.

"What does that mean?"

"Captain, you're alone in that cockpit and we both know it. I've been talking to the hijacker all along, haven't I? You had to know I was going to figure it out eventually."

Kat held her breath. She could hear the cockpit sounds in the background as his hand fidgeted with the small cell phone, but there was no voice.

Finally, a long sigh broke the silence.

"How'd you know, Bronsky?"

Kat felt her heart skip a beat. She'd suspected. She'd gambled. But to hear the cold, brutal confirmation was a profound shock.

"I . . . was dealing with too many pieces that didn't fit, Captain. But now that we both know what's happening and who's in control, we can really talk."

She heard a snort on the other end.

"Talk about what, Bronsky? So I'm unmasked. So what? It's over for me, anyway."

"What do you want, Captain? What's the bottom line?"

Thirty seconds of silence ticked by like some form of slow torture.

"I already told you," he said at last. "Have you arrested that scum in Denver yet? You sang that jolly song about having to hear the hijacker before complying, and you heard the hijacker."

There was a snarl in his voice. Pure, unmitigated rage and pain. She could feel it as well as hear it, and the barrier it raised against her was substantial.

"I did hear the skyjacker, or hijacker, or whatever we want to call the mythical individual you created. But the truth is, I'm not stalling down here. We're truly bending heaven and earth to comply with what you want, but it takes time."

"Sure you are. *Sure* you're working on it! The Easter Bunny's here, too, along with Elvis. Wanna talk to Elvis?"

"Captain, cut it out. Please come back here to Salt Lake and land so we can solve this."

"Why, Bronsky? You'll just shoot out my tires and storm the airplane, or try to bore me into surrender."

"Call me Kat, please. All my friends call me Kat, which is short for Katherine."

"So I'm your friend now? Step number fifteen—am I right, Agent Bronsky?" He adopted an overly officious voice. "*Above all else, the hostage negotiator must try to build a personal relationship with the hostage taker. This relationship will eventually work to the advantage of law enforcement authorities trying to regain control.* Did I get it right?"

A cold feeling of pure fear began to crawl up her middle. He had, indeed, paraphrased one of the manuals correctly, and she realized with a sinking feeling that the game had changed drastically. No longer was this an ally in the common quest of fighting a hijacker, he was someone fully trained in the same techniques of handling hijackings that Kat had just learned at the FBI Academy.

Kat felt the chill of hopelessness envelope her. She was fighting it, but the feeling of being defeated before she could start was already dragging her down, constraining her voice, and freezing her mind, blocking her ability to think clearly.

Suddenly she wasn't the learned professional controlling the game. She was the pawn.

"Captain—"

"If we're gonna be bosom buddies—oh, pardon me, I shouldn't say bosom to a woman, should I?"

"It's okay," she said lamely, her right hand rubbing her forehead.

"Well, *Kat*," he said with as much sarcasm as he could manage, "why don't *you* call *me* Ken? I mean, if we're going to really pretend to care about each other—"

"Captain—*Ken* . . . you have me at a disadvantage."

"Captain Ken has you against the wall, Agent Bronsky. I know your every move. I am, as the hackneyed old movie phrase goes, your worst nightmare, because I know all your procedures and all your tricks."

"We're not using tricks, Ken."

"Yeah, right! And you've got some beachfront property you'd like to sell me at, where, Waco? Oklahoma City? Ruby Ridge? I know government lies, Bronsky. I'm the victim of two years of government lies, and crooked prosecutors and stupid judges."

"Captain, what happened to you? Please tell me what it is you're so angry about. I don't understand."

"In good time, Bronsky, you'll find out."

"Okay, then where are you headed, Captain? Are you coming back here?"

"Oh, what the hell. Go ahead and call me Ken instead of Captain. After today, I'll never be a captain again, anyway."

"Ken, where are you headed? That's the first question."

"Probably to hell, but I'm going to take a couple of real low-life animals with me, and about a hundred and twenty other innocent people if you don't do what I've demanded."

"You still have a goal to achieve, Ken. Don't blow it. Don't give up on this process of talking."

Kat felt a hand on her right arm. She opened her eyes and looked up to see Frank holding a notebook with a note in large block print:

LAB SEZ: THE TWO VOICES RECORDED EARLIER BELONG TO THE SAME PERSON. YOU WERE RIGHT.

Kat nodded and focused her attention back on the desk.

"Ken, listen to me very, very closely. I am not the President of the United States, and I'm not even the director of the FBI. I'm just an agent, and I can't suspend laws, part oceans, or make government policy. I can tell you that if you'll land in Salt Lake, we'll do everything we can to bring this to an end by addressing whatever wrong you're trying to set right, but if you just fly off, I can't promise you anything."

Seconds ticked by as a voice from the hallway echoed toward the office she was occupying.

"Departure control says he's turned slightly toward the mountains at nine thousand."

Kat sighed again, long and ragged. "Ken, are you still there?"

"Yeah, for a few more seconds."

"What does that mean, exactly?"

"You give me no hope, Kat. A man must have hope. No hope, no salvation. No salvation, no airplane. Goodbye, Kat. Sorry you couldn't listen. Maybe with the next one you might learn. Sorry. I don't mean that. I don't want to help hijackers. This is unique. You just screwed up this very unusual situation."

"What, Ken? What did I screw up, and how can we repair it?"

"Too late, Kat. You tell the illustrious Attorney General his cowardice in refusing to act was responsible."

"Ken, we *are* acting! We're trying to do what you said. If you do anything rash, all you'll accomplish is help future hijackers get anything they want. You'll be disciplining us to accede to any demand immediately. You're a captain. Do you want airline captains flying under that sort of expectation? Anyone who wants anything can get it in the future by hijacking an airliner, all because Ken Wolfe couldn't wait it out? You don't want that!" Kat felt perspiration on her forehead.

The line was still open, but Ken Wolfe was saying nothing.

She heard a voice in the doorway softly repeating a transmission from Salt Lake City Departure Control.

"He's turning toward the ridgeline now, and he's not high enough to clear it."

"Ken, please talk to me. At least tell me what you want."

Ken Wolfe's voice came back immediately.

"I'll bet you aren't married, Kat."

She nodded, then remembered to speak. "You're right. I'm not married."

"I hope to God you never lose a child, Kat. Only then can you understand."

"Captain, turn back to the west, right now."

"No, Kat. You had your chance."

"Captain, you're not a mass murderer. Don't even threaten."

"You don't know who I am, Kat. There hasn't been enough time for your people to find out anything about me. My airline doesn't understand what's happened to me. The current President sure as hell doesn't understand, or he'd never consider a lying bastard like Rudy Bostich for Attorney General."

Another voice came from over her shoulder. "Kat! He's headed directly into the top of the Wasatch Range!"

Aboard AirBridge Flight 90. 12:45 P.M.

Annette looked again to the right, calculating their distance from the Wasatch Mountains. She felt her heart leap to her throat when she realized the position of the mountains had changed. They had been alongside and parallel. Now they were ahead at a forty-five degree angle. And the 737 was headed right at them, but at an altitude lower than the approaching ridgeline!

Annette jumped from the seat and moved forward to the front entry way to grab the P.A. microphone.

"EVERYONE STAY IN A BRACE POSITION! REPEAT, STAY IN A BRACE POSITION!"

She could feel the terror in the passenger cabin mirroring her own panic, but there was nothing else to do. She could also see Elvira Gates waving her right arm frantically from her seat in coach as the leader of the fear-of-flying group leaned into the aisle, still trying to maintain a semibrace position.

"What, Mrs. Gates?" Annette shouted.

"Now? Stay down now?"

Annette nodded as she pressed the microphone button again.

"Yes. Now!"

The thought of breaking into the cockpit and clubbing Ken Wolfe resurfaced every few minutes, but having no pilot to fly and land the plane would doom them for certain. They were utterly dependent on their captor now for life, with no clue as to what he was trying to accomplish.

FBI "Command Post," Salt Lake City International Airport.
12:45 P.M.

Kat pressed the receiver to her ear and closed her eyes.

"Ken, even if you're planning to end it, give me enough time for you to explain what you want. What has this Bostich done? How did he lie? Do you hold him responsible for losing a child of yours? If you end it now or cut off communications, no one will ever know what you wanted."

The voice came back too low, the words spaced too evenly, as if he had disengaged.

"The man you must arrest is Bradley Lumin. He murders little girls. He takes them like an animal, keeps them, rapes them, does horrible things to them, then kills them. He takes pictures of them, too, pictures he puts on computers, and probably the Internet. And he's about to strike again if you don't stop him. No one will listen to me. I've begged for nearly two years, but no one listens. Meanwhile, he's killed twice more. I've begged and pleaded, but no one would listen, and the little girls keep dying."

Frank's voice in her ear again. "Kat! He's three miles to impact!"

Sheer panic was crawling up and down her back with claws. Only her words stood between the passengers and the ridgeline.

"Ken, damn you, LISTEN TO ME! Turn that aircraft back to the west long enough to tell me the basics. Don't end this before we at least know what's happened and what to do about it."

"It's all in the record. Talk to Connecticut State Police Detective Roger Matson. He's telling the truth about Bostich. Bostich lied. Bostich covered up."

"Ken, pull up! You're a professional pilot, not a murderer. This is not an appropriate legacy for whomever you've lost."

He said little girls. The murderer kills little girls, and he lost a child.

"It was your daughter, wasn't it? How would she want to remember her father? As a mass murderer? Is that what you want?"

Frank's voice again. "One mile. He's five hundred feet below the ridge." Frank was pressing a phone to his ear, and relaying the word from Salt Lake Departure.

"Ken, what was she like? Your daughter. WE DON'T KNOW WHAT SHE WAS LIKE. WHAT WAS HER NAME? WAS SHE PRETTY?"

Aboard AirBridge Flight 90. 12:47 P.M.

The sight of rapidly moving real estate in a side window caught Annette's full attention. She moved past the wide-eyed woman in seat 1C and crouched down to look forward out the window at a rapidly approaching ridge that was above them and ninety degrees to the airplane's flight path. They were rushing straight toward it!

Bostich was muttering into his phone, asking for someone and demanding connection in a shaky voice.

There would be no time. There was no way anyone below could help influence their fate now. They were too close.

A strange calm fell over her as she sat in the window seat next to the woman in 1C and looked through the glass at the onrushing ridge. The woman looked up at the same moment, her right hand finding Annette's hand and squeezing hard. Annette squeezed back, fully expecting to leave life in her company.

FBI "Command Post," Salt Lake City International Airport. 12:49 P.M.

Kat felt herself go limp at the sound of the cell phone being turned off in the cockpit of Flight 90. She looked over at Frank with a frantic, feral expression, pleading for word that what they all expected hadn't occurred.

Frank Bothell's face had drained of all color. She saw him nod slightly and lower the receiver as he took a stunned, ragged breath.

"Departure says . . . the target has merged . . . with the ridge . . . and disappeared."

"Oh, God!" Kat's voice echoed off the walls of the chief's office as her fist clamped against her mouth.

TWELVE

FBI "Command Post," Salt Lake City International Airport. 12:50 P.M.

Kat stood in shock for nearly a minute with her mind screaming at her:

A *father who was willing to end his career and his freedom to prosecute his daughter's murderer would never be able to resist answering those last questions, no matter how intense his pain!*

Kat moved to the desk in a haze and punched up the same line Frank had used for Departure Control. She could hear the controller coordinating with an inbound United Airlines 757, asking him to overfly the same ridge. She turned to Frank and the others in the room and cleared her throat, aware that her voice was shaky.

"Gentlemen," Kat began, "we've just been conned. He hasn't crashed, and this isn't the end. It's just the beginning of what's going to be a bizarre and, probably, lengthy game of cat and mouse. And he's the cat."

Frank Bothell was staring at her in disbelief. "Kat, we'd better face it."

She shook her head strenuously, hanging on to the logic she knew was right.

"No, Frank. They're safe. He skimmed the ridge, flew over it. He's somewhere on the other side hugging the terrain, flying through valleys. It's too soon."

"Kat, you don't know this guy. You can't be sure."

"I'm sure."

The voice of the United flight crew cut into their exchange.

"Ah, Salt Lake Approach, United Twenty-Two-Fifteen. We're circling the area."

The transmission dropped out for a few seconds, then returned.

"Ah, it appears that . . . there's no crash down here we can see. There's no sign of fire, wreckage, impact, or anything else, and we don't hear any emergency locater beacons."

"You're certain, United?"

"Well, Approach, are *you* certain of the coordinates you gave us?"

"Yes, sir. The Salt Lake V.O.R. zero-three-zero degree radial at precisely twenty-six miles."

"Then we're certain, Approach. No one's crashed anything as large as a Boeing down there. We'd see it."

Kat sat hard in the office chair, her heart racing, as Frank stood in stunned silence, staring at the wall.

"Jeez, Bronsky. You were right. How on earth did you know?"

"It didn't fit, Frank. Someone killed his daughter. He's hurting for *her*, not for himself. Crashing now would only ease *his* pain, not hers. That has to be the point."

Kat had her forehead cupped in her right hand, her mind racing ahead. She had a second chance, but she had to move fast.

Another wide-eyed FBI agent had entered the room with a steno notebook in hand, and Frank nodded to him immediately.

"What, Jim?"

"Our two agents in Colorado Springs just phoned in their report. The details are interesting and the airline's trying to hide it, but this captain has a long history of strange behavior since his daughter was murdered two years ago."

"Is that a case anyone recalls?" Kat asked, her head still cupped in her hand.

Jim nodded, then shrugged. "I don't know. I recall it, because it was so infuriating. It was a kidnap-murder near Stamford, Connecticut, and nearly eight months went by before they collared the bastard, a real sleazebag pedophile with a long record of molestation, child porn, the works."

Frank was shaking his head. "What was the girl's full name?"

"Melinda Wolfe," Jim replied. "They had this Lumin character cold, but virtually all the evidence came from a search of his home and his computer, and when the warrant was thrown out, the case went with it."

Kat looked at Frank. "I'll bet you anything that Mr. Bostich was somehow involved in issuing that warrant."

Jim shook his head. "I doubt it. It was a state prosecution. There was no federal prosecution, or not yet, at least."

Kat looked at both of them, then addressed Jim.

"You said two years ago?"

"I did. I checked the date. This is the second anniversary of her murder."

"Bingo," Frank said under his breath.

Kat intertwined her fingers as she sat in the chair, staring at the floor.

"Frank, there are several corporate air terminals on the east side of the field. One's called Million Air. I forget the others. If we don't have a business jet standing by with FBI pilots, and I'm sure we don't, call the Million Air terminal and beg for help. See if we can commandeer or charter a business jet, one that can keep up with a seven-thirty-seven. I need to be off the ground within ten minutes."

"Kat—" Frank began, a pained expression on his face.

"Trust me, Frank. Don't argue. There isn't time. If I'm not airborne in ten minutes with the ability to talk to Wolfe directly by aircraft radio from above, we'll lose him yet. I can't do it from down here."

There was no sound from Frank Bothell. He was in deep thought. She was wondering what more to say when he smiled suddenly.

"Okay, Kat. Let's get one of the officers here to race you to the other side while I call. Keep your cell phone on."

"Jim, call Approach, get me a stack of frequencies Wolfe might be monitoring."

"Will do." Jim grabbed a phone as Frank pushed past him headed for the hallway. He hesitated in the doorway just long enough to turn back to her.

"Take your weapon, Kat, and don't take any chances."

Million Air Executive Terminal, Salt Lake City International Airport.
1:01 P.M.

Captain Dane Bailey emerged from the plush passenger cabin of NorthLight Industries' thirty-nine-million-dollar Gulfstream IV and entered his high-tech computerized cockpit as the copilot looked up from the right seat.

"Are we into Plan B now, or what?" Jeff Jayson asked.

Dane maneuvered himself into the captain's seat as he handed a fistful of maps to Jayson and nodded.

"I've never seen the FBI commandeer a jet before, but," he inclined his head toward the passenger cabin, "the boss says if they need help, we'll provide it."

"So where are we going, Dane?"

He shook his head and smiled. "There's an FBI agent racing over here right now. I guess he'll tell us. All I know is, this still concerns the AirBridge hijacking, and I've never seen the boss so disturbed about anything. He's trying to hide it, but this has him really upset."

Jayson nodded. "It must, to prompt the vice chairman of AirBridge's board to chase the company's 737 across Utah rather than fly to AirBridge headquarters. I couldn't believe how fast he got here from his office."

Bailey shrugged. "Hey, ours is not to reason why. The man's got about thirty million invested in that airline. He's got a right to worry."

Aboard AirBridge Flight 90. 12:50 P.M.

Annette had expected to die as the 737 approached the ridge and suddenly pitched up. Instead, the ridge flashed beneath them and the 737 pitched over as Ken Wolfe dove down the far slope and began maneuvering along a mountain valley, hugging the trees and the terrain which were passing in an incredible blur.

"What's happening?" the woman sitting next to her asked in a small voice. Annette realized with some embarrassment she'd been squeezing the woman's hand, and she let go as decorously as possible.

"What's your name?" Annette replied.

"Louise. Louise Richardson."

"Stay calm, Louise. I have no idea what's going on, but I don't think he means to kill us. I think he's trying to scare us."

"It's working!" Louise said.

The sound of the P.A. clicking on seemed ominous. They had no ally on the other end of the microphone, only an enemy now.

"Listen up, people. Stay down, stay put. According to our captor, we've got more than one criminal aboard today. He says in first class there's a piece of walking excrement named Rudy Bostich who thinks he's going to be the next Attorney General of the United States. Mr. Bostich is a liar and a cheat and an unconvicted felon, and our captor requires Mr. Bostich's presence on the flight deck. He says we'll tell you more later. Annette, escort Mr. Bostich to the cockpit door. If he won't come voluntarily, tell him our guest says he will detonate the bomb."

Annette leaned forward and looked across at Rudy Bostich, whose face was a study in pure panic. The cell phone had been open in his hand, and it dropped unnoticed to the floor as he looked back at Annette with pleading eyes, swallowing hard.

Annette got to her feet and headed instead for the forward door area to pull the interphone from its hooks and punch the cockpit call button.

"What the hell is it, Annette?" Ken snapped. "Weren't the instructions clear enough?"

"What do you want, Ken? You planning on killing him in the cockpit while trying to fly?"

"I considered it," Ken shot back, "but he's got to live to face charges. Does that make you feel better?"

She closed her eyes and metered her breathing before replying. "When are you going to drop this pretense, Ken? People already suspect. Your voice is too angry, too hateful."

"Bullshit. Stop stalling, Annette. Get that worm by the collar and get him up here."

"Do it yourself, Ken!" she snapped.

Immediately, the 737 began a roll to the right and a sharp pull.

"Want to change your mind, Annette? Or do you want me to fly us into the hills? I don't get him up here, I have nothing to live for anyway."

"Okay, OKAY!" she stammered. "I'll bring him up."

The roll reversed itself.

She replaced the handset and moved back into the first class cabin, feeling like an unwilling executioner.

"Rudy . . ." she said quietly, irritated by the cornered look on his face. Wasn't he supposed to be a big, brave prosecutor? She could use a little show of bravery from him right now, not the pitiful, cringing image of a cornered animal she saw before her.

"What . . . what does he want?" Rudy stammered.

She shrugged. "I don't know, but he did say he wasn't planning to hurt you."

"I can't bring his daughter back!"

"It was a daughter? What happened to her?"

His right hand waved aimlessly at the ceiling. "I—it's a long story. Someone killed his daughter and . . . and the police ruined the case, and he blames me for not filing federal charges."

"Rudy, I don't know anything about it, but if he wants something you can promise, for God's sake, promise it!"

He sat motionless, his eyes darting from her to the cockpit area and back until Annette decided she'd had enough.

"Okay. Come on. On your feet."

"You can't do this! Aren't you supposed to protect your passengers?" he asked in a strained whine.

She felt herself grimace at that. Was she walking a passenger to his death to save the rest, or just complying with what she couldn't change?

If they were going to survive, maybe Rudy Bostich could figure out what to say that Ken wanted to hear. She wasn't an executioner. This was the logical thing to do.

"Come on. It's up to you to talk him down."

"Up to me?"

"He says you're the cause of this, Rudy. That means only you can rectify this. You've got to try."

"And if I refuse?"

Annette looked him in the eye and tried to answer the same question for herself. If he refused, would she look for some burly passenger to help her push him, kicking and screaming, into the cockpit? Or would she just wait for Ken to get mad enough to really fly them into a mountain?

"Rudy? Now. Let's go. I can't reason with him. Maybe you can."

"I . . . can't."

She leaned down to speak directly in his ear.

"Rudy, you're supposed to be a leader. We need you to lead and show some confidence. You're acting like a coward."

The words stung him as she'd hoped, and slowly he got to his feet and moved into the aisle beside her. She pointed toward the cockpit and he moved with a leaden gait to the door. She knocked three times and heard the electronic lock release click, and saw the door swing open.

"Come in, Mr. Bostich, and have a seat," Ken said. The electronic trigger was evident in his left hand.

For a second Bostich stood there, motionless, as Annette thought about grabbing the crash axe, or kicking Bostich forward into the cockpit, or falling on Ken Wolfe with a stranglehold around his neck. All pointless ideas, all born of the panic she had to control.

Slowly, Rudy Bostich moved into the cockpit and looked at the empty copilot's seat.

"Close the door, Counselor," Ken ordered.

Bostich turned and looked at Annette with a trapped, haunted expression, his face a pasty white, as he pulled the door closed behind him.

Million Air Executive Terminal, Salt Lake City International Airport. 1:04 P.M.

Kat Bronsky pointed to a sleek Gulfstream IV business jet sitting in front of the Million Air terminal on the east side of the airport.

"There! Pull up right in front of him."

"That's the one?" the officer at the wheel of the airport police car asked as he checked the taxiway they were about to cross.

"November-Five-Lima-Lima is the 'n' number. That looks like her."

Kat folded the cell phone and stuffed it into her handbag with the note on which she'd scribbled Frank's relayed information. "They're supposed to be ready to start as soon as I can dive in the door."

The officer negotiated a turn onto the Million Air ramp and stomped on the accelerator. "You FBI folks have some awesome power if you just reach out and snatch up a Gulfstream at will."

"I think we're chartering them," she answered. "I just hope I don't have to put it on my Visa card."

He brought the car to a near skidding halt fifteen feet in front of the jet as Kat snapped off her seatbelt and yanked open the door, hurling a last thank you over her shoulder as she grabbed her handbag and the portable aviation radio and leapt from the right seat.

There was a uniformed pilot with three stripes on his shoulders standing by the stairway to the aircraft, and she waved at him as she ran in his direction.

"Five-Lima-Lima?"

"Yes, ma'am," he said.

"I'm Agent Bronsky. Let's go ahead and start."

He hesitated. "You're . . . the FBI agent we're expecting?"

"You were expecting Elliot Ness?" she asked with a slightly sarcastic smile.

Jeff Jayson chuckled as Kat bounded up the stairs to the plush interior with the copilot on her heels. She paused at the top and looked to the right, startled to see an impeccably groomed man in a gray business suit sitting in a large swivel chair.

"Ah, hello," Kat said.

"Hello to you," he replied, getting out of the seat with his hand outstretched. "I'm Bill North."

"Agent Kat Bronsky of the FBI," she said, taking his hand. "Are you one of the pilots?"

He smiled and arched a thumb in the direction of the cabin behind him.

"Nope. I'm the owner."

Kat glanced toward the cockpit momentarily, aware that the copilot had retracted the stairs and was locking the door. She looked back at North, who had shoved his hands in his pants pockets and was leaning against the side of the galley. His eyes were a smoky blue, and they were studying her with a calm intensity.

"I'm sorry," she began. "I guess I'm confused. I thought we were chartering this jet."

Bill North shook his head no. "One of your people called over and said there was a major emergency, you needed a corporate jet fueled and ready to go almost instantly, and here we were on the ramp getting ready to go to Colorado Springs," he shrugged. "I'll send your director a bill for the costs later, but, no, this isn't a charter. Just a concerned citizen."

The sound of the left engine winding up whispered through the heavily soundproofed cabin.

Kat smiled back. "I'd better get up there with your pilots, but, thank you. We've got a hijacked airliner I need to stay in contact with."

North was nodding. "So I was told." He straightened up. "Look, you make yourself at home, tell my guys what you need and where you need to go, and I'm going to sit back here and stay out of the way."

Three minutes later, the sleek Gulfstream was lifting off runway 35 and turning east into a clear blue sky.

Kat knelt on the cockpit floor behind the center pedestal as the copilot offered his hand.

"I'm Jeff Jayson, Agent Bronsky. This is Dane Bailey."

"Hi," the captain said, his eyes remaining on the instruments.

"I appreciate you guys, and Mr. North back there, responding so quickly. What'd I take you away from?"

The young pilot in the right seat glanced at Dane, then grinned as he swept back an unruly lock of sandy hair with his right hand. "Just a last-minute trip to the Springs."

"Besides," Dane Bailey added, "this is the most excitement we've had since Cindy Crawford flew with us last month."

Kat smiled, then sobered. "Okay guys, we've got a deadly serious situation here. I'm going to need to talk on one of the two radios just as soon as we get to altitude. The whole point of this exercise is to try to maintain contact with a seven-thirty-seven that's been hijacked."

Both pilots nodded, and Dane asked, "How do you want to handle this, Agent Bronsky? Departure control says Salt Lake Center will give us any heading and altitude we want, and they're standing by to relay information from a couple of Air Force fighters who're apparently trying to find the seven-thirty-seven. It *is* a seven-thirty-seven, right?"

She nodded. "First item of business is, please call me Kat. Not 'Agent.' "

The two pilots exchanged a glance and smiled at each other.

"Glad to, Kat," Jeff said.

"Second," she continued, "we're chasing him in order to let me stay within radio range so I can talk to him. Let's take up a heading of zero-nine-zero for a few minutes and climb to twenty thousand. I need as high a radio footprint as possible to reach him. I think he's flying through valleys and trying to stay hidden. He's had a pretty good head start, about twelve minutes, and I figure that would put him a maximum of forty-eight miles ahead, and, maybe, with enough turns and twists to his flying, as little as thirty."

Dane nodded. "If we take her on up to flight level three-five-zero or so, we can get her up to around five hundred knots on the ground speed, and basically close the distance in about fourteen minutes."

Kat shook her head. "Too high. He could be going north or south, not just east. If we can't raise him at twenty, then we'll go higher and I'll give you kind of a search pattern to fly."

"You don't know where he's headed?" Jeff asked.

Kat shook her head. "We don't even know if *he* knows where he's headed. How much fuel do you have in hours?"

The two pilots glanced at each other before the captain turned back to Kat.

"Kat, this is a Gulfstream and we've got almost a full load of fuel, so we've got more than eight hours at altitude. But if we stay low, that could be as little as five hours."

"That's great. That's more than the seven-thirty-seven has."

"Basically, we could almost get you to London."

"Understood," Kat said, inclining her head toward a sectional aviation chart the copilot was unfolding. "Is that Utah?"

He nodded. "Utah's full of mountains and valleys leading right into Colorado. If he's down there flying what the Air Force calls nap of the earth, it's going to be pretty hard to find him."

Kat tapped the chart with her index finger. "I don't expect to find him visually. I'm just praying we can get him to talk, and I'm pretty sure he will, because of what he wants."

Dane Bailey turned to look at her. "Kat, truth is, this was all so sudden we don't really know what's going on here, except that it's a hijacked AirBridge flight."

She studied the center pedestal for a few seconds wondering how much to tell and whether to be vague. This was FBI business, but they were potential assets—professional pilots who could understand what she was dealing with and maybe contribute the right idea at a critical moment.

She sighed and looked at both of them in turn.

"Okay," Kat began, "this is all privileged information, but let me tell you what we know so far, and then I'll brief your boss back there."

Dane nodded, as did Jeff.

"Okay," she began. "We're in the middle of one of aviation's worst nightmares, guys. We've got an airline captain holding his own aircraft and passengers hostage and making demands we don't understand. Right now, I haven't a clue as to how it's going to end."

THIRTEEN

Aboard AirBridge Flight 90. 1:16 P.M.

"Bad choice of flights this morning, eh Rudy?" Ken Wolfe banked the 737 sharply to the left and slid around the promontory shape of a bluff rising several hundred feet above their altitude as he glanced to the right at the terrified prosecutor.

He heard Rudy Bostich swallow hard and try to speak, his voice a rasp until he cleared it and tried again.

"What, Rudy? I can't hear you above the sound of your lying hypocrisy. Speak up."

"I asked," Bostich began, "what, exactly, do you want from me?"

Ken yanked the control yoke to the right suddenly, causing the 737 to roll rapidly back to the right, forcing a gasp from the right seat.

"What do I want from you? Well now, I can't imagine. It couldn't be justice. That would be too damn simple. And I guess it couldn't be something as old-fashioned as prosecuting my daughter's murderer and putting the animal on death row. No, that wouldn't do, because that might hurt *Mr.* Rudy Bostich's career, right?"

"Captain, I don't know what you're talking about, and I don't know what you want me to do, but you're frankly scaring the hell out of me flying this low. Can't we climb? There are innocent people riding in this airplane, too."

Ken rolled the yoke back to the left to guide the Boeing down another valley.

"I'm glad you differentiated the folks in the back as being innocent, unlike yourself. What do I want? I want a confession."

"A confession? A confession about what?"

Ken snorted at him. "You sack of shit. Whatever you do, Bostich, don't try to play innocent with me. The name Roger Matson sound familiar?"

Rudy sat in silence for a few moments, then nodded his head. "Matson is a detective, I think, in Stamford, Connecticut."

"As if you had to think about it. That's right. Good. And Roger Matson's a good man, right?"

Rudy shrugged, his raised eyebrows betraying his alarm. "I wouldn't know. He's a detective. My office deals with many detectives."

"Yeah, well you've dealt with Roger Matson, all right, because Roger and his partner got hold of me and spilled the whole story." He looked over at the frightened man in the right seat and glared. "I know what you did, Bostich, and you've got a choice. You're either going to sign a confession up here with all the details and dates and places, or I'm going to take you to hell where you belong."

Rudy Bostich drew a ragged breath and tried to straighten his posture as he looked Ken in the eye.

"I'm not confessing to anything I didn't do, and I haven't done anything. You, on the other hand, are in commission of so many felonies right now I've lost count. Do you realize you can get the death penalty for air piracy?"

Ken's head jerked around to the right, his eyes boring a hole in the side of Rudy's face.

"HEY, shithead! Let's get this straight. I died when that animal killed my daughter. You're looking at an angry corpse that doesn't give a damn. That's point one."

"And point two?" Rudy asked quietly.

"Point two is a question. Can you fly this aircraft?"

Rudy's eyes shifted back to the forward windscreen.

"Probably, if I had to."

Ken suddenly let go of the controls and folded his arms with the Boeing descending slightly into a valley, a thousand-foot bluff standing several miles ahead of them beginning to fill the windscreen.

"Go ahead, Bostich. You've got it. Let's see what 'Probably, if I had to' means."

Rudy looked at the pilot in disbelief.

"WHAT? Look, I don't have any experience with something this big."

"Whoa, another lie, Rudy? You said you could probably fly it."

"With proper instruction, maybe, but—"

"Tough luck, Rudy. You think you're in control of this situation? You, who can't even help convict a murderer! Hey, Mr. Testosterone, the yoke's right in front of you. Put your slimy hands on it."

Bostich pushed himself as far back in the seat as he could, both palms up and away from the yoke.

"Okay. Okay, I admit I can't do this, Captain! Does that make you happy?" Sweat was breaking out in beads on Rudy's forehead as the airspeed increased slightly and the rate of climb showed a descent rate of five hundred feet per minute, the bluff coming up fast in the window.

"You'd better do it, bastard. Either that or confess what you did to Matson to set him up."

"What . . . what do I do here! What do I pull? We're going to hit that mountain, you jackass! WHAT DO I DO?"

"Beats the hell out of me, Rudy. If the big federal prosecutor and cabinet nominee can't remember the basics of truth and confession, then I guess I can't remember how to help you fly."

Rudy closed his hands around both arms of the control yoke. He looked out frantically, then pulled too hard, causing the nose to rise alarmingly as the G-forces pushed them down hard in the seats.

The bluff was disappearing, the nose coming up, and the airspeed was decreasingly alarmingly, but Ken sat with his arms folded and watched.

Rudy pushed the yoke forward sharply, throwing them up against the seatbelts with zero gravity as the bluff once again reappeared.

"I CAN'T DO THIS!" Rudy yelled. "I DON'T KNOW WHAT TO DO!"

"Sorry. No confession, no flying lessons," Ken said.

Rudy Bostich's eyes were huge as he pulled again and inadvertently rolled the Boeing to the left. Once again, the airspeed began dropping as the two-engine jetliner entered a steep climbing left turn. Ken watched the speed diminish through one hundred and eighty knots as the roll increased to nearly ninety degrees, the bluff now passing beneath them by a thousand feet.

"You planning on doing a barrel roll, Bostich?" Ken asked.

"WHAT?" Rudy fairly screamed the response as he struggled to roll the yoke back to the right and once again pulled too hard.

Suddenly both control yokes began vibrating furiously as the stall warning kicked on. There was nothing but blue sky showing in the windscreen as Ken's hands came forward, sweeping the power levers full forward as he nursed the roll back to the left, letting the nose drop to the horizon before rolling back wings level and checking the increasing airspeed.

When the 737 had reached two hundred fifty knots in level flight again, he pulled the power back and resumed flying.

Rudy Bostich was covered with sweat and breathing hard, his eyes wide with fear, his hands still holding the copilot's yoke with a death grip.

"Well, Mr. Prosecutor, what have we established here?"

There was no response.

"I guess," Ken continued, "we've established that when it comes to flying, you're a wus. You can't do it, and if you try, you're going to kill all those innocent people you care so much about in the back. Along with your own ass, about which you obviously care very much."

Ken heard a ragged breath drawn by the occupant of the right seat.

"What's your point, Wolfe?"

"My point? Oh, of course. My point. Well, Counselor, I guess my point is simply this. You can't fight me, because I'm still holding this electronic trigger, and even if you succeeded in knocking me out, the nanosecond I release this, we explode. And since you obviously can't fly, and there are no other pilots on board, I guess you're just stuck big time having to do what I say. In other words, Bostich, you're either going to confess on paper in front of witnesses what you did, or you're going to die. Clear enough for you?"

"I can't believe you're a murderer, Captain Wolfe."

"You're the murderer, Bostich. Remember the little nine-year-old girl in Vermont found floating in a lake last year? You did that."

"What? What the hell are you talking about?"

"You're entirely responsible because you didn't take the murderer off the streets. And there was a thirteen-year-old girl in Provincetown, Massachusetts, six months ago. Remember her?"

"No."

"Figures. You're responsible for that, too, because I'm convinced she was consumed by the same animal who killed my daughter." Ken turned toward him. "Both those girls, you sleazy bastard, would be alive today if you hadn't lied."

Rudy slammed his right hand into the sidewall of the cockpit as he looked at Ken. "What *are* you talking about, Wolfe? I haven't lied about anything! What on earth do you think I did?"

Ken snorted and focused his attention forward.

"I know what you did. I have the proof. But I'm going to hear it from your lips first." Ken snapped his head around again toward the right seat.

"UNDERSTAND? I'm not going to tell *you*, you're going to tell *me*, and in exquisite detail. Or, your lousy ass is going to die."

There was an uneasy silence for more than a minute.

"Are you through, Captain?" Rudy asked in a small voice.

Ken nodded. "Yeah. Without a doubt, I'm finished. But so are you, Counselor."

Rudy fell silent, his right hand massaging his chin. He stared out the copilot's side window as Ken's grip tightened on the yoke, his left hand carefully holding the trigger, his jaw clenched in fury, his mind momentarily far away as the 737 flew alongside a ridge, bucking in the rising columns of air propelled by the heat of the noonday sun.

There was another valley to the right, a broad one leading away to the south, and he banked toward it at less than five hundred feet above the terrain, as he checked again to make sure the aircraft wasn't transmitting its usual radar identification to the air traffic control radars that would be searching for him. With his eyes momentarily focused inside the cockpit, the flock of buzzards just ahead at the same altitude escaped his notice until the last second. Ken looked up just as the flock tried to dive away in all directions. Two sickening thuds rumbled through the airframe as Ken jerked the controls back too late.

"What—what was *that*?" Rudy asked.

"Bird strikes," Ken responded, mostly to himself. He checked the engine instruments, relieved to find them steady. He looked carefully at the left wing then cycled the controls in all directions, satisfied there was no serious damage. One of the impacts had come from over the cockpit, and Ken leaned forward to look up through the small eyebrow windows, his eyes focused on the airframe and missing a sudden glint of sunlight reflecting off the high-flying shapes of two F-16s as they banked tightly over the same valley some ten thousand feet above, spraying tactical radar in all directions in search of Flight 90.

Aboard Gulfstream N5LL. 1:22 P.M.

"Agent Bronsky, you have a call on the Flitephone."

Kat looked around from her vantage point in the cockpit door to find Bill North standing behind her. She knew her face betrayed complete puzzlement, but it didn't make sense.

"Excuse me?"

"We have a Flitephone aboard, and I took the liberty of passing the number to your people back at Salt Lake. One of them, Frank, I believe, wants to speak with you."

"Really? You thought of that?"

North nodded and smiled. "Had to do something to pass the time."

She got to her feet and instinctively straightened the tunic of her pant suit as she followed him back into the luxurious passenger cabin. He motioned her into a plush leather captain's chair and handed her the instrument.

"Frank?"

"Kat, we found him. The Air Force passed the coordinates a minute ago. Got a pencil?"

"Go."

He passed the latitude and longitude. "His heading is roughly southwest, he's down low, about five hundred feet above the ground and running at two hundred fifty knots. He's left a wake of citizen complaints about low-flying jets. We know it's him."

"Great. Any further contact?"

"No. You're it, as you figured."

"Can we keep this line open?"

"I suppose," Frank replied.

"Hang on," she shot back, looking up at the owner. "Mr. North, could I ask you a big favor?"

He spread his hands out, palms up. "If you'll call me Bill."

"Okay, Bill. I'm Kat. Could we keep this line open and have you monitor it in case he needs to pass me something else?"

"You got it," Bill North came out of his swivel chair and took the handset as Kat sprang to her feet and moved back to the cockpit to relay the position.

"Good," Dane said as he studied the flight management computer after entering the coordinates. "He's about twenty miles south of us. What do you think, Jeff?"

"About one-seven-zero degrees?"

The captain nodded as he pushed the power levers forward, then turned to Kat.

"You might want to get on a headset now. The frequency you gave me is in this radio head right here. Your transmit button is on the panel."

"Got it. And we're still at twenty thousand?"

The copilot nodded as Dane turned to her. "When we get to where we think he might be, we probably ought to be around ten or less."

Kat leaned forward and focused on a small spot etched into the matte black of the center instrument console, organizing her thoughts. If Wolfe was able to hear the radio calls she was about to make, how would he react? Logically he should be pleased, but his actions had hardly been logical.

But what choice was there?

She pushed the transmit button.

"AirBridge Ninety, Gulfstream Five-Lima-Lima, how do you copy?"

There was no answer.

"AirBridge Flight Ninety, this is Gulfstream Five-Lima-Lima, can you hear us? Over."

Nothing.

Kat repeated the call several times before lifting her head and realizing the altimeter was already unwinding.

"Are we there already?"

Dane shook his head no. "I'm going to take us up to maximum speed on descent. We should be on him in about eight minutes."

She looked down again, closed her eyes, and tried to imagine what might be going on in the cockpit of the hijacked 737.

How is he going to play this? she thought. *How is he going to try to force our hand? He's got to know we can't arrest people at random or just set up a grand jury and a trial because someone demands it.*

Her eyes flew open all of a sudden. *Of course he knows that, which means that only new evidence, or new information will make it happen. So what does he have?*

"Kat, I think I may see him up here," Dane said.

She thought of the copilot's words from Durango, and the captain's reactions in Colorado Springs. Who was it he had aboard?

Oh yeah, the candidate for Attorney General.

"Kat, did you hear me?" the captain was asking. Her eyes were closed again.

The guy's currently a U.S. Attorney in Connecticut, and that's . . . New Haven . . . her eyes fluttered open. *Which would have jurisdiction over Stamford, Connecticut, where Ken Wolfe lived when his daughter was murdered!*

Dane Bailey banked the Gulfstream slightly to the left.

"I think we may have him about ten miles dead ahead, Kat."

She stood up and followed his finger as he pointed beyond the radome of the Gulfstream. "I don't see him."

"Just a small speck right now, but it's weaving down a valley, and it's too big and fast to be a light plane."

She nodded. "Wonderful. Get as close as it takes, but don't let him see us. You have a Flitephone?"

"Yeah, right here," Jeff Jayson responded, pulling the handset from its cradle and handing it to her. Frank was waiting on the other end.

"We've spotted him, Frank, but so far he won't respond to my calls. I need some quick information."

"Go ahead, Kat."

"What was the name of the U.S. Attorney aboard that plane?"

"Hold on. . . . Rudolph Bostich."

"Check to make sure he's headquartered in New Haven, second that New Haven has jurisdiction over Stamford, third that the jurisdiction over the murder of Captain Wolfe's daughter was the same area, and finally, do we know of any involvement Mr. Bostich had with the Wolfe case?"

"I've got it, Kat. I'll get back to you in a minute. What's your theory?"

"I don't think Bostich is a hostage as much as he is an unwilling source. He's got something Wolfe wants. Remember his first statement about what the hijacker wanted? An end to dishonest federal prosecutors? And the copilot said Wolfe threw up after finding out Bostich was on board. There has to be some kind of link between Bostich and Wolfe's tragedy."

Dane Bailey touched her arm with his right hand and pointed ahead. Kat looked up with the receiver still pressed to her ear and saw the shape of the 737 clearly for the first time, as it rolled into a left turn just a few miles ahead.

Frank's voice filled her ear. "Stand by, Kat."

"Okay. Bill, are you still on?"

"Yes, Kat."

"Could you keep monitoring this line, please?"

"You bet."

She handed the receiver back to the copilot and stood again, leaning forward to see over the glareshield as she raised the microphone to her mouth.

"Captain Wolfe, this is Kat Bronsky. Please talk to me. I know you're still there. Half the homeowners in Utah are complaining about you flying through their clotheslines."

There was silence for a second, then the sound of a transmitter being keyed.

"Seems a strange time for humor, Bronsky."

Kat flashed a thumbs up sign to the pilots as she pressed the transmit button again.

"Hey, gallows humor is the FBI's favorite pastime—when we're not dealing with guys who're trying to change the world, that is."

"That what I'm trying to do?"

"Sounds like it to me, and since you didn't fly into the mountains like you wanted us to believe, I'd wager you still want us to do a few things for you."

"Worked, didn't it?"

"Yeah, you tested our blood pressures, but I already had you pegged, Wolfe. You're not what you want us to believe you are. That doesn't mean you wouldn't do what you threaten, but you don't want to hurt anyone. What you want is to stop your daughter's killer from hurting anyone else, right? Isn't that what this is all about?"

There was silence for a few seconds as she watched the silver Boeing below bank to the right and alter its course southbound, gently rising over an undulating terrain.

"That's part of it, Bronsky. There are a lot of scores to be settled, and that's the bottom line."

"But there's more, isn't there, Captain? You said earlier you wanted an end to unscrupulous federal prosecutors, or however you put it. Right?"

"You mean lying bastards like Rudolph Bostich? Yeah, you could say that."

"Tell me about Bostich."

"I'll do better than that, Agent Bronsky. Kat, wasn't it? In a little while I'll have Rudolph Bostich himself telling you precisely what he did. He's going to spill it all, while he still can."

"We're aware he's on board, Ken."

"I figured you would be. In fact, he's sitting right here next to me in the copilot's seat, wondering when I'm going to bury the crash axe in his miserable skull."

Kat held her finger away from the transmit button and thought hard and fast. Wolfe had taken the man he blamed for doing something regarding his daughter's death and forced him in the copilot's seat. Since Wolfe didn't seem suicidal, the move had to be for purposes of coercion. He was going to try to scare the D.A. into saying something, admitting something, or promising something.

Come on Frank! Get back to me with the basics.

Kat pressed the button again.

"Okay, Ken, I'll admit that's a surprise. Probably a surprise for Mr. Bostich, too. Where do you want to have this little chat?"

"*When* is the question, Bron—Kat. It's a matter of time."

"You've only got so much fuel."

"True, but I've also got a planeload of folks back here and a bomb with an electronic trigger I can't let go of, so when I need fuel, I'll land and you'll make sure I get fuel. How are you talking to me so clearly, by the way? Your radio signal is excellent."

Dane Bailey turned to Kat and pointed urgently ahead. She let up on the transmit button and looked up. "What?"

"He's headed up a box canyon, Kat. Tell him to pull up and get out of there."

"We'll give ourselves away!" she said. "Where is it?"

"There! Hurry, I'm not kidding. Right around that bend the canyon comes to an end in a two-thousand-foot cliff."

They had been in a perfect position, unseen and pacing him from behind, but there was no time to debate it.

Kat mashed the transmit button. "Ken, PULL UP, PULL UP NOW! You've blundered into a box canyon. There's a two-thousand-foot wall ahead you can't see!"

She released the button and waited, her eyes glued to the 737 as it neared the turn in the canyon. The aircraft was less than five hundred feet above the roadway that ran down the middle of the valley.

"KEN, FOR GOD'S SAKE I'M NOT KIDDING! WHAT WILL IT HURT TO CLIMB? PULL UP NOW!"

There was a short burst of transmission from the other radio, but no voice. The Boeing was coming up on the turn now, rolling into a right bank.

Dane Bailey's voice cut in on the frequency as he mashed his transmit button on the control yoke. "AIRBRIDGE, NO SHIT, MAN, SHE'S RIGHT! CLIMB NOW!"

Instantly the 737's nose came up and the ship began to climb as it entered a tight bank to the right to get around the cliff that was blocking Wolfe's view of the sheer wall less than two miles ahead.

"Oh, God!" Kat muttered.

Dane maneuvered the Gulfstream over the cliff that formed the bend in the canyon, and for a few seconds the 737 slipped from view over the far edge, still beneath the altitude of the surrounding mesa. They could see where the canyon ended now, the plateau green and verdant thousands of feet above the valley floor.

Suddenly the silver 737 popped into view, nose high, approaching the rim from below, its wings level, its engines obviously at full power.

Kat felt herself squeezing the microphone in a death grip as the Boeing closed in on the wall of exposed cap rock.

The Boeing was less than a quarter mile away, its altitude close to that of the rim, how close she couldn't tell.

"I think . . ." Jeff began, his voice strained, ". . . he's got a chance."

There was no way to know whether the rim was higher than the aircraft or vice versa in the microsecond before the 737's image merged with the stark promontory of the ridge. Kat felt her breathing stop, waiting for impact, a part of her wondering how she was going to feel about losing them so quickly, knowing this time it was a mistake, not a charade.

One moment there was airspace between the aircraft and the ridge, the next the green of the plateau was slipping safely beneath the 737 as the twin engine jetliner soared over the rim with less than a hundred feet to spare. It kept climbing, then stabilized a thousand feet above the altitude of the mesa ahead.

After a short eternity, Kat let out a ragged breath.

"Jeez, that was close!" Jeff said from the right seat.

Kat reached over with her left hand and patted the captain's shoulder.

"Thank you, Dane. You saved them. He wasn't going to listen to me."

The captain nodded, his jaw clenched with tension, as Kat tried to calm her heart rate.

More than a minute passed before the sound of a transmitter clicking on filled the headset.

"Whoever's back there, thank you. That wasn't part of the plan."

Kat let the statement hang on dead air before she hit the button again.

"I tried to tell you, Ken."

The answer was quick and almost contrite. "You did. You did, Kat. Which means you're shadowing me. So where are you?"

She shook her head and shrugged, holding her finger off the transmit button as she looked at Dane. "So much for surprise."

He looked back and smiled a nervous smile. "Might say the cat's out of the bag, huh?"

She grimaced before punching the transmit button. "Ken, we're behind you, and we're at 'let's make a deal' time. Please. You almost bought it just then."

There was a long period of dead air before the radio clicked on again from AirBridge 90.

"So what do you suggest?"

Kat was not expecting the words to flow so easily from her mind, but her answer was immediate. "Grand Junction is off to the east. They've got a good airport, and we've got no one waiting for us, since no one knew any of us would be here." She let up on the transmit button for a second, then pressed it again. "Remember, Ken, I told you our cooperation officially depends on getting your passengers out of harm's way. Why not land at Grand Junction, let your passengers off, and give me the leverage I need to get you what you want?"

She let up on the button and waited, watching the silver Boeing as it kept running southbound, maintaining a more healthy altitude above the plateau than before.

Finally the transmitter clicked on as the 737 began a sudden left turn.

"Grand Junction it is, Kat. No tricks, no guns, and no Bostich. I'll give you everyone else, but I keep the aircraft and I keep Bostich, until he's ready to confess, that is."

She exhaled heavily and closed her eyes for a second to give a small prayer of thanks. "It's the right way to handle it, Ken. Then we can work on accomplishing the things you want."

She put the microphone down and looked at the two pilots.

"How far to Grand Junction?"

Dane Bailey was already punching the identifier of the Grand Junction Airport into the flight computer, which gave an instant readout.

"One hundred ten nautical miles, Kat. At his—and our—present speed, a little under a half hour."

She nodded and relayed the mileage and time to Frank on the Flitephone extension before peeling her knees off the carpet and getting to her feet. Most of the feeling had drained away from her right leg, and she grabbed the edge of the cockpit bulkhead for balance while she tried to shake out the pins and needles reawakening her right calf and foot.

"Frank, do we have anyone nearby? Is there any chance of scrambling one of our people to Grand Junction in time, but keeping them out of sight?"

Dane Bailey saw her nod in response to the reply on the other end.

"Okay, but warn them, Frank. Warn them how volatile this man is. I'm convinced Wolfe is making this up as he goes along, which means he's not going to trust any decision he makes for more than a few seconds. He'll be expecting at any point to have done the wrong thing, and he'll be ready to change course at the first sign that he's misestimated our reaction. No police, sheriff, or even crash trucks at Grand Junction Airport unless they're hidden in a hangar, okay? We spook him, we'll lose him."

FOURTEEN

Aboard AirBridge Flight 90. 1:30 P.M.

Annette, Bev, and Kevin had been in a frantic huddle in the aft galley when the engines suddenly throttled up and the 737 began a steep climb. They scattered to respective windows, wondering what was ahead, and returned to the galley ashen faced after seeing the cap rock of the mesa whistle beneath them less than a hundred feet below.

The passengers had grown very quiet—young members of the high school band were holding on to each other for support, and Elvira Gates had been busily hopping to her feet to try and comfort the few members of her group who had moved from fear-of-flying to stark terror with each new shock. Others, she had whispered to Bev, were responding like they were on an amusement park ride, and she wondered aloud if her course hadn't succeeded too well. The tour company owner from Seattle had been quiet as a church mouse, but the one passenger whose level of terror was worrying them all was the FAA maintenance inspector. He seemed somewhere close to catatonic.

The near-miss suddenly made a dangerous decision wholly unanimous: The passengers had to know the truth. It was more a spontaneous gut reaction than a reasoned decision, a collective revulsion to the lie that they were the faithful crew of Captain Wolfe. That's what the passengers would be thinking, and that had to change.

Annette hurriedly pulled the battery-powered megaphone from one of the overhead compartments and walked forward to first class, knowing Ken would be monitoring anything she said on the P.A. system. The aircraft seemed to be flying steadily now without any of the weaving and bobbing that had sent a dozen passengers grabbing for their airsick bags.

At the head of coach she turned and looked into the frightened eyes of her passengers, and began briefing them, keeping the volume too low to be heard in the cockpit, holding onto the overhead compartments with her left hand in case Ken Wolfe began some new gyrations.

"There's no easy way to say this, folks. As bizarre as this will sound, we've been hijacked by our own captain. Captain Wolfe is the only hijacker aboard. He's the one making the threats, and the federal district attorney he said so many nasty things about on the PA is his captive, and is up there in the cockpit alone with him. The copilot was apparently left behind in Durango. Your flight attendants did not know any of this until just outside Salt Lake City. I have no idea what to expect next, but I want all of you to stay belted in your seats. Do not try to play the hero. The captain says he had placed a bomb in the forward baggage compartment, and he is holding an electronic trigger in his hand. I have seen that trigger. It does exist, and he claims if he lets go of it, we'll explode. We can't afford to second guess that threat. We have to assume it's valid."

She paused and lowered the megaphone for a second, surveying the wide-eyed disbelief before her.

"Okay, look, I know the main question many of you have is the same one I can't answer. 'Why is he doing this?' " She shook her head in the negative for emphasis. "I don't know. I understand the captain's young daughter was murdered two years ago, and he holds Mr. Bostich responsible for not going after the murderer. I do not know the details, and I don't know why we're caught up in this. I do know Captain Wolfe holds all the cards right now, and all we can do is stay strapped in and pray. Your flight attendants are just as much trapped by this situation as you are, but we're still in charge of keeping you as safe as possible, and that's what we're going to keep on doing."

She walked back ten rows at a time, repeating the same message, putting off questions, aware that the passengers seemed no more stunned than before. It was all surrealistic anyway, being hijacked, cliffs and bluffs and mountainsides whistling by the windows, wild banks and turns, and strange messages from the cockpit.

She'd been waiting for the chance to talk to Nancy Beck, and as she reached row eighteen, Annette knelt beside her.

"Nancy, listen closely. Your husband's okay. I didn't know this until a few minutes ago, but somehow he left the airplane in Durango and we left before he got back aboard."

She looked utterly stunned, and Annette filled the silence.

"So, stop worrying. He's back in Durango, safe and sound, and probably worrying himself to death about you."

She stood, then, and began moving backward up the aisle toward the front, a row at a time, looking carefully at each one of her passengers as Bev followed.

At every row the basic questions were the same: "Do we know where he's really taking us?" and "What does he want?"

"I don't know," was all she could say.

"Somehow it all makes sense now, in a peculiar sort of way," one of the fear-of-flying group said with tears in her eyes. "I mean, after the rest of it, what's another bizarre twist like finding out the captain is a maniac? At least he knows how to fly. I was afraid they were wrestling for the controls up there."

Annette worked her way back to first class. She stood for a while, feeling an eerie calm settle in over the confusion she felt—the sensation of a hand being placed gently on her shoulder seeming too distant to be real. Annette jumped and turned to find herself facing a barrel-chested man in his sixties. Five more passengers, four men and one woman, stood behind him.

"You startled me. Can I help you?"

"Miss, I'm Mike Clark, a retired police officer, and the folks behind me all want to help."

She looked at him in confusion. "Help with what?"

"Look, we've got to take some action immediately. This guy's gonna kill us flying the way he is. Did you see how close we came to hitting that ridge back there?"

Annette nodded slowly as she examined the group. "What do you suggest, sir?"

"We were talking, the bunch of us. Do you have a key to that cockpit door? I thought I saw you open the cockpit door earlier. If we can get in there quickly enough by yanking the door open when he's least suspecting it, I think we could subdue the S.O.B., especially since you say he's the only hijacker."

She shook her head no. "It's locked, and the captain has the only key."

"I can't accept that. There's got to be a way to force that door open."

She shrugged. "I don't know, but it's far too dangerous to try."

There was a flurry of voices as the group behind him all spoke at once, demanding action, the retired cop in the lead summing it up. "We stay back here like sheep, we're gonna get slaughtered like sheep."

Annette shook her head and grimaced as she looked the man in the eye.

"I understand the frustration. I'm frustrated too, but if you disable him, who's going to fly?"

The cop was shaking his head. "No, you don't understand. We know he's the only pilot, but if we could yank that trigger away from him—"

"And if he's suicidal?" She regretted the word the second it left her mouth. The blood drained from the retired officer's face and there were gasps from those behind him as he tried to recover.

"You say he's . . . suicidal?"

"No!" Annette said quickly. "I don't have reason to believe he is, but we don't know. Take away his options and force him into a corner when he's the only one flying, and do we really know what he'll do?"

The man was shaking his head in shock. "I do not believe this!"

"Sir, I'm just as scared as you are,"

He raised his index finger. "I'm not scared, ma'am, I'm madder than hell. This is supposed to be an airline. We trust you not to put maniacs in the cockpit! How the hell did his happen?"

"I don't know. I wish I did."

She tried to meet his eyes, but felt herself turn away, as much in shame, she concluded, as anything else.

He was right. She was AirBridge, and AirBridge was responsible for this.

She wet her lips and tried again. "Sir, please, we can't lose our heads. He says he's got a trigger up there that will blow us up if he lets go of it for a second. I've seen it in his hand. I don't know if it's real, but I don't want to find out the hard way."

The retired cop sighed angrily and turned to look at the others before turning back to Annette. "Did you see how close we came to that damn ridge back there? You stand here and tell me we can't do anything. Are you really that helpless, or just terrified?"

The words were like a hard slap to the face. *Helpless, indeed!* she thought. *But that's how I've been acting.*

Annette snapped her head up and looked him squarely in the eye. From somewhere inside she felt herself mustering up the air of authority that Ken had beaten out of her in the previous hour, a loss that had left her floundering and flustered. She felt her throat expand slightly as she straightened her back and found the familiar tone in her voice that had always exuded command.

"Okay, sir, listen up. Here's the deal. We got too close to that ridge, but the fact is, we're still intact and we're still flying. No, we're not in control of where this man is taking us, but I am in control back here, and I told all of you to remain seated. As tough as it is, you've all got to follow my instructions and stay calm. I know where you are, and now I know who you are." She looked over at the group's spokesman. "If there's a need for your help as a police officer, you can absolutely count on me to come back here and get you instantly. Understood?"

He studied her face for a few seconds in silence without moving, his head cocked ever so slightly to one side as if he were seeing her for the first time.

"I'm in Twenty-one-D," he said with a nod and a thin smile as he turned and made a move-along sign with the palms of his hands to the people behind him. "Okay, folks, you heard the boss."

Aboard Gulfstream N5LL. 1:38 P.M.

Kat had waited to make sure AirBridge 90 was steering a straight line toward Grand Junction before racing back to use perhaps the plushest airborne bathroom she'd ever seen, a leather-trimmed roomette complete with gold-plated faucets, a small glassed-in shower, and a flat-screen color display of the exact point over planet earth where N5LL was flying at that moment.

As she straightened her tunic and checked her face in the mirror while washing her hands, she studied the map. There was a dotted line extending from their position to Grand Junction clearly depicted with the surrounding mountains in relief less than sixty miles ahead now. She could see the Canyonlands Park area to the south, lower mountains to the north, and even the Interstate running east to the same destination.

Kat glanced at her watch, anxious to get back up front, but there were buttons on one side of the screen and she couldn't resist pushing the one marked weather.

Instantly, an overlaid depiction of cloud coverage merged onto the picture. She worked another control and increased the scale, as if pulling up into orbit, the scope of the display now taking in a thousand miles laterally, and then the entire country. The cloud coverage included thunderstorms in the midwest, a veil of cloud coverage over Florida, and with one more touch of a button, temperatures at various spots across the nation.

"Fascinating!" she said out loud, simultaneously feeling guilty for taking the extra thirty seconds.

Kat returned to the cabin and whistled as she walked past Bill North, who was still listening to the Flitephone. "That is one beautiful bathroom, Bill, and I love the display screen."

He smiled and chuckled. "Yeah, I'm a control freak, I guess. I can't stand to be in there and not know where we are. By the way, Kat . . ."

She stopped and turned back to him."Yes?"

"I understand the captain is the hijacker. Wolfe is his name, right?"

She nodded cautiously.

"Well, maybe this is information you can't share, but I'm really curious what you know about this man."

Kat studied Bill North for a few seconds before replying. He had offered his expensive jet and crew without hesitation and had made no move to interfere. It seemed only fair to let him know what they were dealing with.

"Bill, I don't have time to tell you the whole tale right now, but apparently he's trying to force prosecution of a man who killed his daughter and we've got a very disturbed pilot on our hands who may be capable of mass murder himself."

Bill North shook his head, a distant look in his eyes. "You're right to worry, Kat. It amazes me what a desperate man is capable of doing." He smiled suddenly and gestured toward the Flitephone. "By the way,

Frank's waiting to talk to you. You're welcome to take it here, or in the cockpit."

She nodded and thanked him. "I think I'll go up where I can see," she said as she moved back to the cockpit to pick up the Flitephone extension.

"Frank?"

"Answers to your earlier questions, Kat. Ready?"

"Go ahead."

"Okay. Bostich *is* headquartered in New Haven, and yes, he does have jurisdiction over federal matters in Stamford. Now, Wolfe's daughter was kidnapped from Stamford, and her body was found in Connecticut, but there are indications she was tortured and murdered somewhere else over state lines, perhaps in Maine. In any event, if federal charges were appropriate, Bostich could have filed them in New Haven. He didn't. Finally—follow me on this carefully because it's a little convoluted—it was a Connecticut State Police detective who obtained the bad search warrant that later let the killer off the hook. He got the warrant by telling a state judge that he had received a tip from an unimpeachable source, a source he could personally vouch for, to search the computer of a known pedophile named Bradley Lumin. The judge granted the warrant, the police served the warrant and found a treasure trove of evidence on Lumin's computer, including a photo of the victim in the process of being brutalized. There was no other physical evidence found. The whole case depended on the computer evidence. Then, the usual occurs. Some sleazy defense lawyer challenges the warrant before trial, and on examination of the detective, the judge discovers that it was a *telephone* tip, not an in-person tip, and worse, the detective never even asked the identity of the tipster."

"Wonderful. So he lied about knowing the tipster?"

"Not necessarily. He told the judge he didn't ask who the man was because he recognized his voice without question. But, the man the detective said the voice belonged to, when hauled in on subpoena, testified that he had never made such a call."

"How does this tie in with Bostich, Frank?"

"The man who claimed he had never made such a call was Rudy Bostich, the United States Attorney for Connecticut headquartered in New Haven. I had the transcript of the court record faxed in. Bostich was quite clear on the stand that he not only did not make that call, he would have had no access to such information, and even if he had, he would never have passed it anonymously in a phone call to a state cop. That all makes very good sense, Kat. This man has three decades of experience, and fifteen years as a U.S. Attorney. It's unlikely he'd be that stupid. Someone apparently used a fake voice to fool the cop, or just happened to sound like Bostich, and when the judge found out, he threw out the warrant. When the warrant went out the window, so did virtually all the evidence against the killer of Melinda Wolfe, a killer they had cold with the computer evidence."

Kat was massaging her forehead with one hand as she balanced the phone against her ear with the other, imagining Rudy Bostich's dilemma as he sat captive in that cockpit several miles ahead, his life in the hands of an aggrieved father. She'd been worried more about the passengers, taking Wolfe's fury at Bostich somehow at face value. But Bostich wasn't the enemy, it seemed. Wolfe's misinterpretation was.

"Lord, Frank, we've got an even worse problem than I figured. Wolfe is apparently convinced he can force Bostich to confess to something, I suppose to lying about phoning the tip to the detective. But if Bostitch is innocent and Wolfe won't accept that, where do we go from here?"

There was a pause back in Salt Lake. "You're the psychologist, Kat."

She sighed, loud and long. "Any chance we could dredge up some proof Wolfe might accept, like phone records or something? Maybe prove he couldn't have made the call?"

"I'll try, Kat, but you're talking major investigative footwork in a matter a year and a half old, and I don't think we can move that fast. Somehow Bostich is either going to have to fake a confession to get out of this, or you're going to have to convince Wolfe he's got it wrong, or somehow we have to take him out."

"Wonderful. How about Grand Junction assets?"

"Local sheriff and police SWAT team are all we have. We're mobilizing them by phone, and they're cooperating fully. We're going to have them standing by out of sight."

She nodded to herself. "Okay. We're about—hold on." Kat looked up at Dane, who had been watching her in his peripheral vision. He saw the movement and turned toward her.

"How much longer, Dane?"

His eyes flicked forward to the "remaining distance" readout on the flight computer, then back at her. "About twelve minutes or less."

She repeated the words to Frank.

"Kat, Washington may rip this away from me in the next few minutes."

"What do you mean, Frank?"

"Well, if AirBridge was on the ground in Salt Lake, this would be our show. With him practically in Colorado now, the Salt Lake office is no longer exclusive owner of the franchise, so to speak."

"I don't want to be dealing with people I don't know, Frank. I need too much support on this."

"Kat, I hate to say this, but I think you're going to lose control in Grand Junction the second they get another team in from Denver. They're launching someone now."

She felt her face begin to flush, as much in embarrassment as in anger.

"That's nuts, Frank."

"Hasn't happened yet, but be aware it might. The media is all over this. CNN is live, the other networks are doing news breaks, and if we can nail that seven-thirty-seven to the ground in Grand Junction, you can expect a media extravaganza within a half hour. In that atmosphere . . ."

She nodded, her eyes closed, reminding herself both the pilots and her host, Bill North, were listening to her side of the conversation. "Okay, Frank. Whatever the Bureau wants, the Bureau gets, but I need to stay in the loop."

"I'll make the point with FBI Headquarters, Kat. Be careful."

She replaced the phone, aware that his admonition had as much to do with how she handled their bosses as how she handled the hijacker ahead.

FIFTEEN

Aboard AirBridge Flight 90. 1:46 P.M.

Rudy Bostich dabbed his forehead with a handkerchief and watched in silence as Ken Wolfe retarded the throttles and began a slow descent, his eyes on the distant horizon toward what had to be Grand Junction, Colorado.

For nearly ten minutes not a word had been spoken, and without a headset, Rudy could hear only the captain's side of the conversation.

Wolfe's voice was more subdued after their close encounter with the ridgeline. Obviously, Rudy concluded, the captain had been shaken by that near-fatal mistake. Rudy had watched him sweating through the whole episode as he firewalled the throttles and pulled hard on the control column while the two-thousand-foot wall of rock loomed in front of them, then barely passed beneath them.

That meant Wolfe was vulnerable, and not completely crazy. That meant he could probably be reached with reason. Rudy wondered if Wolfe realized his life as a pilot and a free man was over.

And he wondered if Wolfe had any idea how alone he was, an enemy to everyone.

Wolfe was craning his neck again and looking up through the small eyebrow windows in the cockpit ceiling. He'd been doing that since the ridgeline, and Rudy concluded they were probably being followed, maybe by Air Force jets. Someone must be up there and talking to Wolfe on the radio. At least he hoped so. Even if they couldn't physically help, it would be comforting to know someone was out there watching.

He felt numb now, not paralyzed with fear like before. He was ashamed of his earlier reaction, but being marched to the cockpit had felt like an impending execution. Slowly, however, he was becoming aware that Wolfe's main purpose wasn't killing him, it was finding a way to convict the monster who killed his daughter, and in that, their goals had always been the same.

Rudy glanced over at Wolfe again, this time more boldly. "Captain, may I ask you a question?"

Wolfe shot him a withering look of hatred and disdain, but Rudy held an even expression, being careful not to show either fear or confidence.

"What, Bostich?"

Rudy swallowed hard and realized he had licked his lips, a nervous signal he should have stifled. "Isn't it possible you could be wrong?"

Again Wolfe glanced quickly his way, this time more in curiosity. "About what?"

"About me. About whatever you think I've done."

"I know what you've done, you bastard."

"You said that, Captain, and I'm sure you *think* you know something about what happened in relation to your daughter's death, but—"

"Get to the point, Bostich!"

The impact of Wolfe's voice, sharp and angry and at full volume, caused him to flinch.

Wolfe suddenly looked to the left and flicked something on his control yoke, then banked the 737 sharply to the left, pulling enough G-force to push Rudy down in the seat.

Just as quickly they were back to stable flight and Wolfe turned angrily to him again. "I said, get to the point!"

Rudy kept his eyes on the scene ahead. He nodded slowly. "The point is, I honestly don't know what it is you think I've done, and even a condemned man is entitled to know the charges against him."

Wolfe's head jerked to the right, a sour smile on his lips. "So, you think you're condemned, huh?"

"Aren't I? You're apparently planning on releasing everyone but me, and you want me to confess to something I don't even understand, unless all this is because I didn't file federal charges against the suspect."

Ken Wolfe adjusted the descent rate of the aircraft and reached down to the center pedestal to reposition some knobs, then glanced back at him.

"Okay, shithead, I'll tell you what you already know. I'm very aware you couldn't file federal charges. No evidence, no charges. But you're responsible for ruining that evidence. You were subpoenaed by the judge and asked if you were the one who called and tipped the detective on who killed my daughter. You knew the warrant, and all the evidence, depended on your answer. You knew if you said no, the murderer would go free. I'm sure you got the original tip about who killed Melinda from some scumbag in the witness protection program, someone you were shielding, someone who knew the underworld enough to finger the killer. Go search this felon's home, you told the detective. Impound his computer and get an expert to look at all the files. The evidence will be there. And it was, wasn't it, Bostich?"

Rudy nodded. "It was there, all right, but I wasn't the tipster."

"Yeah, right. You knew there was no way that state judge was going to force you to disclose where *you* got the information. That's what I can't understand. You knew that telling the truth wouldn't have hurt anything you cared about, but you sat there on that stand, swore on a Bible, and lied! You, a federal prosecutor, a candidate for Attorney General of the United States, knowing that how you answered that question would make all the difference in prosecuting or freeing a murderer of little girls. YOU, you unspeakable piece of scum, lied."

Rudy let out a ragged breath. "I didn't lie. I wasn't the tipster."

"Bullshit! I've got you dead to rights. I've got evidence that you *did* make that call. Why the hell would a thirty-year veteran detective have made that up? He'd worked with you before. He knew your voice. You depended on that when you called him, didn't you?"

"I didn't make—"

"CAN IT, BASTARD! You *made* the friggin' call!"

Rudy was shaking his head energetically, feeling like he was fighting a ghost, dealing with an accusation he had no way of refuting. What evidence? What on earth did Wolfe think he had? Certainly the detective claimed it was him, but that was old news. Discredited news. The word of a state police detective who was on the spot, against that of a respected federal prosecutor who had no apparent stake in the case and no apparent motivation to lie. Deciding whom to believe had been a no-brainer for the judge.

Ken Wolfe reached toward the fuel gauges and pushed a button, then made some other adjustments on the front panel.

Rudy looked over at him again. "Suppose your evidence is wrong? Evidence often appears to confirm one thing, and in fact, the opposite is true. Have you considered that?"

"Yes."

"And?"

"This evidence doesn't lie, unless you were in the habit of making calls to detectives at random every night."

Rudy studied Ken Wolfe's face from the side, his eyes in a squint. "Wait a minute, you think you have *phone* records?"

"I don't *think* I have them, Bostich, I have them. And the originals are safe."

Rudy shook his head. "Captain, phone records can be faked. Where did you get them?"

"None of your damn business."

"Did Detective Roger Matson give you those?"

"I said, it's none of your damn business, until your trial for perjury, that is."

Rudy looked forward and began shaking his head, slowly at first, then with energy as he snapped his gaze back to Wolfe.

"Captain, you've been had! What you apparently don't know is that Detective Matson is a bad apple. He has a long history with his department of cowboyish operations, and a long history with area judges for making up so-called evidence to get warrants. You didn't know that, did you?"

"I don't know that *now*, Bostich. I can't believe a word you say. If you said the sun was up, I wouldn't believe it without an astrophysicist's affidavit."

"Captain, Matson is, in fact, a bad apple. It's all in his record, but I don't happen to carry that record with me."

"Pity. Shut up a second."

Wolfe banked the aircraft to the right and once again rotated a wheel-like thing on the side of the center pedestal as he spoke into the microphone boom attached to his headset.

"Kat? Are you still out there shadowing me?"

Wolfe listened to the response and nodded, his eyes on the horizon.

"Okay. I want to see what you're flying. Now. Pull alongside on my left, one half mile spacing. Then you're going to land first. Understood?"

He nodded again, then turned back to Rudy.

"You have anything more to say?"

Rudy nodded. "Captain, Matson certainly did know me, but you've been so eager to blame me, you never looked into his background. There are an awful lot of things a federal prosecutor can't tell the general public and the media, things that civilians like yourself can't know. God, I wish you would have come to me first before throwing everything in your life away on this . . . this, stupid, pointless reaction."

"I did, bastard. I've been writing letters to you. You never answered."

Rudy shook his head sadly. "You never asked questions in those letters, Captain. You just made accusations. I wish you'd come in person. Now . . . look what you've done."

He gestured toward the front instrument panel while looking at the captain for a response. There was none.

"Look, Ken."

"Don't use my first name, scumbag."

"Okay, okay, I know you've convinced yourself I'm the bad guy, but you're wrong. Look, I've had to sit on Detective Matson numerous times in the past for getting in the way of federal investigations. He knew me well enough to want to discredit me, and this gave him a perfect opportunity. He was on the spot. Some impossibly unreliable tipster obviously told him who did your . . . who killed your daughter, and to get himself off the hook for lying to get a warrant, he invents me as the caller, thinking I'd just say yes. But that would have been a lie! Don't you see, captain? I *was* under oath. I knew the stakes, but I could not lie about it. The fact was, I did not make that call."

Wolfe had turned his head and was staring at Bostich, eye to eye, in silence.

There was obviously a radio transmission Rudy couldn't hear. The captain looked up and said a few words in pilot jargon into his microphone, then banked the 737 to the left a few degrees as he reduced the power a little more.

Ken Wolfe suddenly looked back at Bostich. "Are you trying to tell me those phone records are fake because I got them from Detective Matson?"

Rudy nodded energetically. "That's exactly what I'm trying to tell you. We've both been set up. I never anticipated he would do this to you, a grieving father. It shows what a scum he is! But that's what he's done. He's used faked records to turn you against me, for what reason I have no idea. Maybe just to hurt you, and he's certainly succeeded."

Wolfe had turned his head forward again, and Rudy watched him with rising hope, knowing the captain couldn't have been aware of what he'd just told him about Matson. Rudy remembered the angry letters from Wolfe, always stopping just short of making actionable threats. He'd pushed them aside as innocuous, hysterical, and not worth his time.

Wolfe was shaking his head slowly, and Rudy felt his heart leap. Maybe, just maybe, they could end it peacefully in a few minutes at Grand Junction. He would still recommend charges of air piracy, of course. This would be some other federal prosecutor's jurisdiction, but Rudy would be listened to.

Ken Wolfe's expression was changing. As Rudy watched, a sarcastic little smile began playing around the captain's mouth, and Rudy watched it in puzzlement until Wolfe turned to look him in the eye.

"Nice try, Bostich, I'll give you that. As a snake oil salesman, you're good. Too bad for you there's one small detail *you* didn't know when you concocted that smooth explanation."

Rudy felt his confidence crumbling. "What are you talking about? I've concocted nothing."

"Detective Matson had nothing whatsoever to do with the phone records I've obtained. He doesn't even know they exist."

Aboard Gulfstream N5LL. 1:58 P.M.

Dane Bailey pulled back the throttles and let the Gulfstream slow as it pulled even with the AirBridge 737 at the same altitude of ten thousand feet. Kat was still on her knees just behind the center console, her left hand holding the back of Dane's chair, keeping her eyes on the Boeing as she pushed the transmit button.

"Okay, Ken, we're out here to your left."

There was a pause. She could see the outline of a head in the pilot's window of the Boeing, but she could make out no details.

"A G-four is hardly a government-issued aircraft," Ken Wolfe replied.

"I never said it was, Ken. We asked a concerned citizen for help, and he's lending us his plane and crew. The whole damn country's worried about you, Ken."

She heard the transmitter click on, and she heard a derisive snort. "Sure they are, Kat. What they're concerned about are my passengers. They're concerned the FBI might not be able to get off a clean shot and drop me. The whole damn country doesn't have a clue what this is really all about."

The opening was there and she took it.

"Okay, but we could remedy that, Ken. We could hook you up with a camera crew on the ground and give you all the time you need to tell the country the whole story." She could almost hear the scream of outrage that would come from FBI headquarters if they heard her making such an offer, but it made sense.

"I'll think about it," he said. "Meanwhile, we're ten miles out. You land first."

"Ken, we went through this at Salt Lake with the F-sixteens. What does it matter? We're unarmed, and no threat to you."

"Nevertheless, you land first or I'm not landing. Got it?"

Kat looked up at Dane, who shrugged and nodded, as he radioed the approach controller and began a left turn to prepare for a visual approach.

"Okay, Ken," Kat replied. "You just tell me how you want to handle this on the ground, okay?"

"Remember, Kat. If you've set up any sort of reception committee, you've imperiled everyone. Anyone gets close to this aircraft without my permission, it goes up in smoke."

"Nobody's going to violate your orders, Captain," Kat told him, praying whoever was leading the team below on the ground knew to keep all vehicles strictly behind the airplane once it was on the ground. They had to stay completely out of sight of the cockpit.

Aboard AirBridge Flight 90. 2:08 P.M.

Ken Wolfe lowered the 737's flaps to the five-degree setting and slowed to 180 knots as he orbited to the west of the airport, watching the

Gulfstream land and turn off onto the ramp. When it was down, he positioned the 737 to fly over the airport, along the runway a thousand feet above the surface to look for any sign of a reception committee.

"Grand Junction Tower, AirBridge Ninety. I'm going to make a high-speed pass over the runway. I'll pull up into a downwind for a VFR landing after that."

"Approved as requested, Ninety," the controller shot back, obviously primed to give the hijacker whatever he wanted.

There was no doubt what the FBI's standard procedures would dictate. Con the hijacker into landing, get the passengers off safely, and somehow immobilize the aircraft without the hijacker thinking the FBI was responsible. In fact, he thought, they would be keeping the airport open just to convince him things were normal.

Somewhere out there in the grass by the runway, Ken thought, *there's a sniper waiting to knock out my tires on rollout if someone gives him the signal.*

He knew Grand Junction well. AirBridge had been serving it with 737s for the past six months, and Ken had made many a landing in the arid community. The ramp area was sliding past his left shoulder now at more than three miles per minute, the scene appearing nonthreatening, except for one small detail which might mean nothing. Along the flight line, a large hangar stood with the doors partially open. Normally it was either full open or full closed.

He looked again.

There was a haphazardly parked gaggle of aircraft outside the hangar, as if someone had emptied it in a hurry. Normally the ramp in front of the hangar was empty.

Ken pushed the throttles up and began a climb to the south. He was preparing to push the transmit button when another voice came on the frequency.

"Grand Junction Tower, AirBridge Forty-five with you for the visual."

AirBridge Forty-five? Ken thought. *Oh, of course. The noon flight from the Springs.* Somehow it seemed strange that the airline's flights would be going on uninterrupted, but if the airport *was* being kept open to fool him, adding another AirBridge flight was a convincing touch.

The tower's reply came quickly in his headset.

"Roger, AirBridge Forty-five, cleared to land runway eleven, winds, one-seven-zero at one-two knots."

"Roger, cleared to land."

Ken turned west and flew several miles away from the airport before turning back east toward it. He saw the landing lights of the other AirBridge flight—an identical 737—as it approached the north end of the runway, and he watched it touch down, taxi off the runway, and head back up the ramp abeam the open hangar, toward the commercial terminal.

The other 737 was just passing the hangar. Ken tried to visualize what might be waiting inside. If there were police cars and a SWAT team, the commanders would be standing out of sight.

Ken punched the transmit button, altering his voice slightly to sound irritated. The other 737 flight crew would be on ground-control frequency and wouldn't hear him.

"Tower, this is AirBridge Forty-five about ten miles to the north for a visual. We just heard another flight using our call sign down there. There's only one of us. What the hell's going on?"

Ken turned his aircraft right to a southerly heading to give himself a better view of the suspicious hangar, now four miles distant. He could imagine the exchange of startled looks among anyone waiting down there. If he was right and there was a reception committee hiding in the hangar, there would be a sudden explosion of activity in a few seconds as they convinced themselves that the hijacked aircraft had landed under the guise of a regularly scheduled flight.

"AirBridge Forty-five, we're, ah, confused, sir," the tower controller began. "You say you're still airborne?"

"Roger that, Grand Junction, and we'd like landing clearance," Ken replied.

"Ah, roger, Forty-five, you're cleared to land, runway eleven, winds one-seven-zero at eight."

Ken pressed his nose against the glass of the pilot's side window, startled at the stream of vehicles that rushed suddenly from the interior of the hangar, red rotating beacons clearly visible even miles away, all of them racing after the real AirBridge Forty-five as it taxied innocently toward the terminal past the waiting Gulfstream.

"So what are you planning now to make things worse, Captain?" Bostich asked suddenly.

Ken looked at the occupant of the right seat and raised his left hand, showing the electronic trigger once again.

"Shut up and start thinking about how you're going to phrase your confession, Bostich. By the way, your life is worth something only if you're willing to tell that judge you lied. You don't do that, you don't deserve to live."

"So now you're threatening the life of a federal prosecutor?"

Ken looked over in mock amazement. "You mean to tell me I hadn't made that threat crystal clear before? Lord! Let me make it clear for the record, scumbag. Confess or die. That clear enough?"

Bostich nodded a sullen nod. "Quite."

Aboard Gulfstream N5LL, Grand Junction Airport. 2:17 P.M.

Jeff Jayson lowered the steps of the Gulfstream and Kat scrambled down to the ramp, followed closely by Bill North. The two of them moved around the nose of the private jet and squinted into the sky, looking for the hijacked airliner as the captain, Dane Bailey, brought up the rear with a handheld aviation radio tuned to the tower frequency.

Kat glanced back at the open hangar, assuming whatever police and SWAT team assets the Bureau had been able to gather would be waiting inside. There was no sign of the hijacked 737 to the west now, and she felt her apprehension rising as the seconds ticked by and another flight, AirBridge 45, landed and taxied past them headed for the terminal.

When a *second* AirBridge 45 called in for landing, the conclusion was obvious.

"I'll be damned. He just taxied by us!" Kat said in amazement. "He used the other call sign and we all bought it!"

A line of police and security vehicles were streaming out of the hangar now to chase the 737 as it approached the terminal.

"Where's he going?" Bill North asked.

"I'm not sure," Kat replied, shading her eyes as she watched the taxiing 737 still moving north along the ramp, now pursued by at least twelve vehicles, including an Army Humvee with a gun mounted on it.

North shook his head in amazement. "You know, Kat, I think he's actually going to taxi right up to a jetway. I can't believe it. He'll be trapped unless he can force someone to push him back from the gate."

Kat watched in silence for a few seconds, straining to follow the jet.

"Maybe it really is over, and he's not planning on going anywhere else."

She stood in thought for a second, alarm bells going off in her mind.

"No," Kat said aloud. "This is too easy. This is wrong somehow."

In the distance, off to the southwest, the sound of another aircraft could be heard.

Kat turned her head and searched the horizon, shading her eyes with her hand.

"What is it, Kat?" Bill North asked.

"Sh-h-h!" she responded, pointing to the southwest. "There. Can you make that out?"

She heard nothing for a few seconds, then the sound of Bill North's voice. "Oh, shit."

Kat whirled around to find him looking through a pair of tiny portable fieldglasses.

"What?"

He handed them to her quickly.

"Take a look, Kat. It's an AirBridge seven-thirty-seven. I already looked to the north for the so-called other flight Forty-five. There's no one out there."

She took the glasses and pointed them to the southwest.

"Wolfe," North added, "obviously wanted everyone down here to think Flight Forty-five was Flight Ninety so he could see how you'd react."

Kat lowered the glasses, feeling a deep cold creeping through her body.

"We've tipped our hand," she said. "Damn, damn, damn! He'll run now for sure."

Kat raised the glasses and adjusted the focus. The outline of the 737 was unmistakable, the markings on the tail clearly visible.

She lowered the glasses and shook her head. "Bill, can I talk you into—"

North had already grabbed her elbow to move her toward the door of the Gulfstream with Dane following as he yelled up to Jeff in the right seat. "Get her cranked!"

Aboard AirBridge Flight 90. 2:21 P.M.

Well, well, well, Ms. Bronsky. No reception committee, huh? At least I know I can't trust you.

Ken banked the 737 back to the north and skirted the western face of the Grand Mesa, a huge flat-top mountain standing like a sentinel to the east of Grand Junction. He pushed the power up and watched the airspeed climb above two hundred fifty knots as he hugged the lower foothills and followed the flanks of the huge mesa until he was running along the north face some three thousand feet beneath the top of the cliffs that towered to their right.

He was aware of Bostich sitting wide-eyed and watching his every move in startled silence, but his attention had to remain on the flying until the plan he'd suddenly hatched to slip away had been executed.

Ken snapped on the transponder before rounding the northwest side of the mesa, knowing Grand Junction's approach control radar antenna would pick up the hijacking code he still had set in the window. The sudden appearance of the code and the target in conjunction with the flight identification and low altitude would cause pulses to race in the air traffic control facility as they relayed word to the FBI that AirBridge 90 was racing east just south of Interstate 70 toward Glenwood Springs and Aspen.

That was the plan.

Once the 737 was around the north side, he turned the transponder off again and forced the nose of the Boeing down until it was skimming along less than a quarter of a mile from the mountainside.

Speed three hundred. God, don't let me hit any more birds at this speed. The windshields might not take it.

A small rise in the terrain loomed up without warning and Ken pulsed the control yoke back to bring them safely over it.

Three hundred ten knots. Just about right.

He strained to look up and to the right at the cap rock speeding by above them.

Now!

Ken pushed the throttles almost to the firewall and pulled the yoke back smoothly and steadily until the Boeing had reached almost twenty-five degrees nose up.

"What are you doing?" Bostich asked in alarm.

Ken Wolfe ignored him.

The speed was decreasing slowly, the rate of climb shooting from zero to more than six thousand feet per minute as the mountainside melted away on his right. Ken rolled in the same direction just before the jet popped above the top of the mesa and he pulled hard, bringing them around to a southerly heading and stabilizing just two hundred feet above the trees and lakes and startled campers shooting by beneath them at just under two hundred fifty knots.

Within two minutes, that surface dropped away suddenly as the 737 roared over the southern rim of the mesa and Ken shoved the nose down and yanked sharply left to follow the terrain, hiding from air traffic control radar as he prepared to dash across the wide valley to the south. He let his eyes wander to the fuel gauges again as his mind calculated how long he could remain airborne. Flying at lower altitudes was extremely fuel inefficient in a jet, and the otherwise miserly engines were gulping fuel at a furious rate. He thought he had more, but the gauges now showed less than six thousand pounds remaining.

Forty minutes tops, he decided. *Maybe Montrose would be a good place to get fuel. No way would anyone be expecting this aircraft to drop in.*

Ken's left hand fumbled blindly through his map kit looking for the small binder which listed western airports for private pilots. He had to hold the electronic button tightly and feel with his free fingers, but finally they closed on the binder and pulled it out. He alternated between looking out, checking the airspeed and radar altitude, and glancing at the book as his right hand flipped the pages looking for Colorado and Montrose.

There!

He reached down and punched in the three letter identifier, MTJ, in the flight computer.

The distance remaining showed thirty-eight miles.

Magnificent spires of snow-capped mountains loomed to the south as Ken pressed the Boeing down to five hundred feet and shot across a highway, aiming the jet for the entrance to a broad valley to the south he knew well, a valley that contained a U.S. highway and led to the Black Canyon of the Gunnison River, as well as the San Juan Mountains. He would have about three minutes to decide whether to go to Montrose or veer to the east following the Gunnison.

Unlike Utah, he knew this country. Years of flying commuter airplanes through the Rockies had mapped it in his mind. There would be no blundering into a box canyon this time.

So now what do I do? Ken asked himself. *You've given them the slip, you have half a plan, but how do I crack Bostich?*

Ken rubbed his forehead with his right hand, his left hanging on awkwardly to the electronic trigger and the control yoke. Bostich was still quiet in the right seat, but Ken was watching him carefully in his peripheral vision.

Bronsky will be back in the air looking for me the minute she realizes the other aircraft was an inadvertent decoy. Maybe . . . maybe I should let her find me, or at least try to talk to her again.

The thought of going on the air nationally to expose Bostich was growing, though it was probably too dangerous. There were too many ways they could trick him as he talked into a camera.

Ken banked sharply to the right as he descended over the highway and checked the fuel again. Forty minutes was the maximum. Forty minutes to squeeze a confession out of Bostich or figure out a way to get fuel. He didn't need the passengers now, he only needed Bostich, but how could he get the people off the aircraft without imperiling the whole effort?

And what if Bostich didn't crack? What if there was no way to get Bradley Lumin? How many more little girls would he be allowed to kill?

Aboard Gulfstream N5LL. 2:28 P.M.

"Gulfstream Five-Lima-Lima, Grand Junction Approach. We had a couple of radar hits on him just northwest of the mesa, about ten miles northeast of the field. He was at seven thousand, heading approximately zero-three-zero, and doing three hundred knots. That was four minutes ago. We lost him heading east just south of the Interstate."

Kat looked up at Dane, who was concentrating on the instruments and running the after-takeoff checklist as he banked the Gulfstream to the north and climbed to their clearance altitude of fifteen thousand feet.

She saw him punch the transmit button.

"Thanks, Approach. Five-Lima-Lima."

"Why would he turn his transponder back on?" Kat asked, her eyes on the center panel but her mind in the cockpit of Flight 90.

Dane shook his head. "Maybe he forgot and switched it back on accidentally, or maybe he never had it off and we just didn't hear."

Or maybe, Kat thought, *he turned it on because he wanted to establish his presence running toward Glenwood Springs, which he'd do if he were trying to disappear again.*

"Dane," Kat tugged on his right sleeve and caught his eyes as he turned to look at her.

"Yes?"

"He's going to skim the top of the mesa and run south. The transponder is a ruse."

The captain looked pained. "Are you sure? That sounds pretty bizarre."

"I'm sure," she said. "Please get us to the south as fast as possible, and let me look at a sectional chart. He can't have a lot of fuel left, and there are only a few airports out here he could use."

Dane was shaking his head. "If we run south and he's going east, we'll lose him, Kat. There are some pretty high mountains in between."

She nodded again. "Trust me, Dane." She picked up the Flitephone and asked for Frank, explaining her theory.

"They're throwing things at walls back in Washington, Kat, over losing him in Grand Junction. The decision to let that other AirBridge flight land and pretend business as usual was disastrous."

"Frank, that wasn't my decision."

There was a grunt of acknowledgment on the other end. "I know. It was mine. But it's done now, and he's running east."

"No, he's going to run south."

"Kat, I'm looking at a map. South is where he came from this morning. The Durango area, Four Corners, Monument Valley. I don't think he'd go back there, and besides, you said they had a radar hit on him headed east."

"That was a ruse. He's clever, Frank. Desperate and clever. Nevertheless, get every airport in western Colorado with more than a four-thousand-foot runway up to speed on what's happening. Also, if you can, get AirBridge to stop any seven-thirty-seven service to this part of the state until we know where he is."

"I'll do it, but I want you to head east."

"No, Frank. This is instinct, but I'm beginning to understand this guy, and what he wants requires some time to set up. He needs to buy time, and he needs to buy fuel, and I need you to trust me."

"Kat, the word comes from headquarters. Fly east and try to talk to him, try to shadow him. I'm already taking a lot of heat for allowing you to go off on your own in that private jet."

She sat in thought for a few seconds, gripping the receiver, her jaw clenched.

She raised the receiver again, then stopped.

"Frank, there's a lot of static on this line."

"What? What static, Kat? It's perfectly clear."

"I CAN'T HEAR YOU. If you can hear me, we're heading south to intercept. Please alert the airports. I'll check in later."

She replaced the phone and looked up. They were headed south at fifteen thousand, the expanse of the Grand Mesa's flat-topped terrain now behind them and a broad valley below.

"He might head for Montrose, Kat."

She shook her head. "He'll think of it, but unless I miss my guess on his fuel state, he'll go down the Black Canyon of the Gunnison thinking we'd never suspect that. He'll head for Gunnison's airport."

Dane looked around at her. "You sure?"

"Are you kidding? Of course I'm not sure. I'm just rolling the dice and depending on instinct, which may be wrong, but if you'll set me up again on the radio, I'm going to try to raise him once more."

SIXTEEN

Offices of Davidson Aviation, Stamford, Connecticut. 2:29 P.M. MST, 4:29 P.M. EDT.

Hilda Lungaard winced internally as the click of the intercom on her desk announced her boss's voice.

"Hilda? Get Steve Coberg on the phone, please. That's the Air-Bridge chief pilot in Colorado Springs."

"Yes, sir," she replied as she reached for her Rolodex. She glanced behind her at the closed double doors leading to Tom Davidson's plush office, wondering what had set him off. All morning the tension had been thick enough to cut with a knife.

She punched in the number, navigated the inevitable secretarial barriers on the other end, and announced the call.

On the other side of the heavy oaken doors, awash in the expensive decor of a wood-paneled office full of aircraft models and framed pictures of the owner with various dignitaries, Tom Davidson pressed a portable receiver to his face and paced the thick carpet. In his mid-sixties with a full mane of silver hair and carrying an excess fifty pounds on his six-foot frame, Davidson's craggy face had been chiseled into a perpetual grandfatherly smile.

He pivoted in front of the glass wall lining the western end of his office and moved back toward the other end, his voice low and controlled as it echoed off the walnut paneling.

"Good Lord, Steve, do you have any idea what he's trying to accomplish?"

Davidson suddenly stopped pacing and stood still, listening to the reply.

"You say that came from the FBI?"

He took a step forward and turned, leaning his body against the edge of the desk.

"Jesus! I didn't know he'd been screwing up out there. Why didn't you call me?"

Davidson turned and pulled a notepad across his desk and fumbled with a ballpoint pen.

"Give me the fed's name and number, Steve. Wherever they have their command post. I'm going to need a patch to his cockpit. I need to talk to Wolfe."

Aboard AirBridge Flight 90. 2:31 P.M.

Ken turned toward the right seat.

"Look at me, Bostich!"

Rudy turned his head slowly. "What is it?"

"I want to know something: Do you have children?"

Rudy looked back to the front of the cockpit and nodded. "A boy and a girl, now both in their twenties."

"What's the girl's name?"

"Captain, this isn't—"

"WHAT THE HELL IS HER NAME?"

Rudy swallowed hard and frowned as he shook his head and studied the rudder pedals. "I . . . all right, if you must know, her name is Annie."

"You care about Annie? You love her?"

Bostich glanced at him. "What kind of question is that? Of *course* I care about her, just as I know you cared deeply for your daughter."

"You know the details of how my Melinda died?" Ken asked through clenched teeth.

Bostich nodded. "The overall profile, yes."

"You know about the six days of rape and torture, the burns on her eleven-year-old body, the . . ." Ken coughed to cover the struggle he was having, then continued. "The other things that animal Lumin did to her."

Bostich was nodding.

"Have you ever pasted Annie's face on Melinda's mutilated body? Mentally, I mean? Have you? What would you do, Bostich, if someone pulled a morgue drawer out and showed you that mangled body with Annie's face on it, and then said, 'We know who did it, but he's going free?' "

"I don't know."

"Yes you do! Look in your mind at that body. That's *Annie* on that slab."

Rudy was shaking his head, trying to expunge the image.

"I can't imagine . . ."

"Yes, you can! You *are* seeing it, aren't you? Annie Bostich. There she is, Rudy! The sweet little girl you've loved all her life, battered, ruined, dead, mangled, lying there in front of you. Remember how she looked at eleven?"

"Captain, stop it!"

"What's left of her hair's matted with things you don't want to identify. Her face is contorted in a frozen scream."

Rudy turned to him, eyes flaring. "STOP IT! Damn you, leave my daughter out of this."

"Why, Rudy? There she is before you in your mind now, Annie Bostich, dead, destroyed, used up by an animal, her blue lips frozen in a scream as if she's asking 'Why, Daddy? Why didn't you keep me safe? I'm your daughter. Annie. You were supposed to protect . . .' "

"ENOUGH! DAMN YOU, ENOUGH!"

"What would you do, Rudy?"

"I'd hope for prosecution—"

"She's been raped and murdered, Rudy. That's your Annie on that slab, and no one will prosecute the murderer. What would you do? WHAT WOULD YOU DO?"

Rudy snapped his head to the left, his eyes burning coals boring into Ken's, his voice a constrained roar.

"All right, goddammit, I'd probably take a gun and go blow his fucking head off, after shooting off a few strategic body parts first! Okay? I'd probably go completely crazy and end up in prison!"

Rudy turned back toward the forward panel in silence and put his head in his hands, the images Ken had created still swimming through his mind.

"Exactly," Ken said quietly. "That's exactly what the normal father would do. But I couldn't."

Rudy's face was still in his hands, his reply muffled. "What?"

"I couldn't do it," he repeated. "After you ruined the case, I started stalking Lumin. I thought I could prevent more murders, but I couldn't be on him every day. I had to earn a living. I was flying, and I had to be away a certain amount. Melinda was coming to me almost every night in my dreams, asking that question. 'Why, Daddy, why?' Then two more little girls were killed the same way, as I told you, and the police wouldn't listen. No one would listen. Lumin hadn't been found guilty of murder, so there was nothing that could be done, even with a long list of child molestation convictions. Finally I realized *I* had to finish him off. For Melinda. For all the other little girls that were going to suffer her fate. I bought a gun. I picked the time. I drew a bead on him, but I couldn't pull the trigger."

Rudy Bostich looked up slowly at Ken Wolfe, his eyes reading the anguish on the man's face as he diverted his attention back to flying.

"You . . . you tried to kill him?"

Ken nodded.

"And you didn't?"

"I couldn't. I could not pull the trigger." Ken tried to suppress the tears welling up in his eyes. "I . . . didn't care about me. I *don't* care about me. As I told you, I've already died. But I couldn't pull the trigger! Can you imagine that? Can you imagine how helpless and impotent and useless that feels? After everything that's happened, knowing he did it, knowing what he did, and I can't pull the damned trigger!"

Rudy took a deep breath and nodded. "But that's good, don't you see? You didn't sink to his level. You're not a murderer. Even now, regardless of the bomb you say you've got below, you're not a murderer."

Rudy tentatively reached out a hand and Ken recoiled instantly.

"Don't even think about touching me, Bostich."

Rudy withdrew his hand quickly. "I'm sorry. I was just trying . . ."

Ken's eyes were on the terrain as he banked the Boeing to the left toward the Black Canyon of the Gunnison.

"I wouldn't have been a murderer. I would have been an executioner. Better yet, I was exterminating a rabid dog that had killed my child. But that's not the point, you see. The point is, I couldn't save my daughter, I couldn't stop you from ruining the case, I couldn't get Lumin prosecuted, I couldn't stop Lumin from killing again, and then

I couldn't even muster the courage to kill him." Ken looked over at him again. "Until God arranged for you to walk on my aircraft this morning, Mr. Prosecutor, I had been totally helpless. But that ends here, you see. You're going to confess and give that judge back in Connecticut the grounds he needs to reverse that ruling and reinstate the evidence, or you and I are going to die together."

"Captain—"

"AND I'd consider killing you the moral equivalent of putting down a mad dog."

Aboard Gulfstream N5LL. 2:36 P.M.

"Ken, this is Kat Bronsky again. Are you listening?"

The distant image of the 737 some ten miles ahead maneuvering at less than a thousand feet near the Gunnison River had been difficult to spot, but she had been right. He was running south.

"I've been expecting you, Kat. You don't give up easily, do you?"

"No, not when someone stands me up."

"Good personalization of the issue, Kat. You're doing well. It's just unfortunate you've got such a knowledgeable opponent. Are you behind me again and in sight, or is it asking too much to get an honest answer from the FBI?"

"Yes, Ken, we're behind you and above you, and we know you've got to land somewhere soon for fuel."

"True, but this time, I'm not going to be dumb enough to tell you where."

"You don't need to," she replied. "Every airport in Colorado suitable for a seven-thirty-seven has already been notified you might be dropping in. Look, Ken, there's just no point in running like this. Please get her on the ground and let those passengers out. I know you don't want to hurt them."

"They'd be on the ground safe in Grand Junction now, Kat, if you'd kept your word."

She sighed loudly and punched the button again. "Ken, I promised no intervention. I didn't promise there wouldn't be law enforcement units on the ground. You can expect a small army anywhere you land.

But back there in Grand Junction, they weren't about to violate your orders. You panicked for nothing."

"Are you in touch with your headquarters, Kat?"

She glanced at the Flitephone and thought the answer through carefully.

"Ah, periodically, yes, but with you running so low to the ground, it's hard to stay in contact. I'm trying to reestablish contact right now to see if that arrest has been made."

There was silence on the channel for nearly a minute.

"When it has, call me back."

Kat had replaced the microphone and was reaching for the Flitephone to report back to Frank when Dane's voice rang out.

"What the hell is he doing *now*?"

"What?" Kat looked up and over the glareshield, following the captain's finger.

"He's climbing suddenly like a missile, and turning left. He doesn't seriously think he's going to lose me back here?"

The Boeing was still climbing and turning, its left side presented to the oncoming Gulfstream.

"What's our altitude, Dane?" Kat asked.

"Twelve thousand, and he's got to be coming through eleven right now."

"He's turning back in this direction," Jeff added from the right seat.

Kat watched the rising jetliner ahead as she tried to imagine what was going on in Ken Wolfe's mind. He wanted to land unobserved to discharge the passengers and keep Bostich. What was she missing in that equation?

"Kat?" Dane's voice rang out louder than normal, and she jerked her head back up to see the 737, which had leveled its wings at their altitude and was now headed straight for them.

"What on earth?" she exclaimed.

"That's what I was about to ask you. He's seen us, and now he's aiming straight for us. Might be a very good time to talk to the boy."

Jeff was holding the microphone out to her, his eyes getting larger by the second.

She grabbed the microphone and punched the button. "Ken, this is Kat Bronsky again. Are you trying to tell us something, or just create a midair collision?"

No answer.

"He's about four miles away," Dane added. "Our closing velocity is over nine miles per minute."

"Ken? Kat Bronsky. I know you can hear me. What on earth is this going to solve?"

Dane was shaking his head. "I'm going to have to veer off here in just a few seconds!"

"Ken? Answer me!" Kat knew her voice had grown tense, but the 737 was looming ahead, getting bigger by the second.

"Okay, that's enough!" Dane said as he rolled the Gulfstream into a right bank to change headings, and realized the 737 was altering its course in the same direction to maintain the intercept.

"Ken, please, tell me what you're trying to accomplish? If we jerk this aircraft the wrong way, it might not be what you planned."

Jeff Jayson's voice reached her ears. "Dane, better break right. He's serious."

The Boeing was less than a mile away, pointed directly at them as Dane rolled the Gulfstream to the right and pulled hard, simultaneously shoving the thrust levers almost full forward. The powerful business jet leaped into a climb as the Boeing closed on them, its five-hundred-mile-per-hour passage marked by a sudden muffled roar as the 737 passed just aft of the Gulfstream's tail.

"Jesus Christ!" Dane said through gritted teeth as he pulled the power back and entered a left turn while Jeff Jayson notified Denver Center what was happening.

"Roger, Five-Lima-Lima, I see the skin paint target that just passed you now behind you and in a left turn. He appears to be coming around to follow you."

Dane looked back at Kat in utter amazement. "*Now* what is he up to?"

She raised the microphone to her lips and pressed the button.

"That was too damn close, Ken, and it was unnecessary. Now that you're on our tail, and since you don't have guns or missiles aboard, tell me precisely where you'd like us to lead you?"

His voice came back rapidly, calm and collected. "Turn left to a heading of one-seven-zero degrees, Kat. You're going to lead me south to Albuquerque."

Aboard AirBridge Flight 90. 2:44 P.M.

The sound of a seatbelt being released startled Wolfe, and he looked to the right with disbelief to see Rudy Bostich climbing out of the copilot's seat.

"Where the hell do you think you're going, Bostich?"

Rudy stopped with his leg half over the center console and looked Ken in the eye. "I've had about enough of this. Maybe if I'm back in the cabin, you won't be pulling any more stupid stunts just to scare me."

"Sit down, Bostich!"

He remained half in, half out of the seat.

"Or what? You going to explode the jet and kill us all because I climbed out of the seat?"

Ken transferred the control yoke to his right hand and raised the trigger into view with his left. "That's exactly right."

"I don't believe you, Captain. I don't think you'd do it. You know I'm still aboard, I can't get out, and therefore you still think you can pressure me into a false confession, and who knows, maybe you can. In the final analysis, it wouldn't be worth anything. If you weren't aware of it, coerced confessions are worthless."

"Don't forget I've got evidence," Ken said, true alarm beginning to form in the back of his mind.

Rudy Bostich snorted. "Bullshit! If you had real evidence, which, of course, you couldn't, you'd have already presented it to that judge, not put yourself on death row by hijacking your own aircraft."

Ken was shaking his head, trying not to look as desperate as he felt. In his peripheral vision, the Gulfstream IV remained in the proper place in the forward windscreen as he flew formation on it, staying behind and out of their visual range.

"I only received the evidence a few days ago. There hasn't been time. Besides, that evidence you don't believe I have may ultimately convince the judge, but your confession will reverse his ruling instantly. Of course, it'll ruin you professionally if you're exposed, but a confession with some sort of explanation might just get you off the hook in the public arena."

Still Rudy remained frozen halfway out of the seat. "I'm touched by your concern for my career, Captain."

"I don't have any damned concern whatsoever for your career, but I have to admit that if you're going to be exposed—and you are—you'd be a lot smarter to do it yourself and put your own spin on it. I don't give a rat's ass as long as that warrant and the evidence are reinstated."

Slowly, Rudy's right foot resumed its arc toward the alcove behind the center console, and once more Ken thrust the trigger into view.

"Don't try it, Bostich! I am not kidding, and you can't take the chance that I am."

Once again the leg stopped.

"You've basically told me you didn't know I was going to be on this plane this morning," Rudy said, carefully monitoring Ken Wolfe's reactions. "Unless you always carry a bomb along when you go fly, why should I believe you suddenly found a way to plant one?"

Ken lowered his left hand into his brain bag on the left side of the captain's seat and pulled out a small rectangular package, then tossed it to Bostich, who caught it deftly in midair.

"What's this?"

"Look inside, Rudy."

Still half out of the seat, Rudy Bostich supported his left shoulder on the seatback and pulled open a portion of what appeared to be a burlap wrapper. Inside was a block of pliable material which resembled an off-white plastic, and was soft to the touch. Somewhere he had seen such a thing before. In fact, it looked a lot like . . .

"Be careful with that," Ken commanded. "It's fairly stable, but it's what's left from the lot I have downstairs in my bag, a big block of it with an electronic detonator."

Rudy's eyes had grown large. "You . . . you mean to tell me I'm holding *plastique*?"

"C-four, actually. I couldn't get plastique."

Rudy Bostich handed the block back as if it were a live cobra and swung himself back in the seat, his eyes locked forward, his breathing rate increased.

"Good God, man, I didn't think a pilot would . . . would . . ."

"I've been checking the reservations computer daily for a long time,

Rudy. Suddenly your named popped up. I knew where to find this stuff, and I know how to use it. I just needed a few hours."

Rudy looked at Ken Wolfe with a wild expression. "You got this through security?"

Ken let out a derisive snort. "Airline pilots have to go through the same screening as everyone else, which is asinine, and useless. The whole block, the detonator, everything, went through security."

"Good God! I thought you were bluffing. You really *are* crazy!"

Ken nodded. "You said it yourself, didn't you, Rudy? What would you do? Probably go crazy. I've had two years to deteriorate to this, thanks to you."

"What do you mean, two years?" he asked in a sullen voice.

Ken turned and stared with an intensity that froze Rudy's blood.

"Two years ago today," Ken began, "in a forest in northern Connecticut, my beautiful eleven-year-old daughter was killed, and her body dumped. Lumin destroyed a monitored electric fence in a state wildlife preserve when he dumped her, which is the only reason we know the date. Her body was found months later. That's how I got my daughter back, Mr. Prosecutor."

"I'm truly sorry," Rudy said in a quiet voice.

Ken turned back to the panel, barely holding on to his emotions.

"You're damn right I'm crazy, Bostich, and you'd be well advised to help me do something about it, because I've got nothing left to lose."

SEVENTEEN

Aboard AirBridge Flight 90. 2:48 P.M.

The sound of Ken Wolfe's voice on the P.A. took everyone in the cabin by surprise.

"Folks, this is the captain. In a few minutes I'm going to be landing somewhere, hopefully, to let you off—all of you except one, that is. Rudy Bostich stays here to face the charges. Now, it's time I told you the unvarnished truth. This is hard for me, because this is the last time I'll ever sit in the left seat of an airliner. Truth is, the only hijacker up here is a heartbroken airline pilot who's terrorized everyone to try to catch a killer. I fully realize what I'm going to tell you is neither legal nor moral justification for what I'm doing, but I want you to know anyway."

Annette had been sitting quietly on the arm of a seat in the forward part of coach when the P.A. began, watching Kevin and Bev continuously moving up and down coach trying to calm and soothe the passengers as best they could. In that instant, though, everyone in the cabin was looking toward the ceiling at the speakers, their faces impassive masks of tension, their minds riveted on what was being said.

Ken Wolfe's voice was sad but steady, and as he unfolded in excruciating detail Melinda Wolfe's kidnapping and murder, and the saga of the botched search warrant, Annette watched in amazement as waves of shock, grief, and outrage played in sequence across the faces of her passengers, many of them barely holding back tears as he finished.

"The federal D.A. who lied about making that call is the man sitting next to me here in the cockpit, Rudy Bostich, who, until today, was the leading contender to be U.S. Attorney General. As I've told Mr. Bostich, my life is forfeit, but I can't let Bradley Lumin kill again, and I can't let my little daughter's death go unpunished. I have the evidence on Mr. Bostich, and I have no choice now, the rest of this day, but to do whatever it takes to get him to tell the truth to the judge back in Connecticut. He's shaking his head up here and denying he lied, but I know differently. I have the telephone records from the phone company showing his call to Detective Matson the very night and the very time the detective said the call was made. Bostich says the detective is a liar and a bad apple, he claims Matson has a long history as a cowboy cop and that somehow Matson colluded with the phone company to falsify the call record. However, I have never heard anything bad about Detective Matson, who, I believe, is an honorable and honest man. For his part, Bostich claimed under oath that he was home alone that night, and that he never called Matson about anything. The police checked the phone records for his home number, but they didn't know he had an unnamed, unlisted cellular phone. His cell phone record proves he lied, and because of that lie, a serial killer is still free right now."

A sudden movement in coach caught Annette's eye, as the retired policeman who'd approached her earlier moved out of his seat and rapidly up the aisle, pushing past Bev and Kevin, his eye on the distant cockpit door.

She rose to block his way.

"Sir? Where are you going?"

He pointed to the speakers overhead as Ken continued.

"Folks, I hate it that I've had to involve my passengers and threaten you and load a real bomb in the belly. There is one there, by the way, and I do have the trigger up here."

The man was breathing hard, and was obviously agitated.

"He mentioned Roger Matson in Connecticut!"

"Yes?"

"I've known Roger all his professional life. He's a member of our police association."

"Okay, but—"

"I want the captain to know that. Anyone speaking ill of Roger is definitely a liar."

"Sir, this is a very delicate situation."

The P.A. came on again, drowning them out.

"I don't want any of you to think any of this has been a bluff. It hasn't, and it isn't. I am holding a live trigger, and I am endangering you, and for that I am sorry. But there seemed to be no other way to force the authorities to act. I had already tried everything else. It's just important to me that you know why."

The police officer pointed to the ceiling again, irritated at being restrained.

"Look, I've got to talk to him."

"Why, sir?" Annette asked, her curiosity rising.

"Because, Miss, if Roger Matson said that Jesus Christ himself had come back, I'd say hallelujah without a second's hesitation and head for the nearest church. The man's incorruptible and the most honest cop I've ever known."

For several seconds Annette searched his eyes.

"This captain has hijacked us, sir."

"Dammit, I know that. But when he mentions a man I know that well, I've got to let him know he's right to trust Matson. Your captain may end up in the chair for what he's doing, but I'll bet anything he's right. I remember Roger being in agony over this case, and over having his reputation tarred by that arrogant fed. He was horribly hurt to be called a liar by the judge."

"What do you want me to do?"

"I want to talk to the captain. Now."

Annette nodded and inclined her head toward the front as the P.A. clicked on again. There was a pause and the sound of the P.A. microphone contacting a metal surface in the cockpit.

"Folks, earlier I turned off the seat phones. I just now pushed in the circuit breaker and turned them back on. You're free to call whomever you like, and tell them what's happening. Just please, tell them why. Tell them my story. Tell them about Rudy Bostich. If I don't succeed with

this, more little girls are going to be killed, all because a politically ambitious lawyer doesn't want to embarrass himself by doing the right thing."

Ken clicked off the P.A. as Rudy Bostich shook his head vigorously.

"You just won't understand, will you, Wolfe?"

Ken glanced at him. "You thought up a new explanation for the phone records yet?"

"It's still Matson. He's a detective, he probably has a buddy in the cellular phone company and they diddled the computer records. That proves nothing."

"Do you have the original records from your phone bill?" Ken shot back. "That could prove real quick whether the phone record I've got was changed from the original."

Rudy fell silent for a few seconds in thought. "I . . . I may, but I'm not a pack rat. I do throw things out."

"After only two years? Phone bills and records? Not unless you didn't want something to be seen."

"Dammit, that's trying to prove a positive with a negative. I don't have them, therefore they corroborate the false record you say you have."

"Interesting," Ken said, his eyes on the listing of Colorado airports as he dialed a new frequency into the second radio head.

"What?"

"Interesting that you shifted almost instantly from, 'I might not have them,' to 'I don't have them,' which is what a guilty man would do. An innocent man would have grasped at straws and at least told me the original phone bill was probably still in his desk at home, or in a box in his attic, and that it would show no calls to Matson's number. I might have been swayed by that, but once again you've tipped your hand."

The sound of the cabin call chime rang through the cockpit, and Ken looked at the interphone handset in confusion before grabbing it, surprised to find Annette on the other end.

"Captain, I've got someone here who wants to talk to you. He's a friend of Roger Matson, the detective you mentioned. And he's a retired police officer himself."

Ken glanced at Rudy Bostich, who was watching him with a worried expression as he hunched over the copilot's yoke, unable to hear the other side of the interphone.

"What does he want?" Ken asked.

"He wants to tell you that Matson is an extremely reliable man."

"Put him on."

Aboard Gulfstream N5LL. 2:50 P.M.

"But where *is* he?" Kat asked.

Dane Bailey shook his head. "I assume he's pacing us back there, but since his transponder is turned off—that's the little device that pings back identification information every time a radar beam hits—"

Kat had her hand up and smiled. "I know what a transponder is, Dane."

"Sorry. Anyway, without that, Denver Center has been watching only a raw radar reflection from the aircraft."

"Skin paint, they call it?"

Dane nodded. "Right." He punched the transmit button and asked Denver if they still saw the 737 on their scopes.

"Negative, Five-Lima-Lima. He was right behind you, then the target merged with yours. He's probably still there, but too close to separate from your radar return."

Jeff Jayson pointed to the west. "That's Telluride on the right, Kat."

She followed his gaze through the right window and down to a spectacular bowl of snow-covered mountains.

"The airport?"

"Yeah, and the town."

"Any chance he'd try to land there?"

Both pilots shook their heads no as Dane replied. "Far too high, runway's less than seven thousand feet. You could get a Boeing seven-three-seven in there, but I'm not sure he could take off."

Kat's own words to Frank came back for quick review. "Call every airport in Colorado suitable for a seven-thirty-seven" she'd requested, and Frank had reported it done.

Kat sighed and pointed to the west where Telluride was supposed to be. "If it's not suitable for a Boeing, then he won't head there. I'm guessing, but I think he's headed for Durango, and he'll try to peel off without our noticing, which we're going to let him do."

Aboard AirBridge Flight 90. 2:54 P.M.

Ken adjusted the throttles to hold his position just behind and beneath the Gulfstream and reached down to punch a button on the communications panel, certain Kat Bronsky wouldn't be monitoring that frequency.

"Telluride Regional Unicom, AirBridge Charter Seventy-two-twenty."

Rudy Bostich turned toward the left seat, puzzled by the call. Without a headset or earpiece, he couldn't hear the reply.

"Ah, AirBridge, what, a charter?"

"Yes, sir. Seven-two-two-zero, out of Colorado Springs. We've got a small problem on planned delays ahead and need to drop in for some more fuel."

"Okay, ah, how much do you need, AirBridge? I assume you're a Saab three-forty."

The image of the far smaller turboprop commuter flashed across Ken's mind, the only type AirBridge used to service the smaller airports. But if he said yes and taxied a seven-thirty-seven into the ramp, the confusion factor would be a problem.

"Negative, Regional, we're a Boeing seven-three-seven. Can you give us, say, twenty-five thousand pounds of Jet A?"

The voice sounded shocked, but the reply was what he wanted to hear.

"Ah, yes, sir. We only have one fuel truck and it holds twenty-two hundred gallons, about fifteen thousand pounds. But we can use that, then fill the truck back up."

"How long to refill?"

"About twenty-three minutes."

"Okay, please get the truck ready. Don't bother dispatch, I've already coordinated, and they want as fast a turnaround as we can get."

"Roger. What time are you estimating here?"

Ken looked over the right side of the nose at the San Juan Mountains and calculated the remaining distance.

"Twelve minutes."

"We'll be ready, but, ah, are you sure you're okay to land and take off on this runway at this altitude with a seven-thirty-seven? We've always joked around here you could get one in, but you'd have to take it out on a truck."

"I've checked the density altitude and the weight. We're okay."

Ken clicked off and rechecked the position of the sleek Gulfstream IV as it hovered in the top visual perspective of the windscreen less than a hundred yards ahead and barely fifty feet higher. He inched the throttles up and closed the distance some more, staying around eighty feet below the jet as it seemed to move backward until the tail section was directly over the 737's nose.

"Captain, if this is another 'scare Rudy' demonstration, don't bother. I'm as terrified as I can get."

"Not my purpose this time," Ken replied.

"So where are you going to land?"

Ken snorted softly. "Telluride. The highest commercial airport in North America, one that everyone will consider unsuitable for seven-thirty-sevens."

"Is it?" Rudy asked. "Unusable, I mean?"

Ken nodded. "Probably."

He pulled the power back slightly and began a descent, carefully keeping the 737 directly under the Gulfstream and its radar image, bringing the rate of descent to six thousand feet per minute as the Boeing dropped from sixteen thousand feet toward the ten-thousand-foot terrain below. When the highest mountain peaks were significantly above them along with most of the radar beams from Denver Center, Ken punched Telluride's identifier in the flight computer and banked sharply to the west, aiming for a preplanned low spot in the ridge east of Telluride near the tiny mining town of Pandora.

"Not again?" Rudy Bostich was tensing in his seat as the ridgeline approached.

Ken shook his head. "No, not this time. I'm just keeping low until we get closer. We'll clear it by five hundred feet."

Aboard Gulfstream N5LL. 2:57 P.M.

Kat Bronsky had left the cockpit for a minute to brief Bill North. Suddenly she was back with North behind her.

"Dane, would you please try something for me?"

"Sure, Kat. What?"

"Tell Denver Center you're going to turn off your transponder for a moment. See if he can spot two skin paint targets up here."

Dane nodded and smiled as he punched the transmit button and turned off the transponder simultaneously.

The answer came back within thirty seconds.

"Negative, Five-Lima-Lima. I've got only one target on skin paint, steady, and in the same position your blip occupied."

She nodded. "I should have known. I ruled out Telluride for the same reason he was ruling it in."

"Want me to relay to Frank?" Bill North asked.

Kat shook her head. "Not yet. Dane, can you turn around and head for Telluride? And can we land there?"

"Yes, to both questions," he said, clicking off the autopilot and beginning a descending right turn as he punched the button to inform Denver what they were about to do.

"If he lands there, Kat, he may not be able to get it out," Bill said quietly as they stood for a moment in the alcove behind the cockpit.

She nodded. "I know. I'm hoping that's all he's doing. Get the passengers off and hope to sit there and negotiate knowing we can't get much equipment in, at least not rapidly."

"What would you need, normally?"

She bit her lip. "FBI SWAT team preferably. Maybe armored equipment. Manpower. There are a variety of ways to handle it, but Telluride . . . I've only been there once, I don't think they've got anything but the county sheriff and some town marshals." She fell silent, her eyes vacantly looking through the side of the aircraft, her mind back on Ken Wolfe's flight deck trying to discern his next move.

Bill North inclined his head toward the main cabin. "You want to check in with your guy at Salt Lake?"

Kat followed him back into the plush surroundings and placed the call to Frank Bothell, who sounded strained.

"He's going into Telluride, Colorado, Frank. We'll need to scramble what we can there."

"Kat . . ."

"What?"

"I'm told to direct you to call Clark Roberts in Washington. I'm out of it."

"What's going on, Frank?"

"The national coverage is increasing, the pressure is increasing, and Headquarters is getting nervous that we're screwing this up."

"Good Lord, Frank!"

"I know, Kat, but I warned you we might lose control."

"What, are they upset with me?"

"Well, they're not happy with either of us for what happened in Grand Junction, and there's a lot of second guessing going on as to what, precisely, you're doing in that bizzjet."

"How about tracking and trying to control the situation?"

"Kat, there's something I'm not sure you know. Is Bill North still on the line here?"

"I don't know. Bill, are you on?"

There was no answer.

"I guess not, Frank. Why?"

"Are you aware that Bill North is the vice chairman of the board of AirBridge Airlines?"

"What?"

"He'd filed a flight plan to Colorado Springs to race to AirBridge headquarters in response to this very hijacking."

"No, Frank, I didn't know that!"

"I'm not sure it makes a difference."

"I'm not sure either," she replied, her mind racing back through the various exchanges with North, wondering if she'd disclosed anything she should have kept to herself.

But he was listening to most of our exchanges anyway.

"Kat, a caution, okay? Remember one of the first things I told you about the Bureau when you walked in the door? If it ain't in the book, someone is going to challenge you for doing it. Innovation is not always rewarded here."

"I remember."

"Look, we're wasting time. Call FBI Headquarters. I'll stand by if you need me for anything, but as command and control, I'm out of business."

"Thanks, Frank."

"Be careful if you get Wolfe on the ground there. You know the priorities. Get the passengers off safely, then stall until the cavalry arrives. If you can get Bostich out of there in the meantime, please do, but it sounds like we've got a good chance of losing him."

"Frank, have they made the arrest in Ft. Collins?"

There was silence on the other end for too long.

"Frank, did you hear me?"

"I heard you."

"So what's the answer? That's step one for this guy."

There was a sigh on the other end.

"Washington wouldn't let me do it. Justice is involved and they vetoed it. The usual we'll-never-give-in-to-terrorists thing."

"This guy isn't a terrorist, Frank. I need to give him something. I can't tell him that! You want to lose Bostich, that's the way—"

"KAT! Calm down. I did it anyway."

"Had him arrested?"

"No, I called the Ft. Collins police chief and explained things. He sent two of his men out there to at least surveil him."

"And?"

"That's the problem. The place is empty. This is a ratty little single-wide trailer on the edge of a fallow farm quite a ways out of Ft. Collins, toward the Interstate. They're watching it, but so far there's no information on where this Lumin has gone. But Kat, they found something really interesting outside."

"They didn't look inside of course? No warrant?"

"No warrant, no search, but outside in some trees they found an unfired thirty-ought-six bullet someone had dropped, and indications someone had been out there stalking the trailer for some time."

"Any bullet holes in the trailer?"

"None. No broken glass. No empty rounds. No blood outside, but a lot of footprints in the dirt and various car tracks. Nothing, however, to justify going in. They did look through the windows. It's a small trailer. What's your guess, Kat?"

"He's been taken. Somebody else snatched him, probably to kill him."

"My thought exactly."

A wave of hopelessness swept over her at the thought of Ken Wolfe throwing everything away to convict a killer who might already be dead.

She sighed loudly. "I'll call Headquarters, but Frank, unless we can prove he's dead or find him, I've got almost nothing concessionary to hand this pilot."

"Other than what he already has—Mr. Rudolph Bostich, whom even the White House likes."

EIGHTEEN

Telluride Mountain Village. 3:05 P.M.

The staccato sound of someone channel-surfing the hanging TV set echoed through the Java Shack, causing Deputy Gary Goodwin to look up momentarily from his mocha. He looked back at the waitress—Julie, the raven-haired dropout from Colorado State whose feminine allure had been drawing him daily for the last few months. She finally settled on CNN and replaced the remote on the counter.

"Is that okay for you, Gary?" she asked as she adjusted her peasant blouse, well aware where his eyes had been.

"Whatever," he grinned back, paying little attention to the CNN anchor covering the breaking story of AirBridge 90.

> "Just after this hijacking began, we were able to bring you a dramatic report from the passenger cabin of the aircraft as CNN's Chris Billings reported live on an airborne telephone."

Gary picked up his oversized coffee cup and moved to the counter opposite where Julie was busily working the espresso machine.

"There's, ah, something I'd like to ask you, young lady."

She smiled and glanced at him before looking back at the machine. "And that would be of a personal nature, I assume?"

> "Chris has been out of contact for more than an hour, but we've reestablished the connection."

"Well, I was just wondering—" he began.

"Hold that titillating thought for a second," she said, inclining her head toward a customer waiting for his order. She handed over his coffee and took the money as Gary glanced up at the TV, trying to look casual.

> "We're going live now to the cabin of AirBridge Ninety. Chris? Can you hear me?"

A burst of static filled the speakers as a male voice cut in and out in the background, only a few words understandable.

> ". . . on descent right now as . . . have little idea . . ."

Finished with the transaction and wiping her hands on a towel, Julie appeared beside him. "So, you were in the process of asking whether I wanted to go out with you, and do some boy-girl stuff . . ."

He smiled at her self-consciously as the voice on the TV cut in again.

> ". . . into Telluride, Colorado, where . . . think there is a chance . . ."

Gary looked back at the TV. "Hold it a second!" He held up his hand and Julie, too, shifted her focus to the TV as CNN attempted to reestablish the connection.

> "Chris, we're having trouble hearing you."

Suddenly the voice of Chris Billings returned in the clear.

> ". . . possibility that all the passengers will be released in Telluride, when the airplane gets on the ground. At this moment, I'm looking out the window on the left side at a stunning array of snow-covered mountains and what appears to be a very deep mountain valley to one side. I have no clear idea of where we are in relation to the Telluride airport, but our flaps are coming out, and . . . right now I'm hearing the landing gear extending as we appear to be descending. This odyssey has been perhaps the strangest in the annals of the airline industry, with the admission a few minutes ago by the captain over the public address system that he, in fact, is the hijacker, and

his explanation of why he has become perhaps the first captain in U.S. airline history to hijack his own aircraft."

Gary Goodwin was on his feet and reaching for his handheld radio.

"What are they talking about?" Julie asked.

"There's a hijacking. I heard about it earlier, but it sounds like he's coming in here, for Chrissakes! I've gotta go."

Her eyes were still glued to the screen.

"Julie?"

"Yeah?"

"Would you monitor what they're saying? I'll call you in a few minutes from my cell phone for details."

She nodded as he raced out the door talking to the San Miguel sheriff's dispatcher on his handheld as Chris Billings summarized the killing of Melinda Wolfe and her father's desperate gamble to force prosecution of the accused murderer.

Aboard AirBridge Flight 90. 3:07 P.M.

Ken checked his airspeed again as he lowered the 737's flaps to the thirty-degree landing position while guiding the Boeing through a left turn back toward the airport. The east-west runway was visible in the left half of the windscreen as the 737 began to line up finally with the 6,870-foot runway, a hundred-foot-wide strip of asphalt cut along the top of a mesa.

Antiskid on, flaps down to forty degrees, gear is down, landing check complete. Ken hurriedly pushed the power up and worked to stabilize the airspeed. The landing would be very fast, the tires hitting the surface at a speed of just under a hundred and seventy miles per hour because of the thin air. There was no margin for error. Any hesitation in reversing the engines or going to maximum braking could send them skidding off the opposite end of the runway and off a thousand foot cliff.

He was five hundred feet above the mountainside, concentrating all his attention on the landing, but marginally aware of a white Bronco-like vehicle with lights flashing on top tearing up the mesa on a road just below, apparently headed for the airport.

He gauged the remaining distance to the runway, the speed, and the Boeing's sink rate.

Okay, concentrate. One hundred feet, a little slow, pull some power off, hit the very end like a carrier landing, twenty feet maximum altitude over the runway threshold. Here we go, don't flare, don't flare, hold it . . .

The last of the approach lights disappeared at a dizzying speed as the 737's main landing gear slammed hard onto the surface some fifty feet down the runway from the threshold.

In the right seat, Rudy Bostich watched with dry mouth and wide eyes as Ken's right hand lashed out like a striking snake, yanking the speed brake handle back to full deployment, then moving with blinding speed to the thrust reverse levers, pulling them into the max reverse position. At the same time, Ken shoved his feet full forward on the brakes, causing Rudy to lurch forward as the fifty ton jetliner decelerated with frightening efficiency, the runway environment flashing by but slowing, arriving finally at a sedate taxi speed with several thousand feet of runway left.

"Good Lord!" Bostich murmured.

Ken snorted, his hand shaking slightly on the yoke, his body full of adrenaline. "You think that's impressive, wait'll we try to get out of here."

Rudy looked at him in mortal alarm, but said nothing.

Last Dollar Road, Telluride, Colorado. 3:10 P.M.

Deputy Gary Goodwin had used lights and siren to race out of the Mountain Village area to the highway and on to the airport while alerting as many of the nine other deputies as he could raise.

The San Miguel County sheriff's dispatcher was taking a call from the FBI at the same moment.

Gary had been too busy to call Julie back for information, but somehow, on her own initiative, she'd relayed word to the dispatcher, who in turn was briefing everyone over the radio.

Within minutes Highway 145 out of town was alive with three white sheriff's Broncos, all racing from the town toward the turnoff for Last Dollar Road, which connected the highway with the airport.

Gary raced up the road ahead of the formation and was nearing the airport when the 737 whistled overhead on short final approach. His speedometer was topping eighty as he rounded a curve too fast, nearly lost control, then settled the Bronco back on all fours as he braked hard and steered back to his lane. The airport was less than a half mile away now.

"What does the FBI want us to do?" Gary managed to ask on the radio.

The dispatcher's voice came back strained and unsure. "I don't know. They say there's an agent on her way in another airplane, but there are no specific instructions."

Gary nodded, reviewing the procedures he knew. *Unknown situation, the FBI in charge, this is a capital federal crime, the hijacker appears to be the plane's captain, and a bomb's on board with the captain holding an electronic trigger.*

Gary picked up the radio microphone again. With the sheriff out of town, his position as chief deputy meant he was in charge, but the small prestige of that position now seemed a bit double-edged in the pressure of the moment. The decisions, and the responsibility for getting it right, were his, while the FBI and the whole world would be looking on and second guessing his every move.

"This is Goodwin, everyone. We do not intervene until we have more information. Set up a perimeter on the airport road and keep everyone out. I'll take the point on the airfield, but no one draws guns and no one tries to approach the aircraft without my approval. Dispatch, you still talking to the feds?"

"Affirmative. I'll relay back and forth."

"Roger."

The aircraft was turning onto the taxiway by the time Gary crested the hill by the east end of the runway. He instinctively slammed on the brakes and stopped in the middle of the road, flipping off his overhead lights as he checked to make sure anyone coming up behind would have enough room to stop without plowing into him.

There was a distant whine of turbine engines overhead, and he glanced up to see another jet, still very high over the airport, headed west. He wondered if they were inbound as well. The FBI had said someone was coming in another aircraft, so maybe that was the plane, and his position as de facto on-scene commander could be passed to the feds.

With no control tower at Telluride Regional Airport, there was no way to quickly shut down the airport, which is what the FBI would probably want.

Gary tromped on the accelerator again and headed for the terminal building with his emergency lights off, calculating where to enter the fenced-off area and how close to get to the aircraft when it parked. There was always a possibility of gunfire in a hijacking situation, and he let his right hand go down to his holster to verify the presence of his Colt .44 Magnum.

Aboard AirBridge Flight 90. 3:12 P.M.

"I know what you're probably thinking, Bostich. You're trying to figure how to escape now that we're down." Ken glanced at him. "Get this straight. You hold the lives of everyone aboard in your hands. If I see any attempt to escape, I'll let go of this trigger instantly and explode the weapon. Even if you're outside running, the shrapnel will kill you, as well as wipe out all of us aboard. Don't think I'm bluffing. I'm not."

"I don't think you're bluffing, Captain."

"Good."

"I also don't think you realize the FBI has the ability to neutralize that trigger with radio waves. They're hardly amateurs, you know."

"Yeah, they've had so much time to prepare a welcome here and set up all their exotic equipment."

Ken steered the 737 toward the ramp in front of the metal passenger terminal as Bostich spoke again.

"Don't sell the FBI short. I work with the Bureau all the time, and they're extremely clever. They're also honest, and if you cut a deal with them, they'll keep their side of the bargain. I'm always losing prosecutions because of some deal they've arranged to get bigger fish."

Ken looked at Bostich and snorted. "In other words, I ought to be so-o-o worried about their catching me I'll just surrender in return for their promise to, what, *think* real hard about someday arresting Lumin?"

"Look, what I mean—"

"I *know* what you mean, Bostich. You mean to look for a chance to save your miserable hide, and you hope the FBI will give you the opening." He shook his head. "Fact is, they don't even suspect the frequency this switch uses, because it was custom built. And, they run a huge risk of trying to find out by trial and error, because any radio energy focused on us could trigger the firing mechanism in the bomb."

There was a flicker of fear on Bostich's face. "I think they probably know that," he said.

"Oh?" Ken shot back. "And how would they know that, since no one, including you, has been close enough to this transmitter to accurately describe even the external housing?"

The fuel truck was waiting in front of the terminal, which sat on the north side of the runway. A fueler was in the cab just as Ken had ordered. He taxied the 737 past to the east, then turned to point the nose of the Boeing back to the west, putting the fuel truck by the right wing where the fuel receptacle was mounted.

Bostich remained silent as Ken set the parking brake and surveyed the scene outside. The sheriff's car he'd spotted on final approach was pulling onto the ramp now on his left. It approached cautiously and stopped about a hundred feet off his left wing, the deputy remaining inside.

Obviously he's been told to keep some distance, Ken thought. *If I can at least get them pumping gas, I've got a chance.*

Aboard Gulfstream N5LL. 3:12 P.M.

Kat had reached Clark Roberts, Assistant to the Deputy Director in Washington, only to be told to stand by. There was no time to stand by, so she disconnected and dialed information in Telluride, and then the emergency number of the sheriff's department to relay a quick explanation of what was going on.

The woman at the sheriff's office seemed perplexed. "We've already been talking to FBI headquarters in Washington, I believe, ma'am. They told us pretty much the same thing."

"Did they tell you the deputies should remain out of sight?"

"Negative, but one of the deputies has said that."

"Okay, please tell them again."

"How . . . do I know you're legit?" she asked.

"How did you know *Washington* was legit?" Kat shot back, regretting her tone immediately. "Look, I don't have time to either beg or prove myself, but I am an FBI agent and I need you RIGHT THIS SECOND to get on your radio and tell all your people who might be headed to the airport to kill their lights and sirens, stay back, stay away from the aircraft, stay away from the airport, and wait for instructions."

There was a telling hesitation on the other end. "Okay," the dispatcher said at last.

"Someone's already there, right?" Kat asked.

She heard the dispatcher calling one of her units in the background and heard his response. "This is Goodwin. What do you mean, remain out of sight? I'm already here."

Kat's heart sank.

"Dispatch, this is Agent Bronsky. Can you patch me through to that unit?"

There was a gentle hand on her shoulder and she looked up into the eyes of Bill North, who tipped his head toward the cockpit.

"They're getting ready to land, Kat. You want to take the extension up there again?"

She nodded and leapt to her feet as she handed him the receiver.

"Thanks, Bill."

Jeff was waiting for her with the Flitephone extension in his outstretched hand, and Kat pressed it to her ear as she knelt in time to hear the San Miguel dispatcher say, "Stand by, I'm patching."

"Deputy Goodwin here," a male voice said on the other end.

"Deputy, can you hear me?"

"Yes, ma'am. You're FBI?'

She passed her name and position, and asked if he could see the Gulfstream on approach.

"Yes I can, Agent Bronsky. You're across the valley, and I can see your landing gear coming out."

She explained what had happened in Grand Junction. "You've got to stay back and out of sight unless I need you in there."

"Well," he replied. "I'm right out here on the ramp about a hundred feet from the aircraft, but I'm still in my truck. What are you expecting from him?"

"Stay in your truck! He's going to release passengers and get fuel, and when he sees me land, he'll talk to me. Stay on this frequency and wait for instructions, okay? And please don't let any more police or deputies on the ramp. Whatever you do, do *not* get out or let anyone else get out carrying a rifle or looking like they're going to storm the plane, and do nothing that might be interpreted as trying to block the aircraft's exit route."

"Okay, you got it. The plan isn't to immobilize him, then. But if he can be seen, do you plan to take him out with a sharpshooter?"

"No! Absolutely not!" Kat explained the bomb and the dead man's trigger.

"Okay. I understand. All other units, do not approach the aircraft, do not attempt to block him or intervene or even look threatening. This is Goodwin."

"Since you're already there, Deputy Goodwin, tell me if you see anything happening."

"Nothing yet. I can see someone in the pilot's seat, and heads in the passenger windows, but no doors have opened. A ground service guy is by the right wing standing on a ladder and opening what may be a fuel panel or port."

She could see the 737 on the ramp ahead now in the distance as Dane and Jeff settled the Gulfstream in on final approach and floated in over the highway.

"Agent Bronsky, you still there?" Goodwin's voice crackled over the phone.

She pressed the handset to her ear again. "Yeah, sorry."

"You want to taxi up alongside my position when you get here so we can talk?"

"Will do. We're landing now and I'm going to disconnect. When we drop our steps, please come aboard immediately. I've got radio contact with Flight Ninety."

NINETEEN

Telluride Regional Airport, Colorado. 3:15 P.M.

Ken looked toward the sound of a decelerating jet and saw the sleek Gulfstream IV slowing along the runway. The fact that they'd figured it out so fast wasn't particularly surprising. Kat Bronsky was an interesting, tenacious, dangerous adversary, and he knew she'd be calling momentarily.

Ken pulled the P.A. handset from its cradle as he shot a stern glance at Rudy Bostich. "Don't move a muscle!"

> *"Folks, this is Captain Wolfe again. I told you a while ago, with regret, why I was doing what I'm doing. I also told you I did, in fact, have a large load of plastic explosives wired and primed in the baggage bin, and that I'm holding a trigger that will explode the bomb if I let go of it. All of that is still true. Don't anyone even think of touching a door without my approval. I have lights up here that will tell me instantly if any door or hatch, including the emergency exit hatches, are opened. I hate to say it, but I have no choice. If I see any one of those lights turn on, I'll let go of the trigger, and the end will be immediate and tragic for all of us. Now, stay seated and don't even undo your seatbelts. I have some things to accomplish before I can decide when and how to let you off this airplane."*

Ken replaced the P.A. handset as a familiar voice came through his headset.

"Ken Wolfe, this is Kat Bronsky. Can you hear me?"

He snorted and shook his head slightly as he punched the transmit button.

"What kept you, Kat?"

The answer was rapid. "Oh, a small matter of our wingman not telling us he was planning on leaving. Do you have built-in stairs on that seven-thirty-seven, Ken, or should we order some portable airstairs for you?"

"Why do we need stairs, Kat?" he asked with feigned innocence.

"You were going to let the people out of there in Grand Junction, Ken. Telluride's just as good, and steps seem like a better idea than making them jump."

"All in good time, Agent Bronsky. First, let's get this straight. Anyone who approaches this airplane from any angle kills everyone aboard. I see a door light go on, I'm releasing the button, and boom, it's all over. Every single hatch and door is wired. Try to shoot, touch, deflate, or monkey with the tires or landing gear, try to immobilize this aircraft, or stop the refueling, and it's all over."

"Ken, we understand."

"I don't know who 'we' is, Kat, but it better be everyone." Ken closed his eyes for a second, trying to decide whether the thought that had flitted across his consciousness should be spoken.

He opened his eyes then and pressed the transmit button, the decision made.

"Kat . . . triggering this bomb would create enough outrage to force a thorough investigation of every single aspect of my allegations, expose Bostich, and convict Lumin. Letting go of this trigger is another way to accomplish my goals, so please don't think I won't do it. Don't make that mistake. I'll die with it, but you, on the other hand, would have to live a lifetime with the miscalculation."

There was a lengthy silence before the Gulfstream's transmitter kicked back on.

"I understand, Ken. Believe me, I do understand."

"Okay, Kat. Tell that deputy sitting out here he'd better stay back. I parked here because I can see all of my airplane reflecting in the terminal windows. I can see anyone approaching, understand?"

"Ken, no one's going to approach you."

"One more thing. I'm sure you'll have some sharpshooter show up in a minute who'll have my head in his crosshairs, and yes, he could kill me with a single shot. But not even Bostich would be able to stop me from releasing the trigger, and detonation would occur instantly."

"There are no sharpshooters, Ken. We're not crazy. The deputy's alone out here. No one else is going to approach from any angle, I promise you. The deputy is going to come aboard my airplane. I'll keep him strictly under control, okay?"

"Kat, I'd better hear real fast from you that Bradley Lumin's been apprehended and a grand jury's been convened."

Rudy Bostich shifted position uncomfortably in the copilot's seat and Ken's head jerked instantly to the right to see what he was doing.

The pause from the Gulfstream was too long, and Ken turned back to the left and pressed the transmit button.

"You're not *really* going to tell me he hasn't been arrested yet? Not after more than two hours?"

"Ken, Lumin is gone. We can't find him."

Ken inhaled sharply. He hadn't expected that. Obviously it was a clever ploy. Maybe they'd even told Lumin to run.

He jammed the transmit button down in anger. "Jesus Christ, you think I'm an idiot? That trick's not about to work, Kat. Tell the fools in D.C. this equation is as simple as it gets: No arrest, no indictment, no trial, then no passengers. That's the bottom line. Why don't *you* tell these nice folks they don't mean enough to their government to rescue with a simple arrest?"

"Ken, it's not a trick! Honest. Officers were dispatched to Lumin's trailer, just as you asked, but there was no one there."

"Bullshit! I was going to let these people go. I *wanted* to let them out, but now I can't, until that animal is in custody and you stop trying to manipulate me with lies."

Her tone was pleading. "Ken, I'd be an idiot to lie to you at this point. I'm telling you the gospel truth. They went, he wasn't there, and they searched the area. Don't hold those people hostage to something we can't control. Please!"

The Gulfstream was coming to a halt on his left side, right behind the deputy's vehicle. Ken sighed and shook his head as he muttered to himself, "I don't believe this." He rubbed his temple for a second, keeping an eye on Bostich in his peripheral vision before pressing the transmit button again.

"You people are crazy! How many agents back in D.C. did it take to think that one up? Here I sit with the ability to kill us all in a microsecond and the goddamned FBI and Justice Department refuse to arrest a murderer. You've tipped your hand, Kat."

Dane shut down the Gulfstream's engines and quietly ran through the checklist with the copilot as Kat fingered the microphone and tried to find the right words.

"Ken, you've got this all wrong. Let me tell you the details."

She described the trailer and the distance from Ft. Collins as Frank had relayed it. "Ken, we wouldn't know all that unless someone had been out there."

"Yeah, right," he shot back. "So they sent someone out with a notepad. Did they search his pigsty trailer?"

"They didn't have probable cause, ah . . ." her eyes widened in horror.

Oh, No! Damn, damn, damn! Wrong thing to say! Kat kept the button depressed and tried to recover.

". . . which is to say, Ken, that they hadn't received the warrant yet to go inside, but while they waited for it, they were able to look in the windows and there wasn't anything amiss."

The response from the cockpit of the 737 was all too rapid, the voice even more suspicious and sarcastic.

"Oh, of course, they must have left the warrant in their other pants. Jesus Christ! They went out there without a *warrant*? Obviously, then, no one had the slightest intention of arresting Lumin. On top of that, what the hell do you mean, 'there wasn't anything amiss?' What were they doing, checking on his damned *welfare*?"

She sighed as she pressed the button once more, keeping her voice even and steady, making certain not to betray the seismic emotions roiling her stomach.

"Ken, wait just a second, will you? Let's stay calm here. Let me explain precisely what went on. First, while they were waiting for the warrant, they went out to place him under surveillance to make sure he didn't slip away, and that's when they found he'd left. His car wasn't there, there was no sign of him in the trailer, and no indication of where he'd gone." She released the button with her heart fluttering. How had she gotten herself into a corner so fast?

The frequency was quiet for several long, agonizing seconds before Ken's voice filled the speaker.

"Remember I told you over an hour ago, Kat, that I was your worst nightmare because I knew all your tricks? Okay. Lesson number one for hostage negotiators is learning to delay the game and wear the guy down. Kat, get it through your skull that isn't going to work with me. Take a look at your watch. Mark where the big hand is. Add thirty minutes to that. That's your deadline. If Lumin isn't in custody by then, we're out of here, one way or another."

"Ken, if you know the procedures that well, you also know we're not allowed to lie to the perpetrator. They did precisely what I told you, and now we're tearing around Colorado trying to find Lumin, but God only knows whether it's been a day, a week, or a month since he left." She released the button and was shocked at the rapid reply.

"No more than ten hours."

Kat hesitated. "What?"

"Ten hours, maximum, Kat. He couldn't have been gone more than that."

"How . . . how do you know that?" she asked, truly puzzled. If Lumin had been kidnapped, could Wolfe somehow be behind it?

"I just know."

"But *how*, Ken? That isn't good enough. Did you call him this morning on the phone? If so, you need to realize that he could have forwarded his line to somewhere else."

"Trust me, Kat. Lumin was there at midnight. He couldn't have gone far. His car was missing a tire."

Kat felt a strange blush of recognition engulf her, as an obvious connection she should have seen earlier finally coalesced. There were tracks outside, Frank had said, along with footprints and an unused bullet, as though someone had been stalking Lumin.

And it was the second anniversary of Melinda Wolfe's murder.

She closed her eyes briefly and shook her head in disgust that she hadn't connected it right away.

Kat pressed the microphone button with her mind racing.

"Ken," she began, slowly, "around midnight last night, out there in the cold with that rifle, what made you change your mind?"

· · ·

In the cockpit of AirBridge 90, Ken Wolfe let his head loll forward as he closed his eyes, the entire agony replaying in his head.

She'd put it together.

Rudy Bostich's voice caused him to jump slightly. "What the hell are you discussing, Captain, and with whom?"

Ken didn't respond.

"Captain?"

He rubbed his forehead, feeling the hopelessness again.

"You all right?" Rudy tried again.

Ken snorted suddenly and opened his eyes, slowly looking to his right.

"Do you have any idea, Bostich, how incredibly stupid that sounds? Here I am with your life literally in my hands, and there you are a lying bastard holding back the very thing I'm committing all these crimes to accomplish, and you want to know if *I'm* all right?"

Rudy looked embarrassed and shrugged. "I just wondered, you know—"

"When you tell me the truth I'll be all right, and so will all those people back there," Ken gestured to the back as Kat's voice returned to his ear, her tone very soft.

"Ken? Are you there?"

He took a deep breath and pressed the button again.

"I'm here."

"So why, Ken?"

He held his forehead again and pressed the transmit button, startled at the involuntary sob that preceded the words he wanted to say.

What the hell! Tell her! he decided, and the same explanation he'd given to Rudy Bostich tumbled out along with the pain and anger and the utter, complete, devastating realization in the middle of the night that he was powerless to even end the murderer's life.

Lumin had won. He'd killed them both.

Kat's voice was slow in returning to the channel.

"So, this morning you suddenly found Rudolph Bostich on your flight, the man you're convinced screwed up the prosecution of Bradley Lumin, and it was all too much to take, especially after last night's failure."

Ken nodded before remembering to punch the button. "You're very perceptive, Kat. But please don't tell me that proves I'm not a murderer, or in this case, executioner. If I could go back tonight, that trigger would be pulled."

"I understand."

He exhaled suddenly and gripped the microphone with resolve. "Just like I'll carry out my threats here and now if my demands aren't met. This is the last chance I have, Kat. I'm not going to back down. I can't. You either comply directly, or I blow us up and let public outrage provide the momentum."

"I need to come over there and talk to you in person, Ken. That okay? I'll leave whenever you want."

Involuntarily he jerked his head to the left, wondering why she would make such a request. That couldn't be in the procedures, or was he overlooking something?

"No!"

"Think about it, please?" she pleaded. "I'm unarmed, and it wouldn't matter anyway, would it? You've got that infernal trigger. Even if I had a Howitzer I couldn't use it, so I'm no threat, but it's hard talking to you this way, having to push to talk, and waiting for every reply."

Ken let out a short laugh as he checked the fuel gauges. The fueler had already loaded over eleven thousand pounds and was still pumping, probably wholly unaware of what was happening.

Ken hit the button again. "Kat, you're still forgetting I know the routine. If I let you over here, you'll have a chance to work on my head, try to pretend friendship and caring and bonding, and hey, I'm a normal male and you sound like a normal female, so maybe I'd fall for that chemistry, too. No. You can't come over here. There's nothing to talk about until you and Bostich both give me what I want."

"Then let me talk to Bostich. Maybe I can convince *him*."

Rudy Bostich couldn't hear her request, but he could see the utterly strange look that crossed Ken's face as he suddenly turned his head toward the right seat, then reached up and flicked on an overhead speaker before pressing the transmit button. "Stand by, Kat. I'll set it up, and I'll be listening to every word."

"Understood," she said, the answer booming through the cockpit at earsplitting volume as Ken's hand shot out to turn down the volume control.

He pointed to a microphone hanging to the right of the copilot's seat.

"Pick up the mike, Bostich. Agent Kat Bronsky wants to talk to you."

A look of alarm crossed Rudy's face.

"Why?"

Ken snorted. "Hell, Bostich, I don't know. Maybe at last the FBI is onto you."

"What do I do?"

"Pick up the microphone and press the button on top to talk, release it immediately to listen."

Bostich did so tentatively, as if the microphone were about to shock him.

"This is U.S. Attorney Rudolph Bostich," he said in a slightly forced tone, still holding the transmit button.

"Release the button," Ken snapped.

Rudy looked to the left, startled. "What?"

"The transmit button. Release it to listen."

Rudy looked down at the microphone and let go of the button suddenly.

Kat's voice returned as she introduced herself and assured him that the FBI was aware of all aspects of the situation.

"So, what do you want to talk to me about?" Rudy asked. "I just want out of here."

"Sir, I have to tell you with all due respect, that if you are, in fact, holding back any information on the Lumin case, you're imperiling yourself and everyone aboard."

Rudy snorted. "You trying to intimidate me, Agent?"

"No, sir. But we have a serious accusation against you made the first time, I'm told, in a Connecticut court by a police detective, and now repeated in a major hijacking, and demands are being made here that are being heard all the way to the White House. I'm not allowed to come over there physically and talk to you, so I have to use this method. Mr. Bostich, I've been given a quick synopsis of the Connecticut hearing that led to the invalidation of the search warrant. I'd like to ask you about that." She let up on the transmit button, and Rudy punched his immediately, a look of amazement contorting his face.

"Are you aware who I am, young lady?"

Kat's reply was immediate.

"Yes, sir, you told me who you are. Now. In reference to Detective Matson's claim under oath in that hearing—a claim that you called him with a tip that Bradley Lumin was the murderer of Melinda Wolfe—could there be the slightest truth in that claim, sir? Think very carefully before you answer, please, because this is a formal investigation."

Rudy shook his head and smiled sarcastically. "What hick town police department did you come from, Agent Bronsky? You're speaking to a United States Attorney, and a candidate for U.S. Attorney General. I'm not the goddamned hijacker here, woman! Captain Wolfe is. How *dare* you presume to question me, and on an open radio channel?"

Rudy sensed a reaction from Ken Wolfe, but he was unprepared to see Ken laughing.

"What?" Rudy asked him in an offended tone.

"What?" Ken replied. "*What*? Listen to yourself, you overblown, lying, pompous sack of shit! You're about to lose your life here, you and I both know you're lying about that tip, and you've got the audacity to try to intimidate *her* because she's just a little female FBI agent and you're a big, badass, male prosecutor! Jesus Christ, Bostich, you're an egomaniacal bastard! Your arrogance simply knows no bounds, does it?"

"I don't know what you're blathering about, Wolfe."

"Oh, yes you do, and I think you probably just alienated the only friend you've got in this equation, fool. Go ahead. Pick up the microphone. Snarl at the woman some more. After all, she doesn't count, does she? She's just a little female, like my daughter. Just a little female, and females are so much baggage, aren't they Rudy?"

"Her questions are nonsense," Bostich stammered.

"Well, please explain that to her in acid detail, Rudy. Because when you're through demonstrating your total disdain, she'll probably come over here and shoot you herself. Save me the trouble."

Bostich snorted. "You don't have a gun, just that electronic thing."

Ken looked at him in deep thought for a few seconds, then leveled his index finger at him.

"You know, you're right about that."

He turned back toward the Gulfstream and clicked off the overhead speaker.

"Kat, I'm sad to report the big candidate for Attorney General doesn't like you very much. In fact, I think Mr. Bostich is a misogynist."

"I'm just trying to get at the truth, Ken. What do we do now?"

He drummed the fingers of his right hand on the glareshield for a few moments before answering.

"I see the deputy coming aboard. Send him back out. I want him about twenty-five feet to the side of my forward entry door, his hands on his head where I can see them at all times."

"Why?"

"I'm not going to tell you, but I can assure you I'm not planning on hurting him, Kat. You be sure to explain to him, though, that he can't hurt me without blowing up everyone."

Ken pulled what appeared to be a small handheld radio from his map kit with his right hand, then snapped off his seatbelt as he looked at Bostich and raised the electronic trigger into view with his left.

"The first sign of movement out of that seat, Bostich, and I let go."

Rudy shook his head disgustedly. "I'm not going anywhere. Apparently."

Ken clipped the small handheld to his belt and stepped over the center console to stand in the small aisleway between the console and the cockpit door. Without warning, he reached out and yanked the shoulder harnesses on the copilot's seat from their stowed position. Rudy flinched at the vibration and began to look around.

"Freeze!" Ken commanded. "Get your eyes back forward."

Rudy complied, his eyes focusing on the instrument panel as Ken reached down to the base of the copilot's seat and adjusted something, then handed the shoulder harnesses over Rudy's left shoulder.

"Here. Grab these two straps and pull hard."

"Why?"

"Don't argue. Just do it."

Rudy took the straps in his right hand and pulled them to their maximum length.

"What now?"

"I've wedged the trigger into the shoulder strap inertial reel at the base of your chair, Bostich. The pressure you're putting on that strap is holding the button down. As long as you keep constant tension on those harnesses, the button will remain depressed."

"No!" Rudy cried out. "You can't leave me like this!"

Ken snorted in disgust. "What, in suspended agony, like you left me when you lied to that judge? I can leave you any way I want to, scum."

"What are you planning?" Bostich's voice was an anguished whine.

"What am I planning? I'm planning to use the lavatory, and I don't want you thinking about leaving. Any attempt to pull that trigger out without knowing precisely which button is depressed, and we're all gone."

Rudy was breathing hard. "After you use the bathroom, you're coming right back? Right?"

"Maybe. Maybe not. I may evacuate this aircraft and leave you like this until I get a confession. Or I might get the people off and set it on fire to let you make your own decision whether to blow up or roast. I haven't decided, except for one thing."

"What—what's that?"

"You sign a confession, you walk away. Think about it."

Ken leaned behind the left seat and pulled the circuit breakers for the communication radios.

"Remember, Bostich. Even a slight lessening of the tension may trip the trigger. And don't get any ideas about the radios. They're turned off."

TWENTY

Aboard AirBridge Flight 90, Telluride Regional Airport, Colorado. 3:27 P.M.

With Rudy Bostich afraid to move in the copilot's seat, Ken Wolfe reached down to the back of the center console and pulled up the P.A. microphone.

"Folks, you're going to see someone come out of the cockpit. Make no attempt to stop him, approach him, talk to him, or otherwise interfere with him. Stay in your seats. That includes the flight attendants."

Ken looked through the peephole before moving out of the cockpit and into the adjacent lavatory. He emerged again rapidly and glanced back up front, satisfied that Bostich was holding onto the straps for dear life, totally unaware that the trigger was still in Ken's left hand.

"I just want you to know, Bostich, that we're all depending on you," Ken said mockingly.

The passenger cabin was quiet, with several sets of startled eyes following him. Annette was nowhere to be seen, so Ken reached down to the same panel Annette had used constantly to talk to him and rang the rear galley. Annette answered almost instantly.

"Are you all three back there?"

"Yes," was the icy response.

"Okay. You're going to feel the pressure change as the front door is opened. Stay back there! Do NOT come forward, and do NOT let any passenger stand up."

"We get the idea, Captain."

"Just one thing. I'll have the trigger with me if I step outside. If I see any human being open a door, or worse, try to leave the aircraft, I'll detonate."

He replaced the handset and looked through the small window on the door. The deputy was visible on the tarmac below, his hands on his head as requested.

Ken disconnected the automatic exit slide and worked the door handle before flipping the switch that extended the self-contained boarding stairs. The sound of motors whining finally ended, and he swung the door open and stood for a moment in the doorway, half expecting the impact of a bullet.

Instead, the flow of a cool breeze washed over him as he stepped outside and raised his left hand. "You see this black plastic thing, Deputy?" he yelled.

"Yes," Goodwin replied.

"Did the FBI agent brief you that it's a trigger?"

Goodwin nodded.

"Okay. I'm coming down these stairs. If anyone's waiting with a gun, you'd better stop him. I get shot, we all go up in one horrendous explosion."

"No one else is close, Captain. I told all my people to stay away. What do you want?"

Ken reached the bottom and stepped onto the ramp, immediately dropping to a squatting position to inspect under the 737 and around behind it.

No one there. So far, so good, Ken said to himself as he stood.

He turned back to the deputy. "I want your gun, Deputy. Take it out of the holster with two fingers and place it on the ground, then back off. I see any sudden movement, or see your fingers closing around it, I'll trigger the bomb."

"No."

"No?" Ken said, his head inclined to one side in surprise. "*No?*"

"I can't give you my gun, Captain."

Ken looked down and shook his head before looking back at Goodwin.

"I don't think you thoroughly understand the situation here, Deputy. What's your name?"

"Gary Goodwin."

"Don't try to be a hero, Gary. You're going to give me that gun, or you're going to be the cause of a hundred and thirty deaths."

"No, sir," Gary said, shaking his head.

"*Why?*"

"Because you're an airline captain, sir, and I just can't believe an airline captain would really do that."

Ken was shaking his head in wonder. "Believe it, Gary. This one will." He gestured toward the Gulfstream. "Did the FBI agent up there tell you I'm too desperate to really give a damn what happens?"

"No, sir."

"See, Gary, live or die, blow them up, save them, I could care less at this point. She tell you that?"

Goodwin shook his head.

Ken paused, a sudden flash of an idea in his head.

"Gary, didn't she tell you how many people I killed last night near Ft. Collins?"

A wide-eyed look of shock spread across Goodwin's face as he tried to stammer an answer. He'd heard nothing about any multiple murder, but then again, he hadn't listened to a radio or TV newscast in the last week.

"Are you willing to gamble all their lives, Gary, on the unpredictable actions of a maniac like me?"

"Why . . . why do you need a gun if you've got a bomb, Captain?"

Ken could see faces pressed against the Gulfstream's windows and suddenly an attractive woman appeared on the top step of the business jet, holding the handrail and looking alarmed, her hair blowing wildly from the stiff breeze whipping across the tarmac.

He pulled the handheld radio from his belt.

"You see this?"

The deputy nodded.

"It's an amplifier. It's part of the trigger mechanism. The trigger in my left hand doesn't have a timer. This base unit does. It's like nothing even the FBI has seen because I modified it myself." Ken fiddled with the buttons on the front and set it down on the ground beside him, then began walking slowly toward the deputy.

"What are you doing?"

"We're going to play a little game of electronic chicken, Gary. I've set it to go off in less than a minute. Remember, I still have to hold this trigger down in my left hand or the bomb blows immediately, but in less than fifty-five seconds, if I don't get back to this unit and punch in the disarm code, it's all over."

"Look, Captain, I can't give you this gun." It was more of a plea now, Ken noted, and less a battle cry.

"Okay, then I'll take it out of the holster myself," Ken replied, "and if you delay me with a fight, you'll bear the responsibility for blowing up the hostages you'd like to rescue."

Ken continued walking steadily toward Goodwin, whose eyes were getting even wider with indecision.

"Stop right there, Captain!" Gary's voice had become slightly shrill, slightly less assured, and Ken understood the tone.

"I'm giving the orders here, Gary, and you're just making it more difficult for me to return to the timer before it goes off."

Eight feet remained between the two men.

"Look, Captain—"

"It's not a wise idea, Gary, to gamble with a dead man who's got nothing left to lose."

Five feet remained.

Kat's voice rang out from the top of the Gulfstream's stairs.

"Ken?"

Ken continued walking slowly toward Goodwin.

"What's it going to be, Gary? We've probably used up twenty seconds, and it'll take me at least five to run back to turn it off."

The deputy glanced nervously at Kat, then back at Ken, licking his lips as he tried to decide what to do.

Ken was three feet away, moving steadily, his eyes locked on the deputy's eyes.

In his peripheral vision he could see Kat descending the Gulfstream's stairs in a hurry.

And suddenly he was standing nose to nose with the startled deputy.

"We've probably got twenty seconds left," Ken said. "Want to continue arguing?"

There was a two-second pause before a single word exploded from the deputy's lips.

"Damn!" Gary spat the word off to one side as he shook his head, then glanced down to his right. "Take it. Take it quick. Just . . . get back to that radio."

Kat was moving slowly across the tarmac toward them, trying to decide what was happening.

Ken reached over with his right hand and slipped the .44 from the holster, then turned and moved swiftly back across the ramp to scoop up the handheld unit. He jabbed at one of the buttons, then turned back to see Kat stop next to Goodwin.

"Timer disarmed . . ." Ken announced, holding the base unit aloft, ". . . with eight seconds left."

"Ken?" Kat Bronsky called out, smoothing her hair back with her right hand as she held her position some thirty feet away

"Yes, Kat. Have they found him?"

She shook her head reluctantly as he glanced at his watch, then back at her.

"Sixteen minutes left, Kat."

"Then what, Ken? Suppose it takes us just a bit longer than that?"

He shook his head. "The deadline is non-negotiable."

"You want Bostich, right?"

A sudden gust of wind from behind Kat cascaded her hair around her and she fought for control of it, pushing it off her face as Ken glanced around him, making certain no one was creeping up.

He turned back to her. "You know I want Bostich. I want him to confess so I can get Lumin convicted. You know that already."

"If you'll give me some time, I can crack Bostich. I agree he's probably lying."

Ken checked over his shoulder again. The fuel truck was nowhere to be seen, and the fifteen thousand pounds of fuel they'd already loaded wouldn't get him more than two and a half hours of flight time. He looked down at the large handgun he'd taken from the deputy, who'd dropped his hands to his hips and was standing slightly behind the FBI agent.

"I'm not kidding, Ken," Kat said. "I know about the hearing, and I know about the detective, and I believe Bostich is lying. But if I can't talk to him eye to eye, I don't have a prayer of proving it."

She started moving toward him with the same slow, steady speed he'd used to approach the deputy.

"What do you suggest?" he asked.

"Cut me some slack, Ken. Give me some time to come aboard and question Bostich. He doesn't like me, I don't like him, and let's just see where it leads, okay? If it doesn't work, I'll leave. You can kick me out of the airplane at any time and I'll return to the Gulfstream and talk to you on the radio, okay?"

As she came closer, he could see the wind whipping her blouse against her body, revealing her feminine contours, and confirming the fact that she wasn't wearing a shoulder holster.

"The deadline still holds, Kat."

She nodded. "Okay, but then what? Are you going to blow everyone up while there's still a chance of success? That's pretty lame."

"I've got a better plan," he said, the words causing a flicker of uncertainty to cross her face. "You wondering why I haven't stopped you from walking over here, Kat?"

"No," she said. There were ten feet separating them.

"Have you thought of your own safety? I'm armed with a bomb and a gun, I'm desperate and dangerous as hell. Why get too close to me? Are you that brave?"

She let out a short laugh and looked off to the side in reaction before meeting his eyes again.

"Brave? *Brave?* Are you kidding, Ken? My knees . . . are literally *shaking* here! You're scaring me to death, but I can't talk to you very well over the radio, and I can't question Bostich that way either, and despite what you think I'm trying to do, I want to help you get to the bottom of your daughter's murder as well as end this . . . this . . . hijacking thing."

He smiled for the first time as she came up to him and stopped, her arms folded in front of her.

"I guess," Kat began, "I've always had this blind trust thing about airline captains, y'know? Call me crazy, but it's this nutty idea I get when I buckle up in a commercial airliner that my captain probably isn't going to kidnap me today."

"This is bizarre!" Ken said, looking off to the left at the sky and shaking his head. "Really bizarre."

"Hey, fella, you're calling the tune," she said. "I'm just trying to keep dancing."

He looked her in the eye, the smile gone. "Kat, don't think for a moment I don't know what you're up to."

"What am I up to, Ken?"

"You're an FBI agent, for chrissakes, despite the soft, feminine package. Don't you think I know you're trained to kill people caught doing what I'm doing?"

She laughed suddenly, a short chuckle, somewhat forced but incongruous enough to throw him off guard even more.

"What am I going to kill you with, Ken, my bare hands? I probably couldn't even reach around your neck."

"Nevertheless, keep those arms folded."

"Okay, okay. You're right. They could be lethal weapons."

He smiled again, in spite of himself.

"You're trying to con me, young lady."

"No I'm not, Ken!"

"You want me to believe you're suspicious of Bostich, but you don't believe he lied any more than I believe he's telling the truth."

She shook her head, her face serious. "Not true. There's something in that man's voice that's beyond a reaction to fear."

"Yeah, he's a pompous ass to begin with."

"Let me try, Ken. Please! I'll leave anytime you decide it's not working."

He looked at her once more, studying her eyes, wondering if there was a way to let her try, but still keep control. Maybe there was a way to let her probe Bostich while avoiding the web of endless delays she'd been taught to weave.

Ken took a step back and pointed the .44 into the air just over Kat's head, startling her as he nodded toward the airplane.

"Okay, Kat, you can join the group."

She cocked her head to one side as she tried to interpret his words. "You mean, it's okay to come aboard?"

Ken shook his head. "No, Agent Bronsky. I mean you've just become a hostage."

TWENTY-ONE

Aboard AirBridge Flight 90, Telluride Regional Airport, Colorado. 3:30 P.M.

For several minutes after the captain left the cockpit, Rudy Bostich sat perfectly still, holding the shoulder straps tight and trying to interpret the sounds filtering through the closed cockpit door. After the opening of the forward entry door and hearing muffled voices outside, he finally concluded Wolfe had left the airplane.

The problem of the electronic trigger seemed simple enough. Provided he could maintain perfect tension on the shoulder harnesses at all times, it didn't matter where his body might be; the button would remain pressed.

Slowly, carefully, he held the harnesses in the middle of their length with his left hand while threading the ends around a handle just below the copilot's window with his right. When he was sure he had the tension right on the makeshift pulley, Rudy unfastened his seatbelt and ducked his head under the straps to get them over his right shoulder, then carefully lifted himself out of the seat and over the center console until he was standing behind the seat.

Satisfied the straps were still being held tightly enough to keep the trigger depressed, Rudy ran his right hand down the back seat to the inertial reel at the base, gently probing for the trigger device.

He ran his fingers underneath the unit and around, and leaned over even farther, wholly unprepared to lose his balance.

Suddenly his feet slipped on the metal floor and in an instant he was falling, his left hand grasping for a better hold on the shoulder straps that were holding the bomb at bay. Gravity was yanking them away, pulling them at last from his fingers.

Rudy could hear the straps retracting automatically as his mind waited for the impact of the explosion.

Nothing.

He had landed on his side. He lay there for a few seconds, afraid to move, probing finally at the back of the seat with his left hand before grasping the top of the copilot's seat with it and pulling himself up. He looked for the small electronic trigger, around the seat, behind the seat, under the seat, and everywhere else he could think of.

The conclusion was startling, but inescapable.

The bastard! It's not here. It probably never was here.

Rudy finally pulled himself to his feet and stood, shaken, behind the center console.

There was a small peephole in the cockpit door and Rudy pressed his eye to it. He could see the daylight streaming into the front entry area from the open door, and he could see the heads of some of the passengers in the distance, but there was no sign of Ken Wolfe or any of the flight attendants inside.

He leaned forward cautiously over the pilot's seat to look out the side window to the left. Wolfe was there, standing twenty feet from the door with his back to the airplane, talking to a young woman who was walking toward him. Wolfe's attention was thoroughly diverted. Maybe, Rudy thought, he could slip out, get to the back doors of the Boeing, and open one of the exits.

A small, distant twinge of conscience rippled through his mind, a recognition that he'd be leaving a plane full of hostages behind, but he pushed it out of his mind. He refused to believe Wolfe's words—that blowing up everyone would eventually accomplish his purpose. That was just posturing. The challenge of explaining the abandonment of people who were being held hostage primarily because of him crossed his mind, but he dismissed that as well.

But, if there were no Rudy Bostich to batter at, there'd be no reason to continue the hijacking, so why would Wolfe hurt anyone?

That's a defensible explanation, he concluded. *If something happens after I get out of this aircraft, that's what I'll tell them.*

Rudy opened the cockpit door and peered around the corner of the forward lavatory to the open entry way. He could see Wolfe outside, his back to the plane.

Rudy crept past the door in a crouch until he reached the forward portion of first class, then stood and moved to the rear galley as fast as he could walk, ignoring the sea of questioning eyes that followed him down the aisle.

He reached the rear galley and barged inside, startled at Bev's instant response.

"Sir! Why are you out of your—?"

Annette silenced Bev with a look as she stood. "Rudy, what are you doing back here?"

He gave her a wild-eyed look as he moved to the right rear door and put his hands on the door-opening lever.

"What in heaven's name do you *think* I'm doing?" He shot back. "I'm going to get the hell out of here and remove his reason for hijacking this airplane."

Annette crossed the galley and stood facing him, her right hand on the same handle as his.

"Didn't you hear his warnings?"

Rudy Bostich snorted. "He's full of warnings, but I've been sitting up there watching the criminal bastard for the last hour, and I can tell you he's not after anyone but me."

"He says he has a bomb in the forward compartment."

Rudy saw an iron-willed look in her eyes as he remembered the small block of plastic explosive Wolfe had shown him earlier. He licked his lips nervously before replying, his eyes looking away from hers. "I'm sure the bomb is real, but I'm also sure he wouldn't actually use it."

"Did he tell you that? Did he give you some reason to believe he wouldn't use it?"

Rudy scowled. "Look, dammit, I'm a good judge of people, and I'm telling you he won't use it. Trust me."

"Why?" Annette asked, searching his face. "Why should I trust you? Why should *we* trust you? I don't know who's right or wrong about what Ken said on the P.A. regarding you and that warrant and everything, but I can't trust your opinion because it comes from a panicked man who's trying to save himself."

He sneered at her and shook his head. "Yeah, right. Spare me your amateur psychology and move away from this door, unless you want to be an accessory to kidnapping and air piracy."

Annette's grip tightened on the handle as Kevin stood and approached from the side.

"You're not going anywhere until it's safe to do so," Annette told Bostich. You want to call that being an accessory, go right ahead. I call what you're doing being a coward."

"She's right," Kevin added. "Stand away from that door. You're imperiling all of us."

Rudy Bostich snapped his head to the right and snarled at Kevin. "Stay out of this, sonny!"

Kevin reached out quickly and grabbed the handle—his hand next to Annette's—as he raised his eyebrows in mock surprise.

"*Sonny*?" he repeated in a mocking tone.

Rudy's eyes shot back and forth between the two of them for a few seconds before he relaxed his grip and let his arm drop. "Okay, look. He's outside. What he's doing I don't know, but this is the ideal time to—"

"To what?" Annette asked in amazement. "Just deploy an emergency exit slide and *run*, with him able to see you? Leaving all of us in here?"

Rudy shook his head. "I was going to wait until he came back aboard and found me gone." He explained the ruse with the trigger and the copilot's seat. "He'll be frantic to find me, and while he's racing down the aisle, I can get out."

"And go for help, right?"

He started to nod before realizing Annette meant it derisively.

"No, not go for help, just remove the reason for the hijacking."

Annette stared at him for several very long moments, until Rudy looked away.

"Let me ask you a question, Rudy," she said quietly.

"I've had enough questions—" Rudy began, leaning against the side of the galley, his eyes on the floor.

"Nevertheless, answer one more."

He looked up. "What?"

"I heard what the captain said on the P.A. about that warrant. Did you call that detective, and for some reason not want to admit it?"

Instantly his expression became a sneer. "You gotta be kidding me!" he said as sarcastically as possible. "You, too?"

"Did you?" she repeated evenly.

He stood away from the galley wall.

"Why should I answer such a stupid question? I'm a federal prosecutor, for God's sake."

"Did you?"

"Of course not, but even if I had, I certainly wouldn't stand back here and admit it to you."

Annette glanced at Kevin, who looked startled, then back at Rudy, who was trying to fathom her reaction and remember exactly what he'd just said.

"What?" he asked.

"I think . . ." Annette said quietly and slowly, her mind racing. "I think you just answered my question."

The confusion on his face deepened. "Are you going to help me get out of here, or what?"

"Sit down, Rudy."

"*What?*"

"Sit down in the last row back here. You're stuck with us, and I'm afraid we're stuck with you."

At the same moment outside the forward entrance of the 737, Kat Bronsky was looking at the barrel of a powerful .44 Magnum pointing just over her head as Ken Wolfe's words echoed in her mind like the vibrations of a struck gong.

"You've just become a hostage," he'd said.

She looked him in the eye. "You are joking, right?"

Ken shook his head side to side slowly. "No, Kat."

She raised the palms of her hands. "Ken, what . . . what good is *this* going to do? I mean, I'm the negotiator, for crying out loud!"

"So, we'll go aboard and you can negotiate. Come on, m'lady. Get up the stairs."

"I do *not* believe this!"

Ken snorted. "I think I just had the same conversation with the shell-shocked deputy over there. Kat, I'm dead serious." He inclined the gun barrel toward the top of the stairs and she began climbing in trance-like confusion, wondering how she could explain to Frank what had just happened.

Oh God! The Bureau will disown me for this! They'll go crazy! They'll never take me seriously again!

Kat stopped halfway up and turned around toward Ken.

"How can I be your link with the government and help get you what you need if I'm here *with* you?"

Ken smiled at her, not unkindly. "Come on, Kat. That was never your mission to begin with and we both know it. Besides, we've got phones aboard. Plenty of them. You get Bostich to confess, you can chat with the Pope if you want."

"I'm not Catholic," she replied.

"Keep moving, Kat," he said.

She turned and climbed the last few steps to the entry way and stepped inside, aware that Ken had reached the top step right behind her.

"Stand in the galley there for a minute, Kat."

He turned back to the door and threw a switch. She heard the whine of a motor as the stairs retracted, and the slight bump of cabin pressure as he closed and secured the door. He turned to her then with an index finger up.

"Stay there. Don't move." He opened the cockpit door with his left hand, keeping an eye on Kat, then leaned in for a second, emerging with a strange expression on his face.

"What's the matter?" Kat asked.

"Seems Bostich figured out my little ploy and ran to the back."

"What ploy?"

He looked at her and shook his head. "Never mind. Kat, get up front and strap into the right seat."

"The copilot's seat?"

He nodded. "Now."

"What are we going to do?"

Ken looked at the ceiling and shook his head before looking back. "We? Kat, let's get our roles straight here, okay? I'm the hijacker, holding a gun and a bomb and giving you orders. You're the hostage. Stop sounding like my accomplice."

"What, I'm confusing you?" she asked in mock surprise.

"YES, you're confusing me! *Absolutely* you're confusing me."

"Good," she said, smiling slightly despite her knotted stomach and the appalling picture playing in her mind of the impending reaction at FBI Headquarters when they found out their agent on the scene was a hostage herself.

Ken shook his head, a rueful expression on his face. "Damn, lady, you are *very* good at this."

She looked up at him with surprise in her mind and an inadvertent look of innocence on her face.

"I'm just trying to figure out what you want, Ken."

He pointed with the gun toward the front. "Cockpit. Copilot's seat. Now. Go."

She hesitated, catching his eyes. "What are *you* going to do, Ken?"

"Just get up there."

Her hand came up in a stop gesture.

"Ken, don't go back there and do anything stupid."

A look of disgust crossed his features as he glanced over his shoulder at the cabin, then looked back at her.

"What, like shoot the only bastard who has the information I need? Hardly. Kat, get up there now!"

"Or what? Or you'll gun *me* down?"

The sound of the .44 Magnum being cocked shot through her consciousness. The fact that his finger was nowhere near the trigger did not register in Kat's mind. She heard herself inhale sharply, involuntarily.

"I've got one last chance to get Lumin by cracking Bostich. There will be no second chances for me. Get in the way of that mission, and yes, Kat, I would kill you."

"Okay," she said quietly.

"Don't confuse what happened last night with Lumin. Last night there were other options. Today there's only one."

He carefully uncocked the hammer.

Kat nodded. "I'm moving."

She moved into the cockpit and sat awkwardly in the copilot's seat as she tried to suppress the shaking in her limbs. She could hear Ken somewhere behind her in the entryway. Up to a few seconds ago she'd been confident she could talk him away from the brink. There had been a connection there, however slight, established in spite of his resistance.

But that confidence had evaporated in the face of the cocked pistol. Now she wasn't sure. The level of desperation she'd witnessed frightened her, cutting through the procedures and the psychology and the empathy she was beginning to feel.

Kat's eyes moved around the interior of the cockpit quickly as she tried to familiarize herself with the various controls.

Her head was still whirling, and she thought of her handbag, now sitting in the Gulfstream. Her gun was in there. The gun she needed now. So were her FBI credentials, her credit cards, and the one piece of paper she instinctively knew Ken Wolfe must not see: her pilot's license.

Communications panel. Where is it?

She ran her hand along the center console to her left until she located the buttons.

VHF number one and two, Navigation radios, P.A. button, and interphone. Okay. I need a headset.

She looked to the right, finding the copilot's map kit and the cord from the headset jacks on the panel running back to a place on the floor where the copilot's tiny Telex headset had dropped.

Kat leaned to her left and looked through the partially opened cockpit door. She could see Ken in the forward part of the cabin pulling a briefcase out of the overhead compartment.

She picked up the copilot's headset and put it on as she punched the transmit button on the control yoke.

"Five-Lima-Lima, can you hear me?"

"We're here, Kat," Jess replied. "What's your situation?"

She hesitated for a second, wondering whether to lie about her status as a hostage. Perhaps she could talk her way back out. Yet . . . they needed to know.

"I . . . I think you'd better call Frank in Salt Lake and let him know what's happened," she said in little more than an animated whisper. She let up on the button, waiting for a response.

"Kat, we saw the gun. Did you go aboard voluntarily?"

"No," she replied, "but I'm going to try to defuse this situation. Tell him to inform Headquarters and stand by."

A sound to her left caused her to turn around to find Ken Wolfe standing in the doorway, holding a briefcase.

"You crack Bostich, Kat, and I guarantee you'll defuse this situation."

She searched his eyes, finding no anger there.

"You did say I could use the phone."

He snorted. "That's the radio, as you obviously know. Stay put."

"Ken, where *is* Bostich?"

He gestured over his shoulder. "In the back. Cowering in one of the seats."

"Shouldn't I go back and talk to him?"

Ken ignored the question as he slid into the left seat and worked the levers to slide it forward toward the yoke, adding to her confusion.

"Ken?"

He was fastening his seatbelt now, glancing every few seconds out the left window, then down at the fuel gauges.

"Yeah?" he said at last, his eyes studying the overhead panel.

"When can I question Bostich?"

"When we're airborne," he said simply.

Kat felt her heart skip a beat.

"Ken?"

His right hand came up in a wait gesture. "Just a minute. I've got a few things to do."

"Ken, you promised to let the passengers off!"

He shook his head while flipping through the aircraft's performance manual. "No I didn't, Kat. I said I wanted to, but you and your people back in D.C. didn't keep your end of the bargain. I can't release the people until Lumin's in custody."

She swiveled halfway around in the copilot's seat, leaning forward to catch his eye. "Ken, dammit, *look* at me!"

He stopped and looked over with a neutral expression. "Yes?"

"You can't leave here with all these people aboard. You've got to give us something. You've got me, you've got Bostich, you don't need them."

There was something in his eyes she hadn't noticed before, a distant, almost haunted look, as if he were looking through her, as if she didn't really count in the equation that was governing his thoughts and actions.

"The people stay, Kat."

"Dammit, at least let a few off. There's a wife back there whose husband you sent on a wild goose chase in Durango. The poor guy's petrified because she's pregnant and scared. *Please*, Ken! At least let her off."

"And while I'm at it, a few more, right?"

Kat nodded, aware that he was hesitating and thinking it over.

"There's no difference between keeping twenty or a hundred and twenty, Ken, except that releasing a hundred gives the FBI reason to give you something in return."

"First it's a single frightened wife, now it's a hundred.

"The point's still valid, plus you're too heavy to take off with a full load of people and fuel."

Ken glanced at the right window. "You see a fuel truck out there?"

Kat looked around at the ramp. "Yes, there's one there."

Ken nodded. "And he's still pumping. As soon as he's finished, we're out of here."

A very cold feeling was spreading down her back.

"Ken, a hundred thirty passengers, baggage, and fuel and according to that Gulfstream crew, there's no way you can lift this seven-thirty-seven off this runway. You'll kill all of us trying!"

"I guess we'll see, Kat."

She stared at him as he adjusted the air conditioning and pressurization panel overhead, then pulled the P.A. microphone from the pedestal and pressed the button.

"Folks, there's going to be a small delay in my ability to let you off the aircraft. We may need to fly to another airport to do that. In the meantime, just so no one will be tempted, I've pressurized the aircraft. None of the doors or emergency exits will open, so please don't try."

He reached down to replace the microphone as Kat shook her head. "I don't believe you."

Ken stopped and glanced up at her. "What?"

"What about the kids?"

He straightened up, a puzzled look on his face.

"What kids?"

She gestured to the back, a short, angry, staccato gesture. "There are kids back there you've been virtually terrorizing for the past few hours. The ones who're now in tears and shaking and holding on to their parents. Is this how you avenge Melinda's death? Your little girl was terrorized, tortured, and murdered. You're threatening to do the same to these kids."

She'd been trying to spark a small explosion, and she'd finally succeeded.

"Shut up! Goddam you, just shut the hell up!" he snarled at her. "How *dare* you compare a brief inconvenience for anyone back there to what Lumin did?" His eyes were wide with anger, his left hand gripping the glareshield for control. "You want to talk about kids? Let's talk about kids! *This* one, for instance!" He reached in his shirt pocket and removed something, slapping it down on the center console. Kat looked at the pretty face of a smiling young girl.

"Melinda?" she asked.

He nodded. "That's the kid I care about. Besides, how the hell do *you* know whether there're any kids back there?"

Kat kept her voice low and steady. "Because it's true, and you know it. To get Melinda's killer, you've blinded yourself to the effects on all those people, and blinded yourself to the effect on the kids—the children just like Melinda."

Ken replaced the picture in his pocket and shook his head violently. "You're guessing!"

"Call your flight attendants. I assume they're still back there somewhere. Go ahead, Ken. Call them. *Ask* them. Find out!"

He straightened up, glowering at her, and slammed the palm of his hand into the padded edge of the glareshield, causing Kat to wince.

"Dammit, Kat, don't push me too far! I forced you in here to break Bostich, not to take over. You're on thin ice here."

She nodded, trying to keep the butterflies in check.

"I know, Ken. You've got all the cards. You've got a bomb and you've got a gun, I already know that. You're willing to take my life to get what you want, and kill everyone aboard. But I also know what you're trying to accomplish here, and right now you're embarrassed that you didn't think about the kids, and you know I'm right, and one more—"

"That's ENOUGH!" he yelled in her face.

"NO!" she yelled back, eyes flaring. "It's *not* enough! You don't *need* the kids aboard to get this done. Ken? Ken, listen to me! The FBI needs progress in the form of released passengers, and those kids back there need off of this nightmare. Don't you think they're terrified watching their parents being scared? Don't you think they can understand what it means when the pilot gets on the P.A. and threatens to blow them up?"

She saw him transfer the small electronic trigger to his right hand, his finger carefully sliding onto the depressed button, his left hand disappearing toward his map case. The flash of chrome from the barrel of the deputy's gun caught her by surprise. He pulled it out and looked at her, breathing hard, his jaw set, his eyes aflame. Kat felt her heart racing as she watched the barrel, expecting it to descend toward her accompanied by the sound of the hammer clicking in place.

Instead, Ken Wolfe turned the barrel to the side until it was pointed at his own temple. His index finger slid to the trigger.

"Ken, NO!" Her eyes dropped to the trigger device in his right hand.

"Kat . . ." he closed his eyes briefly then opened them and swallowed hard. "Maybe I should finish it here and now. If I can't get Bostich and I can't get Lumin, then I might as well. I'm not going to live past today, anyway."

"Ken, Jeez, at *least* defuse the bomb first!"

He glanced down at the trigger and nodded.

A burst of conflicting thoughts ricocheted through her head. Letting him defuse the bomb and shoot himself would end it, but what of Bostich and Lumin? If she talked him out of it, would she be perpetuating the hijacking? Would she be almost an accessory? Would she be responsible if something terrible happened later?

She almost missed the fact that he was lowering the gun, his finger off the trigger, saving her from the decision.

Kat took a deep breath. "Ken, defuse the bomb before your finger slips and you kill us all. Let the passengers out, and then let me question Bostich here, on the ground."

He paused, his eyes on hers. "Kat, don't—"

"Don't what, Ken?" she asked quietly. "Don't interfere? Come on. You know you miscalculated about the kids. Let them off. Let that poor man's pregnant wife off, and put that gun back in your case. You can't even consider shooting yourself until this is concluded, and you need to defuse that damn bomb. Suppose you tripped and dropped the trigger?"

He nodded slowly as he reached around to drop the gun in the bag, transferred the trigger back to his left hand, then reached for the interphone to call the rear galley.

Kat kept her eyes steady on him.

"Annette, do we have children aboard?" Ken asked into the interphone handset.

The feminine voice from the rear galley was cold and even, Kat thought.

"Of course."

"How many?"

"I haven't counted them, Ken, but at least one infant, a scattering of young children under ten, and probably three, maybe two, very young teens, like, say, eleven to thirteen. We also have a high school band. Why?"

Ken's eyes were squarely on Kat's, but there was no mockery. "All the kids, their parents, and the woman whose husband we left in Durango are going to get off. The high school band, too. Kids and chaperones. Everyone else stays."

He replaced the interphone and unsnapped his seatbelt as he looked at her again. "Fasten your seatbelt, Kat, and keep it fastened. Do not get out of that seat." He reached back for the gun and stuck it in his belt as he swung out of the seat and left the cockpit to open the door and extend the stairs.

Kat pressed the transmit button immediately, speaking in little more than a whisper.

"Dane, Jess, are you there?"

"Yes," Dane's voice responded instantly.

"He's going to release kids and parents. Could you take them aboard your bird, or get them to the terminal?"

"We'll arrange it."

"Did you talk to Frank?"

"Yes, Kat. He said the command passes now to Washington and help's on the way to immobilize."

"*No*, Dane! Call him, tell him they can't risk that! I'm working on Wolfe. They must *not* put anything or anyone in here that will spook this man."

"I'll relay it, Kat, but your friend Frank thinks it's too late."

"Then call Washington. Get the number from Frank. Explain I'm making progress, but tell them I need all the background they can get on Rudolph Bostich."

"How will they talk to you?"

"Don't know yet. Hold on."

She could hear Ken making the P.A. announcement, asking all families with children to get their things together and stand by to leave.

"We see the door opening, Kat."

"They'll be coming out in a moment. He's made a P.A. Tell Washington I'll either call them on a cell phone or relay through you and your Flitephone."

"The Flitephone won't work here, Kat, but we've got a satellite phone Bill says we can turn on when you need it."

The sound of passengers and a crying baby greeted her ears as she turned and looked through the partially opened door. She heard the P.A. coming on again.

"I know all of you want off, and I wish I could let you off. But the coward you saw run down the aisle some time ago, Rudolph Bostich, the prosecutor whose lies let my daughter's killer go free . . . until Bostich confesses, and I mean signs a confession and admits what he did on a telephone to the judge in the case, I can't let all of you go. Melinda . . . that was my daughter's name . . ."

Kat heard a choked sob as the P.A. went silent. Through the door she could see Ken's left arm as it hung down by his side, his fingers still pressing the button on the small plastic trigger device, and she could hear him clear his throat.

The P.A. clicked on again.

"Melinda would not want me to scare children, so for the young people on board, I'm truly sorry. In about five minutes I'm going to lower the stairs and have you take your parents and go. And the lady whose husband was left behind in Durango, I'll want you to go, too. Just, please, remember what I've told you, remember my daughter. What I'm doing is against the law, but the law has failed, and I have no choice."

TWENTY-TWO

Aboard AirBridge Flight 90, Telluride Regional Airport, Colorado. 3:50 P.M.

Annette watched the last family pull their bags out of the overhead bins and move forward anxiously, the wife turning to squeeze the free hand of an older gentleman across the aisle.

"Go on, now. I'll be fine," the older man said to her.

As the family passed the middle of the cabin, a youth Annette had spotted—a teenage boy—stood and looked around uncertainly, until he saw Annette coming up from the rear. He pointed to himself and raised an eyebrow, watching Annette's face as she moved to him.

"How old are you?"

"I'm . . . ah . . . fourteen, actually fifteen, this month. Can I go?"

She nodded and pointed toward the front. The gossamer hint of a smile flickered across his face, and he turned and walked forward briskly, watched, Annette saw, by Blenheim, the obnoxious tour company owner in the bulkhead seat who stood as the boy approached. The man put a hand on the boy's shoulder and leaned over to say something to him in a voice Annette couldn't hear. The boy looked around, a startled expression on his face, then nodded at the man, who grabbed a briefcase and moved into the aisle, his hand tightly clasped to the boy's right shoulder.

They were thirty feet ahead of her, but she broke into a trot, covering the distance quickly.

"Sir?"

He pretended not to hear, moving with the boy toward the entryway where Ken stood watching the exodus.

"Sir! Stop!"

The passengers who were being left behind began turning to look as Annette reached them.

Blenheim turned and hesitated, holding the boy by the shoulder as he looked back with a startled expression.

"I'm trying to leave with my boy, here," he said, sounding pained.

"This is your son?" Annette asked, pointing to the boy, who was looking terrified.

Blenheim nodded. "What, now I need a birth certificate to please you?"

Annette looked the boy in the eye.

"Is this your father?"

There was a panicked hesitation before Blenheim jumped in. "This is ridiculous. Of *course* I'm his father!"

"I didn't ask you, sir."

She motioned to the boy to step around Blenheim and come back toward her, and she leveled a finger at the tour company owner before he could speak.

"Keep quiet, sir, and stay there."

The last family to leave was rounding the corner in front of Ken and moving toward the steps. Annette leaned over to speak in the boy's ear.

"You have to tell me the truth, son. Is that man really your father?"

The boy shook his head. "No, ma'am."

"Is he related to you in any way?"

"No."

"You ever see him before he jumped to his feet and told you to pretend you were his son?"

"No, ma'am. But I don't mind."

"I do." She whirled on Blenheim, who'd been nothing but trouble since takeoff. "YOU! Step back, NOW!"

She ushered the teen safely past the man and watched until the boy had turned the corner and started down the steps.

Ken had been watching the exchange from his position in the entryway some twenty-five feet away.

"What's the problem, Annette?"

Violently conflicting emotions washed over her as she looked at Ken. He was the hijacker, yet he was the captain. She could have helped another passenger escape, yet she had held him back. She glanced at the obnoxious man, remembering his withering arrogance and insulting behavior at the first of the flight, and the decision suddenly became easier.

Blenheim stood wide-eyed in shock, backing up into one of the first class rows.

"Who is that, Annette?" Ken said.

She looked forward at Ken. "This is the Mikey I told you about in Colorado Springs who hates everything." Her eyes snapped back to Blenheim. "He just tried to sneak out pretending to be that boy's father."

Blenheim turned to look at Ken, who stared back for several very long seconds.

"Annette," Wolfe said at last, "strap him in a coach seat, then get on the P.A. and tell everyone on board what he tried to do, and tell them his name and the name of his company."

She smiled for the first time in hours. "With pleasure, Ken."

Aboard Gulfstream N5LL, Telluride Regional Airport, Colorado. 3:52 P.M.

In the cockpit of N5LL, Bill North and his two pilots watched the brief exodus from Flight 90 in suspense, hoping it might continue. But when the steps began to retract, fewer than half the people had left.

"Dane, if we're in agreement with what we discussed, hand me the mike, please."

"We are," he said, putting the microphone in North's hand.

"Kat, this is Bill North. Can you hear me?"

There was a brief hesitation. They could see Wolfe once more through the captain's side window on the 737, apparently getting settled in his left seat.

"I'm here, Bill. So is Ken Wolfe," Kat responded.

"Understood. It's Wolfe I want to talk to."

Dane looked up at his boss and nodded again, then glanced back through the door as Jess helped several more of the passengers aboard the Gulfstream.

"This is Ken Wolfe. Who's speaking?"

"Bill North, Captain. I own the Gulfstream, and as you may know, I'm vice chairman of AirBridge Airlines. Look, I've got a proposition for you."

"What are you doing here, Mr. North?" Ken's voice carried a shocked tone.

"I've been here all along, Captain. I was getting ready to fly to our headquarters to respond to this thing when you popped into my home airport at Salt Lake."

"Mr. North, look—"

"Bill, please."

There was a long silence.

"Okay. Look, I'm sorry for all of this, but I've got no choice."

"I want to offer you something, Ken."

"I'm not after money."

"I'm not offering money. I'm offering a trade. Let's swap aircraft. You leave the rest of those folks over there, bring Kat and your other hostage, and come take my bird. My pilots have volunteered to fly you wherever you want to go, I'll stay as a hostage, and I'm sure you know the Gulfstream Four can get you almost anywhere."

"No thanks, Mr. North."

"Captain, come on. You and I both know you can't get that Boeing out of here safely. The temperature over the runway is rising, the density altitude is above eleven thousand feet, and you're going to risk everyone's life if you try it. Those are our passengers. You're a responsible airline captain. You simply can't imperil them with a wild takeoff attempt. This Gulfstream can hop out of here just fine. Your Boeing can't."

Dane pointed toward the right window, his voice a stage whisper. "The fueler is finished loading. He's sucked up two trucks. About thirty thousand pounds worth."

More silence. Bill North found himself searching frantically for a different approach.

"Ken? You know I'm the majority stockholder in Tom Davidson's airline, don't you?"

"Yes, sir."

"Did you know I personally helped Tom get you the job with AirBridge and move you to Colorado?"

"I'm . . . grateful, sir. No, I didn't know that."

"Well, I did. And I want to help now. Please, Ken, let those people go, and let's handle this between you and me."

Ken's voice returned, neither strident nor anguished.

"The subject's closed, Mr. North. If you want to help, then yank some strings with the government to get them to comply with my demands. This is my last day as a pilot or an employee of yours. We both know that. I can't back down until those demands are met."

"Well," Bill replied, glancing at Dane and raising an eyebrow. "Why don't you tell me exactly what those demands are?"

There was no answer.

Bill called twice more, and on the third call Kat's voice responded, subdued and metered.

"Thanks, Bill, but he says no."

"He's really going to try it then?" Bill asked her.

The response was hesitant. "I . . . don't know. He wants me to stop talking now."

"Kat, we don't have the performance charts over here, but Dane is type-rated in the seven-thirty-seven, and in his opinion, a takeoff attempt would be suicide."

There was a short click of the transmitter, but no voice.

"We're here, Kat," Bill added, "if, you know, there's anything more we can do."

Bill North and Dane Bailey sat in silence for nearly a minute, their eyes on the adjacent Boeing, their thoughts on how to prevent Ken Wolfe from attempting a takeoff.

"We could taxi out and block the runway, I suppose," Bill said.

Dane was shaking his head. "No way. We don't want to corner a man with a bomb. God knows what else might push him over the edge, but blocking the runway, or shooting out his tires, or anything like that is exactly what would push *me* over the edge. That's . . . intolerable to a pilot."

Bill North searched Dane's face carefully. "Why, Dane?"

He snorted softly. "Boss, you're an aggressive chess player. I've watched you. You don't like to lose. In chess, in business, in anything."

Bill North smiled in response.

"So how do you feel when someone checkmates you?"

"I'm not following this, Dane."

"How do you feel in that crystalline moment of shock when you realize you've been boxed in, when you recognize that there's nowhere to move, nowhere to go, no strategy left to employ, nothing left but admission of defeat? Checkmate or stalemate. One second you're conducting a battle with a myriad of options, the next, because of a strategic or tactical oversight, you've lost it all. How does it make you feel?"

Bill North cocked his head. "In a word? Panicked."

Dane was nodding aggressively. "Exactly. A strong, controlling individual is panicked. 'This can't be! I can't be out of options.' And when you realize you are, there's a fatalistic urge to regain control by bailing out of the game, resigning on your own terms."

"And pilots are controllers."

"To the depth of our being, Bill. Just like you are in business. If we block Wolfe, we're stalemating him, and his only option to regain control is to trigger that bomb."

Bill North sighed. "How about *getting* to that bomb? Didn't Kat say it was supposed to be in the forward cargo bin? Couldn't someone open the bin and get all the bags out?"

Dane was shaking his head. "Not without turning on a master caution light and a light on the overhead panel. He'd see that master caution light in a split second and know what was happening."

"And you can't defuse the light from outside?"

"No," Dane said sadly.

"Then . . . she's truly on her own." He stood. "Let's get the folks we brought aboard safely escorted into the terminal so *we've* got options if, somehow, he does get that thing off the ground."

"Bill."

"Yeah?"

He sighed heavily. "Look, despite everything I just said, the FBI needs to know that stopping him here and taking a chance he's bluffing about the bomb might be a better bet than letting him attempt a takeoff. That's got to be *their* decision, because it's a real crap shoot."

"A takeoff is that risky?"

The captain looked up at the owner. "If Wolfe tries to lift off this sixty-nine-hundred-foot runway with this eleven-thousand-foot density altitude at his weight of over a hundred and thirty thousand pounds, we'll have a fireball off the departure end."

Bill North shook his head as he gazed at the 737 through the windscreen.

"If he was the only one on board over there, that might be the best solution."

Dane Bailey turned in his seat with a startled expression, his eyes studying Bill North's face.

Aboard AirBridge Flight 90, Telluride Regional Airport, Colorado. 4:01 P.M.

"Kat, would you reach over and get that briefcase behind me, please? First, pull your seat back on the rails so you'll have enough lap space to open it."

Ken Wolfe motioned to the tiny jumpseat behind his chair. Kat had noticed the case when he'd brought it in, but somehow it had seemed unimportant at the time.

"What's in there?" she asked.

"That is exactly what I want to know." Ken looked over at her. "It belongs to Rudy Bostich. His laptop computer should be inside, and we're going to go on a small fishing expedition."

"For what, Ken? What would he have on his computer that could help you?"

He balanced the checklist on his lap as he ran through familiar patterns on the various panels with his hand, setting the electrical, hydraulic, air conditioning, and fuel systems for engine start. For a while he didn't answer, his attention focused on the checklist. He looked over at her then.

"Guys like Bostich are arrogant beyond reason. They always carry too much sensitive information in their personal databases, and very few of them know enough about computers to know that password protection of a file can be easily broken. Bostich probably has names, numbers, references, and God knows what memos in there, and something might just be a smoking gun."

She retrieved the case and laid it on her lap, aware that he was watching as she snapped open the two clasps. The clasps were gold, the exterior fine hand-tooled leather, the interior rich with the aroma of expensive cowhide.

In the middle, as predicted, was a powerful laptop computer and several manila filing folders.

Kat closed the case again immediately.

"Ken, if I find anything in here that might be evidence to help your case, I'll contaminate it, because I'm the FBI."

He paused and glanced over at her. "You're telling me you need a warrant to search a briefcase?"

"I'm . . ." she shook her head. "I'm telling you that on the outside chance there's something here, it would probably be inadmissable in a court because I found it without probable cause and without a search warrant."

"Okay, what if I ordered you to look?"

She shook her head. "I'm not a lawyer. I don't know."

"How about if I pressed the keys while you held it in your lap?"

"Ken, I'm telling you I don't know the legal ramifications well enough to predict. I just know that the FBI can't go poking around just anywhere. We're still governed by laws, and the laws are very strict on what constitutes probable cause."

"Okay, Kat. Just hold it on your lap for a few minutes while I get the engines started."

She looked over at the Before Starting Engines Checklist he was using, and reminded herself what he was doing.

"You're going to start the engines?"

"Yes."

"And try to take off?"

He nodded without comment.

"Ken, please! Don't try it! You looked at the performance charts a minute ago. You know it would be suicide, don't you?"

Ken snapped off a toggle switch and she heard the air conditioning system go silent. He reached up to the forward overhead panel, then, and turned a rotary switch and the sound of the left engine winding up reached her ears.

"Ken, you're an experienced professional airman. You're a conservative airline captain. Like North said. Why would you take a wild chance that's almost certainly doomed to fail?"

"Why didn't you tell me the vice chairman of my airline was in that plane?"

Kat looked startled. "You didn't ask. And it was immaterial. I commandeered him." She watched his hand still holding the start switch. "Ken, are you going to listen?"

There was no response. The first switch automatically clicked off, and he rotated the adjacent one to start the right engine.

With her stomach in a tight knot, Kat watched the second engine wind up to idle power as Ken finished the start procedure, turned the air conditioning back on, and craned his neck to make sure they were clear on the ramp.

The options were limited. She could reach down and cut off the engines, but he could simply start them again. She could try to grab the trigger from his hand, but if she missed, the bomb would kill them all.

But to try a takeoff . . .

"Ken—" she began again. His right hand came up in a stop gesture.

"Not now. I've got to get out to the runway."

"That's what I'm trying to talk about," she said. "You can't *do* this."

"We'll talk about it at the end of the runway," he snapped, pushing the power up and using the steering tiller by his left knee to guide the 737 ahead, and then to the left around the parked Gulfstream. He turned left then, and accelerated the Boeing to the east down the long taxiway leading to the end of runway 27 as he reached for the interphone and punched the rear galley call button.

Kat heard Annette answer in her earpiece.

"Where is Bostich, Annette?"

"I put him in the last seat in coach, a window on the left."

Ken nodded to himself. "Okay, have him stand in the aisle by his seat. I want to see him."

"Ken, what are we doing?"

"Whatever I need to do to finish this without hurting anyone. Did you make the P.A. about that blowhard in coach?"

"Yes. I thought you heard me."

"No. But I'm glad you did it. Is he still seated?"

"Yes, Ken. Angry, embarrassed, and frightened beyond belief, but, ah, thank you. That felt very good."

"Get Bostich on his feet, Annette. Please. So I can see him from the cockpit door."

"Okay, Ken. Just—"

"What?"

"Ken, I . . . didn't know the details about Melinda. I'm so very sorry. I can't agree with what you're putting us through, but . . . but good Lord, what a terrible ordeal."

"Thanks, Annette."

There was an awkward hesitation, and Kat could hear the interphone receiver being shifted to another hand. "Okay, Ken. I'll get him to stand."

At the end of the taxiway Ken guided the 737 onto the runway surface sideways and braked to a halt, carefully searching the sky to the left before turning the Boeing a hundred and eighty degrees to the right. When he stepped on the brakes, they were facing the taxiway to the north.

He straightened the nose wheel steering and set the parking brakes.

"What are we doing, Ken?"

"I'm protecting my flanks, I'm sure, as we speak, your people are sending in some sort of team to deal with me, now that they've lost you. I'll bet you anything we'll see a military aircraft pop up in the pattern in a few more minutes, and I do not intend to give them a runway to land on."

She saw him take a piece of paper out of his pocket, hesitate, then unfold it and read it carefully. She also realized that tears were rolling down his cheeks.

"What is it?"

Ken looked up, his gaze outside, as he held up the slip of paper.

"One . . . one of the departing passengers . . ." he closed his eyes and waved it for her to take, unable to finish.

The handwriting was in highly legible cursive:

To the Captain,

You said you'll be opening the door in a few minutes, so I don't have much time, but there's something I need to say to you.

Thank you for letting my family off. My wife and daughter and I have been terrified, as you suspected.

I listened to the story of your daughter's murder with great sympathy, and with tears in my eyes. We, too, lost a child to crime—a drive-by shooting two years ago, for which no one has been arrested or tried.

You and I know a terrible truth most parents don't: There are two-footed animals out there who prey on children. They're not really human, and why we protect them with laws meant to protect normal humans I will never understand. What you have done today is very wrong, and very criminal, and while I can't condone threats to innocent passengers, I pray you succeed in bringing your daughter's murderer to justice by forcing the truth from whoever holds it hostage. You've been a victim and a hostage, too, Captain, but the last hostage is always the truth.

May God be with you.

Kat dabbed at her eyes and refolded the note as she looked back at Ken. "That's quite a note, Ken."

He was nodding, his eyes still shut. "He's right, you know. It justifies nothing, but . . . at least understanding helps."

His right hand was resting lightly on the throttles, and Kat reached for it with her left, intertwining her fingers with his, dismissing the flash of caution in her head. She squeezed ever so slightly, expecting him to pull back.

Instead, he squeezed back and looked at their hands.

"Thank you, Kat. I appreciate your being . . . human."

She nodded.

"I know you'd have to stop me if you could, arrest me, shoot me, but this . . ." He raised her hand with his an inch. "This helps to stem the rage."

He withdrew his hand, then, and took a deep breath.

"Ken?" she said softly.

He nodded, his eyes on the panel. "I know. I know, you don't want me to risk a takeoff. I fully understand, Kat." He looked over at her suddenly.

"Look, there's something you don't know, something about the performance of this aircraft, my knowledge as a pilot, the whole thing, that you can't know. As silly as this sounds, the hijacker asking the FBI agent to trust him, please, on this one point, trust me. I wouldn't risk a takeoff if I had any real doubts I could do it."

"So . . . you're going to try?"

Ken hesitated as he searched her eyes. "Kat, I know they're not going to sit back there in Washington with their feet on a desk and wait for this to be over. They're planning to intervene. We both know that. Truth is, the minute anyone shows up here to deal with me—a line of sheriff's cars, a helicopter, a military aircraft—I'll have no choice. We'll have to go."

TWENTY-THREE

Aboard AirBridge Flight 90, Telluride Regional Airport, Colorado. 4:10 P.M.

Ken Wolfe pressed his face forward toward the windscreen and searched the sky once more before turning to Kat and gesturing over his shoulder.

"I'm going to check on Bostich. I've probably left him standing long enough."

He rolled his seat back as he removed his seatbelt and swung his leg over the pedestal, unlocking and opening the door halfway in one motion. He stood for a few seconds, then returned to the left seat and picked up the P.A.

"Okay, Bostich, you can sit down and strap in again. Folks, we're going to be sitting out here on the end of the runway for a while. I know I've kept you from the restrooms, but now, anyone who needs to, make as fast a run at the nearest restroom as possible. I'm turning off the seatbelt sign, but when I turn it back on, I'll need you back in your seats immediately, because it will mean we're about to depart. Rudolph Bostich, you stay in your seat."

Ken replaced the P.A. microphone and removed Bostich's powerful laptop computer from the briefcase Kat had been holding. He was in the process of punching the on button as the radio came alive.

"Flight Ninety, this is Five-Lima-Lima."

Kat recognized Dane's voice. She looked at Ken who nodded approval to answer.

"Go ahead, Dane," she said.

"Kat, we have an urgent message for Captain Wolfe . . . from your people in Washington, the FBI. They want the captain to call the number I'm going to give you. Do you have a cell phone aboard?"

Ken was nodding, and she answered yes and wrote the number down.

"Got it Dane. Stand by."

Ken was fishing for something in his map case, a small black plastic box with wires that he plugged in overhead. He replugged his headset into the box, connected it to a cellular flip-phone, and handed it to her.

"What's this?" Kat asked, apprehension in her voice.

"Allows us to talk on a cell phone through our headsets and the transmit button on the yoke."

Ken opened the phone and punched in the number, then sat it on the glareshield as the number began ringing in her earpiece and a voice she didn't recognize answered from FBI headquarters.

"This is Agent Katherine Bronsky aboard AirBridge Ninety. I . . . we . . . had an urgent message to call you."

There was a pause and several background voices before the man returned. "Ah, Bronsky, we need to talk to Captain Wolfe."

She shook her head in puzzlement. "Look, I'm the negotiator here, and the captain is listening."

"Agent Bronsky, you are a hostage, right?"

"That's right. Her stomach tightened even further, knowing instinctively what was coming.

"Then you're off the case. Take care of yourself, but pass this line to the captain."

Kat looked at Ken and raised her eyebrows, fighting down the embarrassment of being summarily dismissed from the loop.

He nodded and punched the transmit button. "This is Wolfe."

"Captain, would you please stand by to speak with the Acting Attorney General, Martin Springfield?"

"If he's got something useful to tell me, like you're complying with my demands."

"I know he does, Captain. Stand by."

There were a few clicks on the other end. Ken could envision the sophisticated recording gear hooked up to the line as they opened the line to an office at the Justice Department, where, undoubtedly, a group of people were huddled around Springfield getting ready to prompt him on what to say.

"Is this Captain Ken Wolfe?" a new voice asked.

"Mr. Springfield, I presume?" Ken replied.

"That's right. Look, Captain, let's get right to it. You've demanded we arrest Bradley Lumin. The FBI didn't find him at his home, but we now have a track on him and should have him in custody within ten minutes."

"Meaning?"

"Meaning he's surrounded in a Kmart in Ft. Collins, and we're simply trying to make sure we don't alert him before we nab him, so we can protect innocent bystanders."

"How about the grand jury and the federal indictment?"

"That's the interesting part, Captain. Obviously what you're doing is hijacking, and a capital crime. Normally we would never deal with the demands of a hijacker, but you've triggered an interesting investigation regarding our U.S. Attorney in Connecticut, Mr. Bostich, who I guess is on the airplane with you?"

"Yes, he is."

"And Mr. Bostich is . . . still okay?"

"Yes, Mr. Springfield, I'm not about to kill the man before he confesses that he lied. Are you about to tell me the *government* now believes Bostich lied?"

"No. I'll be frank with you, Captain. We have virtually no reason to believe Rudy Bostich lied in that Connecticut court or anywhere else, but we're quite concerned why federal charges weren't filed against Lumin. That's why we've convened an emergency session of a sitting federal grand jury, and they're in the federal building in Manhattan as we speak looking at the evidence. I can't guarantee they'll indict Lumin, but there's a good chance they will."

Ken took a deep breath and stared at the instrument panel for a few seconds before punching the transmit button again.

"Mr. Springfield, I'm trained in the standard delaying tactics for hijackings. I know all your tricks. Promise the hijacker anything, don't actually lie, but keep dangling hope out there and keep him in one place. I'm also aware the FBI has some sort of force on the way here. Now here's the deal. When Lumin has already been arrested, and that grand jury has returned an indictment, and finally, when Rudy Bostich has confessed here on this aircraft, I'll end this and deliver everyone safely. Until then, all the promises and the assurances in the world will not suffice, and if there's any attempt to block me or take this aircraft, I'll detonate the bomb."

"Okay, Captain, but here's *our* deal. We do want you to stay on the ground there in . . . where the hell are you?"

"Telluride, Colorado."

"Okay. I don't know the area. Keep everyone, including Bostich, safe, stay on the ground, we'll leave you alone until we can report back that the things you've demanded are done."

"Mr. Springfield, are you aware that I have Rudy Bostich's phone records that prove he made the call he claimed under oath he never made?"

There was no answer for nearly thirty seconds, and Ken could imagine the hurried, whispered conference taking place in Springfield's office.

Martin Springfield's voice returned with a surprised tone. "I've reviewed that case against Lumin, and Mr. Bostich's testimony. You're sitting out there telling me that you somehow have possession of his personal telephone records, and that those records, if examined minutely, would prove that a call *was* made to that detective when and where the detective claimed it was?"

Ken was nodding to the instrument panel. "That, Mr. Springfield, is precisely what I'm confirming to you."

"Well, where the hell did you get those records? How do I know they aren't forged?"

"I won't tell you how I got them, but I will tell you they are a telephone company internal record of his telephone calls."

"We'll check immediately, Captain."

"If you find anything different at the phone company, Mr. Springfield, someone's altered them, and that is exactly what I suspect. If so, I've preserved a certified copy of the original computer tape."

"Where? Is it with you?"

"It's safely salted away where the FBI would never find it. Anything happens to me, though, it will be made public, and it has a perfect chain of possession that will hold up in court. That was done just in case someone in the government tried to rewrite the evidence at phone company level."

"Come on, Captain, we don't do things like that."

"Yeah, right. Look, no one's listened to me, Springfield, because everyone assumes a federal prosecutor is perfectly honest. Especially this one. He's too highly placed, he's too politically connected, he's too respected to be human, right? Wrong. He lied. Hard as that might be for you to believe, he in fact lied under oath. I don't know *why* the man lied, but he did pass that tip to an honest detective, then ruined the murder case against Lumin and the detective's reputation when he perjured himself about the call. I have the proof. It's available to you, too. The whole world's going to see it after this."

"When did you get those records, Captain?"

"A month ago."

"Jesus, Captain. You're throwing away your life here and you could just as easily have called the FBI with those records? Why didn't you just fly to D.C. and present it to us?"

Ken looked over at Kat and shook his head slowly before responding.

"Are you not aware, Mr. Springfield, that I did exactly that?"

"What do you mean, you did? There's no record of our having known about any phone records."

"Does the name Julian White ring a bell?"

"Of course. Julian is head of the criminal division here at the Justice Department," Springfield replied.

"That's right. I'd suggest you start by calling Mr. White in for a quick polygraph, with a court recorder present."

There was a long hesitation on the other end.

"I'm not following something here, Captain. What the hell are you talking about? Are you saying I should administer a polygraph to Mr. White? Why?"

"Because three weeks ago, Mr. Acting Attorney General, I *did* fly to Washington, and by appointment met with Mr. White. I gave him copies of the smoking gun records in the presence of a senior FBI official named Campbell. An assistant director, I think."

"I had no knowledge of this. But too often, what civilians like you think are 'smoking guns' very often are so flawed they can't be used as evidence at all."

"I hardly think irrefutable proof of a call like this is flawed. Of course, there's a strong possibility the Justice Department and the Administration want it covered up."

"All right, Captain. What proof do you have that anyone here, let alone Julian White, would participate in a coverup, and of what?"

"Consider the evidence, Mr. Springfield. Mr. White was outraged when I showed him Bostich's phone records. He promised to investigate immediately. He also pledged to be available to me by phone at any time and report back. The very next morning, however, the White House announced Rudy Bostich is the front-runner for Attorney General, something I'm quite sure Mr. White didn't know when we talked. I tried for ten days after to reach him, but despite his promises, every phone call was refused, and faxed requests for a meeting were never answered. Finally, three days ago, I was told by White's office that the United States Department of Justice had looked into my allegations and found them groundless, and that nothing more would be done. That's a ridiculous lie, of course. I demanded to know whether anyone had checked the phone company's records. The underling I talked to wouldn't tell me, but I'm convinced now that the records have probably been altered, possibly by the FBI itself."

"Another wild accusation that's going to be very difficult for you to prove, Captain."

"Well, what no one knew is the fact that even if the phone company records have been falsified, more than two complete, verifiable, intact copies are available, each of them providing irrefutable evidence that Bostich lied . . . and now, apparently, providing circumstantial evidence of a Justice Department coverup as well."

There was a long silence from Washington.

"That's quite an allegation."

"But it's true, and you're not going to weasel out of it. Now, Mr. Springfield, when you've got something substantive to tell me, call me back."

"How?"

Ken passed the number of his cellular phone, then paused. "One more thing, Mr. Springfield."

"Go ahead."

"Tell the FBI they've got a perfectly good representative aboard whom I'm comfortable negotiating with. They want to talk to me, they can talk to Agent Bronsky. Her intervention is the only reason these people are still alive, the only reason people were allowed off here in Telluride, and the only reason we're still talking. They said she was off the case? I just put her back on."

He punched the disconnect button, aware that Kat was staring at him.

"I . . . guess I never expected a recommendation from, ah . . ."

"From the criminal?"

She snorted softly and shrugged. "Yeah, I guess. Thank you for that, I think."

He nodded as he looked down at the computer screen that had been waiting for additional commands, then looked up to scan the sky to the west, north, and east.

"I've got to look behind us."

He handed Kat the computer, moved his seat forward, and released the parking brake as he pushed the throttles up and brought the steering tiller full right, pivoting the 737 through a full 360-degree turn.

"I don't see anyone yet, but they'll be here shortly."

"Ken, I told them not to."

He shook his head. "They wouldn't have been listening to you by that point, Kat."

With the 737 sideways on the end of the runway once again, Ken set the parking brake, repositioned his seat, and put Bostich's computer back on his lap.

Kat watched from the copilot's seat in silence for a minute. The screen was a blank from her angle, and she struggled with the question of whether she should even be watching what he was doing.

If I'm not directing the search in any way, it will probably not affect admissibility, she concluded, then immediately upbraided herself. *This is foolish! You're buying into his fantasy that he's going to find something substantive on there. Bostich may have lied, but he's not a fool. He wouldn't carry a smoking gun around on his laptop.*

Ken glanced at her. "You can't see the screen, can you?"

She shook her head no.

He raised his left hand to show the trigger once more. "You do remember I'm holding onto this, right?"

She nodded. "How can I forget? One heart palpitation away from disaster? Of course I remember."

"Okay. You can unstrap and sit behind me to watch if you'd like."

Kat thought it over quickly and unsnapped the seatbelt. She sat sideways on the tiny jumpseat behind him, aware of how easy it would be to disable him from such an angle—and how potentially fatal with the presence of a dead man's trigger in his hand.

Ken had opened a long list of files and was darting in and out of them, looking at various documents, most of them legal forms, memos, letters, and a financial program. With a series of staccato keystrokes he fired various search requests into the database, using the name "Lumin" in various spellings, "Matson," "Connecticut," and other potential links to the case.

Nothing useful appeared.

"You're rather amazing with that, Ken," she commented, realizing she was practically speaking into his right ear.

"I love computers. So did Melinda. She loved the Internet and surfing the Web."

Kat saw his fingers freeze on the keyboard as he looked part way around toward her. "Lumin lured her in through the Internet, Kat. You probably didn't know that."

"No, I didn't."

"He pretended to be a thirteen-year-old boy who shared her interests. She hid all the e-mail behind a password-protected file, but I knew her password, and when I got in, I found a long, long list of missives the vermin had written to gain her confidence, and I found her long, chatty, innocent answers. She never suspected she was talking to an adult, let alone a monster."

"These were . . . love letters?"

"No. Just pen pal stuff. Mutual interests. That animal had learned how to emulate a young teenage boy incredibly well."

"That was before the charges were dismissed?"

He nodded, launching another search as he typed in a strange sequence of letters and numbers.

"What's that name?" she asked.

"That was his screen name. WWWebster43. It was also his e-mail address, and the police easily traced it to one of his accounts."

The computer churned through a long search routine and repeated the same "No files matching your criteria" message.

Ken leaned forward and searched the skies around them again before dropping his eyes to the list of files once more.

"Just on the outside chance Bostich is a true idiot regarding files, I'm going to try an 'undelete' routine. That restores files the unwary think they've completely erased."

A series of keystrokes started an internal routine on the computer that ground on for nearly a minute before a lengthy list of files popped up.

"Well, well, well. He is computer illiterate." Ken studied the list.

"Ken, what are those files?"

He pointed to the three letters after the period in each filename. "That gives me information on what type of files they are. Wait a minute."

Ken launched a new fusillade of keystrokes into the keyboard and hit the enter button. Page after page of additional files popped up with the same three letters—TIF—as the last part of the filenames.

"What is it, Ken?"

" 'TIF' files are pictures, or graphics. He's got a bunch of them here, and they're all password-protected, and he's tried to erase all of them. I wonder why?"

"How would he have gotten these?"

"If he brought them in with a diskette, I probably won't be able to find out. But if they came in through an Internet connection . . . let's see."

Once again the screens changed in rapid succession as Ken called up more files and programs, then sat back and exhaled sharply.

"What?" Kat asked.

"These picture files came from the Internet, Kat. These aren't official business. These are personal. In fact, he's worked hard to erase the name of the Web site he got them from, which is very interesting."

"I'm not following this, Ken."

He looked around. "There are some Web sites out there a decent person would not want anyone knowing he'd visited."

"You mean sex-related stuff?"

He nodded, returning to the previous list of picture files and typing in a series of commands.

"If I can find the password he uses . . ."

She watched in silence for nearly two minutes as he entered and reentered keystrokes, then sat back for a second and shook his head.

"I'll be damned!"

"What?"

"I thought everyone knew better than to write down a password where someone can find it, but not only has Bostich written it down, he's labeled it."

"Where?"

"In a special word processor file." Ken pulled out a pen and wrote down a series of numbers, 97883PSY, which he then entered as a password.

"First I'm going to check to see if this opens those picture files. I want to make sure this is really his code."

He worked the keys again, opening and closing three files in a row.

"It does. It's his. He's got legal briefs behind this password, too."

Ken launched a graphics program and fired in the command to open one of the recovered picture files, entering the password 97883PSY when prompted. The computer screen dissolved to black for a few minutes, and even over the distant whine of the idling engines she could hear the computer's hard drive chattering away.

Suddenly a picture began to emerge on the color screen. It was just a shadow of a sketch at first, then, as the data transferred from the disk and translated itself into points of colored light on the screen, a more coherent scene.

"It looks like . . ." Kat began, "a shot of a woman, reclining."

Another burst of data brought more detail.

"She's on a . . . a couch of some sort," Kat added, "with her arm around another figure . . . around the head . . . his head . . ."

The computer blinked and added a new screen full of definition, and Kat looked in silence.

"This is going to be pornographic, isn't it?" she asked. "I think she's nude."

He nodded.

"Kat, that's not her arm. That's her leg, and that's an adult male."

A final burst of information completed the picture, and Kat gasped, a feeling of utter revulsion shuddering through her.

"Oh my God!" she said. "Ken, that's a *child*! She couldn't be . . . look at her body! She couldn't be more than nine or ten."

TWENTY-FOUR

Aboard AirBridge Flight 90, Telluride Regional Airport, Colorado. 4:23 P.M.

Wolfe and Bronsky sat in silence, trying not to look at the disgusting color picture covering the screen of Rudy Bostich's personal computer.

Ken cleared his throat at last and shook his head slowly.

"I thought I might luck out and find a letter, a reference, a memo, something incriminating in here. But *kiddie porn*? Even as much as I hate Bostich, I didn't expect this. That little girl isn't any older than Melinda." He groaned as memories of what Melinda must have gone through flooded his mind, consuming him in helpless rage and despair for several moments. With great effort he focused his thoughts once again on the present, rubbed his eyes, and looked over at Kat. "What do we do now, Kat? What do we do?"

With mixed feelings of sympathy for Ken's loss, and relief that he had his emotions under control again, Kat sat back against the wall. "Ken, the mere possession of filth like this is a felony, and it belongs to Bostich. At the minimum, that launches a federal criminal investigation."

Ken turned slightly. "Thanks to your caution, Kat, you had nothing to do with opening those files. Only I did."

She nodded.

Ken fired off another series of keystrokes, saving the one picture to a nonprotected file, then triggering a new one.

Another full color picture of a naked female child feloniously intertwined with a leering adult male swam into view.

"Oh, Lord. I'll bet they're all like this." He triggered a third, and yet another similar color picture emerged.

"Kat, there are at least fifty pictures listed of this type. It would take a while to open them, and I . . . I don't have the stomach for it."

She shook her head. "Nor do I."

Ken looked up from the computer and checked outside before turning to look at Kat, who had moved back to the copilot's seat. He studied her in silence for a few seconds, then took a deep breath and pulled the P.A. microphone from the center pedestal.

> *"Folks, a while ago I forced FBI Agent Katherine Bronsky aboard this aircraft against her will. She's sitting in the copilot's seat right now, and she's been trying her best to end this thing by helping me work out the arrest of Bradley Lumin with her superiors. Now, there's something else you need to know, but first I want Rudolph Bostich to stand in the aisle again by the seat he fled to a while ago. I realize many of you think that since Bostich is a United States Attorney and a big man politically, and I'm just an aggrieved father, I have to be wrong about his lying to a judge, because a man of Bostich's position couldn't possibly have told a lie under oath."*

Ken unsnapped his seatbelt, handed Bostich's computer to Kat, and swung out of his seat just as something moving in the distance caught Kat's attention. As Ken opened the cockpit door, she peered through the left window, making out the outline of a C-130 transport obviously inbound to Telluride.

For a split second she had an impulse to turn and tell Ken, but she stifled it instantly, reminding herself where she was, who she was, and what was happening. The fact that she could have even formed such a thought was sobering.

What's happening to my head? I'm trying to end a hijacking, not help the hijacker!

But the thought of the pictures she had seen sparked a miniature firestorm of anger at a senior law enforcement officer who could even think about possessing such filth.

The C-130 reimposed itself on her consciousness. If the pilots could get in and land before Ken discovered their presence, perhaps they could make a difference.

But Ken's threats rang in her ears, especially the threat to take off if anyone showed up.

She glanced back at him, standing in the door with his back to the windscreen, the cord of the P.A. mike stretched to its limit as he continued to speak.

She looked back to the west again. The C-130 was disappearing to the south behind them. She could see the gray military color, and decided it was probably Air Force, and probably carrying the Hostage Rescue Team at the urgent request of FBI Headquarters.

She reached down to the VHF radio frequency control head and quietly dialed in the universal emergency frequency, 121.5. As Ken pressed the P.A. button behind her, she fingered the transmit switch on the control yoke, trying to decide what to say as Ken's voice rang again in her ears.

"Come on, Bostich. On your feet. I want to be able to see you back there. Annette? Can you hear me?"

Annette appeared just behind Bostich, her hand in the air, her face too distant to read.

"Annette, would you please get the P.A. microphone from the back galley there and stretch it forward so Mr. Bostich can talk to us?"

Ken could see Annette hesitate, then raise her palms to the ceiling and disappear for a second, returning moments later to hand the microphone to a very confused Rudolph Bostich. She talked to Bostich for a few seconds, obviously coaching him on how to press the button on the mike.

"Do you have the mike in your hand, Bostich?"

There were a series of bumps and scrapes with the microphone as Bostich experimented with the button, then held it down.

"What do you want, Wolfe?"

Ken pressed his mike button.

"I want some answers, Bostich, to some simple questions, and folks, please pay close attention. Okay, Rudolph Bostich, do you approve of hardcore pornography?"

Bostich answered instantly.

"No, of course not! What kind of stupid question is that?"

Ken nodded and pushed his P.A. button again.

"The counselor doesn't like the questions, folks. Okay, Rudolph, would-be Attorney General–designate of the United States of America, the second question is: Have you ever purchased, or otherwise obtained, had, or carried around with you anything that could be described as hardcore pornography that clearly involves children under the age of consent?"

Again Bostich's voice bellowed a quick, sneering answer.

"He's insane, people, but for the record, the answer is not only no, but hell, no!"

Ken pressed his button.

"Okay, again you answered no. Now, Rudolph, a little while ago I confiscated your briefcase from the first class overhead compartment over your seat. Inside that briefcase was your computer. So happens, working out the intricacies of computers has long been a hobby of mine, so I went looking in your computer files to see if I could find any evidence you'd lied to that Connecticut judge. By the way, folks, those of you in the rear of the coach cabin, please turn around now and watch his face on this one. Rudolph, do you recognize the personal computer file password 97883PSY?"

Standing in the rear aisle of the 737, with one hand holding the mike, the other on his hip, and a furious scowl on his face, Rudy Bostich at first looked confused. The few dozen passengers who had turned to watch him saw the blood drain from his face and his eyes grow large, his mouth gaping open for a second before he caught himself and tried to return to the fierce expression. He raised the P.A. mike back to his lips.

"NO!"

In the cockpit door, Ken nodded again as he raised the mike.

"Rudolph? One more. Are your answers as truthful as the answer you gave that Connecticut judge when he asked if you had phoned Detective Matson?"

The answer was slow in coming from Bostich.

"Yes, damn you!"

Ken imagined he could see the beads of sweat on Bostich's brow. He glanced back over his shoulder, aware that Kat had leaned around and was watching him with wide eyes.

"Okay, folks. Rudolph Bostich says, in effect under oath here, that the three answers he just gave are all true, just as true as those he gave that Connecticut judge. Well then, Rudolph, can you explain why on your computer I found more than fifty-one picture files downloaded from the Internet, and apparently purchased by you, each one protected by a password, the very same password you just denied you had ever heard about, 97883PSY? Can you tell me why I also found that very same password guarding some very routine legal files with your name on them? The only logical conclusion—in fact, the only feasible conclusion—is that the password you just told us you never heard of is actually your personal memorized password that you know very well, indeed. Folks, for those of you who don't use computers, a password is just a string of numbers and letters that the user memorizes. When you try to look into a computer record later, if it's password-protected, you have to remember

the password to open it. People use passwords when they don't want anyone else to find or read their files."

As Ken spoke, he saw Bostich stagger back and lean against the aft bulkhead.

"You see, I found his password code and opened up three of the picture files which had been protected by Rudolph Bostich's personal password. I wasn't prepared for what I found. All were color photographs. All three showed separate naked adult males in the act of committing unspeakable sexual acts on the same naked little nine- or ten-year-old girl."

There was an audible gasp throughout the aircraft, heads turning to the back, passengers lifting themselves up in their seats to look around at Bostich, who was shaking his head in shock.

"Folks, the mere possession of hardcore kiddie porn is a federal felony."

Ken paused and let his words sink in as he bit his lip and tried to keep the emotion out of his voice.

"So, the bottom line is this. You heard Rudolph Bostich tell you he was AS *truthful with my questions as he was in Connecticut, and you now know for a fact he has just lied to you on all three of my questions. He not only has possessed pornography containing children, he currently carries a computer full of felonious child pornography. He not only knew that password and lied about it, it's his personal password. And, he obviously not only approves of smut, he supports it. Now, folks, ask yourself, who—Bostich or the detective—is more likely to be lying about that Connecticut phone call, a lie that let my daughter's killer go free?"*

Ken let go of the microphone button, not expecting Bostich to press the other microphone against his mouth in sputtering rage.

"You fucking felon! How dare you fabricate an outrageous story like that? There's no truth to that at all, people. He's lying! If there's anything on my computer that shouldn't be there, he put it there, or somebody else did! I would never—"

Ken pressed his mike button again and cut him off.

"Tell you what, folks, let's go one step further. Annette? Take that mike away from the child pornographer back there and get him back in his seat. I'm going back in the cockpit here and I'm going to hand the microphone to FBI Agent Bronsky, who witnessed my excursion through Bostich's computer, although she had nothing to do with the search, since she didn't have a warrant. Agent Bronsky? Please tell the people whether I'm giving them the correct information."

Kat looked up at him with an expression of complete confusion, but she pressed the button and brought the mike to her mouth as Ken nodded, urging her to answer.

"Ah . . . I'm Katherine Bronsky . . . as, ah, Captain Wolfe told you. I am an FBI agent. Look, it isn't my role to be acting as an advocate, but to the extent it might help to know this, yes, what he says . . . what Captain Wolfe has told you about his search, not mine, through Rudolph Bostich's computer, is absolutely accurate. Mr. Bostich's name is on the outside of the computer, so I believe it to be his, and the password that I saw Captain Wolfe find and use unlocked not just the picture files, but normal files as well, which indicates that the pornographic files weren't just accidentally placed there. I also saw something that Captain Wolfe may not have noticed—the date and time one of the password-protected document files was last opened, and that was this morning, apparently at a time just before you would have been boarding the flight in Colorado Springs. So it's pretty damning evidence, and based on what I've seen, the FBI will begin an immediate criminal investigation into Bostich and why he is apparently in possession of such material."

Kat paused, the button still pressed, then put the mike back to her lips.

"One . . . one other thing. You would not believe how stomach-turning this . . . this . . . filth is. These are just little girls, and there are many, many more pictures on that disk that I didn't see."

TWENTY-FIVE

Ft. Collins, Colorado. 3:40 P.M.

"This is command one. No one, I repeat, no one moves until I give the word."

Greg Villias, police chief of Ft. Collins, put down the microphone and raised the fieldglasses to his eyes again, bringing the entrance to the familiar Kmart store swimming into view. Somewhere in there was a fat slob of a child molester known as Bradley Lumin, a two-time East Coast loser suddenly propelled to the FBI's ten most wanted list—and spotted by one of Villias's off-duty officers shopping for socks in the next aisle.

Villias looked down at the unoccupied right seat of his unmarked car, reassuring himself that the warrant was there—a ridiculously routine arrest warrant for jumping bail on several traffic tickets back in Connecticut.

He lifted the fieldglasses again, resting an elbow on the edge of the steering wheel to steady the view.

His officers were excited, and that meant a potential mistake. Lumin was probably not armed, and probably only dangerous to little children, but they couldn't take a chance. Arresting him in a store full of people wasn't the safest method.

Two more customers emerged from the store, a young woman, little more than a child herself, wheeling two infants, followed by her husband pushing a loaded shopping cart.

"Command one, this is four. Subject is finishing at the checkout stand now."

Villias lowered the glasses and found the microphone.

"Shift into position, plain clothes only. Four, you and six stay back."

"Roger."

He started the car and slipped it in gear, rolling slowly toward the entry, the microphone balanced in his right hand as the automatic door began opening, the shape of the unkempt subject visible right behind it.

"Okay, NOW!" he ordered, mentally chiding himself for sounding excited.

A young man in blue jeans began ambling in from the left, a man in a business suit from the right. A female officer carrying a shopping bag moved into the doorway behind. Effortlessly they closed around the corpulent man, the officer in jeans smiling and saying something innocuous as the other leveled a cocked service revolver at his head and the officer behind pulled out the handcuffs.

"Mr. Lumin?"

"Yeah?"

"Sir, I'm Officer Wallace of the Ft. Collins Police, and I'm placing you under arrest pursuant to a warrant from the State of Connecticut. You have the right to remain silent . . ."

Villias could see the man blinking from surprise as the Miranda warning rang in cadence to the snap of the handcuffs.

The police chief changed frequencies and keyed his microphone.

"Dispatch, let the feds know we've got him. No resistance."

Aboard Sage 44, Air National Guard C-130. 3:40 P.M.

The aircraft commander of Sage 44 banked his large, four-engine airlifter back toward the west as he kept his eyes focused on the civilian Boeing 737 jetliner below, which was still sitting on the east end of Telluride's single runway.

A male voice filtering through his headset caused him to look to his right toward the small jumpseat just behind the center console. The lead FBI agent had returned and was fastening his seatbelt.

The aircraft commander, a major, pulled his headset away from his right ear and leaned toward the agent.

"I missed what you said."

The FBI agent nodded. "I was asking if we'd heard anything more from her?"

The major shook his head no. "Only that first transmission on the emergency frequency asking us to stay out of the way, and not to land."

The agent bit his lip momentarily as he craned his neck to see out the left windows, then sat back and leaned close to the major's ear to get through the mighty background rumble of the hulking turboprop's engines.

"I've been on the phone to Washington. My orders are to get us on the ground as fast as possible and try to keep that 737 from taking off. The lady down there is one of ours, but she's a hostage, and Headquarters has already decided to override her recommendations. When you've got a gun to your head, what are you gonna say, right?"

The major cocked his head, a worried expression on his face. "Look, with the wind under ten knots and the pressure altitude so high, the air is very thin, and it takes us more runway to land and stop than it would at sea level. That's why I'd rather wait for him to taxi off that runway before I try to land on it. I mean, he's sitting on the east end, and I could come in from the west end and land toward him, and we'd probably stop just fine. But, if anything went wrong with my bird here on landing rollout, we could end up plowing right into that airplane."

"How about landing *over* him from the east? You know, come in from behind, right over him, and set down on the runway in front of him?"

The pilot looked out at Telluride's airport again, now passing under the left wing.

"Only as a last resort, sir. It'd be safer to plunk this bird down on the west end, because otherwise I'd have to be a hundred feet over the end of the runway to make sure I didn't hit him, and that means I'm going to land pretty far down the runway."

"You're staying to the south right now, aren't you?"

The major nodded. The instructions from the FBI agent on the hijacked aircraft had been specific. "This seven-thirty-seven is facing north," she'd said. "Stay south of the field and stay high, and the captain won't spot you."

So far she was right. The 737 hadn't moved.

The major turned back to the agent. "What are you guys going to do down there anyway? Shoot his tires out?"

The agent shook his head. "I'm not sure. It's pretty delicate. I just need you to get us there as fast as possible. Can you make an approach now?"

The major sighed and looked around.

"I'll get ready to come in from the west. We'll make an assault landing on the first hundred feet of the west end of the runway and honk this baby to the quickest stop possible. We'll need all you guys strapped in. This is an impressive maneuver."

Aboard AirBridge Flight 90, Telluride Regional Airport. 3:40 P.M.

When Kat finished with the P.A., Ken replaced the microphone. They sat in silence for a while, Ken trying to make sense of what they'd found on Bostich's computer, while Kat wondered when and where the C-130 would make its inevitable appearance. Like it or not, Washington was probably ignoring her pleas to stay away. The C-130 would try to land, regardless of the risk, and Ken Wolfe's reaction would be dangerously unpredictable.

The ring of the cabin call chime caught them both by surprise.

Ken answered it rapidly.

"This is Annette, Ken. I'm . . . too stunned and numb to even make much sense, but I have a request."

"Sure, Annette."

"Well, you turned on the phones a while back and told everyone to make whatever calls they wanted, but when we landed here, the built-in seat phones wouldn't work. Maybe I shouldn't tell you this, I don't know . . . I'm so damn confused . . . but you seem to want everyone to know what's happening . . ."

"Your point, please, Annette."

"Okay, okay. There's a CNN correspondent back here about to have a coronary because he thinks he's got the story of the century and I took all the cell phones away hours ago and the seat phones are out and he says they're going to fire him, and on and on. If you want him broadcasting, give me back a cell phone or two. There is cellular service here in Telluride."

Ken rubbed his temple and closed his eyes momentarily. "I know. We've been using one up here. Okay, Annette. Come on up. Knock four times, but don't forget, in case anyone back there has any ideas about trying to subdue me, I'm still holding this trigger."

When Annette entered, Ken pointed to the bag of cellular phones behind his seat. "Take four of them. Tell the reporter to tell the story loud and clear, and if he doesn't believe us about the pictures, I'll bring him up here and show him."

Kat looked around.

"Hi," Annette said. "I am—or at least was—the lead flight attendant, Annette Baxter."

"You still are the lead flight attendant, Annette," Ken said, fatigue audible in his voice.

Kat extended her right hand. "Katherine Bronsky. I, ah, don't exactly have a ticket."

Annette shook Kat's hand and leaned over to pull four of the cellular phones from the bag. She stood then, looking deeply troubled, as Ken watched her, convinced her look of utter disappointment was meant for him.

He diverted his eyes. "I know, Annette. I know," he said softly. "There's no way I could ever adequately apologize—"

"No!" she said sharply. "That's not what I was thinking about. I . . . those pictures. You're serious about those pictures? They're really hardcore child pornography?"

Both Ken and Kat nodded simultaneously, and Ken raised an eyebrow.

"Why?"

Annette sighed and looked at the ceiling momentarily. "I feel dirty, Ken. I feel dirty because I sat next to Bostich earlier." She closed her eyes and shivered. "He touched me at one point when you told us to sit, Ken. He pulled me into a seat. Now, finding out what slimy things are in his mind, it makes my skin crawl."

Kat nodded agreement.

Ken drew a deep breath. "You know what I cannot understand? I can't understand the fact that Rudolph Bostich has a grown daughter named Annie, but he must have at least *some* memories of her at ten and eleven, as a little girl. How on earth could a father with such memories ever tolerate, let alone possess, pictures like what we found?"

Kat exhaled suddenly and reached for the cell phone Ken had hooked into the aircraft's intercom system.

"What?" Ken asked.

She began punching in a flurry of numbers before pausing to glance at him, then at Annette.

"I've been sitting here being stunned when I should have been relaying what we found—what *you* found, Ken," she corrected herself, "to other agents out there who can start asking the right questions."

"You mean, start an investigation right now into his possession of that filth?" Ken asked.

"Well, yes. But what's setting off alarms in my head is the unbelievable coincidence here." She laid the phone in her lap without finishing the number. "To you, Ken, this just confirms he's a liar. But you may be missing the fact that suddenly there's an incredible connection between Bostich and Lumin no one knew anything about before now."

"What do you mean?"

Annette was standing in the doorway, listening in silence.

"Look," Kat said with increasing excitement. "We know Lumin's a pedophile with a long record. Pedophiles by nature sexually abuse, molest, or exploit children, and they're often involved in creating and selling child pornography. Now, the only known connection that existed between Lumin and Bostich before today was the phone call he made to that detective passing the tip that Bradley Lumin was the murderer." She looked at Ken for a few seconds in silence. "And yes, Ken, I do believe Bostich is probably lying about that."

He nodded gravely. "Thank you."

Kat inclined her head in response and continued. "Now, everyone assumes that as a U.S. Attorney, Bostich could only have obtained the information about Lumin's crime through his job. Certainly Bostich could have no personal connections to the sick underworld of kiddie porn, right?"

Annette was nodding. "Right. Just like with my first reaction, he's a fine, upstanding, nationally respected U.S. Attorney."

"Okay," Kat continued. "In other words, we would all assume some low-life informer, someone in the witness protection program, someone Bostich would only encounter professionally, had to have whispered in his ear the shocking information about Lumin, which

Bostich then passed to the detective by phone. That makes sense. What doesn't make sense is his trying to hide that fact later on, especially when he saw it was going to destroy the case against Lumin. Prosecutors live for the opportunity to convict, not acquit. However, if there's a *personal* angle, some personal involvement in that sick world, then it *might* make sense that Bostich wouldn't want a judge asking him questions under oath in a courtroom about where he got the tip that Lumin was the murderer. If he swears he never passed on such a tip, then he'll have no questions to answer about its origin. So, suddenly, with what you found in his computer, there's a *second* connection between the world of Bostich and the world of Lumin."

"Which is," Ken interjected, his eyes wide, "that Bostich may have *known* Lumin because he buys kiddie porn?"

Kat shook her head. "I doubt Bostich knew a slimy character like Lumin directly, but the connection is their mutual possession of kiddie porn."

Ken sat forward, his eyebrows raised. "Kat, you may not know they also found . . . the Connecticut police did . . . a picture . . ." He stopped and fought for control, diverting his eyes to the floor for a few seconds as he tried to get his voice steady again. "A picture of Melinda while Lumin had her, a picture he probably intended to sell to people as sick as he. They also found other similar pictures involving other little girls, none of whom they identified. It's all in the record of what they confiscated."

Kat sighed and nodded. "No, I wasn't fully aware of that, but it supports my theory. Lumin was a user, maybe even a provider, of the very sort of sickening smut we've just found in Bostich's computer. Somehow, somewhere, their paths may touch a common denominator, a place, a market, a Web site, an e-mail address . . . something. Maybe even an individual they both know."

Annette shifted her position in the doorway, her eyes on Kat. "Are you saying that since Bostich and this Lumin character like the same filth, even if they didn't know each other, Bostich may have learned about Lumin from . . . from someone else involved in kiddie porn? I mean, say he was secretly running in filthy circles like that, and someone said, 'Hey, Rudy, one of my customers over there did that murder,' or maybe, God forbid, someone offered him a picture of Captain

Wolfe's daughter, he recognized it, and was able to track it back to Lumin?"

Kat turned to look Annette full in the face. "Absolutely, Annette. That's a good theory, in fact. You can see how that sort of connection could easily explain why Bostich would elect to destroy the murder prosecution he, himself, started, rather than admit where he got the information."

Ken had turned to the front windscreen more in reaction than to search for air traffic, but the sudden movement of his head to the left caught Kat's immediate attention. A huge, gray Lockheed C-130 was in a turn to final approach runway nine, the opposite end of the runway they were occupying.

"Oh, Christ!" Ken exclaimed as he yanked at the parking brake handle on the center console and shoved the throttles up.

"Annette? Better go sit down or grab something. I'm going to have to move the airplane." He reached up and snapped on the FASTEN SEATBELT sign.

"Are we taking off?" she asked.

"No, just taxiing fast."

Annette nodded and moved back out of the cockpit to grab the P.A. microphone.

"This is Annette, folks. The captain is repositioning the aircraft, not taking off, but please brace yourselves."

TWENTY-SIX

Aboard AirBridge Flight 90, Telluride Regional Airport.
3:45 P.M.

As Kat Bronsky watched, the C-130 transport carrying the FBI's Hostage Rescue Team turned toward Telluride's only runway, the long, straight wings of the powerful turboprop reflecting the afternoon sun with a sudden flash.

"Ken, what are you going to do?" Kat asked, her eyes on the C-130 as it moved through the final twenty-five degrees of its turn.

"Deny them the runway, Kat," Ken Wolfe replied quietly, his right hand already shoving the 737's two throttles forward as the Boeing began to move.

The engines accelerated and the 737 began to accelerate, lurching to the left as Ken aligned the Boeing with the runway then reached up and snapped on the landing lights.

The C-130 was leveling its wings, fully aligned with the runway and heading straight at them, about a mile from the departure end.

"Call out my airspeed, Kat," Ken commanded, and she found her eyes latching instantly onto the airspeed indicator, the words tumbling out of her mouth before she could mentally remind herself that a nonpilot wouldn't necessarily know what he meant.

"Forty-five knots, fifty, sixty, seventy knots, eighty knots, Ken," she said. At the eighty-knot call he suddenly yanked the throttles back to idle, letting the 737 continue to roll down the runway, the midpoint coming up fast.

The extremely bright landing lights of the C-130 now shone in their faces as the big four-engine turboprop hurtled into the last portion of its approach less than a half mile out.

Ken deployed the speed brake and the thrust reversers as he stepped on the brakes, throwing them forward slightly, the 737 slowing as it neared the halfway point.

The C-130 was still moving toward them, the two aircraft approaching each other with a combined speed of over two hundred miles per hour, the Boeing blocking all but the first thirty-five hundred feet of the runway.

"Blink, dammit!" Ken muttered, his eyes on the approaching C-130.

"Can he land and stop short of us?" Kat asked.

"Not a chance at this altitude. Too much runway needed. Maybe lower."

"What if he tries? Could you get out of his way?"

Kat saw a taxiway to their right leading to the terminal that looked like an escape route, but Ken was shaking his head no as the C-130 floated across the threshold of the western end of the runway, still bearing down on the concrete surface.

"I don't believe it!" Ken cried out. "He's going to try it. He's playing chicken."

Aboard Gulfstream N5LL, Telluride Regional Airport. 3:45 P.M.

Dane had called to Bill North to come forward the second it was obvious the C-130 was going to attempt a landing. By the time he entered the cockpit, the 737 had begun moving down the runway in the opposite direction.

"What have we got, Dane?"

"A dangerous game, it appears. Wolfe is probably going to try to block the runway."

"He's not trying a takeoff?"

Dane shook his head. "God, I hope not!"

Aboard AirBridge Flight 90, Telluride Regional Airport. 3:47 P.M.

"Ken, they won't try to disable you, honest. Go ahead and taxi clear. Let him land."

"No way! They're not listening to you any more, Kat, remember? I wish they were. They're here to attack."

She was shaking her head, the image of the C-130 now flaring less than three thousand feet ahead of them filling her mind. "They won't risk the passengers, Ken."

"They're risking them now!" he said, pushing the power up and releasing the brakes.

The lights of the big Lockheed C-130 were growing huge before them. The aircraft had to be less than three thousand feet from the nose of the Boeing, the wheels not yet on the ground, the oncoming angle mixing with the bright landing lights in a confusing mix of images that obscured the sudden burst of smoke from the four turboprops as the aircraft commander shoved the thrust levers up and pulled back on his yoke, ordering gear up as the C-130 leapt back into the air.

Kat had been holding her breath. She saw the C-130 begin to climb and exhaled loudly. Ken, she saw, was once again stepping on the brakes as the C-130 passed safely several hundred feet overhead with a thunderous roar.

When the Boeing had slowed to a safe speed, Ken swiveled the nose wheel around and turned the 737 toward the opposite end of the runway to watch the C-130 climb out toward Telluride for a half mile, then begin a tight right turn to head back down the valley to the west.

"What now, Ken?"

"You had a phone call to make," he said. "Please make it. I'm simply going to keep taxiing around to keep them off this runway."

She picked up the cellular phone with her eyes still glued to the turning C-130 and her mind in a quandary over whom to call. Frank was off the case, but could probably help. Yet, if she called Washington, maybe she could talk them into waving off this stupid assault effort.

The number of Frank's cellular was clear in her mind, and she entered it and jabbed at the send button, grateful to hear the sound of cellular circuits obediently connecting the call.

Frank's voice answered immediately, and she explained the C-130 first, begging his intervention with their FBI counterparts in D.C.

"Kat, they consider you compromised and they're not interested in my opinion either. I've tried. I, ah, assume the captain is listening to me as well?"

She could see Ken nod in her peripheral vision as he worked on taxiing the aircraft and tracking the C-130.

"He's on as well, Frank, through his headset. He's got this phone hooked into the aircraft's intercom system. Frank, are you wielding a pen near some paper?"

"Anything you need, Kat."

"Where are you?"

"Just arrived back at our offices."

"You have unrestricted use of the normal channels?"

There was a small snort from the other end. "Of course, Kat, I'm not the hostage under scrutiny. I'm just out of the loop."

"Not anymore. Listen closely. I need some creative telephone legwork and probably computer searching. There's a new connection between Bostich and Bradley Lumin."

She described quickly the digitalized pornography found on Rudy Bostich's computer, the fact that she had not contaminated the evidence, and the apparent fact that the pictures had been downloaded over a phone line.

"Jesus Christ! I'm stunned, Kat, and I don't stun easily anymore."

"Frank, can I safely search the database on this computer for tracking information? If I could find an e-mail address or a World Wide Web site, something to track back, it could be the key, but I don't want to ruin the admissibility."

Ken was looking at her suddenly, looking surprised. "You're computer proficient?" he asked.

She nodded. "I could have broken that password even faster than you did, Ken. I'm well trained."

Frank's voice was in her ear. "I can't hear you, Kat. Speak up."

She moved the phone back to her mouth, rearranging the cord that connected it to the aircraft's communication system, and repeated the question.

"Kat, if what you find now is simply part of a trail that leads us somewhere else, I believe we're okay legally. You were right about the picture files. But now that we know about them, this is like finding part of a body on the backseat of a car in plain view. That's probable cause to continue the search. The pictures found by the captain are probable cause. Go to it."

"Great!" she said.

"What can I do here?" he asked.

"The number one question, Frank, is how to connect Lumin and

Bostich. Could you dive into background checks, home towns, schools, proximity of residences, anything you can think of? Maybe Lumin worked for Bostich as a yardman or something. Maybe they did business with an unusual company and we could track the commonality through credit card records. Maybe the smut they're buying came from a source on the Web that takes credit cards. Do anything you can think of, while I surf his database and look for any thread to follow."

"You're convinced there's a direct connection?"

"Frank, you're the one who keeps pounding into me the reality that few coincidences really are. If this *was* a coincidence, it'd be a doozy."

"Understood. How do I call you back?"

She passed the number of the cell phone. "If that doesn't work," she added, "I'll call you back in fifteen minutes."

"Kat, since Captain Wolfe is listening, would he consider just shutting things down there and waiting for us to get this down? After all, if we find this connection, we may be able to show Bostich was lying whether he signs a confession or not. I mean, we're doing exactly what he's demanded and more."

Ken's voice cut in on the conversation, startling Kat.

"Look, Frank, I don't know your last name. This is Ken Wolfe. I'll be happy to wait if you can get rid of this damn C-130 that's trying to drop in here. I know they've got some sort of assault team on board, and I'm not going to tolerate any commando tricks while I wait for you people to catch Lumin."

The response from Salt Lake City was rapid. "I'm going to try, Captain, but you've got to keep those people safe and not harm anyone, even by accident."

"The only ones I want to harm are Lumin and Bostich," Ken replied. "But remind them in Washington I'm one flick of a finger away from blowing this airplane off the map. Don't let them forget that for a moment."

Kat looked back at the forward panel, seeing nothing, her mind darting after a dozen possibilities at once.

"Another thing, Frank," she said into the phone. "Get that detective on the phone in Connecticut. Detective Matson. Tell him what I've found. See if he can connect the dots somewhere."

"Will do, Kat. I'll try to hold off the Air Force plane. If I can't, however, please make the captain understand that no one's going to attack or try to disable the airplane unless he does something very rash."

"He doesn't believe that, Frank."

She disconnected as Ken finished taxiing the 737 to the east end of the runway.

"Where is he now?" Kat asked.

Ken's eyes were searching the far horizon. "He disappeared down the valley back west."

"Good. So he's probably out of here for a while."

Ken shook his head no. "I doubt it. He's probably looking for a wide spot to turn around in without my seeing him."

She reached behind the captain's seat and grabbed Bostich's computer as Ken turned the aircraft back toward the west once more.

"I probably shook him up, Kat, but if his orders say to land here—"

Ken stopped, straining forward, his eyes focused on the far end of the runway as she followed his gaze. Something was wavering just above the grass in the distance, something indistinct and undulating, but moving. Suddenly the shape coalesced into a C-130 as the transport leapt above the edge of the mesa into full view.

"Dammit!" Ken's hand shot to the throttles and shoved them forward again as the C-130 bore down on the far end of the runway, its landing lights off this time.

"Where did he come from?" Kat asked.

"He made a tight turn down in the valley below the level of this runway and then popped over the ridge to catch me by surprise."

The 737 gained speed, and once more Ken reached up and snapped on the landing lights as the big Lockheed transport roared toward them at over a hundred and forty miles per hour.

"Airspeed!" Ken demanded once again.

"Ah . . . forty, fifty . . ."

"Call eighty."

"Okay, we're sixty."

"If he lands and reverses those props, we'll hit," Ken muttered to himself, the power still up as the 737 continued to accelerate.

The C-130 was flaring slightly, its wheels nearing the runway surface, the engine power pulled back as the pilot waited to slam on the runway in an assault landing.

"Eighty knots!" She looked at Ken's right hand, expecting him to yank the throttles back. Instead, he pushed the thrust levers forward even more, his eyes glancing to the center panel to check the maximum thrust readings.

"Ninety knots. Ken, this is awfully fast! We have enough room to stop?"

There was no answer.

The C-130 loomed frighteningly close, its wheels touching the runway in a puff of rubberized smoke, the large machine barreling toward them.

"One hundred knots! Ken, stop!"

Her eyes left the airspeed indicator and snapped to the oncoming airplane in time to see it suddenly pitch up, its huge four-bladed propellers clawing the air as its pilot commanded an instant leap from the surface in the face of the onrushing 737.

"He's off! He's off!" Kat cried, her eyes glued to the underbelly of the C-130 as it hung in front of them, slowly lifting out of the way like a reluctant whale.

But she realized with a hopeless feeling the 737's throttles were still full forward.

She glanced at the airspeed again.

Jesus! One hundred ten!

The end of the runway was visible beneath the hulking image of the C-130, the threshold much closer than she'd figured.

"Ken, he's already off. What are you doing? WHAT ARE YOU DOING?"

"We're too fast to stop, Kat," he said calmly.

The rumble and roar of the C-130 passing just above them sent vibrations of terror through her. She expected an impact with the 737's tail. The whole sky seemed to be filled with C-130. There was no way they could avoid a collision.

But as rapidly as it had smothered them with soul-rattling noise, the C-130 rumbled overhead and was gone without impact.

Now it was merely the end of the runway threatening them, hurtling at them.

Kat's eyes locked on the airspeed indicator.

"One hundred twenty-five knots. What do we need to fly?"

"One forty-eight is rotate speed," he said.

Less than a thousand feet of runway remained. She could see the red lights marking the western end of the runway and the grassy area beyond, a tiny overrun leading to the edge of the cliff. Even if he tried to stop now, they would slide over the cliff.

Time began to dilate, their speed seeming almost laconic, as her mind accelerated into an unreal dimension.

"One hundred thirty-five," she heard herself say. Fifteen knots less than flying speed, and only a little concrete left. She wondered if the 737's wheels would break the red lights when they rolled across them.

The control yoke was coming back in her lap as Ken pulled, the control column touching the edge of Bostich's computer, which she instantly moved out of the way.

The last of the runway disappeared in a heartbeat just as the Boeing's nose jumped up in response to Ken's commands, the deck angle of the 737 increasing rapidly, the yoke back in her stomach as he pulled, the distant roar of the engines sounding too puny to help them now.

We're off the end!

There was a shudder somewhere behind them and a sudden feeling of climbing, rising, but the fact that the main landing gear had lifted from the last few feet of the runway didn't sink in until Ken snapped a quick command in her direction.

"Gear up! Kat. The wheel-shaped lever. Pull it up."

Kat reached forward with her left hand and pulled the lever with the small wheel on it, snapping it to the up position, feeling the instant hydraulic response as the gear began its retraction sequence just as the terrain ahead disappeared and the control column in front of her began to vibrate furiously.

"What's that?" she asked, startled

"Stall warning."

He pushed forward on the yoke, dropping the nose of the 737, and banked the jet slightly to the left as they soared above the edge of the mesa and out over a narrow valley, clawing for airspeed.

A highway was visible to the left, along with another huge mesa, and a cliff somewhat ahead of them.

The control columns were still being shaken by the stall warning system, the 737 on the ragged edge of a stall, its airspeed too little to sustain flight more than a few feet above a flat surface—the phenomenon called "ground effect," which disappeared with the mesa.

They were half-flying, half-falling. Kat felt herself get light in the copilot's seat as the Boeing dropped into the abyss, the passengers and crew of Flight 90 experiencing less than one half of normal gravity.

Ken was banking slightly to the left, trying to line up with the highway that snaked down the valley to the west, trading altitude for airspeed as the jet accelerated.

The vibrating stopped!

Just as quickly as it had started, the control columns stopped shaking, the tiny electronic mind of the stall warning system having declared that they were once again flying.

But they were also still descending, the highway looming large in the windscreen.

Kat felt a surrealistic calm as the hundred-thousand-pound jetliner dropped toward it at well over a hundred fifty miles per hour.

Ken's right hand snaked out and snapped the flap lever partially up to a detent labeled two degrees. He was banking back to the right, the jet aligned over the highway some one hundred feet below them, a cliff on the right, a mesa on the left, the surfaces of both soaring many hundreds of feet higher than they were flying.

He's going to follow the highway and gain speed down the middle of this little canyon.

She glanced at the airspeed. It was showing a hundred and eighty now and increasing steadily, the engines still pulsing a dull roar through the cockpit.

There were cars on the road below, and she imagined the shock of the drivers as they looked up to see the big jet flying at what would seem treetop level down the highway, an image at once undeniable and nonsensical.

Two hundred knots!

She felt gravity once again pressing her down in the right seat as Ken Wolfe leveled the 737 and began to climb. The walls of the mesas on either side began to sink, and suddenly fall away as the Boeing soared above the surface of the surrounding terrain, climbing smartly, the captain pulling back the throttles slightly and adjusting the engines to climb power.

Kat took inventory of her senses and found them abused but recovering. Her heart was pounding, her breathing rapid, but the increasing altitude and airspeed were a magical tonic and a wave of relief swept through her as she leaned back in the seat, cognizant of Ken's hand moving the flap lever to the full up position.

He glanced at her. "Thank's for the help. You did good."

"Thank you, I think."

"You've flown before, haven't you?"

Alarm bells went off in her head.

"I've been in a few cockpits before. You know, FBI aircraft and such. Someday I'd like to learn to fly, but I doubt I can."

Ken searched the horizon before looking hard at her, searching her face, reading, she was sure, the telltale signs that she was lying through her teeth.

"You'd enjoy it," he said at last, looking back at the instruments. "I know I'm going to miss it terribly."

She let a few seconds of silence pass, her mind trying to grapple with the priorities she faced. Three minutes ago she had expected they would remain in Telluride. Suddenly they were airborne again, with a major mystery before her and little or no time to solve it for a disturbed man who wanted the impossible done immediately.

Kat looked at Ken Wolfe, unable to resist the question.

"Was that a guess, Ken?"

He looked puzzled. "What?"

"You said I should trust you about a takeoff, but we almost crashed."

He was shaking his head. "No, we didn't. That was exactly what I expected. Get it a few feet above the runway, suck up the gear, fly it off the cliff and accelerate. Worked perfectly. I just hadn't expected to go yet."

"So what are you planning now?"

He snorted and shook his head as his eyes remained ahead.

"The basic equation is the same, Kat, despite what we've found Bostich carrying. Lumin must be taken, the grand jury has to indict, and Bostich has to confess or be nailed on that lie so the state warrant can be reinstated."

"We're halfway there, Ken."

He turned and looked at her, his eyes tired, wearing an expression of sad determination.

"Kat, halfway isn't good enough to a man who has no time left."

She sighed loud and long. "Look, Bostich is toast after what you found, and Lumin will be arrested any minute. There's no reason to keep this hijacking going any longer. Let's get this thing on the ground and let all the people off safely. You know that the criminal penalties for what you're doing are severe, but if you end it now and without anyone getting hurt, there is hope for you."

He was shaking his head slowly.

"There's no hope for me, Kat. There hasn't been for a long time."

"You don't know that!"

"Kat, it *is* over for me."

She shook her head in disgust. "Stop being fatalistic and assuming your life is finished. Due process takes a long time, and a lot can happen. You just have to wait and see."

"I don't intend to wait."

"What else *can* you do but wait and see?"

"Kat, you need to understand something here," he replied, his eyes on the center pedestal for a while before he raised them up to search hers. "I didn't take that deputy's pistol to shoot Bostich."

TWENTY-SEVEN

Aboard AirBridge Flight 90. 3:52 P.M.

When it was apparent they were going to stay in the air without hitting something, Annette Baxter left the forward jumpseat and moved into the cabin to take inventory of her wide-eyed passengers.

She could see Kevin and Bev doing the same thing in the rear of the cabin, both of them avoiding the last row where Rudy Bostich was sulking.

Louise Richardson, alone now in first class, waved at Annette and motioned to a notebook.

"I'm trying to do something useful. I'm trying to take notes on all of this."

Annette smiled at her and moved into the coach cabin as the P.A. came alive.

> *"Folks, this is Ken Wolfe again. I had not planned on taking off from Telluride, at least not yet. But I had no choice. That roar you heard overhead while we were on takeoff roll was an Air Force transport trying to land to bring in a team of federal agents to deal with me. That's why I had to get us airborne, because this isn't over yet and I don't want to subject you—or me—to possible commando tactics. Now. Where are we going? The answer is, I don't know. I'm waiting for the government to tell me that my daughter's killer is in custody, and that a grand jury has handed down a federal indictment. Both things should be forthcoming. The last item depends on Mr. Kiddie Porn back there. Bostich. I must have his confession to end this. So, if any of you would like to say anything to a man who buys pictures of little children being sexually abused, please be my guest. The sooner Bostich is ready to admit he lied, the*

sooner I'll put this aircraft safely on the ground somewhere and let you go. Oh, and the phones should work again now that we have some altitude, so please use them all you like."

Annette had been looking at the rear of the cabin when Elvira Gates's hand reached for her sleeve, and she looked down to see the fear-of-flying group leader looking up at her with an expression of grim determination.

"You okay, Elvira?"

"That would depend," Elvira replied.

"On what?"

She ignored the question, her eyes boring into Annette's.

"I need to ask you a question, my dear, and I need an honest answer."

Annette knelt beside her. "Of course."

"Is your captain telling us the truth about his daughter?"

"Yes, I believe he is."

Elvira Gates nodded slowly and looked over her shoulder briefly toward the rear of the airplane, then back at Annette. "I'm well aware that what he's doing is criminal, but we've come this far . . ."

Annette shook her head. "What are you saying, Elvira?"

"I took a poll of my people. We're all willing—all but one—to stay hostages until Mr. Bostich owns up to what he did."

Annette was in the process of answering when a flurry of activity several rows back caught her eye.

Mike Clark, the retired police detective who'd spoken with Ken Wolfe earlier, was on his feet, charging toward the back of the cabin with an angry scowl on his face.

Annette stood up, unsure what to do.

Clark brushed past Kevin and moved rapidly to Rudy Bostich's row as Annette began walking in the same direction. She could hear Clark's angry voice ten rows away.

"Bostich, you sorry sonofabitch, you're holding all of us hostage here, and by all the evidence I've heard, you're guilty as hell!"

Bostich's reply was sullen and almost inaudible. "I don't confess to things I haven't done."

"Then you're going to get us all killed."

"Who the hell are you?" Bostich snarled.

"Who the hell am I? I'm Detective Mike Clark, retired. And you, you bastard, are obviously a liar and everyone on this airplane knows it. But it so happens I already know you by reputation, Bostich. You defamed a good friend of mine back in Connecticut. Roger Matson. He's as honest and upright a man as I've ever seen. That's enough reason to distrust you, but now we find out from the FBI you're a child pornography customer to boot. *Jesus*!" Clark had his fists knotted, restraining himself with considerable effort. "You did it, dirtbag, and you're going to confess to it!"

Bostich had his jaw set, his eyes squinted, and his body molded against the seat and window in a defensive posture as he glowered back at the detective.

"I had no such things on my computer. This is some sort of amateurish attempt by the captain to force a false confession out of me, and it isn't going to work."

"So how about the FBI agent up there, Bostich? She in collusion?"

Bostich shrugged. "She's a hostage. He probably threatened her to get her to say those things. If there's anything on that computer that shouldn't be there, Wolfe planted it."

"Yeah, Mr. Prosecutor, like I haven't heard that excuse from every drug dealer I ever met." He raised his voice to a mocking falsetto. " '*Oh, dear! You mean you found three hundred pounds of crack in my basement right next to the methamphetamine lab? What a shock! That isn't mine, Officer. I have no idea where it came from.*' Right, Bostich! Try again."

Bostich snorted derisively. "If that maniac up there really found anything, he'd be looking at the shadowy remains of files that were there once, but were erased before I bought the computer. What are you, anyway, some hick town constable? You planning to rough me up if I don't confess, Marshal Earp? Go crawl back under your rock. The felon in the cockpit is simply manipulating you, and you're too stupid to realize it."

Without a flicker of warning, the detective's beefy hand shot out and grabbed Bostich by the collar, hauling him bodily across two airline seats and pinning him against the back wall behind the last row. Annette moved forward to stop him, then thought better of it and paused to watch as the big man put his face within inches of Bostich's, his voice a guttural growl.

"Get this, scumbag! You're talking to Detective Mike Clark of the Providence Police, thirty-eight years on the force, now retired with no intention of being a victim of your stupidity. I know your type, Bostich. Another slimy, slippery, snob of a legal whore who thinks he's better than the rest of us. Captain Wolfe up there is certainly committing a bag full of felonious acts, but he's sure got *your* sorry hide pegged. You're the one holding us here, and that stops now."

With one large hand intertwined in Bostich's collar, Clark pulled him forward and slammed him back against the bulkhead again.

"You open your arrogant mouth one more time, Bostich, it'd better be to confess you set up my friend Matson and lied in that hearing."

"Or . . . what?" Bostich asked, struggling to get the words out.

The retired detective looked around, aware several other passengers had been gathering behind him. There were at least six men, he realized, and one of them had a ready answer, a furious expression on his face.

"Let's dump this bag of garbage out the door. I don't want to share air in here with anyone who likes kiddie porn."

Another echoed the same idea, and two other passengers, one male, one female, stood in nearby rows nodding agreement as Bostich's eyes began to grow wide with fright.

"That dumping idea sounds good," another passenger suggested, a dead serious expression on his face.

Clark read Bostich's reaction.

"Well, well, well. You're scared of heights, aren't you, *Counselor*?"

Bostich's left hand began clawing for the back of the seat while his right tried unsuccessfully to drag Clark's hand from his throat; but he was no match for the muscular detective.

With utter contempt, Mike Clark propelled Bostich back toward the window seat, letting him fall sideways painfully on the arm rest.

"I'm going forward now to suggest to Captain Wolfe he consider that idea . . . depressurizing and tossing you overboard if you don't talk." He looked around, as if calculating the distance to the nearest exit, then smiled a gleeful smile at the thoroughly panicked Bostich. "And as the man says, I know just which one of these hatches to open."

"Don't be ridiculous," Bostich stammered. "You . . . can't do that! You'd be committing murder!"

Mike Clark raised his eyebrows in mock surprise. "Really? You mean when a hijacker with a bomb orders me to do something or get blown up, that's murder? I don't think so." He turned to the others. "You folks think I'd have a choice?"

A chorus of "No's" reached Bostich's ears.

"They say no, Mr. Kiddie Porn. So do I."

Clark stood and turned to move forward. Annette had been watching the faces of the others in alarm, wondering if the detective knew he was inciting a lynch mob. There were no smiles, only fury—all of it directed at Bostich.

She caught Clark's eye and raised her hand. "Look, we all want this over, but—"

"We're going to give him a chance to admit what he did before we shove him out, ma'am," the detective said in a loud voice Bostich could hear. "But he's not getting away with this."

Clark walked to Annette, his voice dropping to a whisper. "Don't worry, I'm not starting a riot. I'm just trying to shake him up."

She studied his face for a second before nodding and looking at the others crowding the aisle.

"You . . . *talked* to these people in advance?"

He nodded.

"I just don't see how assaulting the man is going to extract a confession from him that would be usable anywhere."

"It won't directly," Clark told her. "But I've dealt with this type of arrogant garbage for decades, ma'am, and they have to be terrified before their little shell cracks. Don't do anything to make him think we *won't* throw him out, okay?"

She shook her head. "I can't participate—"

He raised an index finger and smiled. "Trust an old Irish cop, will you? Just don't damage the illusion."

She nodded at last and he smiled at her. "I'm going to walk to first class now and disappear like I was talking to the Captain. Okay?"

"Okay," Annette replied.

Bostich had retreated back into his corner, his eyes out the window as he rubbed his neck. A well-dressed member of the fear-of-flying group leaned over the aisle seat toward Bostich, causing him to look up. "You *did* recognize that fellow, didn't you?" the man asked, smiling.

Bostich said nothing for several seconds, then shook his head no.

"Interesting, and you a prosecutor." The man glanced forward as if checking to make sure Clark was gone, then looked Bostich in the eye. "On the Providence force he was known as Mad Mike. The mob hated him, but respected him enough to try to hire him as an enforcer after he retired last year. Mad Mike's wiggled out of more police brutality charges than anyone can count, because he always got a confession, and it always held up, though it's true that there were a lot of suicides after his interrogations. Very odd, that. Criminals just seemed to jump off ledges or drown themselves in toilets in his presence." He straightened up. "Think about it, Bostich. We're all tired of you. Mad Mike will encounter no resistance from this group, whatever he decides to do."

The man moved forward up the aisle as Annette caught his arm.

"That was part of the ruse, right? You're not serious about Detective Clark being a rogue?"

The man turned and regarded her with a smile. "Who?"

"Detective Clark. You called him 'Mad Mike' and I—" His reaction finally sank in, and she rolled her eyes and smiled. "Okay, I understand."

He dropped his voice. "Never heard of him before in my life."

Aboard Gulfstream N5LL. 3:52 P.M.

The heart-stopping sight of the AirBridge 737 lumbering down the abbreviated runway and barely clearing the rise at the far end had left Dane Bailey, Jeff Jayson, and Bill North stunned.

The lack of an immediate column of smoke from the same direction had given little hope.

Dane was the first to snatch up a cell phone and punch in 911 to relay what had happened, and what they all suspected. But the sheriff's dispatcher had received no other citizen calls, and no reports of a crash down the valley.

When they'd recovered enough from the shock to wonder if Flight 90 might have survived, Dane Bailey began cranking the Gulfstream's engines for a rapid departure to the west—the same direction the AirBridge flight had gone.

They were airborne within three minutes, climbing west, Jeff spotting the 737 in the distance at last as it climbed rapidly.

All three men exhaled with relief.

Bill North was kneeling where Kat had been between the pilot's seats. He gestured to the 737 ahead. "Do you suppose they're monitoring the same frequencies?"

Dane and Jeff both nodded and Bill reached for a headset.

"Kat, you still there? This is Bill North."

Several moments elapsed before the sound of her voice filled their ears.

"I'm here, Bill."

"Look, we're, ah, we're back here chasing you at a distance again, because I figured you'd need our help in relaying your calls."

"Thank you, Bill! You're absolutely right. I know we're going to run out of range of the cellulars at some point."

"Anything we can check for you now? Does the captain need the weather for anywhere?"

"I'll let you know. Wait, he's motioning to me." She was off the radio but came back on almost immediately. "Okay, we need weather for Denver . . . and Colorado Springs."

"I'll get back to you, Kat."

Bill North glanced up at Jeff Jayson, the copilot, who was already dialing in a special frequency for weather information.

Aboard AirBridge Flight 90. 4:01 P.M.

With word relayed from N5LL that heavy thunderstorms were bearing down on Denver, Ken Wolfe turned the 737 back toward the southwest as he talked to Denver's Air Traffic Control Center and climbed to thirty-five thousand feet, the aircraft's radar transponder now on and displaying their position to the controller.

Kat had buried herself in Bostich's computer, unleashing repeated search requests as she verified Ken's conclusions that there were precisely fifty-one downloaded pornographic picture files that Bostich, or someone barely capable of using a computer, had tried to get rid of, not realizing there was a program in the same computer for putting erased files back together.

All the original names of the picture files had been lost, but they bore the same markings and characteristics, and Kat opened a dozen of them to make sure, trying to distance herself each time from the sick perversions that flashed on the liquid crystal color screen time after time.

One of the filenames had survived in fragments, but it was an indecipherable jumble of letters beginning with W. Promising herself it would be the last disgusting image she looked at, Kat gave the computer the command to display the picture.

There had been no warning voice in her head, no particular intuitive caution to insulate her from what appeared next. The picture of a naked little girl began to assemble itself on the screen, and from the first, she saw it was different. There were no artificial, leering smiles of a victimizer with a child, and no male face in the shot—though a male was obscenely present. The little girl was prepubescent, but there was no sick pretense of fun. She was tied to a chair, her hair matted, burns and cuts on her torso, her face contorted by pain.

There were other things in the picture as well, depraved, disgusting things, and Kat looked away, fighting a wave a nausea as she realized she had seen the little eleven-year-old's face less than an hour before on the center pedestal.

It was Melinda Wolfe.

Kat quickly hit the escape key and removed the picture from the screen before Ken could glance over. Her mind was racing through the possibilities.

She checked the computer's directory again, verifying that the picture bore codes showing it had come through an Internet connection.

It can't be an old evidence file. You don't send evidence files through the Internet.

It was possible the fifty-one shots were some bizarre research project, but not probable. Undoubtedly he would claim all the pictures were either an erased evidence file, or that they had been on the computer before he bought it, but it would be easy enough to check the computer's purchase date and chain of possession.

The presence of a doubt, however, meant Bostich might be able to avoid prison.

If we had the time, she reminded herself. But there was no time to map out a careful investigatory campaign. There was no time for background research.

But why was Melinda's tortured image on *his* hard drive?

Stay focused! she told herself. *Priority number one is to prove Bostich lied to that judge about the tip to Matson. But how do we do that before Wolfe loses patience? How can I give him what he wants so we can end this before his finger slips on that button?*

Kat looked down at the screen, which was now displaying long lists of programs. There was an Internet access program she hadn't noticed before and she opened it.

The program contained a history file of sorts—an archive—that might still contain a list of the Web sites and e-mail addresses the computer had contacted.

Kat glanced over at Ken, who was absorbed in flying. He knew she was trying to find something, trying to help. There would be at least a few minutes to work.

She probed more deeply into the program, trying to remember the particular commands for the archive file, hoping that a computer user like Bostich, who didn't know about the ability of his machine to reconstruct "erased" files, might also have left a clear record of which Internet and Web sites he'd visited.

She triggered the archive file which opened up suddenly, cascading e-mail addresses and sites on the World Wide Web in dizzying detail.

Kat's fingers danced over the keyboard, extracting the dates and times of the picture downloads from the jumble of information, then matching them to the list of addresses until the one she was looking for stood highlighted on the screen.

SHRDLU2.

Somehow it had a familiar ring, but why? The e-mail address was accessed through a major provider of Internet service, but it could belong to anyone with a portable computer and the few dollars a month needed to buy such an address.

Did he rent his own private, clandestine little e-mail address?

A more worrisome reality crossed her mind. A man like Bostich might not know computers very well, but he'd know better than to buy illegal pornography with a credit card. He would use untraceable cash, which meant that either personal contact or use of the mail would be required to transfer the cash for each purchase of porn. Either method would be difficult to trace. She might be able to prove that Bostich had contacted whatever smut merchant lurked behind SHRDLU2, but fail to prove he'd actually paid money for their "product."

Who is SHRDLU2? Where is SHRDLU2? If we can find the answer to that, we may find how Bostich is really connected to Lumin.

"Making any progress, Kat?" Ken's voice caused her to jump. She looked up surprised at how deep in thought she'd been. She related her findings, omitting the discovery of Melinda's image. She reported the e-mail address, disappointed that he shook his head when she asked if it sounded familiar.

"What's that ringing, Kat?" Ken asked. She looked to her right and realized the sound was coming from the small cellular phone she'd been using earlier. She fumbled for it, flipping open the cover.

"Hello?"

"Ah, is this Agent Bronsky?"

"Yes . . . yes it is. Who's this?"

"Detective Roger Matson," he replied, his voice calm and even. "Agent Frank Bothell in Salt Lake called me and gave me this number, and explained where you were, and that you knew who I was. I can't believe Wolfe is doing this!"

"He is, Detective, and I need your help to resolve it."

She detailed what she'd found, and what she needed to prove.

"My God. Hardcore pictures?"

"That's right. Fifty of them in what seems to be some sort of package, and one more that was a separate matter."

"I'm staggered! I knew he was a scum of a liar, but I would never have suspected Bostich of being a fan of kiddie porn. That's . . . disgusting in the extreme."

Kat passed him the e-mail address she'd found.

"I'm writing it down, Agent Bronsky."

"Call me Kat."

"Okay . . . I'm writing it down, Kat, and I'm Roger. You said SHRDLU2, and then the communications address, is that right?"

"That's right. Do you recognize it?"

He paused. "Well, I think SHRDLU2 is an obsolete newspaper word from the old Linotype machines. You know, the gigantic machines that used to set lead type for newspaper copy before offset printing?"

"Okay, *that's* why it's familiar. I've heard about that. The typographers would set some sort of signature line with that word, right?"

"They'd run a finger across the top line of the typewriter-like keyboard, and the letters came out as 'SHRDLU.' It became a kind of signature."

"I'm not sure how that helps us here, unless Lumin was somehow associated with newspapers."

"No, he wasn't. Didn't even finish high school, but somehow became very good with computers, and worked as a programmer in the eighties. Computer keyboards are typewriter keyboards, but not the same layout as Linotype."

"Roger, did you know Rudolph Bostich before the Wolfe case?"

"I'm just blown away by this! Yes, I knew Rudy. I always thought he was a straight shooter until then. That's why I didn't have to ask who it was when he called that night. It was obvious. I'd know his voice anywhere."

"Do you have any idea why he'd lie?"

"Until this moment, no. I assumed he had some witness protection program source to protect, but now . . . to find out he's got a smut habit . . . that may change things. Maybe he lied to protect himself."

"That's what I think," Kat replied. "If he was afraid a deeper probe by that Connecticut judge into where *he* got the information on Lumin might reveal a connection, either directly or indirectly, that might have been motivation enough."

There was a brief silence on the other end. Kat could hear Matson breathing into the phone.

"Wait a damn minute!"

"What?" she asked.

"Let me—give me a minute to get my computer. I've got the entire file from Lumin's computer downloaded on mine. I haven't stopped studying this case, but before I say anything, I need to look at something."

"Go ahead. But in case we get disconnected, give me your number."

He passed his home phone number and put the phone down. In two minutes he was back, audibly excited.

"Kat! I want you to get back to that list of picture files and read me a particular number." He explained the precise number he wanted from each file.

She keyed the computer and began reading the information until, on the eighth file, he told her to stop.

"Now, Kat, open up the first three pictures, and—I'm sorry, but I need this—describe them in detail."

She swallowed hard and complied, nausea almost overwhelming her.

"Okay, that's enough," Roger Matson said at last.

"And?"

"Kat, assuming the rest are as I think they are, Lumin had the exact same files on his computer when he was arrested for Melinda Wolfe's murder. They were in a different area, obviously purchased and downloaded from some source on the World Wide Web."

Kat could feel Ken's eyes on her. For a moment she had forgotten he was listening. She glanced at him now, seeing his eyebrows raised in extreme surprise.

Kat turned back to the phone. "Can we assume, then, that Lumin purchased a package of this smut from the same source that Bostich patronized, or could it be that Bostich simply had the same downloaded file you have?"

"He doesn't, Kat. I'm the only one who ever downloaded Lumin's computer. I know that for a fact, and I had to do that in secret to keep working on the case. Lumin's computer was sealed by the court, at my request, and the internal memory system—the hard drive—was deactivated for safekeeping and removed to a separate property facility. I made the only copy before that ruling. Only the judge knew about it and approved it. Bostich would have needed a court order to obtain another one, and I would have heard instantly."

"Roger, is there a file on that list, a fifty-first file, with the following name and numbers?"

She read him the details of the last picture file she had opened.

"There are no extra files other than the fifty you mentioned, but I recognize that filename. It was on Lumin's computer."

Kat felt a strange buzz move through her, a combination of excitement and dread and where this was going, coupled with the knowledge that Ken Wolfe was listening to every word.

"Have you ever looked at it?"

"Yes. Absolutely. Kat, you may not know, but as part of the evidence, this was the lynchpin—the one piece of evidence only the killer would have possessed. I'm almost shaking here. Where did you get that filename?"

"Roger, you know Ken Wolfe is listening in on this conversation, don't you?"

"I assumed he was. Captain Wolfe, I'm . . . very sorry you've put yourself in this position, sir. I wish I could have helped you so it wouldn't have come to this."

Ken switched his transmit function and pushed the button on the yoke.

"You *are* helping, Detective. You're helping a lot."

Kat raised her hand to silence Ken. "Roger? You asked where I got the filename?"

"Yes! I'm baffled, except for one possibility, which would be staggering."

"It's on Bostich's computer."

Nearly thirty seconds went by before Roger Matson's voice returned, subdued, intense, and shaken.

"You . . . found that on Bostich's computer?" he asked.

"Yes," she said.

"And you recognized . . . the subject?"

"Yes," she confirmed. "I've seen the face in another picture, but I didn't expect to find it here, in this file."

"Kat, do you understand what finding that on Bostich's computer means?"

Kat was shaking her head as she answered. "I'm not sure I do, other than the worry that maybe what I've found is an old evidence file that you didn't know Bostich had downloaded."

"No. Trust me, Kat. Bostich never received, or could have received, a copy of this through any channel after Lumin's arrest. It had to be transmitted *from* Lumin's computer to some other destination before he was picked up, because . . . because of the, ah, special nature of it. You follow what I'm saying? Whoever received this, let's call him Mr. X, would have probably known precisely what he was getting. Therefore, the presence on Bostich's computer of the same picture means Bostich deals with the same person, Mr. X, and Mr. X had to have some additional purpose for giving this to Rudolph Bostich."

"This file isn't something that could have been spread around out of control?"

"You mean the *picture*?"

"Yeah. Like on an Internet bulletin board or something."

"No way! I know this . . . this *shot*. I've seen just about everything out there on the Internet. It's not there."

Both of them paused until Kat spoke again.

"So, who is this Mr. X? Could it be *Bostich*?"

"I doubt it, " Matson replied. "Someone had to give Bostich the tip about Lumin, so I would think that if there is a Mr. X, that's the one who tipped Bostich that Lumin was the murderer. My Lord, that does makes sense! I've always been certain Bostich had a source for that tip. Even the night he called, I remember thinking it must have been unusual for him to have some underworld slug actually tell him something useful. But I never had a clue who his tipster might have been. A Mr. X—someone Bostich bought smut from personally—could well be the explanation."

"Can you check on this 'SHRDLU2' address for me? See if the owner is our Mr. X?"

"Sure can. Just in case, let me start by searching Lumin's file. Hold on."

In two minutes he was back.

"Kat!" Roger Matson's excited voice filled their ears.

"Yes?"

"Kat, the 'SHRDLU2' address is on Lumin's database, too! I just ran a search. E-mail messages were sent back and forth, though I haven't read them. I never caught this before! But then, I wouldn't have recognized that address anyway, and there was no apparent reason to look for anyone else since we were sure we already had the killer. I mean, the photographic evidence on Lumin's computer said it all."

"Can we trace where it goes, who owns that screen name?"

"I know we can," Matson answered. "I warn you, it'll lead to what seems like a dead end, because Mr. X will have used cash and a fake identity to set it up. Many people do that just to protect their real identity, especially when they're doing something illegal. That's why the Internet is such a wild frontier. You never know who you're really dealing with."

"There's got to be some track to whoever was using that address, though."

"Yeah. We *could* get lucky, I suppose. Let me look and I'll call you right back."

"How long? We're in flight, and the captain's holding the trigger to a bomb in the forward cargo compartment. We've got to hurry."

"I will. Twenty minutes, tops. I've done this before. I know who to call, but let me get on it. My Lord in heaven, the chance to nail Bostich to the wall for screwing the case up is reason enough to get excited, but I know you're in desperate straits up there. Ah, Captain Wolfe? Can I talk to you?"

Ken punched his transmit button. "I'm here, Roger."

"Look, Captain, the sooner you can let those people out and end this, the . . . the better it's going to go for you. You're in pretty deep trouble. You know that, right?"

"I know that, Roger. I had no choice."

"Well, look, you know I'll do my best, regardless. I hear you demanded they federally indict Lumin, but Captain, unless the judge reinstates that warrant, that'll do no good. All the evidence was obtained with that warrant."

"I know that," Ken said.

"Then why demand a federal grand jury?"

"I have my reasons, Roger."

There was a pause. "Look, Ken, you're committing air piracy. You need to end this as soon as possible. I don't want them executing the wrong man, okay?"

"Doesn't matter what happens to me as long as Lumin is permanently removed from this world."

They disconnected and Kat sat in deep thought for a few seconds before glancing back at Ken, whose eyes were focused out the forward windscreen, but whose jaw was tightening and untightening constantly, obviously in reaction to the conversation.

Ken returned the glance, locking eyes with her, and she noted the hollow look on his face.

"That fifty-first picture, Kat . . ." Ken said softly.

"Yes?" she replied, her stomach knotting, knowing what was coming.

"That was the picture of Melinda being tortured, wasn't it?"

She nodded, biting her lip. "I'm so sorry, Ken."

He shook his head as he made an adjustment on the forward panel. "It's okay. I know the picture. I made Matson show me all those files from Lumin's computer, and the one picture."

He looked over at Kat, his face neutral. "They could never find the print itself, just a cheap Polaroid camera abandoned in his trailer. He probably discarded the shot after he scanned the picture into his computer. I have every pixel of that photo memorized." He shook his head. "And that picture of Melinda is on Bostich's computer, too?"

"It's one of the ones you restored."

Ken reached forward and calmly punched a flurry of keystrokes into the flight management computer, executed the command, and sat back, letting the autopilot bank the 737 left to a new heading.

"Where are we going?" Kat asked.

Ken sighed loudly. "Phoenix. I was going to head for Denver or Colorado Springs, but there's heavy thunderstorm activity moving into that area, so we're headed southwest. That was where we were supposed to go this morning anyway."

She felt a sudden surge of hope. "That's a good move, Ken. Let these folks out at their destination at last."

He nodded without looking at her.

She waited, then continued. "You *are* planning to wrap it up there, right? I mean, Lumin's arrest is imminent, we've got Bostich all but hung, and even if you land at Aspen and ended things there right now, I think that judge would have enough to reverse himself and reinstate the warrant."

"Phoenix is a good place to end things, Kat, regardless of what happens." He raised the trigger into view again. "Thanks to you, I'm a little bit closer to deactivating this thing, but I'm not stopping short of my demands. Bostich must confess. Regardless of anything else, he must confess, and the confession has to be fully admissible."

"Ken?" Kat's voice had taken on a different tone, he realized, and he looked at her, startled to see her eyes boring into his.

"It must have been quite a shock this morning to find Bostich on your aircraft, right?"

The answer was out of his mouth before he could recall it.

"Yes, it was. A horrible—"

"Which means," she continued, "that unless you're in the habit of toting a bomb around with you on every flight, which I somehow doubt, there is no bomb on this aircraft."

"That's not true, Kat, I—"

"Cut it out, Ken! I've been looking at your trigger. That's a car alarm remote, isn't it?"

He looked over at her in silence, then he raised the trigger into view and transferred it to his right hand, being careful to keep the button depressed. "It's highly modified."

"You've put on an impressive show, Ken, but it's a fraud. Hey! You're the only pilot up here anyway. I'm hardly going to shoot you and kill all of us."

"The bomb is real, Kat." He began fumbling to his left, in his map kit, fishing something out of his map case that he tossed onto her lap.

Kat looked down at the rectangular object which resembled a small block of plastic inside an open package. She reached for it, picked it up and sniffed it, trying to recall the basics of explosives training at the FBI Academy.

"What *is* this?"

"The rest of the block of plastic explosives I put in my bag in the belly."

She looked down again. "Plastic explosives?"

"That's right."

Kat looked up at him and shook her head.

"Ken, as I'm sure you know, this isn't C-four or Semtex. This is *cheese*!"

He looked at her for several seconds in silence, his face a blank. Suddenly he nodded and smiled thinly.

"Tillamook cheese, to be precise, from Oregon. It's a good brand, but it doesn't explode worth a damn."

She stared at him, shaking her head and chuckling. "And the trigger goes to your car?"

He held it up and let go of the button.

"Yes. And the handheld I carried in Telluride is a Radio Shack scanner."

"And all of us have been terrified for nothing?"

He nodded. "Even if I had known Bostich would be aboard today, I could never truly imperil my passengers, even if I knew how to obtain C-four, which I don't."

She was nodding. "I guess deep inside I suspected that back in Telluride."

"Your colleagues would have blown my head off in a second if *they* had figured it out."

"Not without confirmation, Ken. You know that. As you already pointed out, you know all our moves."

TWENTY-EIGHT

Aboard AirBridge Flight 90. 4:20 P.M.

Ken heard Kat Bronsky's seatbelt unsnap before he saw the movement from the right seat. He tensed and looked to his right, preparing for some sort of attack, but she was sliding the copilot's seat back on its rails and carefully closing Bostich's computer. She looked up and handed Ken the cellular phone.

"When Roger Matson calls back, I'd like you to page me."

He searched her eyes for a second, calculating whether to assert control, then simply nodded.

"Where are you going?"

She swung her leg over the center console and stood in the space behind with her left hand on the back of his seat.

"I'm going to go accomplish what I came aboard to do. Interrogate Rudolph Bostich."

He reached over and punched the unlock button for the cockpit door.

"When you want back in, knock six times. Three, pause, and three more."

She nodded. "And you're headed to Phoenix at a reasonable altitude for a change?"

Ken turned partially to see her expression, relieved to find the shadow of a smile there.

"Very reasonable," he said. "Like six miles high."

. . .

The cabin of AirBridge 90 seemed surreal to Kat, as if she'd just stepped from the forward bathroom on any commercial airline flight. Other than the somewhat haunted, wondering looks on the faces of the passengers in the coach cabin who were watching her carefully, nothing seemed unusual.

Annette Baxter was kneeling by one of the rows in coach, talking to a young man with a telephone in his hand. Kat touched her on the shoulder, causing her to jump.

"I didn't mean to startle you," Kat said, as she caught the eyes of the man in the window seat.

"No problem," Annette said as she stood and gestured to the man. "This is Chris Billings of CNN."

Kat nodded.

"And you're the FBI agent?" he asked. She saw his eyes glance to a notebook full of scribbled entries, then back at her. "Ms. Bronsky?"

"Kat Bronsky. Yes. Are you broadcasting?"

He looked at the phone. "Not right this second. They're taking a ten-minute break, then I'll go back live. As she said, I'm Chris." He extended his hand and she shook it. "Ah, Agent Bronsky, could I ask you a few questions?"

"Briefly."

"Okay. When you were talking on the P.A. about the porno picture you found on Bostich's computer I got the feeling you agree with the captain about Rudy Bostich. But I went back and talked to Mr. Bostich a while ago, before a mob started threatening to throw him out of the emergency hatch, and he swore there were no pornographic pictures on his computer when he came aboard, and if you found anything there, it was only because the captain planted it to discredit him. He said the same thing to the captain in that bizarre 'dueling P.A.' episode."

Kat looked at Annette, then back at Chris Billings. "Truth is, there was no time for the captain to plant anything on that computer, Chris." She explained the sequence of events and the fact she'd been in the cockpit from the first moment Ken Wolfe had brought the computer forward.

"And those pictures are . . . that bad?" he asked.

She looked at him in silence for a few seconds, until it was obvious he was becoming uncomfortable.

"Chris, have you ever seen a pornographic photo involving a female child? I mean, hardcore, everything's visible? Illegal stuff?"

He shook his head rapidly. "No. I mean, I'm certainly not interested in—"

She raised her hand to stop him. "I'm not saying you are, but in your reporting career, you've never seen such garbage?"

"Never."

She nodded. "Okay. Just so you'll know, when I go back up front in a little while, if Wolfe okays it, I'll bring you forward to look at the evidence. It will sicken you, I promise."

She straightened up and moved aft in Annette's direction, finding a sullen Bostich in the same window seat looking out the window.

"Mr. Bostich?"

He looked up suspiciously. "Yes?"

"We need to continue our discussion, sir. I'm Agent Katherine Bronsky of the FBI. We talked over the radio an hour or so ago."

He glared at her without moving, his left hand under his chin, his index finger massaging the edge of his mouth as she stood in the aisle and looked at him.

"What do you want?"

"Please stand up, sir. We're going forward."

He shook his head. "I'm not going back to the cockpit with that maniac."

"No sir, I want you to accompany me back to your seat in first class where we can talk in private." She looked around at the number of passengers who had turned and raised up in their seats to hear the exchange. "Or, maybe you'd rather we talk back here where everyone can participate?"

Bostich exhaled and reluctantly pulled himself from the seat with a dark scowl. He followed her through a gauntlet of boos, hisses, and worse to the first class cabin, where she motioned him into seat 1A again and asked Louise Richardson in seat 1C across the aisle to relocate to a seat several rows away.

Bostich assumed the same sullen, defiant position and looked up at her.

"All right, what do you want?"

She sat sideways on the armrest of seat 1B and looked at him. "The question, Mr. Bostich, is what do *you* want? You're in quite a pickle here. Oh, wait a minute. I almost forgot to read you your rights."

He snorted. "I've done nothing wrong! I don't need Mirandizing."

"Nevertheless, this is a formal interrogation, Mr. Bostich. You are suspected of possession of illegal pornographic materials. First, you have the right to remain silent." Kat repeated the entire litany of the Miranda warning as Bostich looked away with a sneer on his face. When she'd finished he looked back at her.

"Are you about done?"

"No, sir, I'm just getting started."

"Yeah? Well, let me fill you in on reality, babe. You're *way* out of your league! That fool in the cockpit is going to end up on a table in Leavenworth with a needle in his arm, but *you*—when I get through with *you*, Miss Bronsky—you'll be lucky to find a position as a crossing guard somewhere."

She smiled and nodded. "I always liked crossing guards, and I've always liked children. And, judging from those pictures on your computer, you apparently like children, too, Mr. Bostich. Female children. Preferably nude and spread-eagled."

"Bullshit!"

"Oh, really? You are obviously aware of what Captain Wolfe said he found on your computer. Do you deny that computer is yours?"

"I have no reason to believe he's even touched my computer."

She raised her eyebrows. "Really? Perhaps you'd like to try to find it in the overhead where you left it?"

Kat stepped back and Bostich got to his feet and pulled open the overhead compartment, slamming it shut with a grunt when he found it empty.

"Sit down, Mr. Bostich," she ordered. "I'll be right back."

Kat moved to the cockpit door and quietly knocked six times in the sequence Ken had requested. The door swung open and she disappeared inside, returning a few seconds later with Bostich's computer, and a tiny tape recorder she'd found in the prosecutor's briefcase.

She sat in the aisle seat on the right side and looked over at Bostich.

"Mr. Bostich, I've borrowed—or commandeered, if you want—your microcassette tape recorder, and I'm turning it on now. Do you acknowledge the fact that I'm recording what you say?"

He snorted. "You steal my recorder to use against me? Sure, go ahead. It'll never be admissible."

She held up his computer.

"This computer has your business card attached to the case, Mr. Bostich. Do you recognize it as your computer?"

He snorted and nodded.

"Out loud, please."

"Yes, it's my goddamn computer, but since it's been stolen by that maniac, I have no control over what's been planted there."

"Did you buy this computer new?"

"Yes."

"Where did you buy it?"

"By mail order from the manufacturer in Texas, I think."

"Has anyone else used this computer on a regular basis?"

"Others have had access to it."

"I didn't ask that, Mr. Bostich. I asked you if this has been your personal computer, used normally by only you."

"Yes. I'm the primary user."

"Stay in your seat, Mr. Bostich." Kat opened the cover, turned it on, and when the computer had finished spinning up, she entered the appropriate commands to bring up the list of recovered files. She triggered one of the first, and waited until the lurid photo had materialized, then moved to the armrest across the aisle and turned the screen around so he could see it.

"Keep your hands in your lap, Mr. Bostich, but look at this screen. Do you recognize that picture?"

"No! Of course not! That's been planted there."

She closed the lid and held the computer in her lap as Bostich motioned to the laptop and then the cockpit.

"He stole my computer. That disgusting image, and anything else that shouldn't be there, *he* obviously put there."

Kat inclined her head as if puzzled. "Well, you have a problem with that explanation, Mr. Bostich, because I'm a witness to the chain of evidence, and he didn't have any time alone with it before these pictures were discovered."

Bostich brightened, a sinister smile spreading across his face.

"Oh, of course! You helped him. Without a warrant or probable cause, you started probing my computer and helped him fabricate these charges. That means that whatever you think you found is inadmissible."

She shook her head. "Wrong. I didn't touch this computer before these files were discovered. Ken Wolfe found the files without any input from the FBI. Once found, they constituted probable cause. You should know that." She leaned forward slightly. "See, Mr. Bostich, despite your arrogant attitude on the radio a while ago, I had virtually no reason to suspect you liked kiddie porn. Nor, for that matter, did the captain."

"I *don't* like child pornography!"

"Then why is this picture—and fifty others like it—on your computer? It does exist. I just showed you one of them!"

He shook his head. "All I can tell you is, to the best of my knowledge there were no such files or pictures on any segment of my computer at any time when I walked on this aircraft! Somehow Wolfe has manipulated you *and* my computer. I can't make it any more clear than that. Why is that picture there? Hell, I don't know, but I didn't put it there, and I didn't know it was there."

There was a movement on her left, and Kat realized Annette had quietly come forward and was standing a row behind, listening. Kat began to ask her to leave, but thought better of it, and looked back at Bostich.

"So, you're telling me, Mr. Bostich, that you were unaware at all times that there were pornographic picture files of any sort on your computer, in any form?"

He shook his head. "That's right. I never had anything like that on my machine. Good Lord, I'm a federal prosecutor. There was no such material on my hard drive."

"There is now."

"The machine was stolen from me by a hijacker who hates me, right? You think for a second a court would consider that uncontaminated evidence? Not a chance."

Kat shook her head. "Perhaps you didn't hear me, Mr. Bostich. From the time I came aboard this aircraft, I have been in constant visual contact with Ken Wolfe, and he never had a moment to manipulate your computer."

Bostich leaned forward with a smirk on his face. "So, Miss Amateur

Lawyer, did you consider the fact that it had to have happened *before* you came on board?"

She inclined her head toward the passenger from 1C who had moved to the back. "I believe you'll find there's a witness who'll testify that from the time your computer was placed by you in the overhead, no one touched it until Wolfe pulled it out and brought it immediately to the cockpit . . . with me watching." She patted the top of his computer and looked up. "You've got a big problem here, Counselor. These files do exist, they are on your computer, they are illegal, and they were not planted here by the captain or by me. So, how can you explain that reality?"

"Look, you idiot! I've already told you. I do not have, maintain, or otherwise possess any pornographic material in my computer. Understood?"

"The pornographic picture files that were found on your computer were locked with your password. Not a random password, but one you've obviously used to lock very routine files as well. Did you hear Captain Wolfe mention that password?"

"I heard him mention *a* password, but I didn't memorize what it was."

"The password he mentioned was 97883PSY."

"Okay."

"Is that *your* password?"

"It *is* a password I've used, yes. But it isn't really secure. I carelessly keep it listed in an unprotected file, which I'm sure Wolfe found, so anyone could use it or plant it."

"What is the significance of those numbers and letters?"

"They're random. Just random numbers."

"And the letters 'PSY'?"

He shrugged. "I can't recall."

"Could that be a contraction for a particular word, Mr. Bostich?"

"No."

"So it has no significance, was picked at random, and in no way is related to the slang term for a particular part of the female anatomy?"

"What are you suggesting? That 'PSY' stands for pussy? No. It doesn't. I think you're obsessed with sex, Bronsky."

She smiled and shook her head in amazement. "I'm not the one who keeps kiddie porn hidden in my computer."

Bostich came forward in the seat, arms flailing, eyebrows flaring.

"Goddamn you! There was no kiddie porn in my computer. I didn't load any, I didn't have any, I never had any, I didn't maintain any, and there were no erased files on that hard drive as far as I know! GOT IT?"

Kat looked at him in silence as Bostich looked back at her, defiantly, unaware what he had blurted. She waited a very long half minute until Bostich blinked and looked away, then she cleared her throat.

"Mr. Bostich, why did you mention erased files?"

"What?"

"Well, if files are erased, they're gone, right?"

"I always thought so," he replied, his eyes darting from her face to the wall and back.

"So why would you feel the need to assure me you hadn't erased any files? I'm curious, because before you brought it up, I never mentioned to you the fact that such files existed."

Bostich leaned back, looking trapped. "I just meant I never had any files on that computer that were pornographic. I didn't want you thinking I might have had some there at one point, and then gotten rid of them."

Kat shook her head as if clearing cobwebs. "I . . . guess I don't understand why you would bring up erased files, Mr. Bostich. Let's see . . ."

She sat back slightly, her eyes on the ceiling as if thinking it through.

"If you never had kiddie porn pictures, you couldn't have had the opportunity to *erase* any kiddie porn pictures. Therefore, you wouldn't be at all concerned with assuring me that you had never erased any such files, because you would know that there never *had* been any such files, active, erased, or otherwise. Does that make sense to you?"

"Just as I told you, Bronsky. There were never any such files."

"Okay, but if you're not telling me the truth and you *had* loaded kiddie porn pictures to look at, then later decided to get rid of them, you would obviously have erased them. It would then be a very frightening shock if someone opened your computer and said, 'Hey, Rudy, we found your kiddie porn pictures!' I mean, *you* would know that those files had been erased. If they were erased, how could they be found? Someone in that pickle would figure, my God, the only way they could be seeing something there is if the computer didn't really obliterate those files when I erased them, and somehow they've been reconstructed. Partially erased files found on a computer hard drive would be conclusive evidence that the files were once active, which would catch the person in a lie."

"I don't know what you're babbling about, but those picture files are not mine. Period."

"Well, Mr. Bostich, logically it comes down to this. An innocent man would scream, 'There were no files there!' A guilty man, who had tried to get rid of the evidence, would say the same thing, but would add the claim, 'There were no *erased* files there, either!' You did the latter."

Bostich looked confused, and the shadow of uncertainty that crossed his face was precisely what Kat had wanted to see. He came forward again, this time with the palm of his right hand out as if to offer a friendly explanation, his voice subdued and concerned, with none of the bluster of a minute before.

"Look, you're misinterpreting me. You claim I had awful pictures on my computer. I know I didn't have any such pictures there at any time, unless someone, unbeknownst to me, loaded them on, somehow used my password to close them, and . . . and then, I suppose, stuck the computer back in my case to frame me. And I don't know when that might have happened."

"These files were downloaded by a telephone line, Mr. Bostich, as you know."

"But I *don't* know, don't you see?"

"I think you do. They were downloaded from a particular Internet address that someone had tried unsuccessfully to erase from the files. In addition, I found that same Internet address in another section of your computer."

"It's part of a plant, a frame. After all, I'm being considered for high office. I have enemies."

"Why did you mention erased files, Mr. Bostich?"

He let out a frustrated sigh and looked around, his palms up in a frustrated gesture. "Hell, you were *pressuring* me. I'm in a horrible situation here. Hijacked, targeted by a madman in the cockpit who's managed to convince an FBI agent and all the passengers aboard that I'm a terrible guy, and it's all false!"

"So you only mentioned erased files because I was pressuring you?"

He nodded. "It's just a mistake, for crying out loud. I misspoke. That was the first time I've even thought about the concept of . . . of erased *anything*."

"That's not true!" Annette said suddenly.

Her voice was a shock to both of them, and Kat turned to look at her, surprised to see the senior flight attendant's eyes boring into Bostich, who looked around at her in amazement.

"Annette," Kat asked, "you know something about this?"

"She knows nothing!" Bostich snapped.

"Be quiet!" Kat commanded, turning back to Annette and nodding. "Tell me."

"In the back, a while ago, I overheard him telling one of the passengers that if the captain had found anything, it would be the remains of files that might have been there once, but were just . . . He called them shadowy remains of files that had to have been erased before he bought the computer."

Kat nodded to Annette and turned back to Bostich, watching the color drain from his face.

"But you bought your computer new. Were those statements a mistake, too, Mr. Bostich? Did you misspeak? Were you misquoted? Or did your words really mean something other than what they said?"

"Ah, to hell with you, Bronsky. I've sat through manipulative interrogations a thousand times, and you're a rank amateur."

She nodded. "Perhaps. But you mentioned erased files back there, and you mentioned erased files up here, and I want to know the real reason why. Did you ever erase any pornographic picture files?"

"No! I'm not going to answer any more questions from you."

"Well, I'm going to ask one more question of *you*, Mr. Bostich. Since I think you've looked long and hard at each and every one of those pictures, I want to ask you why one in particular didn't affect you."

She leaned forward toward Bostich as he plastered himself against the seatback next to the window. Kat kept after him, confusing him, as she moved her face next to his to speak directly into his right ear.

"There was this one shot, Rudy . . ." she began in a whisper. "There was this little girl, tied to a chair, horribly bruised and battered. It was Melinda Wolfe, as you know, and the picture was taken by her killer."

She could feel Bostich tense.

"Get away from me!" he snapped.

She pulled back, watching the combination of fury and emotion overwhelm him as he fought against his own better judgment, letting emotion win out.

"How could you have that picture on this computer?" she badgered.

"I didn't!"

"But it's there. I saw it myself."

"I don't know anything about it."

"You want to see it again?"

"No! I've never seen it."

"Why, it's right here, Rudy! It's on *your* computer, locked by *your* password! The most horrible shot I've ever seen. The picture on your computer right now, as we speak, is the very sickening shot I just described to you. THE SAME ONE!"

"Nothing like that was there, dammit!" He had his eyes closed, his fists clenched, and his jaw set.

"That could have been your little daughter. The same picture! How could you have had that picture?"

"I didn't!"

"Well, I can show the world that you did! Imagine your daughter like that."

He was shaking now, his teeth grinding.

"I—don't—know—WHAT THE HELL YOU'RE TALKING ABOUT!"

She leaned close to his ear again to deliver the last portion of the description.

"In this picture, Rudy, Lumin had already used his knife and butchered her. You know what she'd lost, and you know the picture shows it. Imagine your little daughter sitting there, bloody and butchered."

Kat whispered the last few specifics of the butchery, knowing that the picture in Bostich's computer did *not* contain such details—and knowing that Rudy Bostich knew it as well.

"WHAT?" he yelped in reaction.

"It's right here, in your computer."

"The hell it is!"

"You, a father, with a daughter who was once eleven years old, too. How on earth could you carry such a picture?"

"I didn't! There's no such picture!"

"Are you going to tell me it was an evidence file, Rudy?"

He hesitated, obviously calculating whether such a claim could work, but realized he'd trapped himself. "NO! There's no such picture."

"You can see the ragged skin, the blood, and the agony she's in!"

"Not in MY computer! NEVER in my computer!"

"It's here, in my lap, in your computer. THE SAME PICTURE, DAMN YOU!" she yelled suddenly, watching his eyelids pop open as he came forward to yell back.

"THAT'S A DIFFERENT SHOT THAN I HAD!"

Kat left the stunned silence undisturbed as she watched Bostich's expression change from quaking fury to wide-eyed horror.

She looked down and nodded. "I know it is, Mr. Bostich." She looked him in the eye. "I wanted to make sure you knew as well. You're right, as *you* well know. The picture of Melinda Wolfe in your computer does not show any mutilation, but you didn't know you were going to get any shots of a little murder victim, did you? You thought you were just buying the usual package from your supplier."

His eyes were wide, his mouth open, and there was no attempt to answer.

She glanced down again. "Look, Rudy. Men sometimes have some pretty weird feelings about women, and even though possessing pictures like you have on your computer breaks the law, I know that sometimes that sort of lurid interest begins as a deviant urge and grows, until one day, stupidly, you let your twisted fantasies take over, and you buy something you shouldn't have ever touched. Your supplier sent Melinda's picture as a warning not to expose him, didn't he? DIDN'T HE?"

She saw him moisten his lips, his breathing accelerating as he watched her.

"You see, Rudy, I already know it was the supplier who gave you the tip about Melinda's murderer. You called Detective Matson in all innocence, trying to catch a murderer, but when the judge wanted to talk to you about it, your supplier, who gave you the information to begin with, warned you to say nothing about your source, or he'd expose your nasty little habit of looking at pictures of children being forced to have sex."

"Bullshit! I have no interest in such things!"

"That, of course," she continued, "would destroy your career, so you lied on the stand to protect yourself. Then you discovered Melinda's picture in the latest bunch, you got scared, you frantically erased everything, but you didn't know how to totally obliterate a file. You had no idea those pictures were really still there, just waiting for someone to hit the right button and reassemble them. Have I got it right so far?"

Bostich swallowed hard and pushed himself up slightly in the seat.

"That's all a complete fabrication, Bronsky."

"Oh, and I can't prove any of it?"

"You can't prove a thing because it's not true."

Kat looked over at Annette.

"You've heard everything he's said, haven't you, Annette?"

She nodded resolutely. "I'm going to write it down in lurid detail."

Kat looked back at Bostich.

"And thanks to the loan of your tape recorder, we have it all on tape as well. Okay, Rudy. Here's the deal. We're both still hostages here, as are all the people in the back. Despite the trouble you're in, we all may still die if Ken Wolfe doesn't get what he wants, which is your admission that you lied to that Connecticut judge."

She began counting off points on her fingers.

"One, we have the evidence from your computer, and that's enough to convict. Two, we know who your supplier is, and he's already been arrested and has agreed to testify he was the tipster because Lumin was his customer, too."

"That's a lie!" Bostich snapped without conviction.

Of course it is, you slime! Kat thought to herself while maintaining a neutral expression. *But you can't be sure, can you?*

"We've got him, Rudy, and he'll give you up in a split second for a deal."

She looked at her hand and extended a third finger.

"Okay, and three, we have numerous witnesses to your contradictory statements and your interesting conduct aboard this aircraft." She looked up at him. "I don't think you're going to be heading up the

Justice Department anytime soon, Rudy. The real question here is jail time, and if we survive this ordeal without your help and you're later convicted, I doubt anyone is going to be interested in leniency when you could have confessed and ended this hijacking."

"Go to hell!" he said quietly.

"It's over, Rudy! Face it. Make the best of it. You have some wiggle room to do the right thing for once. Let's get you on the phone to that judge in Connecticut. After all, as long as Lumin is out there, *your* daughter is vulnerable, too."

"My daughter is grown, and I don't even know where she is."

Kat looked concerned. "She won't have anything to do with you?"

"No."

"How about her mother?"

"We're divorced."

"And your daughter lived with her mother after the divorce?"

"No. She ran away at sixteen." There was anguish on his face, and Kat calculated the odds of trusting her premonition.

"Rudy, you know, don't you?"

"Know what?"

"Why she ran away."

"No. I don't know."

"Oh, yes you do. It's been killing you for a long time. Knowing your sickness—and it is a mental problem, Rudy—your sickness is responsible."

He sat rubbing his temple with both hands, his eyes looking up at her in numb defeat.

"What're you saying? That I'm an alcoholic or something?"

"You wish it were that simple, Rudy, but you know it isn't."

He dropped his hands and glared at her. "How the hell can you know anything about me?"

She shook her head sadly. "You really don't understand, do you?"

"What?"

"The syndrome that owns you." She shifted her position and sighed. "I'm a psychologist, Rudy. Men with your fixation travel a predictable behavioral path. It's very sad you didn't know that, or maybe you could have gotten help in time."

"What the hell are you talking about?"

"The perverted desires, Rudy. The midnight desires, the strange images in your mind, and the perverted things you imagine yourself doing to females. Those twisted fantasies have been in your head since you were a little boy, and you've never told anyone, have you?"

He looked away and shook his head in feigned disgust as she leaned forward, speaking in a calm, insistent voice.

"You can deny it to me, Rudy, but you can't deny it to yourself. You've been fighting this all your life."

The overt motions had stopped, but she could see his jaw grinding back and forth as he looked out the window and listened.

"Those awful fantasies were always inappropriate, but they were always compelling as well. They always are. They involve your wife, your mother, and a reaction to all females. When hidden, they erupt in predictable ways, especially in a man who has this illness, doesn't know it, and then ends up entrusted with the care of a young, beautiful daughter."

He looked around at her in silence, his eyes wide. "I don't understand what you're saying."

"Yes you do, Rudy. If you hadn't molested your daughter as a little girl, she wouldn't have left at sixteen."

The explosion was slow to come, but it flared with anticipated fury as he came part way out of the seat, sputtering and spitting.

"Fuck you, bitch! Just—just *fuck you!* It's always the male, isn't it? Always the man's fault. Never the female! Well, FUCK YOU!" He turned his head to the window as Kat nodded sadly and let the silence grow heavy before she spoke.

"Rudy, that is *not* the response of an innocent father."

She got to her feet and took a deep breath as she glanced at a thoroughly shaken Annette.

She looked back at Bostich. "Think it over. When I come back, if you're not ready to talk to the judge in Stamford and clear this up, I'm going to place you under arrest."

TWENTY-NINE

Aboard AirBridge Flight 90. 4:35 P.M.

Kat delivered the prescribed sequence of knocks to the cockpit door, and Ken opened it from within. She closed the door behind her and slid into the copilot's seat as Ken turned in her direction.

"Your phone rang," Ken told her, "but it was Frank, not Roger Matson. He told me Lumin's been arrested and is on the way to the county jail in Denver."

"Good!" she said.

"He also patched me into a call from Connecticut." Ken closed his eyes and winced, shaking his head slightly. "That was the hardest of all, Kat."

"I don't understand."

He looked up at her, the pain clearly visible. "Tom Davidson. The fellow who gave me a job when I desperately needed one years ago, flying his private jet. It was Tom Davidson who stood beside me and kind of forced AirBridge to hire me two years ago."

"How on earth did Davidson get Frank to patch him through?"

Ken shrugged. "North's political pull, I suppose. He has plenty. I'm still stunned that he's out there flying formation. I didn't realize, until Tom called, that North was involved. I mean, I knew he was the billionaire financing most of Tom's airline, but—"

"North didn't tell me," Kat added, "that he was an owner of AirBridge when we asked for his help."

Ken nodded. "I'm not surprised. He probably didn't want you to think he was protecting AirBridge's interests." He glanced at her. "Tom was trying to talk me into landing and letting everyone go, including Bostich. He was thunderstruck to hear what we'd found on Bostich's computer."

"I can imagine," Kat replied, feeling off balance at such a call being relayed into the middle of a hijacking. "Does he know Bostich?"

Ken nodded. "For many years. He said the news that Bostich likes kiddie porn makes him wonder if he could have been connected with Lumin directly. He was very glad to hear that Lumin's been arrested."

"Well, that was one of your major goals, Ken."

"Yes, but the federal grand jury in Denver has said nothing about indicting him, and that has to be done."

Kat looked at him. "Ken, we're in luck. With what I just dragged out of Bostich, I don't think you're going to need federal charges. I think the state of Connecticut will be able to get the evidence back in."

Ken searched her face carefully. "You mean he confessed?"

She shook her head, averting her eyes, feeling strangely let down. "No, but he trapped himself, Ken." She held up Bostich's tape recorder and locked eyes with him, her excitement returning. "I said nothing to him about your reconstructing erased files, but he already knew the files you found were erased, so he obviously knew they were there."

"That's nothing. That's obvious!" A dismissive look crossed his face, punctuated by Kat holding her index finger up in a stop gesture.

"Wait. He also knew Melinda's picture was there, too, and he knew precisely what was on it, and that unintentional admission was before a witness, and openly on tape."

"Anything else?"

"Now, Ken, this isn't hard evidence, okay? But by his reaction to my questions and his prurient interest in kiddie porn, I'm convinced he molested his daughter when she was little."

Ken's eyes had looked haunted from the moment she was forced aboard, but now a searing flash of pain careened across his face like a wave.

"You've *got* to be kidding," he said with obvious disgust.

She shook her head.

"I guess that figures. After we left Salt Lake, I found out he had a daughter named Annie, and his reactions when I pushed were not normal." Ken sighed and looked at her. "But am I missing something here, Kat? How does any of that help convince the judge that Bostich lied about the tip to Roger Matson?"

"It helps destroy his credibility and correspondingly increases Roger Matson's credibility."

He was shaking his head as she continued. "Not enough."

"Ken, look, before today, Bostich could always win against an ordinary detective in a contest of credibility simply because of his position. But not now, not after what we've discovered."

"State judges, too often, are self-righteous bastards with poor legal training, and that one was no exception. Can you imagine the gall of a robed idiot like that to free a murderer just to make a legal point to the police? There's no way he'd reverse himself just because we call from an airplane with allegations about Bostich. Only Bostich himself can cause a reversal."

"Ken," she tried again, unprepared for his reaction as he turned toward her with eyebrows flaring, his voice loud and angry.

"DAMMIT!" His right fist was clenched as he cocked his head to one side and locked his jaw, and just as quickly took a deep breath and motioned for her to wait. "Kat, get this straight! Either Bostich confesses to the judge, on the phone, in the next hour, while we're still flying, or I'm still at square one with no way to prosecute Lumin, and that is NOT acceptable!"

Kat chewed her lip and stared blankly at the instruments, her optimism gone with the gut level knowledge that he was right. Something beyond Bostich's lack of credibility, his criminal possession of kiddie porn, and his reactions to her questions would be needed to reinstate the evidence against Lumin. Even the fact of Bostich's connection to the sleazy world of kiddie porn wasn't enough. Bostich himself had to testify that he called Detective Matson to pass on the tip about Melinda's killer.

She looked up at Ken, who had turned back to the panel and was adjusting the flight computer.

"I'm doing my best, Ken."

"I know it," he said, more sharply than he'd intended.

Kat sighed and picked up the cellular phone, flipping it open. "I was hoping Matson would call—"

There was a characteristic rapid beeping on the phone.

"Damn!"

"What?"

"I'm out of signal range."

"We're about thirty minutes from Phoenix, Kat, and I'm just going to circle until we get something resolved."

"It would be—" she began, then paused, unsure of his reaction.

"I know," he answered. "It would be easier if we were on the ground, especially if I let everyone off. But it's not going to happen, Kat. I'm not throwing everything on the table only to walk away before the game's over."

"Ken, have you thought about the fact that Bostich's cellular telephone record may be enough to convince that judge?"

"I thought about it, and I'm sure it's not, because that stupid judge would have all sorts of questions first, and Bostich would have time to raise the possibility that it was manipulated."

"Was it?"

He snorted. "Hell, no. But it won't reinstate the warrant right now, today. Only Bostich can do that."

"Then there's got to be another key," she responded.

"Meaning that Bostich isn't going to crack, right?"

She shrugged as she turned to him. "Ken, did you really think a guy with that much legal experience was just going to admit he'd perjured himself?"

He glanced at her, then back to the windscreen. "I had hope, Kat, not hard expectations."

"He's a hardened prosecutor, and the last thing he's going to do is actually put his neck in a noose and admit a criminal act."

Ken turned to Kat with a look of desperation, triggering a cold, hard knot of apprehension in her stomach.

"Let me ask you a question."

"Okay."

"Suppose Bostich was hauled in front of a firing squad. The rifles are cocked and loaded and pointed at his chest, and then someone provides him one last chance to admit he lied. Would he? Would he tell the truth at last to save his life?"

"Ken, even a moment before execution with salvation resting on that one admission, Rudy Bostich would probably stay with his lie."

He smiled slightly and nodded. "You're very good, Kat. You think very fast, but I can see in your eyes that's not an honest answer. Bostich is a coward, and cowards blink. I just have to find what it takes to make him blink, and I'm running out of time."

She took a deep breath. "If I can get back in touch with Matson in a few minutes—"

"I'm going to have to do something far more threatening to crack him," Ken said. "I'm going to have to put a gun to his head, literally."

"Ken, that's not a wise idea. If he calls your bluff, are you prepared to commit murder?"

"You mean, as if one capital crime isn't enough?"

"What I mean is—"

"Kat, I'm not worried about me, don't you get it? I'm finished. I'm dead. I just want to get Lumin off the streets. Now, thanks to you, I think maybe Bostich is finished professionally. But this was about Lumin, and without a confession from Bostich, Lumin continues to kill."

"The Gulfstream!" she said suddenly.

He turned. "What?"

"I forgot they're back there. Which radio can I use?"

"That same frequency is still up on number two." He reached over and pressed the appropriate button on her audio panel, and she called the name of N5LL.

"Right here, Kat. This is Dane."

She asked for a relay on the satellite phone and passed Roger Matson's number.

When the connection was made, Matson was audibly relieved. "I kept trying that cellular and it wasn't working. You could say I've been slightly frantic."

"I'm sorry about that. We're on a satellite phone now through a private jet sitting alongside us here in Telluride. The owner, Bill North, or his crew, will relay for us."

"Ah, who did you say?"

"Bill North. Don't worry about it. What do you have for us?" she asked.

She could hear him pause on the other end before replying. "Ah, quite a bit, Kat. Okay, first, I tracked the Internet provider on the other end of that 'SHRDLU2' address. The provider is fairly small, and scared they've done something wrong, so they were more than willing to help. They say this address has been active for about three years, and they don't track anything but the time usage. I've got their records coming off by e-mail and printing as we speak. Now. As I suspected, the name of whoever has been using SHRDLU2 is an alias that leads nowhere. The address is a post office box that they say changes about every three months. Not just the box number, but the city and state, though mostly East Coast. They're sending that information, too."

"So, we're shot down trying to find this Mr. X without staking out a post office?"

"I was afraid that was the end result, but we *may* have had a stroke of luck."

"Tell me."

"SHRDLU2's payments for the account are made in cash sent in an envelope two weeks early every time. A new one had just arrived. I asked a friend in the Rochester Police Department—that's where this provider is located—I asked for an emergency fingerprint check. They rolled the portable crime lab out there, dusted, found a couple of excellent prints, and hopefully are getting ready to scan them into your FBI computer through a modem for an emergency ID check."

"I'm very impressed, Roger. Wonderful work."

"Wonderful cooperation. Everyone's aware what's happening up there, Kat. They want to help."

"I know how long a fingerprint scan takes with the new equipment," Kat said. "We'll know inside fifteen minutes if it's an easy match with anyone."

"Kat, SHRDLU2 is almost certainly owned by Mr. X."

"I squeezed Bostich a while ago up here. I squeezed him hard, and he in effect confirmed he knew about the files being on his computer and having been erased. I also tricked him regarding Mr. X and said we had him in custody ready to roll over on Bostich for a deal. He hasn't admitted he lied to the judge yet, but he's thinking it over back there."

"Good. What'd you use?"

"Melinda's picture, for one. Instead of describing what's really there, I made up some pretty horrible additions which he knew weren't there, and he couldn't resist letting me know the picture on his machine was different."

"Excellent, Kat. I'm sure he has every detail memorized as well, even the trees outside the window."

She nodded. "I'm sure that's true."

Ken's voice interrupted. "We've got company again."

Kat looked at him in alarm. "Where? What do you see?"

Ken shook his head, a thin smile on his lips. "Well, I guess I should feel honored."

"What?"

"I've drawn an Air Force AWACS and they're trying to be unobtrusive." He inclined his head toward the captain's side window where she could see the telltale saucer-shaped radar antenna on top of the four-engine turbojet in the distance.

"I'm sure he's no threat, Ken," Kat began.

He laughed. "You can say that again. They just don't want me slipping away this time."

"Kat? You still there?" Roger Matson's voice coursed through the headset as relayed by the Gulfstream.

"Right here, Roger."

"Two things. First, the Bill North you mentioned, is that the chairman of NorthLight Industries out of Salt Lake?"

"Yes. He and his crew have been invaluable. You know him?"

There was a hesitation on Matson's end.

"By reputation only, Kat. Ah, let me ask you to call me back in about ten minutes. I'm expecting a call any minute regarding the fingerprints, and I'm working this with a single phone line from my home."

"Okay," she replied.

"Kat, one more thing. You're FBI and I'm just a state cop. Couldn't you get a federal warrant to look at Bostich, both his home and office? I mean, considering what you've discovered up there, at least all his computer files and materials should be impounded."

She agreed immediately and asked Dane Bailey to break the connection and dial Clark Roberts at FBI headquarters.

"Stand by, Kat," Dane responded.

Roberts's voice followed a minute later, cold, distant, and suspicious.

"What do you require, Agent Bronsky?"

She briefly outlined the discoveries involving Rudy Bostich and her suspicions regarding the existence of a Mr. X.

"What's the bottom line, Agent Bronsky? What are you requesting?"

"We need search warrants for Bostich's office, home, and car, executed as fast as possible, with special emphasis on computer files and anything that might identify payments made to, or through, the individual behind the e-mail address I mentioned."

There was an extended silence before Clark Roberts replied. "I assume these are the hijacker's demands, Agent Bronsky?"

She felt her face begin to redden. "No, these are my considered recommendations."

"You're off the case, Agent Bronsky. I thought we made that clear."

"I still have a badge and a commission and I'm still functional, so, no, that wasn't clear, and I'm not about to go back and sit down in coach and shut my eyes when I'm right in the middle of all this."

"This conversation is serving no purpose, Agent Bronsky. Unless you have something to relay from the captain, we might as well terminate this."

"Who's making the decisions on this case?"

"As I said, you're not on this case. You're a hostage. Drop it!"

Ken was raising his right hand to stop her as he punched the transmit button.

"Mr. Roberts? This is the hijacker, Captain Wolfe. Can you hear me?"

"Loud and clear, Captain. What can I do for you?"

"A while ago I talked with the Acting Attorney General, Martin Springfield. I want to speak with Mr. Springfield again immediately."

"Stand by, Captain. I'll work on it."

Less than two minutes later the voice of Martin Springfield came on the channel.

"Okay, Mr. Springfield. Here's the deal. The FBI is refusing to listen to Agent Bronsky up here, who is doing a damn good job to try to satisfy my demands and end this. I'm going to put her on. You're going to listen to what she's recommended to her agency, and whatever they refuse to do, you're going to make happen. Understand?"

"Depends entirely on what it is, Captain. You know you almost killed everyone back there at Telluride."

"We're not discussing that right now, Mr. Springfield. Here's Agent Bronsky."

He nodded to Kat and she pressed the button and repeated the same plea for search warrants.

Springfield's voice came back incredulous.

"You've *got* to be kidding me, Agent Bronsky! You want me to believe that Rudolph Bostich is in possession of criminal child pornography? Bullshit!"

"It's here, I've seen it, I have not contaminated the evidence, it will be admissible, and it's real and in substantial quantity, and Mr. Bostich is on tape essentially admitting it."

"On *tape*?"

"I Mirandized him and interrogated him on tape, on his own personal tape recorder, in his sight, with his knowledge."

"And he *admitted* this?"

"Not directly, sir. But what he did say on the record would get an indictment."

There were a few seconds of silence and Kat jabbed the button again.

"Look, Mr. Springfield, you mentioned Telluride. We're still airborne here, the captain is the only pilot aboard who can fly a Boeing and land us safely, he's got a weapon, we've still got a lot of hostages, and this is a damned desperate situation, the successful conclusion of which all depends on satisfying Captain Wolfe's demands before something tragic *does* happen. I know what we've found. For God's sake, trust me! Get those warrants and execute them. If I'm wrong, and I'm not, but if somehow I was, all we'd do is exonerate Bostich."

Ken punched the transmit button. "And don't forget, Springfield, I've got my finger barely holding down the trigger of a bomb. Comply, or all these good people go up in smoke."

Kat snapped her head to the left, her eyebrows raised, her eyes large as she searched the slight smile on his face.

Ken gestured toward the radio, then held a finger to his lips, and Kat diverted her gaze to the instrument panel as her mind furiously battled with the ethical obligation she knew she'd already decided to ignore.

Her finger was poised on the transmit button, but she couldn't bring herself to push it.

There was a disgusted sigh on the other end. "In all my years in the law and law enforcement, I have never experienced a situation even remotely similar to this. A captive FBI agent dictating to the acting Attorney General of the United States. Christ! The answer is not only no, but hell, no!"

"Sir—" Kat began.

Another voice cut in on the frequency.

"Ah, Kat, this is Bill North. I've been listening in, and I'm going to suspend the radio link here for a minute and talk to the A.G. I'll be right back."

"All right," Kat managed, expecting the transmitter to go off. Instead, the owner of the Gulfstream kept the channel open as his voice coursed through the line, identifying himself and his extensive connections with the current occupant of the White House—facts Kat had not known. Bill summarized his involvement, the radio relay, the use of the Gulfstream, and their present position.

"Mr. North, while I appreciate your good citizenship, I fail to see the reason for this interruption."

"Very simple, Mr. Springfield. I'd like to ask you if you've lost your alleged mind?" The words were spoken with great calm.

"What?" Springfield asked.

"Listen carefully, Mr. Springfield. The FBI agent in that hijacked airplane out there has saved those people at least twice today by fast thinking, fast action, and pure bravery. While you sit back there in the Beltway and pontificate about how to respond to hijackers, your front-line troop, Kat Bronsky, is doing this by herself with virtually no support from her superiors in what is perhaps the most scandalous and politically inexcusable example of bureaucratic stupidity I've ever observed. I guarantee you my next call is going to be to the President, wherever in the world he is, and the next call *you're* going to get after that will be directly from *him* ordering you to do what Agent Bronsky has already correctly asked you to do, and what common sense dictates needs to be done. So get off your goddamned high horse, Springfield, and order those warrants! She knows what she's talking about. Bostich is a slime, and with what she's found, he won't last past this evening as a U.S. Attorney, much less as a candidate for U.S. Attorney General. I've been following this. You haven't. Get moving."

"Mr. North, considering I haven't a clue who you are, I could take real offense at your tone."

"And I, Springfield, could make it a major political objective of mine to remove you from this Administration forthwith. Or would you prefer to end a hijacking and keep the President out of this?"

"Why should I believe you're known to this Administration?"

"Call the White House. I've got the backline number, if you don't. Ask for Harry Raddison, who should still be in his office. He's the assistant chief of staff, by the way."

"I know who Raddison is."

"I'll hold for three minutes. I'd strongly advise you to call him immediately. Ask him who the hell Bill North is, and whether you should listen to one of the key contributors to the last campaign."

The line was quiet for a few seconds until Martin Springfield's voice returned.

"Okay, Mr. North. You've made your point. And on consideration, I think perhaps I can endorse your recommended course of action."

"Understand this, Mr. Springfield. It is not my recommendation. It's Agent Bronsky's."

"Whatever. Reconnect us, if you'd be so kind."

"Oh, that'll be no problem at all, Mr. Springfield. Actually, I guess I forgot to throw the switch. She's been listening to this whole dialogue."

THIRTY

Aboard AirBridge Flight 90. 4:49 P.M.

"*You're doing a fantastic job, Chris!*" The accolade from the director back in Atlanta ignited a small glow of satisfaction that Chris Billings allowed himself to enjoy for no more than thirty seconds.

He was, he realized, sick to death of the words "alleged," "purported," and "unconfirmed." It was time to verify for himself whether the pictures on the computer belonging to United States Attorney Rudolph Bostich were, in fact, child pornography.

"I'm going to be off for a while," he told Atlanta. "I'll leave the line open and the receiver here in the seat, but I need to try to get to the cockpit."

He found Annette, relieved that she responded immediately with a nod.

"I heard Agent Bronsky make the offer," she said as she escorted him forward and spoke to Ken on the interphone, motioning him in when the door popped open.

Chris Billings came through cautiously, his hand outstretched to Kat Bronsky, who shook it as Ken looked around and spoke.

"Hello, Mr. Billings."

"Captain. Thank you for letting me come up. Agent Bronsky had told me—"

"I already know, Mr. Billings. I'm happy to have you see what kind of slimy individual Bostich really is. I hope you've been able to broadcast what's going on."

He nodded. "I'll be honest with you, Captain. I've tried to be very balanced, but I'm not sure you'd approve of what I've been saying."

Ken looked at him and smiled slightly before diverting his eyes forward.

"I don't really care what you say about me, Mr. Billings. I very much care what you say about Rudy Bostich, the idiot judge in Connecticut, and about Bradley Lumin, who murdered my daughter."

"You wanted to see these pictures?" Kat interjected before Billings could say more.

He nodded, and she adjusted the computer on her lap and entered a series of keystrokes that brought a list of files to the screen.

"This is the package of smut he apparently purchased and downloaded. Let me open several of them for you." She looked over her shoulder first at Billings. "You have children, Mr. Billings?"

He shook his head no.

"A younger sister you care about, perhaps?"

"Actually, three older sisters I care about very much, and two little nieces."

She nodded, her expression serious. "Then these will be doubly disturbing."

He leaned over to get a close view of the screen, supporting his weight on the center console. The first picture drew a gasp, the second a more subdued reaction, and the third an affirmative "That's enough."

"No, there's one more you need to see," Kat told him, triggering the picture of Melinda Wolfe, which Ken had specifically asked her to show.

The picture swam into view as Kat explained its significance, and Chris Billings swallowed hard and looked away. "Oh, my God!"

Kat closed the file and turned the computer over. "You see Mr. Bostich's card here?"

He looked back around, studied it, and nodded, then looked her in the eye. "Will you be filing charges?"

"I can't guarantee that, since I'm not the prosecutor, but I guarantee the investigation will be unstoppable." She searched his eyes for a few seconds. "And what about your reports? Does this change things for you as a reporter?"

He nodded. "Being an eyewitness to something *always* changes a journalist's reports. But it also . . . changes the journalist. And I have to fight that."

"You know that Lumin, the suspect, has been arrested, don't you?" Kat asked.

"Yes. They relayed that to me from Atlanta," Chris Billings said with a small laugh. "The police in Colorado apparently arrested him on an outstanding traffic warrant from Connecticut."

Kat saw Ken Wolfe's head snap around, his eyes probing Billings's.

"On a *traffic* warrant?"

The newsman was nodding, but looking slightly alarmed. "That's . . . that's what we have so far."

Ken slammed his fist into the padded edge of the glareshield, his teeth gritted. "Jesus Christ! JESUS!"

"What, Ken?" Kat asked, her heart rate accelerating.

Ken gathered up the flight plan from the center console and threw it toward the glareshield.

"DAMN, DAMN, DAMN, DAMN DAMN! They lied to me! I let myself expect some honesty, and they lied to me!"

"Ken, they *arrested* him. Why does it matter how?"

Chris Billings had backed toward the closed cockpit door as Ken grabbed and threw several aeronautical maps, growling and cursing.

"Ken? Ken, please, tell me what's wrong with that?" Kat leaned over the center console and placed her hand on Ken's shoulder, relieved that he didn't resist.

Ken looked at her, his eyes narrowed with fury, his teeth clenched.

"Lumin murdered my daughter, but they can't arrest him on that. That isn't enough. They have to use a goddamn *traffic warrant* to justify arresting the animal. That's INTOLERABLE!"

"They probably couldn't get a murder warrant issued in time," Kat said, thoroughly alarmed.

"NO! They didn't want to comply with anything I've demanded, and this was a clever way to institutionally flip their finger at me once again. GODDAMMIT!"

Chris Billings looked at Kat and back to Ken. "Ah, Captain, I'm sorry to have upset you—"

Ken whirled around to look at him, then pulled the revolver from his map case and pointed the barrel toward the overhead panel. "They've never had any intention of listening to me!"

Kat shook his shoulder slightly.

"Ken, put the gun down. We're close to a breakthrough with what

Roger Matson is working on, what I've discovered, what you've managed to highlight. Lumin's in jail. That's what counts. Don't panic because they used a meaningless warrant rather than the whole charge. The charges will be reinstituted as soon as possible."

"Yeah, when Bostich admits it."

"Or sooner. I think we ought to get that Connecticut judge on the line and—"

"Mr. Billings, please return to your seat," Ken said, running the captain's seat back on its rails and breaking Kat's hold on his shoulder as he punched open the cockpit door.

"Ah, sure, Captain. Thank you for talking to me."

Chris Billings beat a hasty retreat and closed the door behind him. Kat barely noticed his leaving, watching in alarm as Ken Wolfe took the .44 Magnum from his map case and began climbing out of the seat.

"Ken! What are you doing?"

Wolfe kept going.

"Ken, I'm not a pilot, and we're in flight. You can't leave me up here alone. What are you doing?"

"It's on autopilot, Kat. And what am I doing? I'm going to give Mr. Bostich that precise choice we discussed. Sign a confession or die."

She reached out again and took his sleeve. "Ken. You're panicking and overreacting to this."

"Overreacting?" He scowled at her, but kept the same position, half in, half out of the seat. Kat took it as a hopeful sign.

"Ken, you're a consummate professional captain! You'd never leave your command chair unless there was another qualified pilot aboard! Look at what you're trying to do!" She gestured to him, half in, half out. "What if something went wrong up here?"

"Something *has* gone wrong. They've lied to me!"

"Ken, *listen* to me! They didn't lie! *I* didn't lie. No one told you Lumin would be arrested on a murder warrant, they just said he'd be arrested. That's the important point! You aren't a law enforcement officer. You don't know the hell we have to go through to get an arrest warrant. We'll take the shortest distance between two points to get the job done anytime. Okay? It's not a message. It's not pointed."

"Don't you see the method, Kat? They're not going to comply with a single demand of mine! Remember the C-one-thirty?"

"Ken, listen to me *clinically*, if nothing else!"

Slowly he sat back down. "What, Kat? More platitudes?"

"Focus, Ken! What do you want? What have you done all this for? To get Lumin off the street and arrested. He *has* been! Who *cares* what for? He's off the streets. You wanted Bostich unmasked and confessing. Well, he sure is unmasked, and I think we're pretty close to a confession. You wanted a grand jury, and they're meeting, though not even the Attorney General can control what they decide. Ken, you're getting it all done! Don't blow it now, especially since one slip with that gun and we'll *never* know the full extent of what Bostich did."

The radio came to life with the voice of the Gulfstream's owner.

"Kat, are you there?"

She glanced at the radio head in the console, then back to Ken. "Don't forget your goal, Ken. It wasn't to dictate *how* Bradley Lumin was captured and prosecuted, it was just to get him collared and thrown behind bars. Okay? He's there!"

"Kat, can you hear me?" Bill North asked.

Ken looked in her eyes, and she tried to smile through the roiling upset inside her and the self-recrimination that she had forgotten how unstable he really was.

Finally he looked down and nodded, as Bill North called her a third time.

"Better answer him," Ken said.

She nodded and turned to punch the button.

"I'm here, Bill."

"Had me worried, Kat. Detective Matson is on the line. Can I relay for you?"

Her eyes remained on Ken as he sat almost sideways, looking at the center console without seeing it, the .44 held loosely in his right hand.

"Kat?" Bill asked again.

Kat's concentration was on the captain. "Ken? You okay?"

He nodded again and inclined his head toward the glareshield. "I guess I forgot you're not a pilot. You're so competent at everything else, Kat. And I was—" His voice caught, and a tear rolled into view on his cheek as he took a breath and looked up. "I used to look at Melinda, after I lost her mother, and I'd have this image . . ."

Bill North's voice reached their ears again. "Kat, please respond."

She punched the button without taking her eyes off Ken. "Stand by, Bill. Tell him to stand by."

She nodded at Ken. "I understand."

"I had this ideal of what she'd be like as a young woman, you know? Strong, self-assured, beautiful, feminine, and terribly capable."

"I'm sure she would have been, Ken."

He was shaking his head. "No, that wasn't the point. The point was the image. I just realized why you seem so familiar, Kat." He looked up at her, his eyes filled with tears. "You remind me of the Melinda I'll never know."

He turned back toward the yoke and ran his seat forward, carefully replacing the revolver in the map case to his side as Kat fought off a wave of emotion and forced herself to punch the transmit button.

"Go . . . ah . . . go ahead now, Bill. Put him on."

"Stand by."

She turned to Ken. "I'm very honored you would say that to me, Ken."

He shook his head and waved her off gently.

"Kat? Roger Matson, over."

"Go ahead, Roger. Any progress?"

We're supposed to have fingerprint results momentarily, but I don't have them yet."

"Okay, Roger. I made the call about the warrants for Bostich's home and office, and supposedly they're in progress. I have not talked to him again since I last talked to you."

Something was scratching at the back of her mind again, a small incongruity, something Roger had said or mentioned before that she hadn't had time to think about because of other distractions. Something that didn't fit. But what was it?

"What's your status up there, Kat?"

"Stand by a second," she said, closing her eyes to capture the gossamer thought.

Her eyes came open suddenly as her finger pressed the button.

"Roger, something's bothering me. Earlier you said something in reference to that picture of Melinda Wolfe we found on both Bostich's computer and Lumin's, the one Lumin took. You said something about trees in the window."

"That's right. I was just referring to the details in the picture."

She shook her head slightly. It still wasn't connecting. "No, I mean, was that a reference to details that I might have added as red herrings?"

Detective Roger Matson's reply carried an equally puzzled tone.

"They wouldn't be very good as red herrings when they're clearly visible. I would think Bostich would remember them."

"Visible where, Roger? I'm confused."

"In the picture. The window in the upper right hand corner with the evergreen trees visible through it. That's why we think she was taken to some cabin in Maine, because of an analysis of the trees, though it's not conclusive."

Kat cocked her head. "Roger, I don't remember . . ." Kat released the button for a second and looked down at Bostich's computer. "Wait just a second. Stand by."

She flipped open the lid and punched a key to turn on the display. A few key strokes were needed to call up Melinda's picture again, and within thirty seconds it had reassembled itself on the liquid crystal color display, the haunting, tortured image boring into her soul once more, the wicker chair, the bare walls behind, *AND NO TREES!*

"Roger, I'm looking at the photo. There is a window in this photo, but it's reflecting the flash on the camera. There are no trees or anything else visible outside."

"Kat, they're crystal clear! The window takes up perhaps fifteen percent of the background. It's not subtle. Look, are we talking about *the* picture of Melinda?"

"Yes."

"In the wicker chair?"

"Yes. But there are no trees. When I look closely . . . wait a minute. Wait just a minute!"

Roger Matson's voice took on a taut urgency. "What is it?"

Kat glanced toward Ken, whose eyes were straight ahead. She took a breath and looked back at the screen. "Roger, I didn't see this before, and it's pretty grainy on this computer screen, but in the reflection of flash in the window, I can see a hand holding the camera. Do you see the same thing?"

"I have the picture in front of me, Kat. There is no reflection on any flash, and no hand. I've got a window and trees, and you don't. My God, Kat! There was only one picture found in Bradley Lumin's possession. You've just described a *second* picture. Are you certain that's Melinda Wolfe?"

A hand reached across her lap before she could respond and swiveled the computer around. Ken looked closely at the horrid image of his battered daughter, and quietly turned it back toward Kat as he punched his transmit button.

"Roger, this is Ken Wolfe. I checked. It is Melinda. There is no doubt. What are you saying?"

There was a long silence before Matson's voice returned, preceded by a long sigh. "Okay. What am I saying? I'm stunned, but there are a couple of basic realities here. One, the picture I have was the only one Bradley Lumin possessed. Two, the picture you're looking at is a different picture, also taken while she was a kidnap victim. Three, the picture you're looking at could not have been taken by Lumin. The conclusion? Ken, unless we're missing something, Bradley Lumin can't be the killer."

THIRTY-ONE

Aboard AirBridge Flight 90. 4:54 P.M.

"That's not possible!" Ken muttered. "Wait a minute."

He checked the distance remaining figure on the screen of the flight computer, then pressed the transmit button again, his mind in a wild quandary, Roger Matson's words ricocheting around his mind.

"Roger, I can't accept that! Lumin is the only suspect. All the evidence was there! You found it yourself on Lumin's computer. I know there were no other pictures of Melinda found on that machine or in his damn house, but he could have easily made other pictures and . . . and uploaded them to someone before his arrest, then fully erased them and thrown the hard copies away."

Matson's voice came back cautious and metered. "I don't think, Ken, that there's any logic in that. We know Lumin got rid of the hard copy of the picture that I'm looking at, because we found nothing but an empty Polaroid camera in his trailer. You know that. There were no photographs in his place. We know he scanned that one into his computer on his scanner because the record is in the scanner program. But no other pictures were scanned in, unless he spent many hours carefully erasing all the evidence with one of those programs the military uses, and we found no evidence of that. Ken, we looked for erased files, too. I had a world-class expert examine every byte of information on his hard drive. Everything, even the fragments. There was nothing resembling an erased picture, and it's very hard to obliterate all record of an erased picture file. My conclusion from that is that Lumin never loaded in more than one picture of Melinda."

Ken massaged his forehead, his mind in a whirl.

"Roger, how, then, if Lumin *wasn't* the killer . . . how does it make any sense that a picture of Melinda obviously taken by the killer is found on his computer? I mean, you said there was evidence he had scanned it in himself. Doesn't that prove he had to be the one who took the picture, or at least possessed the original photograph?"

"Not necessarily," Roger Matson replied. "Ken, any computer can have stuff planted on it. Someone could have sneaked into his house there in Stamford and put all that we found on his hard drive. That's not impossible. Improbable, maybe, but not impossible."

Kat's voice interrupted them. "Roger, do you have a picture or detailed description of Lumin's hands?"

The reply was rapid. "Yes. His hands are very large, and he has the same large, ugly tattoo on the back of both of them. Dragons, I think. If you can see the back of his hand in that shot you've got, you should see it. The thing covered even his thumb."

Kat studied the picture, looked over at Ken, and shook her head as she pressed the transmit button.

"Roger, in this picture the entire back of the hand is visible. It's murky, but when you look closely, it's visible, and there are no tattoos."

"Then," Matson replied, "it is definitely not Lumin in the picture. And, since pedophile murderers almost always act alone, I can't see how Lumin could be the murderer. It doesn't add up."

Ken stared at Kat for a moment, unwilling to let go of the hatred he'd felt toward Lumin for so many agonizing months, knowing every night that Lumin was still alive, and Melinda wasn't.

But Roger's words kept echoing through his mind, reinforcing the same answer from all directions at once: Lumin did not kill Melinda.

"Then I," Ken said quietly, "almost killed an innocent man last night."

"But you didn't," Kat said quickly. "That's the important point. You're not a killer, Ken. That's why we need to get these people safely on the ground."

"Bostich still lied!"

She nodded. "Yes. He did, but it's immaterial now, isn't it?"

"No, it's not immaterial! Destroying a murder prosecution for your own purposes isn't immaterial, Kat, it's criminal, even if the suspect wasn't guilty. Right?" He was shaking his head as if in a trance. "I . . .

I'm thoroughly confused now. Bostich ruined evidence that would have convicted an innocent man, but where did the evidence come from to begin with?"

Ken pressed the transmit button. "Roger? Are you still there?"

"Yeah." There was a long sigh. "I feel like I just got swept out to sea here. Lumin is a convicted pedophile and a scumbag of the first order, but you remember my telling you, Ken, that I couldn't figure out how he could have put this together and almost gotten away with it? He's just not sophisticated enough. So the rational answer is, he *didn't* put it all together. Someone else did. And that someone must have loaded all that information into Lumin's computer specifically to frame him. That's our killer. He must have had both pictures, and Lumin must have been the perfect patsy for him. Stupid, loathsome, a convict with a long history of luring children and molesting them, Lumin's also someone who uses a computer to get his jollies from looking at kiddie porn."

"If it hadn't have been for that tip from Bostich . . ." Ken began, then paused and let up on the transmit button.

"Which was false," Roger added. "But why would Bostich finger Lumin? How did he even know about Lumin?"

Kat pressed her button. "There's a shocking possibility we'd better get on the table, gentlemen. The person with the greatest incentive to create a diversion is the guilty one."

"What are you saying, Kat?" Roger asked.

She took a very deep breath and looked at Ken, worried about Ken's reaction to what she was going to say, as she punched the button again. "Roger, we have to consider Rudolph Bostich a suspect in Melinda's death."

Ken whirled around, his eyes huge with shock, his expression incredulous. "What? *Bostich*? But he *sabotaged* the case against Lumin. If . . . if Bostich killed Melinda, he would have supported the warrant and the evidence, because he would have planted that evidence. He would have been happy to let Lumin go to the chair in his place."

Kat shook her head. "Consider this. Bostich sets up Lumin perfectly, plants the evidence, then tips you, Roger, knowing you'll find the evidence and arrest him. Indicting Lumin based on that evidence is a slam dunk, but then Bostich purposefully lies to destroy the warrant because if Lumin never gets a trial, he'll stand even *more* convicted in the eyes of the public. Bostich knew that letting Lumin go free on a technicality would spark such public outrage that no one would ever question whether Lumin was the killer. No one, in other words, would ever think about the possibility that someone like Bostich might have done it. It was the perfect smokescreen. How incredibly cunning!"

"You're right, Kat," Roger Matson said. "I never seriously considered the possibility that someone else might have killed Melinda because I was too upset over losing the warrant and the evidence. It never occurred to me. Never."

"And we now know that Bostich has a sick interest in kiddie porn," Kat continued. "And Bostich has a picture only the killer would have, and one that Lumin doesn't have, and if we're right, the picture that was on Lumin's computer—the one you have, Roger—is also in Bostich's home or office."

"Kat," Roger added, "if this is all true, the SHRDLU2 e-mail address will belong to Bostich, and the fingerprint will be his."

She looked at Ken, who was deep in thought. "How far are we from Phoenix now?"

He didn't respond, and she had to repeat the question and place her hand on his arm before he heard her and checked the computer. "A . . . ah . . . little over a hundred twenty nautical miles. I'm just getting ready to start our descent." He still sounded dazed.

"Are we going to land?"

He nodded. "*You* are, yes."

She hesitated, studying him. "What does that mean, 'you are'?"

"I'm already dead, remember?" he said.

"No, I *don't* remember. What are you talking about?"

Roger's voice came over the radio before Ken could answer.

She punched the transmit button again.

"Roger," Kat said, her attention divided by Ken's statement. "Please call us back when you've got the fingerprint ID. We're approaching Phoenix."

Roger Matson acknowledged the request and they broke the connection precisely as the cockpit call chime rang, with Annette on the other end relaying a message from Bostich.

"Go ahead, Annette," Ken said.

"Bostich says he's ready to talk to the judge in Connecticut."

"That's amazing," Kat said, shaking her head. "As soon as we *don't* need him, he cracks. Apparently he listened."

Ken thanked Annette and replaced the handset. Kat located the tiny tape recorder and a piece of paper.

"Do you have a book or something I can use for backing? Oh, wait. The computer top will do." Kat closed the lid and began writing as Ken watched.

"What is that?" he asked, when she stopped.

"Bostich's statement, admitting that he purposefully misled the court, and that he did, in fact, make the telephone call to Roger Matson that night, and that he further relied on the knowledge that Matson would recognize him instantly and would not need to ask his name."

She finished checking the confession, unsnapped her seatbelt, and swung her leg over the console.

"I'll be back. I assume you approve?"

He nodded.

The cockpit door closed behind her, and he found himself suddenly alone and missing her presence.

He checked the distance remaining again and calculated when to begin a descent, and what to do when he got there. The gun was back in his map case, and Ken pulled it out and methodically checked the chambers, all of which were loaded. He examined the ammunition, relieved to find a type of bullet that would expand on impact with anything. There would be a lower risk of even penetrating the skin of the aircraft.

He cocked and uncocked the hammer twice, then placed it back by his side.

I should talk to air traffic control, he decided, dialing in the appropriate frequency to tell them he would be ready to descend in ten miles.

"Whatever you want, AirBridge Ninety," the controller at Albuquerque Center replied. "Just let us know, and maintain a squawk of seventy-five hundred."

He reached up and punched the aft galley call button and lifted the handset. Annette answered rapidly.

"You recall that FAA inspector, Annette?"

"Yes."

"Have you been talking to him?"

"No, Ken. Why?"

"I just wondered what kind of jets he was qualified in."

"He's not a pilot inspector, Ken. He's a maintenance inspector. Why?"

Ken swallowed and shook his head before replying. It had been the perfect solution. He hadn't intended to leave a pilot on board in Durango, but since an FAA inspector had slipped through, he had just assumed the inspector could fly a 737. Now he was going to need a Plan B to get everyone down safely without him.

"Thanks anyway, Annette. You can tell the people we'll be landing in Phoenix in approximately twenty minutes."

Eighteen feet behind the cockpit, Rudolph Bostich held a pen in his hand and hesitated over the crudely written confession Kat had prepared, reexamining his conclusions. His initial instinct had been to deny everything. It was, after all, up to the state to prove a crime beyond a reasonable doubt, and who knew better than a prosecutor how hard it was to convict someone who refused to crack unless the evidence was solid as a brick?

He glanced up at Kat, realizing the futility of trying to protest that child pornography held no interest for him, or that he had been equally horrified to find that the bastard who had tipped him about Lumin had loaded such pictures on his computer—pictures he had tried ham-handedly to erase.

But there was no way he could tell her what really happened.

She was right about one thing. Possession of even erased pornographic pictures of children would create a firestorm that even an eventual acquittal couldn't quench.

Rudy Bostich closed his eyes and ran over the options one last time. If he refused to satisfy Ken Wolfe's demands for a confession and someone got hurt, he would bear a double stigma. Yet, if he signed that paper, he'd be admitting to something he didn't do. He had gleefully accepted what he thought were files of young women in hardcore X-rated activities, but would the distinction save him from public condemnation?

No, the President would have to drop him in a nanosecond regardless.

Bostich looked at the words Kat had written. "I acknowledge that I am in possession of partially erased computer files depicting . . ."

That much was true.

Rudy Bostich sighed and pressed the pen to the paper, watching his name flow in sickeningly clear letters. He could still say it was obtained under duress, of course, so maybe this was the best method. He'd already made the same statement verbally into his own tape recorder as Kat held it in front of him.

Kat realized there was one more duty, and she felt her stomach knotting again as she folded the paper and looked at Bostich carefully, the tape recorder still held in her hand where he could see it. A small wave of loathing washed over her as she looked at him, imagining that same right hand tying a rope around a tortured little girl's neck.

"One more question, Mr. Bostich. The picture of Melinda Wolfe on your computer was taken by her kidnapper and killer, but that person was *not* Bradley Lumin."

"WHAT?" Bostich almost came out of his seat with shock.

She nodded. "That's right, Mr. Bostich. I'm glad you decided to do the right thing and admit you lied to that Connecticut court, but as far as the murder of Melinda Wolfe is concerned, it's immaterial. There's no need to reinstate evidence, because the evidence was planted."

"What do you mean, 'planted'?"

She looked at him carefully, trying to read his reaction, wishing she had Frank's years of experience in sizing up human reaction under stress of criminal investigation.

"Whoever killed Melinda tried to frame Lumin, but the attempt has failed."

Bostich looked dazed. "You mean, this was unnecessary? I've sat back here trying to balance what I should do, dammit, and you were right, I thought. I should give Wolfe whatever he wants, whether it's the truth or not. Now . . . now I find out after falsely incriminating myself to end a hijacking, that it's unnecessary?" He started to say more, but stopped suddenly, his mind racing through the possibilities.

If not Lumin, who?

"Give it up, Bostich. You lied, you've confessed to it, and that's that."

"Who *is* the killer?"

"Hold out your right hand, Mr. Bostich. Hold it palm down."

He complied, reluctantly, and she looked hard at it, comparing the hand with the one in her memory from the picture.

I can't tell for sure, but they could be the same! Kat concluded.

"Put your hand down."

He complied.

"Rudolph Bostich, did you kidnap Melinda Wolfe?"

"Wha—what?"

"Yes or no, please."

"Good God, NO!"

"Rudolph Bostich, did you murder Melinda Wolfe?"

The look that crossed Bostich's face was a combination of utter horror and panic. He began to sputter an answer, but sat back hard, his breathing rapid, as he managed to croak out a reply. "Are you *crazy?* NO! I . . . I . . . could never do anything like that! Why would you think—"

"Because, Mr. Bostich, you possessed a picture that only the killer could have taken. Either Lumin was the killer, or you were. Since we now know Lumin is not the murderer, there's only one explanation left."

She stood then, reaching behind her for the plastic handcuffs she had fished out of the aircraft's flight kit earlier without Ken's knowledge.

"Rudolph Bostich, I am placing you under arrest for felony perjury, and for suspicion of the murder of Melinda Wolfe."

"You're wrong!" he croaked, his voice barely recognizable.

Ken was holding the P.A. microphone as Kat entered the cockpit and slid into the right seat. As she held up the signed confession, he nodded and pressed the button.

"Folks, this is Ken Wolfe speaking for the last time. I'm going to land us in Phoenix, which, of course, is where you should have been this morn-

ing. You've been through hell, and I am eternally sorry for all you've endured. I'm not sure what I've accomplished today, other than the unmasking of Rudolph Bostich, who has now confessed to lying in a court of law under oath. Bradley Lumin has been arrested, but a new discovery appears to show that Bradley Lumin may not be my daughter's killer after all. I don't know who is, but I trust the investigation will continue, and the murderer will be caught and tried."

Ken replaced the P.A. microphone and turned to face Kat's startled expression.

"Ken, what exactly are you planning to do?"

"I said we'd land in Phoenix, and I mean it."

"And you'll let the people off there?"

He nodded. "There will be no one stopping them."

"Meaning?"

He looked over at her. "Kat, I think you're trying to hide the fact that you're trained as a pilot. You know too much. You're too comfortable up here."

She tried not to look startled and waved her right hand at the panel. "I've sat in simulators, Ken, but that's a long way from being a Boeing pilot."

He was pointing to the forward glareshield at two paddle-like switches.

"This is the autopilot, Kat. Either switch in the full up position engages it, like you see it now. There are two independent autopilot systems, but for precision landings, we use both at the same time."

"Why are you telling me this, Ken?"

"Because you're going to monitor the aircraft while it lands itself."

"And where are you planning to be?" She tensed for his answer.

"I'll be . . . only God knows where, Kat. I pray with Melinda . . . and her mother. My body will be in the forward restroom."

She shook her head violently. "Are you crazy, Ken? You know you can't shoot a gun in a pressurized jetliner without—without terrible consequences."

He shook his head. "Not necessarily true, Kat. That's a perpetual misconception. Unloose an assault weapon, and, yeah, you'll create havok. But a single bullet may not even penetrate the outer skin of the aircraft, and even if it does, there won't be a rapid decompression.

Merely a small hole. Just be sure you keep everyone out of that restroom until the pathology team arrives."

"This is ridiculous! I can't fly this aircraft! If you're not here, we're dead."

"Not true. Now listen up, because there are some things you're going to have to do, like put down the landing gear and flaps at the right time."

"Ken, CUT IT OUT! This isn't some stupid movie script where the ditzy blonde lands the plane. I CAN'T DO IT! You're going to have to get us on the ground."

"I don't want to ever touch the ground again. I've done all I can do. I'm leaving."

"And killing us is a reasonable result?"

"This Boeing can land itself, Kat, as long as you put the wheels down once this light goes on." He pointed to a light on the panel. "The autothrottles are engaged, I've already got us on an extended final approach to Phoenix Skyharbor, and the only other thing I need to do is show you how, and when, to lower the flaps."

"So what if the autopilot clicks off?"

"Turn it back on."

"What if it won't come back on?"

He sighed. "Then the solution is simple. Here." He clicked a button on the control yoke twice, disconnecting the autopilot. "Put your hands on the yoke, Kat."

"No. I'm not going to participate."

"DAMMIT, DO IT!"

She complied reluctantly.

"Okay. Flying a seven-thirty-seven is simple. I'm going to let go, and just let you get a feel for—"

Kat rolled the yoke to the left sharply, then reversed the roll just as sharply to the right, rolling the 737 almost inverted as she pulled hard, pushing them both down in their seats.

"Whoa! I've got it!" Ken said, resuming control and rolling the jet back to wings level as he arrested the sudden climb.

"I told you, Ken, I can't do it! I'll kill us all! *You'll* kill us all!"

"No, not true. Not as long as I can get you set up for an automatic landing."

She turned to him. "So we're still debating that?"

"No," Ken shook his head. "I'm convinced you can't fly, so what I'm going to do is set you up on final with the gear down and the flaps set, and make sure everything's working right. I'll head into the restroom just before touchdown. All you have to do when the wheels touch is pull back the throttles, pull up these reverser levers, and when the aircraft has slowed under fifty, step on the brakes. The autobrakes will do all the rest to that point. When you're stopped, pull these start levers out and down to cut off the engines."

"This is stupid, Ken."

"I told you, Kat. I don't want to touch the ground again."

"How selfish can you get?" she snapped. "I can almost understand you doing what you've done today in order to catch a killer, but to imperil all these people just so you can kill yourself a few seconds early is nonsense! It's stupid. And it's selfishness in the extreme."

His hand moved around the forward panel, adjusting various settings for the autopilot and dialing in the instrument landing approach frequency.

Bill North called as Ken was lifting the P.A. microphone, and Kat answered.

"I'm here."

"Roger Matson is calling again. I'll patch you through."

Ken punched the P.A. button.

"There's one more thing I want to tell you, folks. Despite what I said for effect earlier, I did not know when I came aboard this morning that Rudolph Bostich would be on this, or any other, AirBridge flight. I did not plan this."

"Kat? Roger Matson here. Where are you?"

"Getting ready to land in Phoenix, Roger, and trying to keep this suicidal pilot from killing himself before we touch down. What have you got?"

"Last night was the second anniversary of my daughter's death. I decided that the law was never going to get Lumin off the streets, and I had to do it myself. So, I took a high-powered rifle up to Ft. Collins to kill him, because the law wouldn't uncover Bostich's lie and rearrest Lumin, and

because I was convinced Lumin had killed twice more since Melinda's death."

"Do you still have a cellular phone within reach?"
"Yes. Why?"
"You have my number?"
"Yes. *Why?*"
"Call me on it. Now!" The line went dead.

"But something strange happened. I found I couldn't make myself pull the trigger and shoot Lumin."

Kat hurriedly opened the cell phone and punched in Roger's number, relieved that the signal from the ground seemed strong. He answered it immediately.
"I could hear you fine, Roger. Why the—"
"Bill North was listening on that satellite phone, Kat."

"I couldn't figure out why, but now I understand God was holding me back from killing the wrong man."

"So what? He's heard everything else."
"Not this, Kat. The fingerprint doesn't belong to Bostich. They had a real problem finding a match, but they finally came up with a petty criminal in Chicago."

"This morning, when I suddenly discovered Bostich on my flight, it was like God giving me a final chance, and even though I knew what I was about to do was criminal, I took that last chance. My life has been over since Melinda's death, but I had to make sure that her killer couldn't kill again."

"What are you saying, Roger?"
"His name is José Taurus. He doesn't have much of a criminal record, but he works for a shadowy operation that produces pornographic tapes and magazines, and has been under investigation by Interpol for suspicion of dealing in snuff films. You know, the ones

where women who think they're doing a porno film are murdered on-camera."

"I know. The whole subject is nauseating."

"Taurus isn't the murderer, but he's the functionary who sent in the monthly cash for the unlisted e-mail address, SHRDLU2, which our murderer may have been using."

"Look, folks, it's important to me that you know one more thing. Even though I've been threatening you all day long to make sure no one stopped me, there is no bomb on this airplane. I would never . . . could never . . . take the chance of hurting my passengers. I'm sorry I had to convince you otherwise."

Kat shifted the phone to her other ear. "Go on, Roger!"

"I had a buddy on the Chicago force find Taurus and squeeze him hard in the last twenty minutes. The guy was terrified, but he apparently knows nothing else. He says he was told by his boss to do it, and we can't find the boss. In the meantime, I had another friend checking the background of this company, and you won't believe what popped up."

"What?"

"I know I've scared all of you half to death, but you were never in any real danger. The flight was controlled at all times, including my psuedo-acrobatics. Even the takeoff from Telluride was carefully calculated and never in doubt, although I didn't know I was going to have to go that soon."

"Taurus's sleazy corporation is a subsidiary of a Swiss company that publishes skin magazines in various languages for the European market, and it, in turn, is wholly owned by a private multibillion-dollar publishing empire headquartered in Salt Lake City."

Kat felt suddenly off balance. How many major publishing empires were headquartered in Salt Lake? "What's the name, Roger?"

"NorthLight Publications. And guess who owns NorthLight?"

"Bill North?"

"Bingo."

THIRTY-TWO

Aboard AirBridge Flight 90. 5:11 P.M.

Kat gripped the cell phone and closed her eyes, concentrating hard. The idea that Bill North could own a company that was even indirectly involved in distributing sleaze was disturbing, let alone the sudden connection with the SHRDLU2 mailbox. The fact that his offer of help in Salt Lake might have been less than altruistic was also throwing her substantially off balance. She had assumed he was just a concerned citizen before discovering he partially owned AirBridge and was taking care of an investment, but now *this*?

"Roger, do we have any indication *who* in North's outfit might be involved? Surely Bill knows nothing about this."

"I don't have a clue, Kat, and without the time to talk to Taurus's boss, the trail goes cold. His company in Chicago is determined not to cooperate, of course."

"Which means we need North's help. Roger, I know nothing about North's operations other than he said he made his money in publishing. What do you know about him?"

There was a long, telling pause on the other end, and she heard him clear his throat before speaking.

"Kat, I was startled when you said he was helping you. North's holdings include a wild variety of questionable publications overseas. For instance, NorthLight Publications has been under investigation in the Philippines for years for controlling the underground production of hardcore porn of all types, and publishing some really disgusting rags. He also owns three of Europe's and Britain's shabbiest tabloids, the type that keep the paparazzi in business hounding the famous to death—literally, in the case of Princess Di. He's got legitimate interests, too, but a lot of the guy's money stinks."

"I didn't know any of this, Roger."

"No reason you should, unless you'd been researching the international sleaze merchants like I have. Where's Ken? Is he listening?"

"He's giving a P.A. right now, so I don't think so. Should he be?"

"No. Kat, there's one more thing you should know. There's something no one else but me knows about Melinda's final hours. I've held it back, because other than us, only the murderer knows these details, and I always assumed that was Lumin. Look, I'm . . . not entirely sure why I feel so strongly I should tell you this, but I do. Now that Lumin looks innocent, it's critical information. Don't repeat this to anyone unless you're using it to confirm, understood?"

"Go ahead."

"It'll make you ill, Kat."

"I'm already ill."

"So, folks, please relax if you can. This will all be over in less than twenty minutes. And please know that even though I can never make amends, or ask your forgiveness, I am sorry for what I've put you through."

Ken finished the P.A. as Roger Matson finished speaking. Kat closed the cellular phone with deliberate care, trying not to betray the feeling of revulsion that had swept over her as he'd predicted. She thought for a second, the anger rising within, and reached for Rudy Bostich's computer once again, determined to find the key. The reflected hand she had spotted in the picture of Melinda Wolfe was a start. It demanded closer examination.

Something had been bothering her about the hand ever since she'd discovered it, and she ran her eyes now over every part of the image, cataloguing the fact that the hand was Caucasian, obviously male, and somehow distinctive.

She made the picture larger, boosting the size until the hand was an undecipherable jumble of square pixels on the screen before her.

There was a sophisticated photo manipulation program on Bostich's computer, and she used it to enhance the image, slowly watching as the picture coalesced, the computer's tiny silicon brain filling in the blanks with its best guess as to what color and shade each empty pixel should be.

Suddenly the hand filled the entire screen with a startling degree of clarity, showing a distinctive sideways crook in the knuckle of the little finger.

Ken was lowering himself back into the left seat and she glanced at him briefly before returning her attention to the enhanced photo.

One thing for sure: It's definitely not Bradley Lumin, and for that matter, it's not Rudy Bostich.

"What did Matson have to say?" Ken asked. His eyes were on the instruments, unaware of the startled look on her face.

She turned and studied him carefully before replying, aware that he was leveling the 737 at six thousand feet as he aimed for Phoenix.

She repeated the essence of the conversation, along with the fact that the parent corporation of the Chicago sleaze merchant was owned by the man sitting in a Gulfstream several hundred yards to their left.

He looked at her in confusion. "What do you mean?"

She took a deep breath. "Bill North owns the company, Ken, and we need help finding who in his organization ordered those payments for the SHRDLU2 mailbox. Remember, whoever owns that e-mail address is probably the killer, or can lead us to the killer. Of course, I didn't expect this to lead to a company."

The sound of the cellular phone ringing caused her to jump. She swept it open, relieved to hear Frank's voice on the other end.

"Kat, I wanted to update you. The search of Lumin's place in Ft. Collins has been very interesting. They found a cache of porno videotapes, all of them featuring underage girls, all of them meant for commercial underground distribution, and none of them involving any kids currently listed as missing or dead, as far as can be determined. In fact, one little girl is a known runaway who sells herself for such things over and over again."

"He was *producing* those things?"

"Producing is too formal a word, but that's the idea. They found a ledger indicating Lumin would lure them in, pay them, tape them in some remote place, sometimes involving group sex, then market the results."

"So there's no evidence he kills them or tortures them?"

"No. Some of them, and maybe all of them, were probably tricked or coerced, but other than the sexual exploitation, he didn't appear to be killing or torturing them. We do believe he was forcing drugs down their throats. They found cocaine in the trailer. But Kat, one of the girls was videotaped in a cabin that looks very similar to the picture Matson described to me."

"You mean the same place Melinda . . ." she glanced at Ken, who was listening through the headset connection. He motioned for her to continue. "It looks like the place where Melinda was held?"

"It does. I've forced my way back into this case by screaming at FBI Headquarters, and I'm having us fax a still shot of that footage to Matson right now for confirmation."

"In those tapes, there were none, I suppose, of Melinda Wolfe."

"None. Kat, if he taped her, the tape didn't surface in Ft. Collins. Fact is, though, with all the publicity about her kidnapping, a sleaze like Lumin would have panicked and thrown away the evidence."

She thanked him and disconnected, staring through the windscreen in thought for a few moments, trying to make the pieces fit. Lumin made kiddie porn videotapes, but didn't kill his victims, or even torture them, as far as they knew. Somehow the search of his Connecticut house two years before had missed such tapes. Why? It gave strength to the conclusion that Lumin wouldn't have suddenly murdered a little girl he'd carefully enticed into his porno web. But had he suddenly made an exception?

She kept her eyes on the western horizon.

"Ken, did the police ever determine how Melinda was taken? Was she snatched in public?"

In her peripheral vision, she could see him shake his head slowly, and she looked over at him, realizing his face was wet.

"No. She apparently went voluntarily to meet the thirteen-year-old boy she thought she'd been writing to. The last e-mail had set up the meeting in a mall. I was out of town. They figured she was snatched there, or voluntarily went with whoever killed her. She might have fallen for some song and dance about taking her to the nonexistent pen pal. I reported her missing immediately, but it was two days before I found the e-mail record and the police recognized a pattern and sounded the alarm."

"No ransom demands?"

"Never. Nothing. It obviously wasn't that kind of kidnapping. Whoever it was just wanted to use her and throw her away."

Kat looked toward Phoenix, seeing nothing, wondering if Lumin had somehow handed off Melinda to someone else—someone who killed her.

She turned back to Ken suddenly.

"Ken, if you truly want to catch Melinda's killer, you're going to have to abandon this plan to blow your brains out."

He looked at her, an unreadable, unfathomable expression of pain and fury creasing his features.

She tried again. "Ken, do you understand? The key has got to be Bill North."

"North?" He asked simply.

"Yes. North! He can force whoever runs that Chicago company to answer the critical question of who was operating that e-mail address, SHRDLU2. I've met the guy. If you're gone, he won't do it if it threatens his business interests. But he wants to be the hero who ends this hijacking. He'll do it for you, Ken."

He looked to the left at the Gulfstream for several long seconds, then suddenly rolled the 737 into a steep right turn as he pushed the throttles up and keyed the radio.

"Ken, what are you doing?"

He ignored the question as his finger found the transmit button.

"Mr. North, Ken Wolfe. Are you over there?"

Aboard Gulfstream N5LL. 5:19 P.M.

Kneeling between his pilots in the cockpit, Bill North had been mildly embarrassed when Detective Roger Matson suddenly decided to use a cellular line to talk to Kat Bronsky a few minutes earlier, excluding him. He knew his two pilots were wondering what they suddenly had to discuss that North and his crew weren't supposed to hear. North had been deep in thought when Wolfe's sudden call cracked through the speakers.

Bill North nodded to Dane and grabbed the microphone.

"I'm here, Captain. Where are you going?"

"We need to talk. Quickly and privately. I need your help in ending this, and I want you to land behind me at Globe, Arizona, just a few miles back."

"I thought we were headed for Phoenix?"

"We were. Now we're headed to Globe. Please follow me in. If you do, I'll let the people over here go and come aboard your aircraft, as you offered before. I'll surrender to you."

North hesitated, thinking it over for a split second before replying enthusiastically. "Good! Good, Captain! We'll be right behind you, and I'll take you anywhere you want to go. The offer's still good."

"Thank God!" Dane Bailey said as he banked the Gulfstream in pursuit. "I wonder what changed his mind?"

Bill North was usually quick with an answer, but there was no sound from his boss as Dane steepened the bank and glanced around, startled to see the depth of the wrinkles furrowing North's brow.

San Carlos Apache Airport, Globe, Arizona. 5:26 P.M.

The five thousand eight hundred feet of San Carlos Apache's only runway was just enough to accommodate a Boeing 737, so the sight of a commercial Boeing jetliner swooping in from the west with little more than a quick radio call on final approach attracted the attention of the few employees who hadn't headed home.

The Boeing landed and taxied to the end of the runway, where it turned off and moved onto a wider expanse of concrete, its engines sitting at idle as a sleek Gulfstream IV business jet touched down a minute later and taxied alongside the Boeing.

Two curious mechanics stood by their pickup truck and watched as the sound of the four jet engines began to wind down. A line boy from the corporate air terminal joined them, pushing back his baseball cap to scratch his head.

"What's goin' on? You suppose they need gas or something?"

"Anybody call you on the radio, Jim?" one of the mechanics asked, his eyes riveted on the Boeing.

"No."

"Well, if they need you, I'm sure they'll call."

"Door's opening on the seven-thirty-seven," the teenage boy named Jim observed.

"Opening on the Gulfstream, too." The older man turned to his companion. "Say, Don . . . you don't suppose—"

"Suppose what?"

"Wasn't that an AirBridge flight hijacked earlier today?"

There was a brief hesitation before the mechanic named Don nodded with wide eyes.

"What do we do?"

"Call the sheriff for starters. Do it, Jim! Quick!"

Aboard AirBridge Flight 90, San Carlos Apache Airport, Globe, Arizona. 5:30 P.M.

Ken silently ran through the items on the shutdown checklist before turning to Kat.

"Wait in the seat just a second."

She saw him deftly remove the .44 from his briefcase and slip it in his waistband again as he got to his feet and opened the cockpit door. She felt the pressure change as he opened the front entry door and heard the whine of the self-contained stairs as they began powering the steps out.

And she could hear Ken adjusting the P.A. microphone in his hand.

"Okay, folks. This is where it all ends. I'm sorry to leave you in Globe instead of Phoenix, but I know transportation will be arranged shortly. Other than that, I've said all I can say. I'm truly sorry. Please wait until I enter the other aircraft. Then you may depart, all but Rudy Bostich, that is. Mr. Bostich is under arrest, and any attempt to free him is a crime."

Ken replaced the microphone and leaned into the cockpit. "Okay, Kat, come on out."

She complied, surprised when his left arm encircled her shoulders and neck from behind as they stood at the top of the stairs.

"Forgive this one last show, but just in case he's harboring sharpshooters over there, I've got to look appropriately dangerous. The gun isn't cocked, as you know."

"But you're going to aim it at my head, aren't you?"

He nodded, a grim expression on his face as he moved her gently into the daylight at the top of the stairs and looked in all directions, the muzzle held to the back of her head.

"Take it easy, Kat. One step at a time. Together."

They moved smoothly to the bottom of the steps, Ken's eyes darting all around as Kat prayed the sudden diversion to Globe had been unanticipated by her agency or anyone else with guns and the power to create a disaster.

The Gulfstream sat less than a hundred feet away, its left side facing the Boeing's left side. The entry doorway was empty, and they climbed the steps slowly.

"Who up there is closest to the door?" Ken yelled.

A face popped into the entryway, and Kat recognized the captain.

"That's Dane Bailey," she said over her shoulder. "The captain."

"I'm unarmed, Captain Wolfe," Dane said as he put his hands up and backed into the aircraft.

"Where's Mr. North?"

Dane inclined his head toward the passenger cabin.

"And your copilot?"

"Still strapped into the right seat."

Ken nodded as he moved Kat through the door and to the right.

"Any sudden moves, Dane, and I'll have to shoot her."

"No one's moving suddenly, Captain! Mr. North is waiting for you. He's unarmed."

"He'd better be. Where are *you* planning to be?"

Dane shrugged. "Anywhere you want me. We're just trying not to get in the way."

Ken nodded. "Understood. Stay in the cockpit."

"Yes, sir."

As Ken Wolfe and Kat Bronsky disappeared in the door of the Gulfstream, Annette began the exodus of passengers from AirBridge 90 with a quick P.A. announcement, unsure what to expect.

"Please leave the aircraft, and move away from it immediately. Bev and Kevin will be in the lead. Follow them, and follow their instructions. I'll

bring up the rear. Please leave all your carry-on items here. You'll get them later."

She expected quick compliance.

Except for Blenheim—who almost knocked Bev and Kevin over in his rush to get off the aircraft—most of the passengers began moving up the aisle in slow motion, as if they weren't supposed to leave so soon, each of them shaking Annette's hand, or hugging her, or squeezing her shoulder—most asking where Ken Wolfe had gone, and what would happen to him now.

Suddenly Elvira Gates materialized in front of her, followed by all of her fear-of-flying group.

"You've won our hearts, my dear," Elvira said. "You acted magnificently."

"Thank you, Elvira. Are your people okay?"

She glanced around, then nodded. "I'm amazed. Some of them may take the bus from now on, but they've earned their PhD in this course." She patted Annette's hand and headed down the steps.

Mike Clark, the retired detective, brought up the rear, stopping in front of Annette and searching her face. "Should I try to go over to that business jet and help?"

She shook her head. "Stay out of it. I have no idea what's transpiring, but my main concern is getting all of you to safety."

He looked at her thoughtfully for several moments before arching his thumb in the direction of the empty captain's chair.

"The question is, Annette, who's going to get that poor guy to safety?"

THIRTY-THREE

Aboard Gulfstream N5LL, San Carlos Apache Airport, Globe, Arizona. 5:38 P.M.

Bill North was on his feet when Ken and Kat entered the plush cabin of Gulfstream N5LL. His eyes followed Ken carefully as the airline captain dropped his arm from Kat's shoulders. Kat moved toward the chair North had occupied at the rear of the cabin, relieved to see her purse still sitting alongside on the carpet.

"Why don't we sit over here, Captain Wolfe?" Bill North said, indicating the couch running along the right side of the cabin between the two swivel chairs.

"Let's drop the 'captain' bit, okay? Call me Ken. And sit over there." Ken motioned toward the forward swivel chair.

"Whatever you say."

"I've jerked those poor people over there around long enough. They can't help me anymore. You, however, can."

North smiled a thin smile and shrugged. "That's what I promised. What can I do for you?"

Ken glanced toward Kat. "You have the name of that Chicago company?"

She nodded as he repeated the details of José Taurus's involvement, watching Bill North's face as it contorted ever so slightly. When Ken was through, North shook his head energetically.

"I own many companies that own other companies in turn, Ken. I can't keep track of all of them. In fact, I don't even know the name of this one. Elysian, did you say?"

He nodded. "Owned by your Swiss outfit."

Bill nodded. "Okay. Let me get my corporate head of the Geneva division on the phone and get some answers quickly." He hesitated, watching Ken's eyes. "Can I get up and use the phone?"

"Where is it?"

"Near Kat, over there."

"Go ahead."

He leapt from the chair and crossed to the end of the couch, where he reached for the elaborate desk phone Kat had used. She watched as his hand closed around the handset.

Kat looked back at Ken and smiled a thin, unconvincing smile.

Kat forced her heart rate down and looked around at Bill North, who was standing with a hand on his hip, barking orders into the phone in French, demanding an immediate midnight connection with his managing director. North smiled at her briefly, his concentration returning to the call. She let her eyes follow the contour of his custom-made suit against the backdrop of his thirty-nine-million-dollar jet, and wondered what other things North's money had bought.

She replayed the mental image of Melinda in the picture.

North hung up the phone and stalked back to the other chair, where he plunked down heavily.

"He'll call me back in three minutes. Bear with me, Ken. We'll get some rapid answers."

Kat Bronsky forced herself to stand up and calmly move toward North's chair.

"Bill, things have been developing pretty fast in the last hour. Not all of it came over the satellite phone, so I doubt you've heard everything."

Bill North shrugged and gestured palms up. "I haven't been trying to catalogue things, Kat. I was just trying to keep relaying for you."

She nodded and smiled. "I appreciate that, Bill. I appreciate all your help since Salt Lake."

"Glad to."

"Now, however, I want to tell you where we are in this investigation. As Ken has said, we need your help getting information from one of your companies, but while we're waiting for that, maybe you can help me untangle some of these conflicting facts."

He leaned forward, looking slightly relieved. "Sure. What?"

There was a sturdy, hand-carved walnut coffee table in front of the couch and she sat on it carefully as she folded her hands and looked him in the eye. Ken stood quietly against the left wall of the cabin, the gun still leveled in the direction of North.

"First, Bill, Bradley Lumin probably did not kill Melinda Wolfe."

There was a flicker on North's face which progressed to a frown and a quick glance at Ken.

"I heard that exchange, and I was stunned. But I wonder if the conclusion isn't premature."

She nodded. "We were stunned, too, but there's no question that if Bradley Lumin didn't take that picture—and he couldn't have—then he didn't kill Melinda. In fact, he may not even have been involved."

North sat back, looking off balance. "But, there was a picture of Melinda on his computer, wasn't there?"

"Planted," Kat shot back. "Lumin was never there. Somebody purposely framed Lumin."

Bill North looked carefully at Ken Wolfe, then back at Kat. She could almost feel the herculean effort he was making to stay calm.

"Well, who, then?" North asked. "You think someone working for one of my companies knows the answer?"

She shook her head. "No, Bill. I think *you* know the answer personally."

She could hear Ken shift position to her left and almost feel his puzzlement.

North was shaking his head. "Me? I told you, I own a lot of companies—"

She raised her hand to stop him. "There's a cabin in Maine that's been used for some time as a sort of studio for kiddie porn films. We have independent evidence already of that, discovered in Lumin's trailer in Colorado. That's the same cabin Melinda was held in and raped in. Lumin made sex videos there. Of course, that Maine cabin hasn't been used since Melinda's death, but it was a filthy porno studio, and Bill, it was feeding one of your enterprises."

He snorted and looked around as if in awe of her naivete. "Certainly you can't believe the chairman of a distant holding company would have any direct knowledge of such activities, even if that were true?"

"Not only do you know about that cabin, Bill, you own it, albeit indirectly. See, we never knew where to look for that cabin before. Maine's a big place. Now that you're involved, we know where to find it."

Bill North smiled suddenly and shook his head. "Kat, you've got this all tragically wrong. If someone's been doing illegal things in one of my companies, or even if someone bought and misused an insignificant piece of property I happen to own somewhere, I wouldn't have any notification. I'm just the overall owner of a holding company."

"Oh, it gets far worse, Bill, and much closer to your doorstep. Your company in Chicago will eventually tell us how close your contacts were, and we know they maintained the e-mail address called SHRDLU2, which was later used to place a horrible picture taken during Melinda's captivity on Bradley Lumin's computer to frame him, and another one on Rudolph Bostich's computer to warn him to keep quiet, and that was *after* Bostich had been tipped about Lumin. When we get to the end of that corporate chain, we find Bill North himself, and not as just the distant CEO."

North had been sitting with his mouth open and an expression of outraged alarm. He stood suddenly with an air of bravado and shook his head.

"I've had about enough of this irresponsible nonsense. Get the hell off my airplane!"

Ken raised the .44 toward his head.

"Sit down, North! Now! You're going to answer our questions fully, or you're going to die. I've heard more than enough to justify killing you already."

Bill North looked down the barrel of the .44 and swallowed hard, then looked at Kat, who nodded and gestured toward the swivel chair. He sank into it again, his face a study in fury. He shook his head and snorted. "I can see why they don't trust you at the FBI, Bronsky. You're an amateur! You're trying to incite a hijacker by personally connecting an investor with supposed misdeeds of employees of subsidiary companies light-years distant. No prosecutor would listen for a minute to such garbage. And what's worse, you're torturing this poor guy for nothing!" he gestured to Ken.

She stared back hard at him. "Bill, I haven't made myself clear. I'm not saying that someone in your company framed Bradley Lumin and intimidated Rudy Bostich. I'm saying you did so yourself."

"WHAT?" North sat back with a wild-eyed expression.

Ken stood away from the wall suddenly, his voice taut and urgent. "Kat, what do you mean?"

She looked over her shoulder at him. "Ken, Bill North is the owner and user of that e-mail site."

"How do you—" Ken began, but Kat raised a hand to silence him.

"Bill," Kat said, "as of this moment, I have to inform you as an FBI agent that you are under investigation for involvement in the kidnapping and murder of Melinda Wolfe. You have the right to remain silent. You have the right—"

"WHAT? What kind of bullshit is this?" Bill North snapped, his eyes wide with surprise and fury.

She placed a finger to her lips, then finished the Miranda warning.

Ken had remained in the same position next to the left wall, but now he was moving forward again, the gun shifted to his left hand, his right hand suddenly on her shoulder. "Kat, what's going on here?"

She looked up at him with a flint-hard expression of command. "Bear with me, Ken! Just listen. And trust me."

He licked his lips, his eyes shifting to North and back to her. He nodded then, and backed away, keeping the gun pointed in North's general direction.

There was a look of panic mixed with rage on North's face as his eyes darted between Ken and Kat.

"Agent Bronsky, if this is how you repay the efforts of a concerned citizen, then I'd say it'll be a cold day in hell before I'd recommend helping the FBI again."

She looked at him and nodded. "It did surprise me, Bill, that you made your aircraft available so fast. Then I found out you're the vice chairman of the airline involved. Later I discovered that the key to some of the evidence in Melinda's killing lay in your hands."

"Bronsky, what on earth are you talking about?" North asked through the most sarcastic expression he could manage.

She sighed and looked at the thick carpet, then reached out and traced a line along the surface of the ornate coffee table, letting him wait for several moments until she snapped her eyes back to his.

"Bill, let's talk about what really happened to Melinda Wolfe."

He shrugged his shoulders, raised his eyebrows, and gestured to the ceiling with the palms of his hands as he sat back. "*Fine*! Hold a gun on me and talk about anything you want, *Agent* Bronsky!"

"All right. Let's talk about a growing business of providing pornography to a world that seemingly can't get enough of it."

"I suppose that's all my responsibility, too?"

"You service the demand, but you cross the line when your products show children engaged in sex."

"None of my companies knowingly—"

"CAN IT!" she snapped, letting her voice return instantly to a quiet, controlled level. "We already know your companies bought the filthy kiddie porn videos Bradley Lumin made. You provided the studio cabin because these were special porno productions that could bring top dollar. It was all business. You'd personally rather be with a girl physically than just watch, but you're a businessman and such things make money."

"I have no knowledge of any such productions anywhere in my companies."

She nodded. "Oh, yes, you do. Of course you kept a good layer of insulation between you and the operational side, but one day, Mr. Lumin, who worked under contract, snatched the wrong kid. Instead of some female street urchin who'd do the flicks, take the abuse, then take the money and never complain, Lumin snagged a little girl named Melinda who didn't want to roll in the gutter with vermin like him. Lumin's an idiot and a pedophile coward. Suddenly the picture of the little girl he's got drugged and tied up in your cabin in Maine is on every newscast on the East Coast as a kidnap victim. He rapes her, beats her to get her to shut up, then panics and runs when he thinks he's killed her, and your middle man breaks all the rules and calls you in Salt Lake and tells you about it."

"This is fantasy, Bronsky!"

"There are phone records, North," she shot back, satisfied at the impact of her words.

"He tells you there's a mess in Maine, and he's not going to clean it up. In fact, he quits on the spot, and tells you never to call him again. You don't know what to do, and you're afraid the little girl may be dead or dying, so you have to race to Maine and take care of it. Bottom line, you end up in that cabin with Melinda Wolfe."

"WHAT?" The roar of outrage from her left caused Kat to jump, the chance that she'd gone too far with Ken's patience a real worry as she turned to find him moving forward toward North, his hand twitching on the grip of the .44 as he leveled it at North's head.

"Are you saying this bastard killed Melinda?"

Again she raised her left hand to stop Ken, aware that his compliance was tenuous. "Ken, stay calm. Mr. North's got a lot to tell us. Right, Bill?"

"I have no goddamn idea what you're talking about, Bronsky!" North snapped.

She leaned forward, her eyes boring holes in his. "You were in that cabin with Melinda."

"Bullshit! I was never anywhere close!"

"She was alive when you got there, wasn't she, Bill?"

"I wasn't there! Goddammit, what does it take to get through to you? I wasn't anywhere near Maine or Connecticut or anywhere else but Salt Lake City at that time. I can prove it!"

A hesitant, familiar voice reached Kat's left ear from the passageway to the cockpit.

"That's . . . not entirely correct, boss."

Kat looked up to see Dane Bailey standing with a shocked expression next to Ken. Bill North's head whirled in the same direction.

"What the hell are you talking about, Bailey?"

He looked down at a pilot log book in Bailey's right hand.

"I keep all my logs aboard. Two years ago yesterday you woke Jeff and me at two A.M. and had us get the jet ready to fly you to Boston, which we did. I remember it very well because it was my son's first birthday party, and I had to miss it, and I was really ticked off at you. You kept us waiting in Boston for two days, and never explained why it was so urgent."

"That was business!" North snapped.

"Nevertheless," Kat interjected, "it places you there, and we'll find the car you used to dump Melinda's body."

"WHAT?"

Kat sat on the edge of the coffee table again.

"Bill, did you kidnap and kill Melinda Wolfe?"

"WHAT? HELL, NO!"

"Bill, we know you were present in the room with a kidnapped young girl."

He started to protest again, but Kat raised her hand for silence and he complied, his face a mask of purple rage.

"We know, and can prove, that you were present in that cabin with Melinda Wolfe, whose body was later found in a Connecticut forest. She was alive when you were there."

He started to respond, then caught himself, and Kat noticed.

Good! He's moving toward the edge. He's dying to tell me she was dead when he got there.

She moved her face within inches of his. "How could you just take her picture in order to frame someone else, and leave her to die?" She heard Ken suck in his breath and moan like an animal in distress, but she couldn't stop now. She was too close to breaking North.

North was shaking his head vigorously, but beads of perspiration were popping out on his forehead.

"This is insane! These are 'have you stopped beating your dog' questions! I wasn't there, dammit!"

"You stood before her in that same room and just snapped pictures! She needed help. She was alive, and bleeding."

"No!"

"No what, Bill? She wasn't alive?"

His eyes flared open. "I SAID I WASN'T THERE!"

She regarded him in silence for a few seconds. "Did you rape her, Bill?"

The impact of her words was almost physical. He sat back in the chair as if kicked.

"What? WHAT?"

"Did you rape her? The question is clear enough."

Ken moaned again, a feral sound.

North ignored him and yelled back at Kat. "JESUS CHRIST, WOMAN! I DON'T SCREW LITTLE GIRLS!"

"Then," she continued, leaning after him, "why were you there, Bill? Someone raped her repeatedly. Or do you just rape thousands of little girls a year by proxy as a smut merchant?"

"I WASN'T THERE! LUMIN OR SOMEONE ELSE DID IT!"

"GIVE IT UP, BILL!" she screamed at him suddenly, leaping to her feet. "Get this straight, Bill North. We've got you nailed. Why didn't you help her? Why didn't you save that little girl's life?"

"Are you sure, Kat?" Ken asked in a broken voice from the left. She nodded slowly, aware of the risks.

There was total silence in the cabin of the Gulfstream as Bill North froze, his eyes riveted on Kat. She saw his mouth move slightly, then stop. His eyes widened in panic as Ken came forward suddenly with a guttural roar and jammed the barrel of the .44 in North's mouth.

"I'm going to blow the back of your rotten head off if you don't tell me precisely what you did to her, when, why, and how, you bastard! She was my daughter!"

North reached up and grabbed the barrel of the gun, but Ken kept it immovable until Kat reached over and squeezed Ken's arm, indicating with her head to back off. Slowly, reluctantly, he withdrew the gun from Bill North's mouth and stepped back, then leveled the weapon at North's head and slowly, ominously, cocked it.

"This is ridiculous!" North said, running his tongue around the inside of his mouth to assess the damage.

Kat stood up and moved to the aft end of the cabin for a few seconds before turning back to him.

A male voice behind them spoke without warning.

"Bill, you're going to take this fall all by yourself."

There was a scuffle of feet to her left, and Kat's heart jumped to her throat. She turned, expecting the worst from Ken, but was stunned to see that Rudy Bostich had been standing quietly in the aisleway, his hands still cuffed behind his back.

Ken followed her gaze and turned, too, equally startled. "What the hell are you doing here, Bostich?" Ken growled at him.

His eyes turned back to Bill North, who was staring at him with an expression of terror.

"I was listening at the door," Bostich began. "I couldn't believe it when I sat over there after everyone had gone and realized whose jet this was. Of all the sleazy vermin on the planet, guess who showed up at my execution? The slime responsible for framing me."

North was shaking his head. "What the hell are you talking about, Rudy?"

Bostich smiled and dipped his head. "See? He knows me. But, my good old golf buddy, Bill, here, probably hasn't gotten around to telling you that it's regular old adult porno I'm into, not kiddie porn. And I'm damn sure he hasn't told you he planted that kiddie porn on my computer along with that picture of the captain's daughter because he thought I was going to tell the Connecticut judge that Bill North was the source of the tip on Lumin. But my friend here may not realize that he doesn't have any more leverage over me, because he's already ruined my life."

"Bostich, get—" Ken began, but Kat raised a hand to silence him.

"No. Let him continue."

Bostich raised his eyebrows and nodded, his eyes boring into North, who looked panicked. "Well, guess what? I never suspected he was involved with the Wolfe girl's murder, but as I'm standing here listening to you question him, it all makes sense." He looked at Ken Wolfe, then at Kat. "For what it's worth, I'll testify against this garbage on every detail I know about. He did put that smut on my computer without my permission. I didn't buy it, contrary to what you thought. He threatened to ruin me, and I lied to the judge to protect myself and him. But I had no idea he was directly involved in her murder."

"I'm not, you fucking idiot!" North snarled.

Ken turned toward Bostich. "Out of here. Now. Sit at the bottom of the steps."

Bostich shrugged and moved to the entryway as Bill North snorted loudly.

"Okay, Bronsky. I think that'll be all the questioning for today until I contact a lawyer and sue the FBI into penury."

Kat glanced at Ken, who was leveling the gun again at the Gulfstream's owner. "If you want a lawyer, Bill, you'll have to ask permission from the hijacker, Melinda's father here, and I think he would rather have your full explanation right now."

Ken nodded silently, his lips white from the pressure of his grim expression.

Kat looked at the carpet and intertwined her fingers. "As I said before, let's talk about what really happened, Bill. You didn't kidnap her. You didn't even rape her. You raced in to clean up the scene and bury the evidence and any connection with you. But the world knew she was kidnapped, so somebody had to be prosecuted or the trail might lead to your doorstep. As you're driving to Maine from Boston that day, scared out of your mind, you're figuring how to plant a package of evidence on Lumin's computer, and that requires a picture of the girl. I mean, you reason that Lumin kidnapped her, abused her, and left her to die, so he *should* take the fall. You acquire a Polaroid camera and film. You arrive at the cabin expecting a dead body. You find a limp little girl tied to a chair who appears to be dead. You wouldn't have a clue what to do if she were still alive, so you *want* to believe she's dead. You take the pictures you need, dump her body in the trunk, drive to Connecticut, and haul her off into the forest, where you leave her."

"I don't—"

"ZIP IT!" she yelled. "Just stay quiet and listen, because not even you know the rest of the story yet."

He was trying to glare at her, but his hands were shaking ever so slightly as she leaned forward, her face inches from his.

"You broke an electrical fence when you drove into that forest, Bill. That's why we know when and where. You drove in, carried her deeper into the forest, and dug a grave for her, about two feet deep."

Kat could hear a choked sob behind her from Ken. He had never been told.

She kept her focus on North and pressed in further, her voice low and intense. "You dumped her body, Bill, covered it over, drove away, cleaned up, dropped off the car, and reappeared at your airplane. That's what really happened, isn't it?"

North was staring at her in silence, his jaw muscles working furiously.

"Bronsky, you go to hell. I'm not about to be badgered into this fantasy of yours."

She nodded and looked down again.

"Okay, Bill. Then let's get some more of it on the table. Was she dead when you drove her to Connecticut?"

He snorted and shook his head, but she could see the resolve draining away slowly.

"You're aching to tell me she was, but you never checked. You assumed."

"Why are you torturing that father over there?" North asked.

"Oh, I'm not! You've done that yourself." Kat turned around to Ken, trying to judge how much strength he had left. He took a deep breath and nodded for her to continue.

She looked back at North. "Bill, when Melinda died, she was several hundred yards from where you left her. Do you know why?"

He stared at her blankly.

"Because, Bill, she crawled there. You see, you buried that little girl alive."

Kat let the horror of her words sink in, watching the cloud move across North's face before continuing.

"She was unconscious from a minor drug overdose Lumin had given her, Bill, but she was very much alive when you put her in the ground."

North gasped, and a ripple of emotions crossed his face as he struggled to keep his mouth shut even as his eyes glazed.

Kat nodded and continued, mindful of the low gasp from Ken's direction.

"Sometime later, after you were long gone, Melinda Wolfe woke up two feet underground with dirt in her face and mouth. She clawed and dug, gasping for breath, until she found the surface. Fortunately you hadn't packed it too tightly. She was alive, Bill. You buried that little girl alive, and she crawled out on her own and got several hundred yards away before she died from loss of blood, exposure, and the results of her abuse."

Bill North's eyes were enormous, his mouth opening and closing once silently, his eyes darting toward Ken, then back, before he spoke in a low, halting voice.

"I'm devastated . . . to hear what that poor little girl went through. But you're wrong. I . . . I had nothing to do with it."

She nodded. "Your denial is pathetic, Bill. The truth is written all over your face, and we have the evidence."

He remained motionless.

Kat dropped her gaze to North's right hand. She reached out and took the hand, pulling it to her, spreading the fingers apart and tracing the line of his little finger as he watched her in growing alarm.

"Did you break this finger as a kid, Bill?"

He hesitated, then nodded, thoroughly off balance. "Yeah. As a teenager. It didn't set correctly."

"It left you with a very distinctive shape around the knuckle that's easily identifiable. I saw it the first time in Salt Lake. You remember us on the satellite phone discussing the photo you loaded on Bostich's computer? Well, Bill, you want to know how I know all these things? You want to know how I can convince a jury beyond a reasonable doubt? Because I enlarged that photo to look at the hand reflected in the window. There was something distinctive about that hand, and I finally realized what it was. The little finger had a unique shape to the knuckle. I'd seen that hand a few hours before in person, because it's your hand, Bill."

The single explosion of a .44 caliber bullet just to her left was deafening, and Kat dove instinctively to the right as she looked back around to see smoke curling from the barrel.

She jerked her head back toward North, amazed to find him unscathed, a huge bullet hole in the sidewall of the cabin several inches above where his head had been.

She whirled on Ken, her eyes huge. "NO! Ken, this isn't the way! It's far too easy for him."

Ken Wolfe was breathing hard as he resettled his feet and brought the loaded and cocked .44 to a dead aim on Bill North's forehead.

"Step back, Kat," he commanded in a dangerously quiet voice.

"Ken—"

"STEP BACK!" he snapped at her, his gaze remaining on North, who was cringing to his left in the chair.

Kat drew a ragged breath as she tried to assess the options, her desire to get North's confession now secondary to keeping North alive, the image of her purse at the back end of the cabin looming in her mind.

Kat moved quickly back to the swivel chair near the rear of the cabin and sat down, her right hand feeling around on the floor for her purse, her eyes riveted on Ken, who was paying no attention to what she was doing.

Her hand closed around the purse and she drew it to the side of the chair, working the zipper at the top, her fingers slipping inside to the welcome feel of the cold metal of her gun.

"Stand up, North!" Ken was commanding.

"Why?"

"STAND UP, YOU FUCKING MURDERER!" he screamed. "This nightmare just gets worse and worse. Now I find a corporate suit let Melinda die, and on top of that, buried my little girl alive! You could have saved her, you shit!"

"Look, Wolfe, I . . ."

Ken raised the gun to his eye level, then slowly dropped his aim to North's crotch.

"If you tell me the truth right now, I'll let you live to stand trial. Otherwise, I'm going to start blowing off body parts one by one until I hear the truth."

"Look, goddammit," North began.

Another thunderous explosion ripped through the cabin as North yelped and looked down in horror, confused to find everything between his legs seemingly intact.

"I'm a perfect shot, North. That was your last warning. The next one will be a ballistic castration. You killed my daughter! Admit it!"

North's hands were out in a stop gesture, his eyes frantic. "Look, Ken, *please*, you've got to believe me! I didn't kill her. I didn't hurt her."

"You're lying!"

"NO!"

"You raped her and murdered her!"

"NO, NO, NO! I DID NOT! Godammit, listen to me! I had no idea she was alive!"

For a second, Ken stood in stunned silence, the confession in North's words finally registering.

"Oh, GOD!" Ken's agonized voice cut through the cabin, his face contorting in pain, his eyes closing tightly in agony.

Instantly Bill North seized the opportunity, diving to the carpet, his hand reaching out to the side of an end table at the forward end of the cabin as Kat pulled her .40 mm semi-automatic clear of her purse and leveled the barrel at Ken's head.

"KEN! DROP IT! RIGHT NOW! DO NOT SHOOT AT HIM AGAIN!"

Ken opened his eyes, his gun still aimed at where North had been. He glanced at Kat, then down at North, who appeared to be writhing on the floor.

"I haven't shot the bastard yet, Kat."

"And you're not going to! Drop that gun. NOW!"

Ken took a deep breath and shook his head no. "For hours now, I've been trying to tell you my life is already over, Kat. I really don't care if you shoot me or not. Just make sure this murderer is put away if I fail to kill him."

"You're not going to commit murder, Ken!"

"I've already committed a capital crime."

"Then don't make it worse. DROP THE GUN!"

"No, goddammit!"

Ken pointed the barrel at North on the floor. "Get up, you fucking murderer! I'm gonna blow your balls off first."

"KEN!" Kat bellowed. "It won't work! I'll have to shoot you if you show any sign of pulling that trigger!"

"I don't care, Kat," he said softly.

"But Melinda would care, Ken! Melinda would want you alive to see this through. You know I'm right! I know how daughters feel about a loving father, Ken. Melinda would never want you to use that gun. She'd want that bastard rotting in jail for the rest of his life, stripped of all his privileges. Killing him is too easy!"

Ken was hesitating. She could see him blink, obviously confused, as he let the aim of his gun sag. Slowly, agonizingly, the barrel dropped toward the carpet as he turned toward Kat with resignation on his face, his attention too diverted to see the simultaneous whirl of movement near the end of the coffee table.

The blur of motion instantly caught Kat's attention as she realized what was happening. Time dilated, the scene before her shifting into slow motion. Ken let the .44 slide from his fingers as Bill North rose like an angry cobra from behind the table, a deadly sneer on his face, his eyes aflame—and his hand clutching the stock of a silver .45 automatic snatched from a hidden compartment on the side of the end table.

"BILL!" she yelped in surprise.

She could see North's eyes on Ken's head, the aim of the .45 rising as North propelled himself up, his finger on the trigger of the cocked weapon.

Instinctively, Kat swung the aim of her gun to the right, from Ken Wolfe to Bill North, her mind rebelling at the thought of pulling the trigger.

"BILL! STOP!"

North was ignoring her. He raised the barrel of his .45 inexorably toward Ken, who had finally detected the movement to his left and was starting to look around, an expression of surprise on his face as he saw the Gulfstream's owner rising from the carpet with lethal intent.

Ken's eyes flickered to the dropped .44, then back to North, whose finger began to squeeze the trigger.

"BILL! NO!"

The .40 mm's gunsight was resting now on the side of North's head.

"FREEZE, BILL, OR I'LL SHOOT!"

But it was obvious North had a singular mission and the rearward motion of the .45's trigger left no doubt. She had no time to decide. It would be instinct alone.

The explosion rocked the interior of the Gulfstream as the slug from North's gun ripped through Ken Wolfe's right chest.

And milliseconds later, Kat's bullet exploded into flight, the projectile blowing through Bill North's head.

North's body crumpled as Ken Wolfe staggered toward the opposite wall, his eyes huge, a growing patch of crimson on his white shirt above the right breast pocket.

He looked down at North's body, then back at Kat, trying to smile, sliding down the wall to a sitting position as she and the two pilots rushed to his side.

EPILOGUE

FBI Headquarters, Washington, D.C. Two months later.

The Director of the FBI stood up and walked to the window shaking his head, his words clearly audible to Kat Bronsky as she waited in the plush chair on the other side of his desk.

"Agent Bronsky, I've got some real problems here. On one hand I've got rules and regulations this agency has to adhere to, and on the other hand, I have you."

He turned at last and looked at her with a neutral expression.

"Problem one is, you ignored orders, sidestepped procedures, and managed to get yourself captured in the process, as you used what some around here are calling cowboyish maneuvers to deal with this hijacking."

He moved back to the large chair behind his desk. "And, of course, let us not forget the small matter of shooting to death a personal friend of the President of the United States aboard his own jet."

"Sir—"

He raised a hand for silence.

"Problem two is, I also have to acknowledge that an FBI agent saved a plane full of passengers and cracked a major murder investigation in a matter of hours through intuition, intellect, training, and brilliant detective work under fire. In fact, like it, hate it, or however I feel about it, the image of the modern FBI agent you've presented to the public has done this agency a world of good—even if it is rankling some of your fellow agents."

"Thank you, sir."

"Don't get cocky. That's reluctant praise."

"Yes, sir."

"Okay. I've also got to add that the President instructed me personally and very privately to tell you he's damn grateful for your unmasking of Bill North. He hadn't a clue that North was involved in worldwide sleaze. By the way, do you know we now have conclusive evidence linking North personally to the production of snuff films in Mexico?"

"Good Lord, no."

The Director nodded. "Enough to indict, if he'd lived. So that was a well-aimed bullet, Kat, and I'm well aware it was fully justified, as the formal review concluded. The President *also* wanted me to thank you most profusely for exposing Bostich and saving his Administration a major scandal. By the way, you said you had the latest on him?"

She nodded and thumbed through a note pad. "Bostich was removed as U.S. Attorney the same afternoon, as you know. Technically he resigned, but he had no choice. The Connecticut Bar suspended his law license for lying to the judge. And the Connecticut judge reinstated the warrant against Bradley Lumin, which, it turns out, was needed to get enough evidence to convict Lumin of kidnapping Melinda Wolfe."

"So that indictment is secure?"

She nodded and smiled. "Lumin has been indicted for the federal crimes of kidnapping, rape, attempted murder, and conspiracy to commit murder, and charged in Connecticut with aggravated first degree murder for his complicity in the death of Melinda Wolfe. In addition, the publicity has caused more young female victims of Lumin's cinematic work to come forward, and more charges are pending. He'll never walk the streets again."

"Good!"

"Bostich came out okay on one point, by the way. The grand jury no-billed him on possession of child pornography. Seems he just likes lewd pictures of big girls."

The Director sat down and motioned toward the notebook in Kat's lap.

"About the pilot, Kat. I know he was released from the hospital last week into custody, but what's his legal situation?"

Kat nodded. "It's the damnedest situation I've ever seen. You knew the U.S. Attorney decided not to charge Wolfe with air piracy?"

He nodded. "Yes, but I haven't heard why."

"He had no choice," Kat replied. "Incredibly, the airline refused to acknowledge that Wolfe *didn't* have permission to fly the airplane all over Utah, Colorado, Telluride, and Arizona!"

"You're kidding!"

"Nope. Legally, you can't hijack an aircraft you have full authority to fly. I'm told their corporate lawyers made the decision based on which type of negligence they'd rather admit to. With the public outpouring of sympathy for Wolfe, they apparently didn't want to be responsible for putting one of their captains in a death penalty prosecution."

The FBI Director was shaking his head in wonder. "I heard that none of the passengers would press for prosecution."

"Not one. It's amazing. Some of those same people who are probably going to sue the hell out of AirBridge for mental anguish and reckless endangerment wrote passionate letters for leniency. But with Wolfe determined to plead guilty to any charges, it really came down to the decision of the U.S. Attorney in Denver."

"And the bottom line there?"

"This morning Wolfe pled guilty to assault and weapons charges worth up to twenty years, and sentencing is next week. Of course, he's already received the ultimate punishment for a pilot. He'll never fly again. The FAA jerked his license immediately, and there's no chance he'll ever get it back."

"Quite a tragedy, Kat." He looked up and slapped the file folder bearing her name. "Okay. Now, what do we do about you?"

"Director, I—"

Once again he held up his hand to silence her. "Kat, some of the good old boys around here are pretty steamed at you, but mostly for stealing the spotlight." He smiled and pointed to the folder. "In fact, your superiors here solemnly recommended that you be fired for insubordination, or at least suspended, demoted, and retrained."

She nodded glumly. "I expected that."

"But the President won't stand for it, and frankly, neither will I."

"So . . ."

"So, while I need a blood oath from you that you'll at least *try* to abide by the rules in the future, I also need more people around here like you who refuse to limit their thinking in a crisis, and who can make good decisions under fire."

Federal District Court, Denver, Colorado. One week later.

"Mr. Wolfe, would you rise, please?"

The voice of the occupant of the ornate bench rumbled through the packed courtroom, and Ken Wolfe suppressed a shudder as he moved the chair back several inches and got to his feet.

The judge adjusted his reading glasses and peered over the top of a paper in his hand. "Mr. Wolfe, you have entered a plea of guilty to the charges in the indictment, and you waived a reading of that indictment. Is this correct?"

"Yes, your honor." Ken felt his stomach fluttering, which was a surprise. He had been numb for weeks. There had been no reason to fear the sentencing. He would spend the rest of his life in prison, whether one run by the federal government, or the one in his own mind. What difference could it make?

Yet, he felt his middle contorting with apprehension.

"Very well. Mr. Wolfe, this court has the responsibility to impose appropriate penalties for violations of our laws. You have readily admitted to the charges filed by the United States Attorney, and these are serious crimes, but I am also fully aware of the details through the exhaustive, and I might add, very compassionate presentencing report presented to this court by the government. I am also fully aware that you have lost your profession as a pilot, and that loss is, of necessity, permanent."

The judge paused and looked Ken Wolfe in the eye.

"So, Mr. Wolfe, this court finds that you should be confined to a psychiatric facility for six months of treatment, and pending a favorable report from that therapy, I am imposing a sentence of ten years . . . which I will probate."

The judge removed his glasses and sighed. "Captain, your conduct cannot be condoned, but I'm convinced that you are of no further risk to this society, and you have already lost far more than this court could ever take from you. Provided you live up to the letter of the restrictions I will place on you, you may remain free of incarceration."

Ken Wolfe nodded and tried to speak, his face wet with tears he was embarrassed to shed. His voice would not come at first, but he managed a modified croak, his eyes closed.

"Thank you, your honor."

The judge adjourned the session, then stood and left the bench, startling his bailiff by turning away from the door to his chambers and walking, instead, to the defense table where Ken was standing with his attorney, his eyes still closed. The judge put a large hand on Ken Wolfe's shoulder.

"Captain?"

Ken opened his eyes with a start and looked at the judge. "Sir?"

"I read what that FBI agent said to you in the airplane. She said that your little girl would not have wanted you to give up. She was right, Captain. Through their pleas for leniency, your fellow citizens have given you another chance to contribute something more in her name. Don't drown that opportunity in self-pity. There's a sick world out there that needs all the help it can get."

With a final squeeze of his hand on Ken's shoulder, the judge turned and walked away.